P9-DND-267

Acclaim for **ANDREW VACHSS**

"Influenced by lean, socially observant crime writers—Dashiell Hammett, Jim Thompson, Charles Willeford, Iceberg Slim— Vachss' prose is still starker, with rap's hard flow. His New York, a flame-etched, pitch-black wasteland, is a truly hellish vision."
—*Uncut*

"Andrew Vachss, a lawyer who specializes in the problems of child abuse, writes a hypnotically violent prose made up of equal parts of broken concrete block and razor wire." —*Chicago Sun*

"Andrew Vachss is unique among modern writers; no one else comes close to the raw power and intellectual ambiguity that he manifests so elegantly, so coldly." —*The Clarion-Ledger*

"Next to Vachss, Chandler, Cain and Hammett look like choir-boys." —*The Cleveland Plain Dealer*

"There's no way to put a [Vachss book] down once you've begun. . . . The plot hooks are engaging and the one-liners pierce like bullets." —*Detroit Free Press*

"Ah, Andrew Vachss. The man makes other noir writers seem like William Saroyan." —*Fort Worth Star-Telegram*

"Breathtaking, nightmarish and seductive. Vachss's writing is like a dark rollercoaster ride of love and hate." —*The Times-Picayune*

"Vachss seems bottomlessly knowledgeable about the depth and variety of human twistedness." —*The New York Times*

"[Vachss] does to pimps, pederasts, snuff film makers and porn industry purveyors what you know he'd like to do in real life, but seldom can. In other words, he decimates them."

—*The Detroit News*

"Andrew Vachss bursts forth with more of the slashing prose that has earned him a reputation as one who gives no quarter in his exposure of the evils of the human mind. The man knows whereof he speaks."   —*Newsday*

"Many writers try to cover the same ground as Vachss. A handful are good. None are better. For anyone interested in this kind of fiction, Andrew Vachss, sculpting pieces of art out of the scummiest wastes of humanity, must be read."   —*People*

"Vachss enlightens the world . . . [with] chilling stories taken from the real world and made into fiction."   —*Publishers Weekly*

"[Takes us] not simply into the mean streets but into a subterranean nightmare . . . a place as compelling and challenging as any to be found in the best crime fiction today."

—*The Washington Post Book World*

"The best detective fiction being written . . . add a stinging social commentary . . . a Célinesque journey into darkness, and we have an Andrew Vachss, one of our most important writers."

—Martha Grimes

"Tough, terse, vivid, Vachss keeps pouring on until, from equal measure bruising and pleasure, the reader screams 'No more, baby, no more.' If it were any more real you'd get twenty-five to life just for cracking the cover."   —John Ridley

ANDREW VACHSS

EVERYBODY PAYS

Andrew Vachss has been a federal investigator in sexually transmitted diseases, a social caseworker, and a labor organizer, and has directed a maximum-security prison for youthful offenders. Now a lawyer in private practice, he represents children and youth exclusively. He is the author of numerous novels, including the Burke series, two collections of short stories, and a wide variety of other material including song lyrics, poetry, graphic novels, and a "children's book for adults." His books have been translated into twenty different languages; and his work has appeared in *Parade, Antaeus, Esquire, The New York Times,* and numerous other forums. He lives and works in New York City and the Pacific Northwest.

The dedicated Web site for Vachss and his work is www.vachss.com

Books by **ANDREW VACHSS**

EVERYBODY

PAYS

EVERYBODY

PAYS

| stories |

ANDREW VACHSS

VINTAGE CRIME / BLACK LIZARD

Vintage Books / A Division of Random House, Inc.

New York

This book is a work of fiction. Names, characters, places, and incidents either are the products of the author's imagination or are used fictitiously, and any resemblance to actual persons, living or dead, events, or locales is entirely coincidental.

A VINTAGE CRIME/BLACK LIZARD ORIGINAL, SEPTEMBER 1999
First Edition

Copyright © 1999 by Andrew Vachss

All rights reserved under International and Pan-American Copyright Conventions. Published in the United States by Vintage Books, a division of Random House, Inc., New York.

Library of Congress Cataloging-in-Publication Data
Vachss, Andrew H.
Everybody pays : stories / Andrew Vachss. — 1st ed.
p.   cm. — (Vintage crime / Black Lizard)

ISBN 0-375-70743-3
1. Detective and mystery stories, American.   I. Title.   II. Series.
PS3572.A33E9   1999
813'.54—dc21   99-28773
CIP

Book design by Mia Risberg

www.vintagebooks.com

Printed in the United States of America
10 9 8 7 6 5 4

CCU/1

CONTENTS

FROM THE UNDERGROUND SERIES:

FROM THE CROSS SERIES:

NOVELLA:

EVERYBODY

PAYS

PROVING IT

1

Every place I've ever been, there's pigeons.

Even here. Prison.

Rats with wings, convicts call them.

That's not ranking them, not really. You can't disrespect rats. Nobody likes them, but they always keep coming.

Like me.

Even here.

2

They let me out on a Wednesday. They gave me back my watch, the clothes I was wearing when I first went down, the cash I had on the books. Seventy-seven dollars and some change. I was the only white guy in the go-home line. It wasn't like that when I'd first come in.

The bus took us into town, this little stupid dead town that only has a depot and a couple of bars. If it wasn't for the prison, the people who live around here would starve to death—it's the only job there is.

Nobody got met at the depot. We didn't say anything to each other. I didn't know them; they didn't know me. We all got on the first bus down to the city. Same way we came up—only this time there wasn't any steel mesh over the windows, and we weren't chained to the seats.

The other guys made a lot of noise. It sounded like they were talking to each other. Going on about all the women they were going to mount, the fine clothes they'd be wearing, all the action, the big scores. Except they were really talking to themselves. Same as it was in the joint.

And a couple of them, they were already nodding out. Prison's just like the street. Only difference is, Inside, drugs cost more.

I looked out the window.

Port Authority was the same as the prison yard—wolves waiting on every new bunch, waiting to see if there were any sheep.

I walked through the terminal, following the rules: Look down or look hard. Maybe I didn't have friends there, but nobody wanted to try me either. Up where I was, you learned to settle for that.

I walked all the way back to the neighborhood. The candy store was still on the corner, but there was a new sign in the window. Lotto.

The old man's back was to me, arranging something on the shelf behind the counter. I picked up three Milky Way bars, waited for him to turn around.

"How much are these now?" I asked him.

The old man's eyes were sharp behind his glasses. "For you, they're still a quarter," he said.

"Thanks," I told him. Handed him the money. Asked: "Where would I find Mingo?"

"Same place," he said.

I walked the three blocks. The street made springtime sounds, but the only birds I could see were pigeons, picking scraps off the concrete. Maybe they sound different outside the Walls. I never listened to them before I went up.

Mid-afternoon, kids running down the block, sprung from school.

The basement door was the same shade of rust. I pushed and it opened. He was at a card table in the corner, wearing a Panama hat and dark glasses even in the gloom.

"Hey, *amigo!* When did you raise?" he greeted me.

"This morning," I told him.

"I got your stuff."

"I appreciate you holding it for me."

"Hey, no problem, man. Nothing's changed."

It was all in a duffel bag, the same one I'd told him to get and hold for me when he'd visited me in jail.

Mingo was the last visitor I'd had.

I got a room in the neighborhood. Fresh linen twice a week, toilet down the hall.

I went to the Greek's that night. The guy who owns the place is big, with a shaved head. People called him the Greek because of *Kojak,* when it first came out. It's a regular restaurant, though.

I took a table in the corner, looked over the menu. It was strange to see a menu. Choices.

The waitress had long, dark hair, big eyes. I told her I wanted the beef stew. She didn't write it down on her pad, just stood there, hands on her hips, looking at me.

"What?" I asked her, trying to keep my voice gentle. When someone stares at you like that Inside, you have to challenge them, but I didn't want her to think I was doing that.

"You don't know me?"

I looked at her again. Right in her face. Everything was different except the eyes, but soon as I saw them, I knew.

"Alicia?"

"Yeah. All grown up now, huh?"

"I . . . guess."

"You don't see any difference?" she said, smiling.

"Uh . . . sure." I didn't want to look at the difference pushing out the front of her plain white blouse. The last time I'd seen her, she was thirteen years old.

"How come you never answered my letters?" she asked me.

"I . . . couldn't."

"How come? They wouldn't let you write from there?"

"They did. I mean . . . you could. But . . . I didn't know what to say."

"Because I was a baby?"

"I was going to be there a long time. I didn't want to . . ."

"What?"

"I don't know . . . connect. I needed to just work on being there. Getting through it. I knew you'd stop, sooner or later."

"You know a lot, huh?"

"Why are you mad at me?" I asked her. "I didn't do anything to you."

"To *me*? No, nothing. In fact, that *was* me to you, yes? Nothing. So why did you do it, then?"

Somebody shouted something at Alicia from one of the other tables. She ignored them. I heard a bell go off, the cook yelled "Pick up!" Alicia just stood there, watching me. Waiting for the answer.

I didn't know the answer.

I don't know why she'd done what she did.

I don't know why I went with it.

What happened was, a man had come into the after-hours joint where I got my jobs. I'm a thief. He walked right up to me, where I was sitting in a booth near the door. Everyone went quiet.

"You a grown man," he said to me. "You mess around with my little girl, I take your life, understand?"

I *was* a grown man. Twenty-two. But I didn't know who he was talking about. So I didn't say anything. We looked at each other for a minute, then he turned around and left.

"Who was that?" I asked Mingo.

He told me. But the name didn't mean anything to me. I didn't even have a girlfriend, so it didn't make sense. But I didn't deny anything when the man had said all that stuff—it would have looked weak.

A few days later, I was back in the same place. That's when Mingo told me he'd asked around. And the man who'd come in and sounded on me, he had a stepdaughter: Alicia. And this Alicia, she was a little girl, and she'd been going around telling everyone I was her boyfriend. That must have been what started it.

I went and found her. I knew where she'd be. All the kids went to the same places I went to when I was a kid. Because the block was the same as it was then. But I didn't have to ask around. When I walked in the candy store, this little girl with dark hair and big eyes came right over to me. She took my arm and pulled me outside. I let her do it.

There's an alley next to the candy store. It's empty there in the afternoons. At night, it sometimes isn't.

"Why'd you tell him that?" I asked her. "That I was your boyfriend?"

"So he'd leave me alone."

"I don't get it."

"He . . . bothers me. I told my mother on him, but she slapped me for even saying it. I'm not allowed to go on dates. He . . . controls everything. I wanted him to stop. So I told him you were my boyfriend."

"Why me? I'm too old—"

"I knew he would—I'm sorry—I knew he would try and get you to . . . leave me alone. But I saw you. I asked about you. You were . . . in jail, right?"

"Yeah. So?"

"So I figured you wouldn't be afraid of him. Maybe he would be afraid of you, even. He's never been in jail."

"I can't be your boyfriend," I told her. "You're just a kid."

"My *pretend* boyfriend," she reminded me, looking up from under long eyelashes.

"Not your *pretend* boyfriend, either."

Her face got all twisted up then, like she was going to cry. But she didn't. Just said, "I'm sorry," and walked away.

I started to go after her, but when I came out of the alley, her stepfather was there. He was angry, making a lot of noise. She was next to the door of the candy store, in front of a little crowd. He slapped her so hard she went to the ground.

"I warned you," he said to me, one hand slipping into his jacket pocket.

I could have told him then.

But what happened was, I killed him.

The Legal Aid told me, if I hadn't had a record, I could probably beat the charge. He had a knife—I had a knife. We fought, and he died.

But I did have a record. And for something with a knife. It happened in a gang fight. Mostly it was chains and pipes, so many people screaming and swinging it was hard to tell what was happening. A couple of zips popped off, but nobody got panicked— you have to be real close to hurt someone with one of those things. In the middle of the rumble, me and Sonny Trion got split off from the rest. He was the other club's Warlord. I knew him from around, but he lived a few blocks away. Another country.

Everyone, like, stopped—they watched us dueling. My blood was so high I was seeing him through a red cloud. Sonny cut me, but I got in under his ribs and he died. I was fifteen, so they couldn't send me Upstate, but they put me Inside.

Everybody had knives in there. They called them shanks, and they made them out of anything—spoons, files, even toilet-brush handles—but they worked the same.

By the time I got out, I was grown. And I knew how to steal. I was too old for gangs. I mean, the gang was still there, but they didn't even expect me to come back to them.

I never used a knife again until that day. But I always carried one.

The Legal Aid told me I could take a plea. To manslaughter. It would be five years. If I went to trial, if they came back with murder, it would be life.

I took the five years. I was a graduate of the gladiator school they called a reformatory, so I knew what it would be like Inside. More knives.

What I didn't know was that the five years the Legal Aid told me about—well, it was five years until I saw the Parole Board, not five years until I got out.

You maybe can scam the Board, fake like you got religion or something. I don't know that for a fact, but some guys said you could. What I did know was that you couldn't scam the other cons. You couldn't just pretend to be hard in there. You had to prove it. They *made* you prove it.

So the Board kept giving me hits, keeping me in. I had a pretty good record the last few years before I first saw them, but I'd had to use a shank a couple of times when I'd first come in. I wasn't mad at anyone. It was just so they'd leave me alone. Just like that first time.

Inside is the same as on the street—you have to keep proving it.

The way it works, you do enough of your sentence, they *have* to let you go. I had a little more than eight years in when it happened to me; when they let me go.

When I first went in, there was nothing. I didn't expect anything. Mingo was my partner, and I knew he'd take care of my stuff, but that was all.

The letter from Alicia came a few months later. It took her a long time to find me where I was. She wrote the letter like I was her boyfriend.

She was just a baby, thirteen. And I was twenty-two, a man. But that wasn't why I didn't answer her. I remembered the last time I'd been Inside. If you had a girl to write to you, to visit you, it made you feel better. But when she stopped—and they all stopped, sooner or later—then you felt worse.

Some guys went crazy behind that. Hung up in their cells. Or jumped the railing off a high tier. For the rest, they just got sad. Deep sad.

I just wanted to get through my bit. I didn't want to get crazy, or be that sad.

I didn't know how to tell her all that now, looking right in her face. But I did the best I could.

"He didn't give me any choice," I said.

"Sure, he did," she told me, leaning over the table so her face was close to mine. She smelled like the syrup in the cans peaches come in. "He was just huffing. You could have told him I was making it all up. You didn't even know me. And that would have been it. For you, anyway. Me, he would've just hit me some more and . . . you knew that."

"I . . ."

"You *knew* that," she said again.

The Greek came from behind the counter and walked over to the table. He pulled at her arm. "What the hell do you think you're—?"

He stopped when he saw me. "Oh, you're back. Jesus, Alicia, I'm sorry. I know how long you been waiting."

"Now I'm done waiting," she said quietly.

The Greek was looking at me. "I got no beef with you," he said. "I'm just trying to run a business."

Alicia took off her apron, handed it to the Greek. "You owe me for three days," she said.

"You gonna walk out right now? In the middle of—?"

"He's home now," Alicia told him.

The Greek went over to the register. Tapped the keys to open it. Handed Alicia some bills. "If you want a few days off, you can always—"

"Come on," she said to me.

The building was only four blocks away. "I never moved," she said to me. "I wanted to be sure you could find me."

I just walked along with her.

She had a key to the apartment. When we walked inside, a woman was sitting on the couch, watching TV. She was short and fat, wearing a housecoat. She had a bottle of beer in one hand. When she saw me, she said: "Oh, he's back. And now you're gonna—"

Alicia walked right past her like she was furniture, pulling on my hand for me to come along. At the end of the hall was a room with a padlock on it. She had the key. It was a bedroom. Hers. It was real small. There was a mirror sitting on top of a chest of drawers. My picture, the one the newspapers ran when I got arrested that last time, it was taped to the bottom corner. She took a suitcase out of the closet, started packing her stuff. She didn't have much.

She had four stacks of shoeboxes already tied together with some string, maybe five in each stack. She cut the string with a little scissors, then she put all the stacks together and tied them up again. It made a big bundle, but it didn't look heavy. "You take the suitcase," she told me. She took the shoeboxes.

"Who's gonna pay the—?" the fat woman said as we walked past her on the way out. Alicia didn't answer.

"Do you have a place?" she asked me when we were in the street.

I told her where I was staying.

"Let's go," she said.

3

"It's extra for two," the old guy at the front desk told me when he saw Alicia and the suitcase.

"How much *extra*?" Alicia asked him, her voice hard.

"Uh, twenty-five a week."

She handed him the money without asking me.

We went upstairs to my room.

Alicia put her shoeboxes down. I put her suitcase on the floor.

"There's only one—"

"That's okay," she said. "I want you to sit there anyway."

"How come?"

"So you can see."

I sat in the chair. Alicia used the little scissors and cut the string. Then she gave me one of the shoeboxes. "Look," she told me.

Inside were envelopes. A whole long stack of envelopes. Every one with my name on it. And the prison address. But no stamps.

"I wrote to you," she said. "Every day. I told you what I was doing. Every day. Now you can read them. You can see for yourself."

"How many of these—?"

"Two thousand, nine hundred, and forty-one," she said. "I didn't get to write you today yet—I always do that after I get off from work."

I didn't know what to say.

"In the last box, there's a little more than thirteen thousand dollars. I saved some, every week."

"Jesus."

"You never got your meal. At the Greek's, I mean. I'll go out and get some food," she said. "You can start reading the letters."

"But there's—"

"After you read them, every one, then you decide."

"Decide what?" I asked her.

"Decide if you really were my boyfriend. *Been* my boyfriend all these years. If I waited for you, faithful. If I loved you."

"Alicia . . ."

"If you decide you were, that I waited all this time, we can go together, get an apartment. I'm not too young now. If you don't, the money's yours. I saved it for you. So you could start over."

"How could you—"

"Me, I was never pretending," she said. "And there's the proof."

for Emily Lyon Segan

REACHING BACK

1

"I want to see her," the woman said.

"Lots of people want to see her," the man replied. "Lots of people want lots of things. It ain't that simple."

"Stop playing me like *I'm* simple, okay?" the woman retorted. "It took me a long time to find you. A lot of money, too. Just tell me what the ticket costs and let me get on the train."

The man was not so much fat as blobby, flesh oozing from his clothes as though it might flow like lava at any moment. His eyes were buried in pockets of obscene obesity, but their glint wasn't piggish; it was reptilian. He was plopped in a huge armchair, a clipboard held on the puddle of flesh that should have been his lap.

He regarded the woman standing before him with the icy objectivity of a slave trader. She looked somewhere in her twenties, a little less than medium height, ash-blond hair pulled back and held in place with a thick black elastic band. Impossible to tell the shape of her body under the loose-fitting Army field jacket she wore. Her posture was straight, turquoise eyes unblinking. Her face was clear of makeup, her mouth a straight line.

"Take off that coat," the fat man ordered.

The woman did as she was told. She was wearing a black T-shirt and khaki pants, a thick leather belt around her waist.

"Come on, come on," the fat man said impatiently. "You could be wearing a wire, all I know."

The woman slipped the T-shirt over her head in one smooth motion, so quickly she seemed to maintain eye contact through-out. She unhooked the belt and the waistband of the khaki pants blossomed so widely she was able to simply step out of them. A black jersey bra and a pair of modest white briefs were revealed to the fat man's eye.

"Okay, now turn around," he said.

The woman did one slow turn. Her calf muscles were sharply defined, the thighs thick with corded muscle. Her upper body was softer in appearance, breasts straining against the soft con-tainer. She completed the turn as smoothly as she had removed the T-shirt, maintaining the impression that her eyes never left the fat man even while her back was toward him.

The fat man licked where his lips should have been, eyes flit-ting over the woman's body like a spider's legs climbing a wall. "You ready to pay what it costs?" he asked her.

"Yes," is all she said.

"Then get over here."

The woman walked over to the fat man. Kept coming until she was only inches away.

"Get on your knees," the fat man said.

The woman dropped to her knees so quickly and soundlessly the fat man wasn't sure he saw the movement.

"You ready to get to work?" he asked.

"I want to see her," the woman said.

"All right, bitch. You're gonna get what you want. But first, I get what *I* want, understand?"

"Yes."

"Okay, now take my—" The fat man hesitated as though he'd been interrupted, although the woman knelt in silence, looking only at the fat man's third eye.

"You . . ." the fat man began. And again stopped speaking.

The woman's gaze remained locked to the same point, right between the fat man's eyes. She didn't speak.

The fat man broke into a heavy sweat, his stench suffusing the narrow basement room.

The woman didn't move.

"Ah, forget it," the fat man said, his voice brittle around the edges. "You wouldn't be any good anyway. Ten grand, that's the price. You got it?"

"Yes," the woman said, not moving.

"You got it *with* you?"

"Yes."

"Where?"

"In my jacket."

"Show me."

The woman got to her feet. She bent at the waist and reached into the side pocket of the field jacket. When she straightened up, her left hand was clenched into a fist. She walked the few steps over to the fat man's armchair. When she opened her fist, gold glistened in the dim light.

"Krugerrands," the woman said. "Thirty-five of them. They're worth around three hundred apiece."

"Worth to *who*, bitch?" the fat man sneered, back on safe ground. "They were trading at two seventy-nine and change this morning. You're about three yards short."

The woman opened her right hand. Two more gold coins were on her palm. "Keep the change," she said.

2

The woman climbed the steps up from the basement and entered an alley. The sun was dropping. At the mouth of the alley, two white males were sitting on garbage cans. One was playing with a stiletto, idly testing the point against his palm. The other held a length of bicycle chain, swinging it like a pendulum from one end.

"You got any money, honey?" the knifeman asked softly as the woman approached.

The woman kept walking as though she hadn't heard.

"Man asked you a *question*, whore!" the one with the bicycle chain spat out, getting to his feet.

The woman produced a blue steel semi-automatic pistol and pointed it at his belly. Her face was as calm as her hand was steady. The man backed up until he felt the garbage can behind him. Then he sat down.

The woman walked out of the alley.

3

The crone looked old enough to be Cain's sister. And evil enough to have taught him his tricks. She was seated behind a block of stone that looked as though it were an extension of the cellar walls, a dark, moist slab.

"You went to a great deal of trouble to find me," she said to the blonde woman.

The woman didn't answer.

"You want to reach back, yes?" the crone asked. "Bring someone up through the gate?"

"Yes."

"If you came to me, you must know how it works. The only

ones who can come back are those who did great harm. You do understand that, don't you?"

"Yes."

"And you have to bring me what they took. You understand that as well?"

"Yes."

"Tell me the name," the crone said.

"Bobby. Bobby Wayne Foster."

"Close your eyes," the crone commanded.

The blonde did as she was told. She heard sounds she couldn't identify: a metallic liquid crackling; a high-pitched, almost inaudible whine; something like a captive bird's fluttering feathers.

Time passed.

"He took seven," the crone finally said. "A serial killer. Rapist and murderer both."

The blonde opened her eyes. "I know," she said.

"You have found the Gatekeeper," the crone said, "not the gate. He took seven, and he was finally taken himself. We have him. If you want to reach back for him, you must take another seven. Do you understand?"

"Yes."

"You understand it all? If you yourself are taken while you are harvesting for us, then—"

"I know," the blonde said.

"Yes, you know," the crone replied. "But we know *all*. We know where you came from. And war does not count. You must take as he took."

"The same . . . ?"

"No. It does not have to be the same way. But you must kill *to* kill—that is the only purpose permitted. The killings must not be sanctioned. Do not waste our time as others have. If you found work as an executioner, killing those on Death Row in some prison, it would not count. If you kill to defend yourself, it would not count. If you are a police officer and you kill a felon, it would not count."

"I agree."

"Ah, 'agree,' you say. You understand this is a contract, then?"

"Yes."

"Seven *separate* killings."

"Yes. How will you know if—?"

"We will know," the crone said. "Do not attempt to return here. This place will no longer exist after you leave. If you succeed, you will be returned to me."

4

"I told them," the little girl said. "I told them all, just like the lady said to. But they didn't believe me."

"Some of them believed you," the blonde woman said. "The jury was deadlocked—some of them must have voted for a conviction."

"Yes, the vote was ten to two," the little girl's mother said, bitter-voiced. "But it almost killed Lila, that terrible ordeal. And I'm not going to put her through it again."

"How long were you married?" the blonde asked.

"Less than two years," the mother said. "Lila isn't his child. I thought she needed a father. He had such a good job, his own business and all. He's a plumber. I thought he could give her a better life. I realize now what I did. To her."

"Don't cry, Momma," the little girl said.

5

"Where's the guy who called me?" the plumber asked.

"He had to go out," the blonde said. "He told me to show you where the leak is."

"I can find it myself. Just tell me—"

"No. I mean, it's not here. It's in one of the outbuildings. About a half-mile from here. Can we go in your truck?"

"Sure," he said, eyeing the woman appreciatively.

A ten-minute drive brought the two of them to what looked like an abandoned shack standing just outside a copse of trees. The plumber turned to the blonde woman: "What the hell is *that*? Looks like nobody's been here for years."

"That's right," the blonde woman said, showing him the pistol, now fitted with a tube silencer.

6

"I did my time," the pudgy woman said. "They took my kid away from me, too." Her facial expression was flat, her skin so taut and shiny it looked glazed. "How come you're nosing around with all these questions now?"

"Just routine, ma'am," the blonde woman said.

"Yeah, well, the hell with your routine. I'm not even on parole anymore. I know my rights. I'm calling my lawyer." She turned and picked up the telephone.

The bullet caught the pudgy woman precisely at the base of her skull. She fell to the floor, the telephone still in her hand.

7

"You don't look like no major player to me," the black man said. "You said *weight*, okay? That's keys, not ounces. You want to deal, you got to show me something."

"I've got it," the blonde woman said.

"Where? I don't see nothing yet. Just a lot of talk."

"It's right here," the blonde said, taking out her pistol.

8

"You'll like it, honey," the dark-haired woman said. "There's a big market for these bondage flicks. Four, maybe five hours' work for five thousand bucks. In cash. Where're you gonna get a deal like that?"

"I don't know. . . ." The blonde woman hesitated.

"Oh, *forget* what you heard, all right? Lymon had nothing to do with what happened to that girl they found. The scene is full of sickos, I'll give you that. But this is strictly legit—well, except for the IRS, of course." She laughed. "Come on, what do you say?"

"Where is the studio?"

"Oh, it's just outside of town. In this warehouse Lymon has all fixed up. I can take you out there myself."

"No, that's okay. Just give me the address."

"I can't do that, honey. That's not the way it works. What do you say, want to give it a try?"

"No," the blonde woman said, pulling the pistol from her purse.

9

"You some kinda social worker?" the heavily muscled Latino asked.

"That's right," the blonde woman said.

"Yeah, well, you wanna hear me go through the whole damn thing again? She made it up—most of it, anyway. Yeah, sure, I gave her a slap or two. The mouth on her—what was I supposed to do?"

"You didn't have to beat her up."

"Beat her up? I just slapped her, I told you. That hospital, they was just looking for business, you know what I mean? The Welfare pays them extra when somebody's gotta stay overnight."

"Her cheekbone was broken."

"Yeah, that's what they said. It's not like I shot her or nothing, right?"

"Right," the blonde woman said.

10

"How old is your daughter?" the slender, well-dressed man asked.

"Four," the blonde woman said.

"And you're sure she's never been . . . ?"

"Nobody's ever touched her," the blonde said.

"This is a release," the slender man said. "For photographs and video. If you ever go to the law, you'll be in it as deep as we are, understand what I'm saying?"

"Yes. You have the money?"

"Of course. But first we have to see the goods. Not just a picture. When you bring what we agreed on, you'll be paid on the spot."

The blonde put three bullets into the slender man's midsection. Then she knelt and fired another slug just behind his ear. She was getting to her feet as a woman entered the room, a camcorder in her hand. She dropped the camcorder and raised her hand to her mouth in a gesture of shock. The blonde raised the pistol.

11

The last was a middle-aged Eurasian woman. As she stepped out of her house toward the garage, the last thing she saw was the blonde before the bullet entered her right eye. She was dead before she hit the ground.

12

"Seven, as promised," the crone said. "You took nine, but only seven counted."

"I know," the blonde woman answered. "Now bring him back."

"You did it very quickly. Where did you learn such skills?"

"In the Army."

"When we reach back, he can return at any age, as I told you. He was twenty-three when he was taken. That was almost four years ago. The aging process continues even . . . there. How old do you want him to be when he passes through the gate?"

"I want him to be a baby. A newborn baby."

"Yes. Ever since this started, thousands of years ago, people like you have been called vigilantes. But it's not for justice, is it? It's always for revenge. What did he do that you want to kill him as a baby? Are you related to one of the victims?"

"Not one of the victims," the blonde said. "Him. He's my brother. We were separated when I was five and he was only a year old. They put us in different homes. I didn't even know he existed until . . . it was in the papers. My parents, the ones who adopted me, they never told me."

"And you want to reach back for him, have him pass back through the gate as a baby, so you can kill him yourself? For what he did to your name?"

"No," the blonde said. "I want to *raise* him myself. So he can honor it."

for David Hechler

LAST DATE

I was on time for our Thursday-night date, but Bonnie never showed. I know things like that can happen, so I wasn't worried, not at first. The thing is, I couldn't find out *what* happened to her until the next Thursday, a whole week.

So I was a little early the next Thursday night. I figured I might stay a little later, too—I held on to the money I was going to spend on her from the week before, and I was really loaded.

She was late. That's what I thought, at first. But I didn't do anything with anybody else. I never do—not since I found Bonnie. That would be cheating, and George Steckle never cheats. Ask anyone. My boss, the guys in the shipping room, my landlady— anyone. I pay all my bills, right on time. In fact, I'm debt-free. That's very important, to be debt-free. It means you don't owe anybody anything.

When it got past midnight, I knew she wasn't coming. I was really upset. Sad and upset. Bonnie would never break a date with me, I knew that.

I'm ashamed of myself for what I did next. I went back on a different night. Not on a Thursday, the way we always do. I went on a Friday. The very next night, I admit it. That's a busy night, usually. I know that from before—before I met Bonnie, when I used to go a lot.

But she wasn't there. I sat there for hours and I never saw her. And if she had been there, I would have seen her. I know the place like the back of my hand—I had been going there for years before Bonnie came.

The way I figured it, something was wrong. Maybe Bonnie was hurt, or in the hospital or something. I knew she wasn't on vacation, or gone home to visit her family, or anything like that—she would have told me first. I mean, Bonnie isn't the kind of girl who would just stand you up on a date. She has very good manners, and she's very considerate as a person. You can tell she was raised right—her parents did a good job.

But I didn't do anything. Not then. I just figured, okay, I'd come back when I was supposed to. On Thursday night, I mean. And then everything would be all right.

I could hardly wait for the next Thursday. I mean, I wasn't jumping up and down or anything. And the guys at work didn't say anything, so I know they didn't notice. They really get on your case if they notice things; that's the way they are. The way everybody is, I guess.

I always wear my good suit when I have a date with Bonnie. I only have the one, but I keep it real nice. And I have different ties, so it looks different when I wear it at different times, if you know what I mean. So I got dressed up, and I went for our date.

But Bonnie wasn't there again.

I didn't know what to do. This was the longest time I hadn't seen Bonnie since we started dating. I decided I would go home and think about it.

Where I live is a good place to think. It's small, just the one room. But there's plenty of space for my magazines and my radio. I like to read the magazines while I listen to the radio. Sometimes, they talk about what's in my magazines on the radio. They don't even know they're doing it, but I know. I never call the radio shows; I just listen. My landlady says I'm her favorite lodger. Because I'm clean and quiet, I guess. And I always pay the rent on time.

My landlady says she'll be sorry when I get married and move out. I mean, this place wouldn't be enough for two people. I never say anything when she says that, but I thought, she would really like Bonnie. And maybe I'd bring Bonnie around to meet her before I moved out.

I have money saved. I always saved money, but I didn't know why, exactly. After I met Bonnie, I knew. It was to buy a house. I always wanted to live in a house. Bonnie said she did. Live in a house, I mean. When she was at home, before she went out to work, on her own. I told her about getting a house, and she said it sounded perfect.

The more I thought about Bonnie not showing up, the less sense it made. The magazines I have, they're mostly detective magazines. About crime and stuff like that. I knew things could happen to a girl. Especially a young, pretty girl like Bonnie. She was the kind of girl they usually have on the covers of the magazines I read, so I knew she could be in danger.

I wanted to investigate. I never did it before, but I knew a lot about it from the magazines. The only thing was, I didn't know where to start. I didn't know where she lived, or who her friends were, or anything. Just where she worked. And she wasn't there anymore.

My head hurt from trying to think about it. I felt lousy all week. But I went to work every day. I never took a sick day, not in eleven years. It's a company record. The boss even said so, once. I have a lot of vacation time all stored up, too. So I could have taken time off if I wanted. But I didn't know how I could use the time, so I just went to work, the way I always do.

When Thursday came around again, I went back. I didn't have my hopes up anymore, so I wasn't even surprised when she wasn't there. I decided I had to do something, so when one of the other girls finished up front, I waved her over to my table. She asked me if I wanted a dance. I told her I just wanted to talk. She gave me a funny look. Like Bonnie had, that first time. But I put money on the table and she smiled. Then she sat down and talked to me.

I asked her, did she know what was wrong with Bonnie? Because she hadn't been there in weeks. The girl I asked, she said she didn't know anybody named Bonnie. I knew the girl I asked, she had been there for a long time, even longer than Bonnie. So I knew she must have known her, but her face didn't look like she was lying, so I didn't know what to do.

Then I figured it out. Of course! Bonnie was her real name. She only told me about it because we were dating, because we had a relationship. She used another name for work. A stage name, that's what she called it. Because she was a performer, and they all had stage names. I had a hard time remembering Bonnie's stage name—it was so long ago. I put more money on the table, and I described Bonnie to this other girl. But she said it didn't ring a bell. That it could have fit so many of the girls. I didn't understand this. None of them looked anything like Bonnie.

I was getting nervous. I didn't want the other girl to leave, but I couldn't think of any name but Bonnie. And then it came to me. Tanya. Tanya Towers. That name was a joke, she told me. Bonnie told me, I mean. The other girls called her that because of her . . . chest. So she made it a stage name. Anyway, I asked this other girl, had she seen Tanya?

The other girl told me Tanya quit. She was working at another place. I asked her, but she didn't know the name of the place. There are lots of places like this one in the city.

I told the other girl we had a date. Me and Bonnie, I mean. For Thursday nights. The other girl said I could have a date with her instead, wouldn't that be okay? I felt bad. I didn't want to hurt her feelings. So I told her about me and Bonnie. About the plans we made.

The other girl, she said something very nasty to me and she got up and walked away.

In a minute, a big, mean-looking guy came over to my table. He told me it was time to leave. I asked him, why would he say that to me? I was sitting quietly; I wasn't bothering anybody. I was just waiting for Bonnie.

The big guy told me Bonnie wasn't coming back. Only he didn't call her Bonnie, he called her Tanya. He said Tanya's boyfriend took her back on the circuit because she was all played out in that place—I mean, the place where we were talking. Where I used to have my dates with her.

I didn't understand a word of what he said. It didn't make sense. Bonnie didn't have a boyfriend. Otherwise, she wouldn't have been having dates with me. The big guy sat down next to me. His face got softer. He said that the girls could only work the same places for a little while. Then they needed fresh ones. That's what he said, fresh ones. He told me Bonnie was never going to come back there. And I shouldn't either.

That was almost six months ago.

I learned a lot since then. About the circuit. And the places, how they work. And the girls, too.

My boss at work says there's something different about me, but he can't say for sure what it is. He wasn't complaining—my work is still perfect. He said he was . . . concerned. That's the word he used.

I get different magazines now. I study different things too.

I need all that information. I go to work every day. Every night, I go to the places. I made a grid. Of the whole city. I check and cross-check, because I know none of the girls works every night. I spend a little money, but mostly I save it.

What I do now is, I look for Bonnie. As soon as I find her, we'll go on our last date.

for Charles

TAG

"Hey! What the fuck is—?"

"This? It's just a sprayer, punk. Like what you carry. Only this one sprays bullets instead of paint."

"What d'you want?"

"Same as you."

"I don't get—"

"There's three of us. One of you. You try and run, we just blast you and leave your body right where it sits. It's nice and dark here. Nobody'll be around for hours. Just like you planned, right?"

"I wasn't gonna—"

"Sure you were. We're the only ones wearing the masks here. You, you're 'MRR88.' That's your tag. Now we got a face to go with it."

"You got the wrong—"

"Uh, don't be stupid. This is the third place you've done tonight. We've been right there with you. Now just put up your hands."

28

. . . .

"And here's your little notebook. With all your punk plans to ruin people's property with your mess. What's 'MRR88' stand for, anyway?"

"I'm not—"

"Yeah, you're not talking. Too bad. 'Master Race Rules!' How's that for a good guess? And would the '88' stand for 'HH' by any chance? 'Heil Hitler'?"

"It's just a—"

"Joke? This time it's on you, punk. Get in the car."

"Where're we—?"

"Just a warehouse. Few miles from here. You'll recognize it. . . . It's where all the amateur taggers practice. Nice big walls, nobody around. Of course, nobody around means nobody gets to *see* it, so it's not for the top guys. Not for you, huh?"

"I just—"

. . . .

"Get out."

"Look, you guys. I wasn't—"

"Keep walking."

"What is all this? Look, I won't—"

"You *won't* do anything, Percy. That's your real name, right? Percy?"

"I—"

"Look, punk, we know this isn't about being a Nazi, all right?"

"Right! I mean, I just wanted to—"

"—leave a mark, right?"

"Yeah! That's all it is. You leave your mark on a place, people know you're . . ."

"You ever think about the people who bought those houses? How much it costs them to fix every time you fuck them up with your 'art'? How bad it makes them feel that they try and keep their places so nice and you and your boys keep coming back? Over and over again?"

"We . . . I mean, I wasn't—"

"You think it's okay, don't you? Leave your mark on other people's property."

"Not . . . really. I mean, it's just—"

"That's okay, punk. We understand. You just want to leave your mark."

"I . . . Hey! What's that he's holding?"

"That? Ah, that's a tattoo needle. It's not gonna hurt much, but you gotta hold real still. You jerk your face and the needle slips, it won't be your forehead, it'll be your eyes. Then you wouldn't be able to run around leaving your mark no more."

for Alan and Sue

DRESS-UP DAY

I am an only child. When I was real small, I thought I was the only child there ever was, because I didn't know there were any others. When I finally started going to school, some kids from big families would tell me how lucky I was. To be the only child. They would have so many kids in their families that it was hard for them to get any attention, or have any privacy. I never told them the truth. I would just nod, like I understood what they were saying.

A lot of kids thought I was stupid at first, because I nodded a lot when they talked. But the teachers knew different, because I could read and write faster—I mean, I *learned* to read and write faster—before the other kids did. Math too, I was quicker.

I *did* understand what the other kids were saying. About being an only child. By then, I knew I wasn't the only child. And I listened to other children, so I knew that we weren't all alike. But even the ones who were wrong about me were half right. I *did* have a lot of privacy. Even when I was very, very small. I remember the privacy. I used to cry and cry for my mother, but she never came. It wasn't until I was older that I understood she wouldn't come. She wasn't even in the house. When she *was* in the house, she usually had a man with her. They didn't want to see me. If I kept them from seeing me, I would be okay. If they saw me, one of them would hurt me, usually her. One time, this man—all I remember about him was he had red hair—he told my mother not to slap me. He said I was just a baby and I wanted my mother. That was a natural thing, he said. My mother told him to mind his own business. She said I wasn't *his* kid, so shut the fuck up. The red-haired man slapped her then. Real hard—she went flying. He grabbed her by the hair and dragged her back and slapped her again. He asked her, did that feel good? Did *she* like that? My mother licked her lips where they were bloody and said something to the man I didn't understand. She was on her knees. The man turned around and went out the door. He never came back. I remember that night especially well. It was the first time my mother ever burned me with a cigarette.

It was always like that until I stopped being stupid. I had to live in the house with her. That was the law. But I stayed away from her. And she never came in my room in the basement as long as I didn't make any noise. I got pretty good grades and I read a lot. I knew the only answer was to be very strong. I tried a lot of things to be strong, but none of them worked. I asked the school nurse once: How come I never got any bigger when I lifted weights and all? She looked very sad. She was very nice. I don't remember what she said, not much of it. But I remembered one of the words, and I looked it up. Malnutrition. From when I was real small. Before I could get food for myself.

Everything changed when I got to be thirteen. I got bigger. Not as big as some of the kids, but not the smallest, not even close.

The next year, I'm not sure why, girls got very important. Different boys did different things to have girlfriends. I really couldn't do anything. I wasn't good at basketball, I couldn't dance, and I didn't really like to fight. And, of course, I never had money to get very nice clothes or buy girls presents.

That's when I got the idea about stealing. I read everything I could about it. I studied it. Then I started. I only took money. Cash money. Never anything else. Sometimes, I would go in a house at night and there would be no money. That was okay. I knew that would happen. It would happen if someone were to break into my mother's house, too, I guess.

I never spent the money. I mean, I never spent a lot. So nobody noticed. But I always had a little. I mean, enough. I bought some nicer clothes. But I still had plenty of money left. And I thought all the time about being stronger. My mother didn't hit me or hurt me anymore, but, sometimes, one of the men she had would if she asked him to. So I spent most of the money I had on stuff to make me stronger.

I don't know how it happened with Darla. She was in my class and all. I had known her for years. Not really *known* her, but . . . well, it's a small school and I guess I knew just about everyone. I never went up to any of the girls. But Darla asked me a question once. In the library. And I talked to her. After a while, she said she was real thirsty, so I asked her could I buy her a soda and she said yes.

After that, it just . . . happened. I don't know how. But it was the best thing in the world. Darla was my girlfriend. Not my secret girlfriend either. Everybody knew. I bought her a lot of nice stuff. Once she told me I shouldn't do that. Her parents were worried, she said. She was just fourteen, and she shouldn't be getting such expensive stuff. It was just a CD player, but I guess it made them nervous. So I stopped. I met them and everything. Once they met me, they liked me. I told them I got the money for the CD player by mowing lawns and washing cars and other stuff I knew kids did. I told them I had saved up. They said that was fine, but I shouldn't spend so much money on a girl at my age. I said all right, and they smiled.

I bought Darla an ID bracelet. Sterling silver. She could only keep it at school, because her parents would get upset, but that was okay. She always wore it at school, and everyone knew it was mine.

A couple of times, her parents said I was maybe spending too much time with Darla. Calling her too much. I guess maybe they were right. But I wanted to be with her all the time. I said they were right, though, and they felt better. I could tell.

Darla and I were going to be married someday anyway, and then I'd be with her all the time.

I don't know who did it. I don't know who to blame. Maybe it was the guidance counselor. I saw my file, the one she kept. I wasn't that curious, but I had already broken into the school. Lots of teachers leave money in their desks. In my file, it said: ATTACH-MENT DISORDER. And the words "unhealthy relationship" a lot. About me and Darla. So maybe it *was* the guidance counselor. Or it could have been Darla's parents. But I know that it wasn't what *she* said—that she just wanted to have dates and stuff with other boys and maybe we were too close and she was too young to make a commitment. I know Darla would never have said anything like that unless someone had told her to do it.

I didn't say anything. I didn't go back to school the next day. I had to think things over.

It's Friday now. The last Friday of the month. That's Dress-Up Day at school. Girls can wear makeup and high heels and boys can wear suits and all. Some of the boys don't do it, but all the girls do. I knew Darla would be all dressed up, but not with my bracelet. She gave that back. I have it with me. I always have it with me.

I'm getting dressed up, too. I have a full set of camouflage gear that I bought. And an M-15 rifle. It looks just like the ones they used in Vietnam, but it doesn't fire on full-auto—you have to pull the trigger each time to make it shoot.

I have four full clips. I taped one to the magazine, like it showed me in this book I bought through the mail, and I put the other two in my belt.

I don't know who did this to me and Darla. But, after today, it won't matter. I'm going to fix everything, and then they'll be sorry. They'll never know why. I know what I have to do when I'm done.

And when they come here to tell my mother, they'll see where I started.

for Chet Williamson

HOMELESS

When I was a little kid, I saw this demonstration in the park near my house. A lot of people, screaming and yelling. Most of the men had long hair. The man who lived with my mother said they were fags. There was a big sign. *BRING THE WAR HOME!* it said.

I thought if those fags could live with me they would know it already was.

I hated them because they didn't.

Hate was easy.

When I was a kid, I liked fighting. I was real good at it. I don't feel pain much. My mother's boyfriend taught me that.

Crying only made him happy. Hurting me made him happy.

I always made him happy until the day I killed him. I thought that would make me happy, but it didn't, not really. He died so quick, and then there wasn't nothing more to do to him.

They put me in a place they called a Juvenile Home. It wasn't so bad. They let the kids fight a lot. The bosses liked that. On Fridays, they let us fight with gloves on. Sometimes they even had people from the outside come in to watch.

I was pretty good at that, even with bigger kids.

One day, a man came in to watch. He said he would take me out of that place. I could go and live with him. He was going to train me to be a fighter.

I was almost sixteen then, so I said okay. The man fixed it with the bosses, and they let me go.

Where this man lived, it was like a farm. "This is your home now," he said.

All my life, I was in homes.

He trained me all the time. I wore the mouthpiece all day long, so I would always breathe through my nose. I did sit-ups with a heavy thing around my forehead, so my neck would get strong. He showed me how to use my hips when I punched. How to punch through things, instead of just at them.

That didn't make sense to me except when I could spar. I liked to punch through people.

He put me in amateur fights. Big pillow gloves and headgear. It was hard to really hurt somebody—if you got them hurt even a little bit, the referee would step in and stop the fight.

I hated it when they did that.

The man wanted me to win medals, fighting amateur. But I would get too excited when I hurt someone. I got disqualified in a lot of fights. After a while, they wouldn't let me in the tournaments.

The man said that was okay—I could turn pro when I was eighteen.

I did that. I won a lot of fights quick. One time I was fighting this black guy. He was real slick. I couldn't hurt him no matter what I did. I lost the fight, but that wasn't what made me mad. I was mad I couldn't hurt him.

I kept fighting, but I hated it. The rules, that's what I hated. If I couldn't hurt them, what good was it?

So I went away. I just got on a bus and went away.

I had some money. Not much. I didn't need much. I found a room. I got a job in a car wash, but I got fired.

A whore asked me what I did, so I told her I was a fighter. She told me about these fights. In a basement. No gloves, just fighting. The people watching bet on the fights.

I liked that better. Nobody stopped the fights.

I could see the people watching got excited, too. That made me mad. Hurting people was just for me.

I started doing that.

It always made me excited. The more I did it, the more I liked it.

At the first trial, they said I killed a lot of people. I got sentenced to life. The judge made a speech. He said the prison was going to be my home forever. He wouldn't look me in the face. He was too scared.

They didn't have the death penalty there, so another state asked for me. They took me out in chains, and I had another trial.

They said the same thing, but this time the judge said I had to die.

Since then, I've been here. A long time. In this one room. People write me letters. Women want to marry me. They write disgusting things to me.

It used to make me frustrated, being here. It was hard to hurt anyone. I got one guy, on the way to the showers. They don't let me out when there's other people around anymore.

A doctor came to talk to me once. He asked me why I did it. I told him I liked it. He asked me why I never killed women. Like he was disappointed. I tried to get him to come into my cell, but he wouldn't.

A priest came, too. He told me there was things I could do. Before they killed me. Things that would make it all right later. If I didn't do the things, I would go to hell.

He wouldn't come in the cell with me either.

They're going to do it tomorrow night. Lethal injection, that's what they use in this state.

The warden came to the bars. He asked me, did I want anything before they did it. He called me "son." I wanted to hurt him so bad that I felt it deep inside my body.

Some organization sent me a copy of a telegram they sent to the Governor. They're against the death penalty.

There are people outside—I can see it on the TV they have in the corridor. A demonstration. People carrying signs saying they shouldn't kill me.

I hate them all.

I just want to go home.

for Gary Lovisi

MISSION

"I don't get it," the cop said to me. "What's the point? You come in here, you say you want to confess to the . . ."

"Killing," I said, finishing his sentence.

"Yeah, okay, the homicide. You understand, we get all kinds of . . . people who confess to things. Especially when it hits the media so big. But where they always slip up is on the details."

"What details?"

"Details beyond what was in the papers, all right? Something to prove it was really you that . . . did it."

"I did it."

"Yeah, yeah, I know. That's what you told the desk sergeant, that's what you told the uniforms. And that's what you've been telling me. Only that's *all* you've been telling me. You did it, prove it," he challenged.

"I don't have to prove anything," I told him, staying calm in my center. "That's your job."

Another cop walked into the interview room. A big man with a moon face and small, flesh-pouched brown eyes. The first one was dressed in a midnight-blue Armani one-button suit, longish dark hair carefully gelled and styled, a gold chain loose around his left wrist along with a matching Rolex. His cologne overcame even the haze of cigarette smoke that hung in the room. He hadn't offered to shake hands. I'd already forgotten his name—Detective Something. The new one's wardrobe was strictly bargain-basement, right down to the clip-on tie and the wash-and-wear shirt that looked like it had seen more wear than wash.

"My name is Nexor," he said. "Al Nexor." He held his hand across the table for me to shake. I took it, measuring his strength, masking mine.

"Adam Stone," I replied.

"Mr. Stone," he said, "the reason I'm here is that some things don't add up . . . and I thought you might help us straighten them out."

"What things are those?"

"Robbie Malton, he was in your school, wasn't he?"

"Yes."

"And you knew him?"

"Yes."

"He was how old? Nine?"

"Yes."

"But he'd already been studying with you for a couple of years?"

"Yes."

"What is all this ying-yang?" the slick-haired cop cut in. "We don't need no yes-and-no from you, pal—we need the details, like I told you before. Now cut the crap!" he snarled, slapping one palm hard against the tabletop.

I looked through him. The wall behind was the color of dirt-laced cream, some of the plaster peeling. It looked like the age-spotted back of an old woman's hand.

"Robbie's mother enrolled him in your dojo?" Nexor asked, as though the other guy had never spoken.

"Yes," I answered him the same way.

"Because he was getting bullied?"

"Yes."

"And had no father at home to teach him how to defend himself?"

"Yes."

"And could he?"

"Could he what?"

"Defend himself."

"Against kids his age," I said quietly.

"What is this 'dojo' stuff?" the slick-haired cop asked Nexor.

The big man turned to face the other cop, talking like I wasn't in the room. "Mr. Stone is a martial artist. A very high-ranking *karateka*. Fifth-degree black belt in shodokan, sixth in tae kwon do. He fought on the Thai boxing circuit. And he was the first European to study t'ai chi in a Buddhist temple."

Slick Hair started to say something, but Nexor rolled on, uninterrupted. "Mr. Stone eventually developed his own style: Shen Chuan. He's one of the youngest Grand Masters ever to be certified for his own school. His dojo has been operating ever since . . ." He turned his large head toward me, asking: "Nineteen eighty-eight?"

"Yes," I answered him.

". . . when he returned from Japan," Nexor continued, as though there had been no interruption. "Mr. Stone remained in Southeast Asia after the war."

"You was in Vietnam?" the slick-haired one asked me.

"For a while," I said softly.

"You seen any action?"

I laughed at him. His face flushed.

"Mr. Stone was with SOG," Nexor said to Slick Hair. "Special Operations Group. He was in Cambodia, too. And Laos, yes?"

I held his eyes. If he had dug all that deep, he would know I wouldn't answer that question.

"What's that mean?" Slick Hair asked.

I looked into his eyes, telling him everything he needed to know—if he had the background.

He didn't. "Mr. Stone worked alone," Nexor said to Slick Hair. "Behind the lines. Taking out targets. With his hands."

"You was one of those ninja guys?"

I laughed at him again.

"I met plenty a guys like you," Slick Hair said, his face darkening. "Black belts, big deal." He took a heavy slapjack out of his inside pocket, patted it against his palm. "I never seen one yet who could karate his way out of a real fight. You know what I mean, pal? No referee, no gloves, no nothing."

"Put it away, Johnny," Nexor told him. "You're embarrassing yourself."

"Hey! This isn't your—"

"It is now," Nexor told him gently. "That's what I came in to tell you. The Captain's taken you off the case."

"You think so?" Slick Hair challenged. "You know this one's a goddamn slam dunk, so you're gonna hog the spotlight? Big man cracks the Malton murder case. Well, forget it, Nexor. You got your rabbi, I got mine. And the Captain ain't the boss, the Chief is, you catch my drift?"

"Drift on *out*," Nexor told him calmly. "Do whatever it is you think you can do. I'll be right here."

Slick Hair slammed the door to the Interrogation Room behind him as he exited.

Nexor turned so he was facing me squarely. "I've done a lot of work on this one," he said softly. "I never spoke to you before today, but I know you. And I know you didn't kill that little boy."

"How could you know that?" I asked him mildly.

"Because I know who did," he shot back, watching my eyes.

He was looking in the wrong place. I kept my *ki* in check, stayed down in the windless part of my center. "Who?" is all I said.

"Samuel G. Parnell. Age thirty-four. Six foot, one inch. One hundred and seventy-four pounds. Brown hair, blue eyes. Tattoo of a snake on the back of his right shoulder. Parnell tells stories. Sometimes he's an ex–Green Beret. Sometimes he's a private investigator. Or an agency official. Or an undercover agent for the feds. Only thing that's consistent about Parnell is that he always lies."

I didn't say anything. Just watched and waited.

"Parnell's got a black belt. I don't know what style, or even if it's true—his stories change a lot, like I told you. But we do know one true thing about him."

I kept watching.

"We know he's a child molester. Two prior convictions. He's a camouflage specialist. Loves those volunteer organizations that work with fatherless kids. Boys. Parnell only does boys. Never does *time*, though. He's supposed to be in some kind of special psychotherapy. On probation, too."

I didn't move, staying true—to my name and to my training.

"And we got a witness. A stand-up, disinterested eyewitness. Someone who saw Parnell with Robbie just before the kid went missing a few weeks ago."

"What does Parnell say?" I finally asked him.

"Parnell? Well, see, we can't find Parnell. I figure he's moved on. Changed his name again. Made up some new stories about himself. Maybe he's back to working the Internet. No way to tell. Parnell knew he wasn't gonna get probation on this one. He was headed straight for Remora. You know what that is?"

"No," I lied.

"It's a maximum-security prison for baby-rapers. Hard, *hard* time. Yeah, they get all the therapy they want, but no privileges. They have to live like monks. Nobody wants to go there. Nobody gets paroled from there either. They're all pariahs. Dangerous, degenerate freaks."

"I did it," I told him.

"Then tell me about it," he countered.

"No."

He stayed silent after that, just sharing the space with me.

Time passed.

"We couldn't get DNA," he said suddenly. "Parnell wore a condom, I guess. There's no forensics at all. But we found something inside . . . the body. Deep inside—it didn't come out until the autopsy."

"A Thai coin," I said softly. "A ten-baht piece. Silver around the edge, copper in the middle."

Nexor's face lost all its color. His body seemed to deflate right before my eyes. He tried to speak, but he couldn't swallow.

I waited for him.

"I don't . . . I *studied* you," he said. "From the first time you tried to confess. I was . . . overseas, too. I still got friends in the . . . Company. I know you reupped once. Then you got . . . sick of it, I guess. I know you drifted around, studying. Seeking the Way, yes?"

"Yes," I told him.

"I heard about you. Even back then. Everyone over there knew you. Or knew your work, anyway. Then it all stopped."

It never stopped, but I couldn't explain that to him. How I wanted to atone. How I learned I could not. Ever. I rejected their missions, but I needed one of my own. That's when I came back. Opened the dojo. Started what I thought was my path to the Way.

"You're a bushi," Nexor said. "A warrior. You served your country. You're a man of honor, that's what everyone said. Everyone. It'll be gone now. Your dojo, your life. Your *name*. How could a true warrior . . . ?"

He walked out of the room, his face wet with tears he didn't even know were there.

They'd never find Parnell.

It had taken a long time for that foul creature to tell me everything. I didn't want to make him talk. I hated when they did that to captives when I was . . . over there, doing that work. But he wouldn't tell me until I made him.

I didn't want to know it all, but I had to listen. He got in that zone where they talk and talk, where they *want* to tell you every-thing. You have to pick out the pieces you need from the flowing stream. He told me about hunting. He was a hunter, he said. But he wasn't alone. He had brothers. A whole tribe. Humans just like him.

When he told me about the coin, he died.

That's when I realized it wasn't enough. His death wasn't enough.

I owed Robbie more than that. I knew he was watching.

Nexor was right. But he didn't understand the truth of his own words. A true warrior's only ego is his mission. To find the Way, and to follow it. I knew where Parnell's brothers lived.

And, soon, I would be among them.

Seeking the Way.

for Professor Joe R. Lansdale

GOING HOME

1

The battered bondo-gray Chevy Impala was parked at the bottom of a shallow valley formed by a gently curving street flowing between a pair of stubby hills. Luxurious houses sat well back from the curb, nestled on lush landscaped lawns. The Chevy was twenty hard years out of the showroom, sagging on its tired suspension as if depressed by its prospects. A faint plume of oily smoke burbled out of its exhaust, quickly lost in the low-lying smog from nearby LAX.

A sleek new Ford Crown Victoria sedan with SECURITY SERVICES discreetly lettered in gold along its black flanks sat in the Impala's blind spot at the top of one of the hills, watching.

Behind the wheel of the prowl car, a narrow-faced man in his twenties peered intently through the windshield. "Can't see a damn thing in there. You think it's going down?" he asked, his voice throbbing with tension.

"Think *what's* going down?" the older, heavyset man in the passenger seat responded. They were both dressed in dark-blue police-style uniforms, complete with Sam Browne belts and 9mm semi-automatic pistols holstered at their waists, but without badges or insignia except for brass nameplates on their breast pockets.

"I dunno. A B&E maybe. Even a kidnapping. You know what they said at HQ. We gotta be alert for—"

"Yeah, right," the older man said, his voice tired. "Arab terrorists, too."

"Look, Mack," the younger man said, "I know I ain't no retired police *sergeant* like you was, okay? But that Chevy ain't from any of the houses in *this* community, and I say we—"

"And *I* say we watch and see, Horace, all right? Whoever they are, whatever they're up to, we'll see soon enough."

A patch of moonlight puddled on the Chevy's broad roof, its luminescence dulled by the faded paint. The window glass stayed blank. Another ten minutes slid past. Then a cigarette lighter flared inside.

"Damn! That was too quick. I couldn't make out anything. You, Mack?"

"A woman. White woman."

"What do you think she's—?"

"Let's go find out," the heavyset man said.

2

The black sedan slipped smoothly from its mooring at the top of the hill and approached the Chevy from behind, running without lights.

"When we get around the next curve, hit the flasher," the heavyset man instructed.

"That'll maybe spook 'em," the younger man protested. "And we got no backup. They could make a run for it."

"We don't get paid to do car chases, Horace. Don't get paid to get shot at, either. We get paid to keep outsiders away from all these fine, expensive houses, understand? They see the lights and they want to cut and run, that's okay—we've already done our job."

"But . . ."

"Remember what *HQ* said," the heavyset man sneered, sarcasm thick in his tired voice. "We don't take risks. We don't pull our guns. And we *don't* get sued. Now, do what I tell you, okay?"

The narrow-faced man opened his mouth, then closed it silently. As he steered into the curve, he reached down and hit the switch: The red-and-white light bar on top of the cruiser came to life, bathing the Impala with its warning glow. As the cruiser came to a stop, the younger man trained the side-mounted spotlight on the Impala's driver's-side door and slowly climbed out, adjusting the bill of his cap and squaring his shoulders. His partner was out ahead of him, moving smoothly despite his bulk, circling toward the passenger side. Despite his own admonition, the older cop's pistol was in his right hand, shielded by his hip, pointed at the ground.

The younger man stopped in his tracks as the Impala's driver's-side door opened with a protesting squeak. A spike-heeled boot hit the street in the bright spotlight, red leather with white snakeskin toes. Then a slim, blue-jeaned leg. Then the woman. Medium-height, slender with a tiny waist, thick long midnight hair curling out over the top of a white Western-cut shirt with rhinestones forming a V to the cleft between her breasts. She turned toward the narrow-faced man, shielding her eyes from the spotlight.

"What is this?" she asked, the Appalachian twang clear in her voice.

"Keep your hands where I can see them," the narrow-faced man said.

"And why should I do *that*?" the woman challenged, taking a step closer to him.

"Because I—"

"It's all right, Horace," the heavyset man interrupted, coming up behind the woman from around the front of the Impala. "Car's empty."

The woman whirled to face him. Her face was heart-shaped, set in hard, lovely lines. If she was self-conscious about the dark mole just to the side of her wide, lipstick-slathered mouth, it didn't show in her clear blue eyes. "You're not cops," she said suspiciously.

"Private security, ma'am," the older man said. "We work for the local community. Saw you parked here. Thought you might be having some car trouble, that's all."

"Well, I'm not," she said.

"Let's see some ID," the younger man said, moving close behind her.

"See some what?" she said over her shoulder, eyes still on the older cop. "I don't have to show you nothing. I was just . . ."

"Just *what*?" the younger man demanded. "You don't live here. You can't just—"

"Easy, ma'am," the older man said gently. "You know what it's like, doing a job, right?"

"Right . . ." the woman said. Slowly, as though she was acknowledging a difficult truth.

"Well, we're kinda under the gun here," the older man said, holstering his weapon for emphasis. "We got bosses, we got orders. . . ."

"Oh, all right," the woman said. "My purse's on the front seat."

Before either cop could say anything, she bent at the waist and leaned through the driver's-side window, holding the pose while the younger man visibly relaxed and grinned appreciatively. And the older man's hand crept back toward his holstered pistol.

The woman's upper body emerged from inside the car, a thick pink vinyl wallet in her hand. "Step to the side, would you?" she said to the younger man. "Let me have some of that light."

In a minute, she extracted a driver's license, held it out to him.

"LaVonda Greene, that's you?"

"It is," she said, a proud ring to her voice. "My name, my momma's before me."

"You hillbillies got names just like niggers, huh?" The younger man smirked.

"Ask *your* momma," the woman shot back.

The older cop laughed.

The younger one glared.

"You all done playing with me? Okay if I go now?" the woman asked the older cop.

"Yes, ma'am. Sure thing. I wonder, though, if you wouldn't mind . . . ?"

"What?"

"Well, ma'am, you got to admit, it's a bit . . . unusual to see someone just parked out here, doing nothing. I mean, if someone was parked in front of *your* house, you'd be happy if an old fool like me rolled by to check it out, wouldn't you?"

"You ain't *that* old. And you damn sure ain't no fool." The woman smiled. "Why you want to play me like I'm one?"

The older cop grinned self-consciously. "You got me, ma'am. Sure enough. But you see how it is, don't you? We need to know what you're doing here. Just for the report, okay? I mean, your name doesn't have to come into it or anything. But if you'd just . . ."

The woman took a step closer to the older man. "I'll tell *you*," she said, a thin vein of honey in her steel-guitar voice. "Not him."

"Well, that's fair enough."

"Can we sit in my car?"

"Uh, how about if we sit in mine, ma'am? I got some hot coffee in there."

The woman held his eyes for a long moment. Nodded.

"Horace, you just give us a couple of minutes, all right?"

"I'll check the grounds," the younger man said, walking off to save face.

3

"It's my husband," the woman finally said.

"Your husband?"

"He's been tomcatting around. I just know he is. But I didn't know where. And then my girlfriend Mary Beth, she heard he was . . . involved with this married lady."

"What's her name?"

"Mary Beth, I just told you."

"No, the woman your husband's supposed to be—"

"Oh. I don't know her name. But I know where she lives. Right there," the woman said, pointing at the house across from where her car was parked. "Eleven Morningstar Place. I figured I'd just sit here and watch. See for myself. It could be just gossip, I know that. But I had to see for myself. And if I see his car coming . . ."

The older cop's laugh was a dry thing in the darkness of the prowl car.

"What's so damn funny?" the woman asked in a hurt voice.

"Ma'am, I hate to tell you . . . but even if your husband was getting it on with some other woman—and I have to say, from the looks of you, he'd be blind *and* stupid if he was—you're not going to catch him here."

"And why not?"

"This isn't Morningstar, ma'am. It's Morning*side*. You're on the wrong side of town."

"Damn!" the woman said softly. "I can't do nothing right. I . . ." She started to cry then.

4

An hour later, the ancient Impala nosed its way through a junk-yard until it stopped between a pair of abandoned wrecks waiting for the chop shop's day shift to complete their demise. The woman got out, snapping a lighted cigarette into the darkness. From her purse, she took a small ratchet wrench and went to work on the Impala's license plates. She put the plates into a blue gym bag. Then she pulled the black wig off her head and shook out her shoulder-length chestnut-brown hair. She pulled a pre-moistened towelette from her purse and scrubbed her face hard. The mole came off with the heavy makeup. Next she unbuttoned the Western shirt and stood stork-legged in a white bra as she pulled off the boots one by one. As soon as she slipped on a pair of scuffed white sneakers, she was five inches shorter. From her purse she took a small compact, popped it open, and surveyed her face. Deft movements with her fingers removed the blue contact lenses, revealing lustrous brown eyes. Finally, she pulled an oversized white sweatshirt over her head, pulled it down until it covered her hips. Then she started to walk through the junkyard.

5

A red Camaro IROC was parked a couple of blocks away. The woman unlocked it, climbed inside, and took off with a chirp from the rear tires.

Fifteen minutes later, she pulled to the curb next to a Goodwill bin. Stepped out and tossed the boots inside.

A Dumpster a few blocks down got the Western shirt. And a sewer got the wig.

As she drove away, she shredded the LaVonda Greene driver's license in her long-nailed hands, allowing the wind to scatter the pieces out the window.

6

"You're a genius, Vangie," the man said. "A pure genius, I swear it." He was tall and whip-thin, long black hair combed straight back in waves from a high forehead. His green eyes dominated a handsome face—prominent cheekbones, a slightly hawkish nose, cleft chin. The man was wearing a black silk shirt with mother-of-pearl buttons, sitting at a pink Formica-topped kitchen table. Before him sat six short stacks of gold coins. They looked like a millionaire's poker chips.

"Nobody saw you?" the woman asked.

"Not a soul, honey. It was just like you said. I swear, I don't know where you find stuff out."

"People talk in beauty parlors," the woman said. "They just talk and talk. They never expect the poor girl with her hands in their ratty hair is actually listening."

"But keeping those rent-a-cops with you so they couldn't patrol . . . I mean, that was . . ."

"All right, Chandler. Spare me the Vaseline. How much we got there?"

"Got one hundred and four of these things, baby. What they worth, anyway?"

"Those are one-ounce Canadian Maple Leafs. Two sixty to two eighty each, depending on the market. But we want to dump them all off at once, we're looking at maybe two hundred each."

"So that's . . . ?"

"About twenty thousand."

"All right!"

"Of which you owe the lawyer five, and two to the bondsman. And we owe Pablo for the car."

"Yeah, honey. But still—"

"But still *nothing*," the woman said. "I'm done with this. I told you—this is the last time. And I got to be at work in a couple of hours."

The woman got to her feet. She was wearing a man's flannel shirt and nothing else. She lit a cigarette, walked barefoot over to the kitchen window, and sat down, watching the sun struggle to come up.

7

"You don't know nothing about dope," the woman said to the man at her kitchen table the next evening.

"Pablo said—"

"Pablo's good with cars, baby. But just 'cause he's a Mexican don't make him no expert on marijuana."

"Vangie, there's nothing to it. Pablo knows a guy, he can bring it in. Ten grand will get us *fifty* on the street in no time. Then we can get—"

"All you're gonna get is your fool self killed, dealing with those people. I am thirty-three years old, Chandler Torrance. I been waiting a long time, living like this. I want to go home. I want to go back where it's green. I want to have girlfriends like I used to. I want to see my momma face-to-face, not over the damn phone."

"I know, Vangie. Me, too, I swear. But if we just had us some real cash, we could go back in style. Buy us some ground, and . . ."

"And what, sugar? You gonna *work* that ground? Or get a job, maybe?"

"It's not my fault," the man said sullenly. "You try and get a job when you're an ex-con. . . ."

"Chandler, I've had my brand on you since I've been fifteen years old. I waited for you when you went to the County Farm because *you* couldn't wait to buy a car to drive one. And when you decided you were gonna stick up a liquor store instead of working in one, I waited for you when you went to the penitentiary too. When that was over, I came out here with you, like you wanted. So you could start over. But you never did."

"Honey . . ."

"There's never been another person had his hands on me in my life, Chandler. Can you say that?"

"Well, I'm a man, honey. You can't expect—"

"You're not a man, Chandler. You're a little boy. My little boy. My pretty little boy. And I've been taking care of you, all these years, waiting on you to be what you always was in my eyes. But I don't believe it's ever gonna happen now. And I'm going home."

"Evangeline . . ."

"I mean it, darling. I know I said it before. But I mean it this time. Look in my eyes. You know I don't lie. Not to you. Look close, Chandler. I am going home."

8

The red Camaro was packed and waiting, the woman standing next to it, keys in her hand. Night was dropping fast.

"I'll be coming, Vangie, I swear."

"You know where I'll be," the woman said, her face soft and sad. "But I'm done with promises, yours and mine. You understand what I mean?"

"Even if you're with another—"

"If I'm with another man, Chandler, I'm gonna *stay* with that man. You tap at my back door, I ain't opening it, understand? You want to make it otherwise, you get in this car with me. Right now. We can be home in three days if we drive straight through."

"I've gotta meet Pablo. In"—he glanced at his watch—"about a half-hour. But after that, I'll—"

"Goodbye, my pretty boy," she said.

9

Chandler Torrance stood next to a short, stocky man who was wearing a Day-Glo–orange sleeveless shirt and a gray porkpie hat with a bright-red feather sticking jauntily from the band. They were at the mouth of an alley; a chopped and channeled '51 Mercury coupe gleamed in forty coats of dark-purple lacquer to their right.

A white '56 Buick Roadmaster lowrider pulled into the alley. Two Latinos got out of the front seat, one carrying a duffel bag over his shoulder.

The four men stood close together, talking. Cash flashed in the dim light. One of the Latinos held out the duffel bag. Chandler took it.

As Chandler was opening the trunk to the Mercury, the first shots took him in the back and he crumpled. Pablo turned, frozen. The two Latinos cut him down like wheat. One of them got out and ran toward the Mercury's open trunk. The red Camaro charged into the alley, engine roaring. A gun flamed through its driver's-side window. The Latino next to the trunk dropped. The other ran toward the Buick.

Sirens cracked the night open. The Buick fishtailed out of the alley. Vangie dropped her pistol and knelt beside Chandler on the blood-smeared pavement, begging him to come home with her one last time.

for Kelly

THE REAL THING

The middle-aged, middle-sized man sat behind a steel-gray metal desk. Venom-yellow glare from the naked fluorescent tubes over his head turned his complexion a sickly shade of ugly. The top of the desk was cluttered with paper: tear sheets from the personals column of a local tabloid, phone bills, a porno magazine with the cover ripped halfway off, the local Yellow Pages.

The man took a hard puff on the remaining stub of his cigar. He made a sour face, as though the taste had betrayed him. Then he started rooting through the paper clutter for an ashtray. After a few seconds, he made a grunt of disgust and dropped the burning stub on the nicotine-colored linoleum floor. He was grinding it out with his heel when the blonde walked through the office door.

"You're a genius, Lester," the blonde said, throwing an extra touch of throatiness into her husky whiskey-and-cigarettes voice as she crossed the room and parked one silk-sheathed hip on the edge of the desk. The man she called Lester opened his mouth to respond, but the blonde took a deep breath first, pulling his flesh-pouched eyes to her chest. The blonde listened to the silence, as if assuring herself it would hold. Then she crossed her muscular legs slowly and smoothly—the rasp of nylon was the loudest thing in the room.

The sex-sound made the man gulp, clearing his throat. "Uh . . . thanks, Delva. But I don't know what—"

"Oh yes, you do," the blonde interrupted. "I mean, you're the *boss* around here, right? Who else?"

"I don't exactly get your—"

The blonde twisted her torso. Her cantilevered breasts jutted at an impossible angle as her head swiveled to face the man.

"The kiddie stuff, Lester. That was real genius."

"Oh. *That*. It wasn't no big thing. To figure it out, I mean. There's a big market there. Different strokes, right?"

"You mean me?" the blonde purred, licking her lips.

"Cut it out, Delva," the man said. "You wanna be a lez, that's your business, okay?"

"So it's the same?" the blonde asked softly.

"Huh?"

"Some people are gay, some people like to meet-and-beat, some people love shoes, some people like to fuck little kids . . . ?"

"What's the damn difference?" the man replied, more life in his voice now. "I mean, it ain't *real* anyway, okay? It's a fake. A hustle, that's all. We don't do no out-call stuff here, not like some of those joints where you can just order pussy delivered like a goddamned pizza."

"Yes," the blonde said, a quick smile slashing across her full lips. "But the genius part was getting a real live little girl for the phones. I mean, it's just *amazing* that those child-molester freaks can tell the difference."

"Huh?"

"Oh, come *on*, Lester. You know as well as me that the rest of them can't tell. You got blimps like Marcia cooing into the phone like she's the hottest piece of stuff in town. You think if the marks could *see* that fat slob they'd still get turned on?"

"Yeah, I guess maybe you're right, Delva," the man said, an

undercurrent of sneer in his voice. "I mean, if any of the guys you phone-fuck knew you was a dyke, that'd sure—"

"Oh, bullshit." The blonde laughed. "Truth is, it'd be a big turn-on for them. They'd think they were so hot, they got me to go over, change sides, right? Besides, men *love* lesbians, don't they? You can get guys to watch girl-girl stuff all day. Try to get a bunch of girls to watch two gay guys getting it on—they'd fall asleep."

"Maybe you're—"

"Oh, you *know* I'm right, don't you, Lester? I mean, *you* know it."

"Look . . ." The man gulped. Sweat cracked under the hair-sprayed strands carefully combed to cover his bald spot, but the practiced sneer stayed in his voice. ". . . they're all the same in the dark, Delva. Pussy is pussy—and yours ain't gold."

The blonde leaned forward again, twisting her body even more radically, her face only inches from the gray man's. Her red silk sheath rose to just past mid-thigh, displaying thick black bands around the tops of her fishnet stockings. "You sure . . . ?" she whispered.

"Cut it out already!" he snapped. "You think I'm a trick?"

"No," the blonde said calmly. "I think you're a genius, like I said. How'd you ever get a little girl to be such a good actress? I mean, I heard her on the phone a couple of times—you'd swear she was really into it."

"She *is* really into it. What can I tell you? That's one grown-up little girl."

"Where'd you ever find her? One of the ads?" the blonde asked, pointing a long red-lacquered fingernail at a newspaper column circled in red: HELP WANTED.

"Not that way! Jeez, how you gonna put an ad like that in the paper? What we do, it's all legit, top to bottom. You know that. There's nothing illegal about any of this. Like I told you when you signed on, all you girls are independent contractors, right? There's a First Amendment, too, maybe you don't under—"

"So how *did* you find her, Lester?"

"I got an ad running. 'Phone Hostess,' you know. Anyway, this woman calls me, right? Regina, you remember her?"

"Uh-uh," the blonde said, a puzzled expression on her heavily made-up face.

"She was only here a few weeks. Anyway, one day, she comes in to get paid—that's the only reason any of them would come *here*. Hell, that's why *you're* here, right?"

"Ah, you know me so well." The blonde smiled. "So what happened next?"

"Next? Oh, you mean with the . . . Okay, she comes in. And she's got this little girl with her. She was, I dunno, eight, nine, ten . . . whatever—I can't tell with kids. So this Regina, she says the kid wants to *work*, okay? I thought it was a gag, but I figured, what do I got to lose? So I give her a tryout. Right here. And let me tell you, Delva, this kid's a pro. She was talking so hot to the marks that called, I couldn't believe it. And once the word got out, we were *smoking*, I'm telling you. There's nothing like the real thing."

"And then—"

"Let me finish for *once*, all right? It's true. What you said. The diddlers really *can* tell the difference. The word got around—now little Lolita's the hottest thing in town. You know what her rate is? Four ninety-five! That's a buck sweeter than we can get for anybody else, including *you*, Delva. And the beauty part is, it's all legal. One hundred percent legit. The kid's an *actress*, see? I don't know how her mother got her trained so good, but—"

The blonde got to her feet, stood facing the man, hands on hips. "You got my money?" she demanded.

"Sure. I got it right here. What'd you think, I was gonna run out on you?"

"No, Lester," the blonde said. "I know you're a man of honor."

The man flushed under his gray complexion. "You think you're better than me? You're a phone whore—I'm a phone pimp. I don't *make* nobody do nothing. You don't like the deal, you can just haul your fat ass out of here, go find a place where they'll treat you better."

"I'm sorry, Lester," the blonde said softly. "I was only playing."

"Don't play like that, bitch!" the gray man said. "You don't insult a man's honor in his own place. You know better than that."

"I *said* I was sorry, Lester," the blonde replied. She took a step forward, leaning one hip against the front of the desk. "You running a new ad?"

"That's right," the man said, only slightly mollified. "And this ain't for no sex stuff either. You know what's hot now? Psychics. Astrologists. Tarot cards. All that stuff."

"But you can get all that on the street," the blonde said, a puzzled tone in her voice. "Why would they want—?"

"Look, everybody knows, the Gypsies, they're just gonna rip you off. Besides, what if you want to talk to someone, say, two in the morning? Who's open then?"

"Yeah, but . . ."

"We got this all on *computer* now, would you believe that, Delva? Square business: You tell your birthday, all they got to do is push some buttons and they got like a whole *report* on you. Computers, it's like magic. They got *everything* on them. It's amazing."

"Yeah. I guess so, but . . ."

"What?"

"You ever try it? For yourself, I mean?"

"How could I—"

"You know what I mean, Lester," the blonde said. She stepped back from the desk, and began to walk in little circles, round and round, as if she were on a turnstile. The gray man's eyes followed—his gaze never reached her eyes. "You give everyone a tryout, right?" she said. "The way you did with me? You get their home number, then you call them and you act like a trick. So you can see how they do."

"What's that got to do with—?"

"You try them *all*, right? Even this little girl—what's her name again?—Lolita?"

"That's not her *real* name, for Chrissakes! What's wrong with you?"

"Me? Nothing. I was just thinking. You always have to test people, right? See how they do on the real thing?" The blonde stopped mid-stride, her back to the gray man, peering over one shoulder. "I just thought you could call one of those psychics," she said, "find out what's going to happen to you."

"Happen to me? What—?"

"Like are you going to win the lottery; stuff like that."

"Oh. Yeah, well, why should I? It's all bullshit, like you said."

"I meant, just to see how they come across. Look, forget I mentioned it—it's probably a stupid idea. Give me my money and I'll get out of here. What time is it anyway?"

"Exactly two-sixteen a.m.," the man said, pulling back a cuff to display a gold watch with diamonds circling the face. He started to paw through a metal box which held a number of index cards. "Let's see. You were on Monday and Tuesday, then you—"

"I sure hope this thing works," the blonde said, fumbling in her purse.

"What works?" he asked, looking up.

"This," the blonde said, pulling a semi-automatic pistol from her purse. "The silencer, I mean," tapping the long tube that extended from the front of the barrel.

"Delva, look . . ." The gray man's voice spasmed.

"Keep quiet, Lester. Keep *real* quiet. You keep quiet, you *stay* quiet, and I'm out of here in a minute, no harm done."

"It's in the safe," he said, a resigned tone in his voice. "If you needed cash, you could've always—"

"No, it's not in the safe," the blonde said. "It's in your records. I want this 'Lolita's' real name. I want her mother's name. I want where they live. I want it all—everything you got, okay? And *fast*, Lester—this whole thing makes me nervous."

"Sure, Delva—whatever you want, okay? It's right in here," he said, holding up the metal box with the index cards. "Let me just . . . here! I got it."

"Put it on the desk," Delva said. "And keep your hands where I can see them."

She moved quickly to the desk, swept the three index cards up in one hand, and glanced down to read the cards, holding the pistol steady all the while. "Okay," the blonde said. "That's it. You wouldn't do something stupid, would you, Lester? Like calling them yourself and telling them what just happened here?"

"No way, Delva," the sickly-looking man promised. "They won't hear nothing from me—you got my word."

"That's good, Lester. Don't worry, I'm not mad at you. This whole thing is all fake, right? Just like you said. It's all an act. Me too. I'm acting, too. Don't worry about the gun—it was just a joke. This pistol, it isn't any more real than what you sell."

"Delva . . ."

"That's not my real name," the blonde woman said. The pistol in her hand made a sound like an enormous champagne cork popping. A red dot blossomed on the gray man's forehead.

for Joel "Doc" Dvoskin

SLOW MOTION

I have to wait for the fear before I start my walk.

There's an Eastern man in town. Came by train. Dressed like a banker. A flashy banker. Says he's a writer.

Someone must have told him about me. Probably over at the Lucky Lady. One of the gamblers, one of the drunks—it don't matter.

He says he wants to write about me. Says people where he comes from, they're all interested in gunfighters. Lot of money in it if I'd tell him my story.

I asked him what a lot of money meant to him . . . what the words coming out of his mouth meant. I always do that when I'm striking a deal. I like to make sure.

He said I could get five hundred dollars if I told him everything.

I told him to give me the money.

He said, no, he'd have to hear what I had to say first.

We settled on half in advance, pretty much like I expected.

That was a week ago. I've been lying to him every day since then.

Now he's waiting to see one happen. Said I'd told him enough—all he needed was to see one happen so he could write about it from his own eyes. Then I could get paid.

That's why I do it, he thinks.

See, the way people talk, you'd think you could make a living being a gunfighter. You can make a living with a gun, all right, but not fighting.

Killing, that's what pays.

People talk different where the Easterner comes from. But they're just as wrong. They think gunfighters go around having duels just to see who's the fastest.

I didn't even know what a duel was until he told me. He said they do it back East, too, only they do it different. Two men start back-to-back. Then they step off while another one counts out loud. When the counter gets to the right number, both men turn and fire.

It's a matter of honor, the Easterner told me. If someone does something against your honor, you challenge him to a duel.

I never fought a man for honor.

Some do. Some men, you call them a coward or a thief or even a liar, they'll want to step out into the street and face you.

I've been called a lot worse than that, but it never got me into a gunfight.

A man in Kansas said things about my mother. I didn't do nothing. He kept on. I told him if he was truthful about wanting to fight me he could prove it. And not by calling my mother no names.

He couldn't call the vicious whore enough names to measure up to the truth, anyway.

But I didn't tell him that. What I told him was, put up a stake and I'd match it. Then we'd go out into the street like he wanted. Winner takes the stake.

He didn't have no real money. So I used on him what he was using on me. I told him he was a coward. Everybody knows I only fight for money. So him challenging me when he didn't have none—that showed his true color.

He was a young one. Stupid. He came back in a couple of weeks and put fifty dollars gold on the table right in front of me. Right in front of everyone.

I matched it. Then we stepped out. And it happened the way it always does.

He got at one end of the street and me at the other. Then we started to walk to each other. My legs always tremble terrible when it starts. I have to walk real stiff, so it won't show. When the *real* fear hits me, I go right back there. Where it first happened.

I feel it inside me. A red wash comes over my eyes. I keep walking. I have to get very close. People don't understand it, not at all. I have to wait for the fear to take over complete. One man has to draw first. They say it's never me. Because I'm so fast. But I keep walking because I can't do nothing else. I get stiffer and stiffer as I walk, like adobe hardening in the sun.

It usually takes them a long time to draw. Everybody knows if you draw too soon you ain't going to hit nothing. Cowards, they start shooting from a long ways away. It's a big thing to keep walking, get close. I get credit for that. But they don't know I can't do nothing else.

I keep walking until the other man draws. Then it all slows *way* down. Just like it used to before, when it happened to me. I can see every move the other man makes. Like he's doing it underwater. Then the fear rips and jolts and blood fills up my ears and I can't hear nothing and my gun comes out. Usually the other man shoots first. Not always. I've been shot a few times, but never one to finish me.

I always finish them. When I shoot, I don't miss.

And I *keep* shooting. Every man I fight, he gets all six.

Tomorrow, it will happen again. The Easterner can see it all. He can write it down. He'll pay me my money then. People always pay me after I do the work.

People fear me. And I know what they say about me. That I ain't afraid of nothing.

They don't know my secret.

For every man I kill, I feel less fear when I start my walk the next time.

That's the only thing I'm afraid of. One day, I won't be afraid enough. Things won't slow down.

That's the day all this stops.

for Tony

TRUE COLORS

1

After tonight, everything will be different. Nobody called for a fair one this time. Turk said that Panama has a pistol. A real one. His father was supposed to have brung it home from Korea, and Panama got it when his father took off. I don't believe it. I mean, why would anyone leave a real pistol behind? His father probably never even lived there. With him and his mother, I mean.

I don't know nobody who's got a father. In the same house, I mean. We all got fathers. Sugarcane, hell, he *is* a father. That baby Rhonda has, everyone knows that's Sugarcane's. Everybody but the Welfare. If they knowed about it, they'd do something to him. I don't know exactly what they do, but everybody knows you can't tell them nothing. They're just like cops, only without the blue and the steel.

It's funny when you think about it. I mean, Rhonda don't have no father, but her mother's boyfriend, he lives there, so he's kind of like her father. I know he tried to stop Sugarcane from coming around there. He was real vicious about it. I don't know why he gives a damn. It ain't like Rhonda's his own kid or anything. But he don't have no job or nothing, so he's always around the house.

Anyway, Rhonda lives on the block, so she has to be with one of us. That's just the way it is.

You can't Jap nobody where we got the meet set for. I heard one time there was this big meet Uptown. They made it for under the El. And one club, they got a couple of men in first. Up top, I mean. They just waited there. And when everyone got into it, they dropped stuff down on the enemy. Heavy stuff, like cinder blocks and all. Like concrete rain. So, anyway, ever since that, nobody makes meets except out in the open. This one's for the vacant lot off Forsyth. It ain't in our territory, and it ain't in theirs, either. I mean, one of us could claim it, but it wouldn't do no good, 'cause there ain't nobody living there.

It's better this way. There's something about walking to a meet with your boys. All together. You feel like nothing can hurt you. Some of the guys make a lot of noise. Some of them are real quiet. But the thing is, we be flying our colors. Everybody see us walking, they see us together, they know what's coming down.

It's funny how everybody knows except the rollers. I mean, *everybody* knows it's going to happen tonight. Even the teachers at school. But the rollers won't show until we're into it. I would never say this to anyone, but I think we all glad when they come, with their sirens and all. 'Cause if they didn't come nobody could leave.

Panama isn't the one I'm thinking about, even if it's true that he has a pistol. Mystic is the one. He's the head man of the Enchanters. The one who gives them heart. I don't think he's their best fighter. I mean, I don't know for sure, but he's not the biggest one. Usually, it's not the best fighter who's the head man, anyway. Like with us: Ramón is the best fighter. He *loves* it, man. I think if he wasn't in the club he'd be fighting all the time. With one of us, even. But Torp is leader, and Ramón never tried to take it from him. Ramón, he's a good man in a rumble, but he can't scheme. And if you can't scheme, you can't be leader, everybody knows that.

Me, I'm nobody. I mean, nobody in the club. I'm somebody on the street. I'm not no coolie, no off-brand. I'm in the Latin Savages. I wear the jacket, and everybody can see my true colors. What I mean is, I don't got no title. Not Warlord or Minister or nothing like that. So I never get to go first when we pull a train. And when I talk, they listen, but you know they waiting on some bigger man before they go one way or the other. And even the debs, they got their own . . . order, like. So I wouldn't get one of the best ones.

I think that's where I first got the idea. Lucy Ann just moved into the block. I didn't even know she was here until I saw her in school. She was very nice. Very polite. I told her all about the school and the teachers and the candy store and everything about the neighborhood, you know? We was getting along real good until she asked me about my jacket. It's silk. Black and blue. That's our colors. The debs wear the same jackets, only theirs are blue and black. Reversed, like. So she asked me, was I in a gang? Nobody ever asked me that before. I mean, everyone's got to be in a club or they ain't even like real people. I thought she would be impressed, but she didn't say nothing.

I saw her in school a lot. I mean, I don't go to school all that much, but she went every day. I found that out, so I went so I could see her.

I couldn't take her to the candy store, 'cause she wasn't a deb yet. So I talked to her in school. And after school one day, she said, did I want to walk her home? I figured that was it, you know? I mean, she didn't need no protection, not in the daytime. So why else would she ask me, right?

But when we get to her apartment, her mother is there. She works nights. Her mother, I mean. So she is home in the day. She was very nice, just like Lucy Ann. But she didn't like my jacket, either. I could tell that. She didn't say nothing, but her face got all funny.

She gave me food. *Good* food, man. Lucy Ann told her we was going to do our homework. Homework, that was funny. I figured, okay, *now* it was gonna happen, right? But Lucy Ann does her homework in the kitchen. There was only one bedroom, and that was her mother's. Lucy Ann told me she sleeps on the couch. It folds out, like. I didn't know what to do. I mean, I didn't have no books or nothing. So I just sat there with her while she did her homework.

I did that every day after that. I even brought some books with me. I mean, I can read and everything. A lot of guys can't, but I can. I used to like it when I was little. Before I was even a Junior in the club.

After homework, we would talk. Just me and Lucy Ann. Her mother never came in, 'cause she was getting ready to go to work. Sometimes I was even there after she left, but we never went out of the kitchen, me and Lucy Ann.

Bongo, he asked me once, was I cutting Lucy Ann? This was on the corner. Our corner, the Latin Savages' corner. Right outside the candy store. Now, there ain't no rules about it. I mean, it wasn't like you could only make it with a deb or nothing. Jaime, he got a girl way over in Brooklyn. That's okay. But I was . . . stuck, like. I mean, I wasn't gonna lie and say I was having Lucy Ann. And I wasn't gonna get ranked behind spending so much time and not getting any. So I told Bongo it wasn't his business. He gets mad behind that. But he don't say nothing more. I ain't the toughest one in the club, maybe, but I will go . . . and everyone knows that. I got heart. I proved in a long time ago, when I was just a little kid.

One day, Lucy Ann told me about her brother, Hector. She showed me his jacket. It was like mine, only gold and red. It said Dragons on the back. Underneath it, it said Warlord. I was . . . I don't know . . . shocked. The Dragons are a *big* club. All the way over in East Harlem, but we heard of them. Everybody heard of them. They was even in the newspapers. I asked her, was they coming here?

She said no. They weren't coming down here. She said her mother moved to get away from that. I didn't understand. I mean, how can you get away from what's everywhere? I couldn't see no

Warlord moving just because his mother did, anyway. But if Hector stayed Uptown, how come they had his jacket? That's what I asked her.

"They wanted to bury him in it," Lucy Ann told me. "But my mother took it out of the casket. Right in front of them. In the church."

"He was killed? In a bop?"

"Yes," she said. Her eyes were wet. I guess he had been a good brother.

I didn't know what to say. I could see, right then, that Lucy Ann didn't want to be no deb. And I know what the debs would do if she tried to be independent. You can't have that. I mean, if you let people not be in the club, then nobody's really gonna respect you. So I knew Lucy Ann was going to be a Latina Savage. And I didn't want nobody else to have her.

That's when I got my idea.

But Lucy Ann had an idea too. "There is a way out, Sonny," she told me.

"What way?" I asked her. "What you talking about, anyway?"

"For you," she said. "A way out."

"Why would I *want* to be out?" I asked her.

"So we can get married," is what she said.

I couldn't believe she said that. I mean, she wasn't even my girl. She wasn't in the club. And I never made it with her either, even going over there for a couple of months. Nobody gets married. You have to have a job for that. How was I gonna get a job? I am seventeen years old and in the tenth grade. I ain't gonna graduate. I got no . . . skills, I guess you call it. Even in shop class, I was no good.

"You will go in the Army," Lucy Ann told me. "It's four years. I asked the man in the booth. The one in Times Square. He said you would get an education. And you would only be twenty-one when you got out. The Army will teach you how to do something. They have all kinds of trades you can learn."

"I don't wanna go in no—"

"And every month, you would send me some of your pay," she said, like I hadn't said nothing. "I would save it. When I graduate, I will get a job. And I will live with my mother, so I could save most of my money too. When you come out, we will get married."

I knew guys that went in the Army. Right from the block. Sometimes, the judge will let you go in the Army instead of to reform school. But I never knowed nobody who ever came back here with nothing. José, he went in like that. But he was back in a few months. And he's still a Latin Savage. Just like the rest of us.

Your mother has to sign papers for you to go in the Army if you're seventeen. But that's nothing. My mother, she would sign anything. I don't even really see her much.

But I told Lucy Ann she didn't understand. I had a plan. If it worked, then nobody would bother her. She asked me what the plan was. I wouldn't tell her. But I told her I would protect her.

She said she trusted me. Nobody ever said that before. I mean, I guess the club trusts me. I got heart. Everybody knows Sonny will be there when it comes down. But this was different.

It was a couple of weeks later when they grabbed me. Right off the street. They was in a car. An old beat-up crate, a Mercury, I think. I was just walking home when the car pulled up and they all jumped out. They was Dragons, flying their colors like they knew nobody was gonna do nothing to them. Dragons walk anywhere. And the pistol they showed me, it wasn't no zip gun. I didn't say nothing.

We drove a long way. I was in the back seat, between two of them. They didn't say nothing. The best I could do was be a man, not say nothing myself. I wasn't going to sound on them, but I wasn't gonna be no bitch either.

They had a real big clubhouse. A whole apartment just for them. It was on the top floor. In the Projects. I'd never been there, but I'd heard about it.

We walk upstairs. It was a long way. There was Dragons on the staircase. Like guards or something.

The Projects is big, but they smell just like my building. I guess they all smell the same.

Inside, there's a man. He's in a chair in the corner, away from the window. I know who he is. Who he has to be. Durango. The head man of the Dragons. He tells me to sit down. Not like I'm a prisoner or nothing, like he invited me into his crib. A . . . guest, maybe.

But he doesn't offer to slap skin with me or nothing. Just looks at me for a minute. I look back at him. Not hard, but not scared, either. That's what I was trying for, anyway.

He asks me about Lucy Ann. I wasn't even too surprised. Not after what I knew about her brother. I told him the truth. About everything.

"They giving her a long time to choose," Durango says. Like he's wondering why.

I knew he meant the debs. "She don't go out," I told him. "You never see her on the block. So she's not in their faces, you know."

"But summer's coming," he said. "Won't be no school."

"That's right."

"And that's when they make their move, right?"

"Probably," I told him. It made sense, but I didn't know for sure. They got their own ways, the debs.

"It's on with the Enchanters, right?"

I was surprised for a minute. I mean, everybody in the neighborhood knows, that's true. But this was a long way from there. I was kind of proud—I mean, a big club like the Dragons knowing we was going to war. But I told him, sure, it was on.

"Hector was *mi corazón*," Durango said. "I was with him when he went. There was three guys hacking at him. Hector stood alone against them, but when he slipped, they had him. I stayed even after the rollers came, holding him. I watched the light go out in his eyes. His mother, she doesn't understand."

I didn't say nothing. I mean, sure, Lucy Ann's mother don't understand. But it wasn't my business.

"You want her in the club?" Durango asked me.

"No," I told him. "She don't wanna be no Latina Savage. I know that."

"So they gonna jump her in?"

"I dunno," I told him. Truth. "But you right. Summertime, they got to do something."

"Can't be on the street without showing your colors," Durango said. "You fair game then. Everybody take a shot. You don't want that for her neither, right?"

"No. That'd be worse. But I got a plan," I told him.

"What plan you got, Sonny?"

I liked it that he used my name. I didn't have no permission to use his, but it was respect he was showing me. So I explain. I take out Mystic. By myself. That changes things. I move up in the club. Maybe not to no title or nothing, but up, you know?

Durango, he just nods, like he can already see where I'm going.

"Then, when Lucy Ann comes in, I claim her," I said to him.

"You don't do no train for initiation?"

"No!" I told him. "We ain't like that. It's funny, right? I mean, we call ourselves the Savages, but we don't go for that rape stuff. And the Enchanters, that *is* what they do. Their debs, they all gotta do at least six, the way I heard. Gotta do six right in a row. Word is, it's their debs who made that rule. It don't make no sense to me, but I never talked to one of them, so I don't really know. But nobody gonna rape Lucy Ann."

"But your debs carry, right?"

He meant, they bring the weapons to the bop. And they take them away when it's done. Sometimes, even in school, they bring the stuff, when everyone thinks it's gonna jump off. I told Durango that was true.

He nods his head like this all makes good sense to him. Nobody else says nothing. It is very quiet in their clubhouse, not even no music playing on the radio.

Finally, he looks at me. "We got a rep," he says. "Citywide.

Clubs in the Bronx, in Brooklyn, even, they know us. If we was to take in an outsider, he would have to *earn* in. Earn big, you understand?"

I nodded like I understood, but I didn't. Not really. I mean, sure, you want to be with the Dragons, you couldn't just walk in and sign up. Like with the Army. I heard some of the colored clubs was citywide. Not just with rep, for real. I mean, they had men all over. But we don't got no coloreds where I live, so I never seen it for myself. They all colored, and we all PRs, and the white boys, they had their clubs too. But it wasn't about *your* color, it was the colors you fly. Those be your true colors. Everybody knows that.

"Give me the piece," Durango says.

One of his boys hands him a pistol. A real little pistol. He looks at it for a minute, then he gives it to me. It had two barrels, one over the other.

"That there's a derringer," Durango says to me. "Only a twenty-two. Just like a zip, but this is a real one, understand? I mean, it ain't gonna blow up in your hand. But it's like a zip 'cause you got to be very, very close for it to work. You can't blast nobody across the way with this. Even if you hit him, you don't take him down. You ever been hit with a zip?"

"No," I tell him. "Sometimes, when we're into it, I can hear them . . . pop, like. But I don't know nobody ever got hit with one."

"I was," he told me. He opened his shirt and he showed me. Just a tiny little dot on his chest. "It didn't go in deep," he said. "I didn't even know I was hit until later. Didn't have to go to no hospital or nothing. We just dug it out."

"Okay," I say.

"Okay? Nah, that ain't where it is, Sonny. There ain't but one way you be with us. You got to bring us something, understand? You bring us Mystic. Like you planned."

"But I—"

"We ain't looking to take over your club," Durango said. "We don't care nothing about no . . . What you got, anyway? A dozen men?"

"Fifteen for sure," I told him. "For the meet, maybe twenty or more."

"And the Enchanters, they got a couple more, but it's about even?"

"About even," I agreed with him.

"This is how it is," he told me. "You can't even *show* the piece until you get right on top of him, understand? You got to fight your way there. What you use?"

I knew what he meant. Some guys use knives, but most of them use baseball bats or pipes. Something long. Maybe they carry a knife just in case, but knives, they more for one-on-ones. "A chain," I told him.

"Good. Walk *right* for him. Let him see you coming. You got to cut off your own Warlord, 'cause he's gonna want him. So you go right to him, got it?"

"Yeah," I said.

"Don't be cocking the piece," he said, taking it out of my hand and showing me what he meant, "until you ready to use it. And make sure you get him in the head. You got two shots. Don't be wasting one."

"All right."

"You get Mystic and you a Dragon," he said, looking around the room like he was waiting on a challenge. But nobody said nothing.

"I . . ." I didn't know what to say. I mean, this wouldn't fix nothing.

"You be with us then," he said. "For maybe two, three weeks. That's all it's gonna take."

"Take for what?"

"For you to go in the Army," he said. "They gonna be looking for whoever dusted Mystic anyway. And you be gone."

"But Lucy Ann—"

"Lucy Ann gonna be flying colors, Sonny. Next day, walking to school, Lucy Ann gonna be wearing Hector's jacket."

That was fair, what he said. If I was a man, if I loved Lucy Ann, I had to take care of her. That was my plan. Now they was telling me she was safe. No matter what.

2

So it's tonight.

I can see them coming. Just like a black blot, moving toward the open ground. The debs are over to the side, watching. I got my chain. Got my hands wrapped in tape. Got the pistol in my jacket pocket.

I see Mystic.

It's my time now.

Time to show my true colors.

for Wendy

UNDERGROUND

CURTAINS

I am very patient. I know I have to wait. It's not enough to be patient. . . . I have to *be* patience. The way they taught me in the temple.

At first, I tried to edge a little closer every day—inches only, but then I realized the Questioner was just playing with me. So now I'm unpredictable: one day I move a foot or so toward her, the next an inch or two back. Sometimes sideways. And, for days, I don't move at all.

I don't respond to anything except her voice. The softer she speaks, the closer I come to her. The Rulers call this a Siren Call. I don't know why they call it that. Nobody knows why the Rulers call things what they do. It's not important now. What's important is that she thinks she's controlling. And what I found was, as long as she thinks she's in control, she's not afraid.

I need her not to be afraid. I send my calm out to her—in gentle waves, lapping against her spirit.

The men and the women of the Rulers are different. To calm the men, you have to let them feel your fear. For the women, you have to let them feel your gentleness—they have to know that you won't hurt them.

I wonder how the men and women of the Rulers ever have sex, then. But maybe they don't. The whisper-stream says they don't—it says they clone. But that's only because you never see any of the Rulers in the Sex Tunnels. Except the Police, of course. And they never take any, that's what people say. But the Book Boys don't write that on the walls, because we never write rumors.

If the Book Boys ever wrote a rumor on the walls, it would become the truth. So we could never do that.

The gentle waves I send are like the tide, in and out. Now they're all coming in from behind her, washing over her back.

But because I send the tide, the undertow is within me, too. And it's very deep. I can call it in. When it locks on, everything will go under. And stay there.

I keep a journal. In my head only—they read everything in here. But I write stuff, too. For them to read. That helps to keep them calm.

They asked me if I wanted to write on the walls, but I told them I didn't have any paint. That's when this started, really.

The Questioner is one of them. Another drone who thinks she's a leader because she has a title, an office. The Rulers don't call her what she is.

I'm in here because I called things what they are.

That's the part of my training they know about. In the temple, truth is God. That was a religion once. Before the Terror. Outside. They called the religion "Journalism."

And some say—the legends say, anyway—that when Journalism stopped worshipping Truth, that was the start of the Terror.

The Rulers know about the temple. They know it's somewhere in the Uncharted Zone. But they didn't know where it is. Their scouts could never find it. Because it's not in one place anymore.

A lot of years after the Terror, a new crew started up in the tunnels. None of the others know exactly when that happened, because the new crew was just *there* one day . . . like it had always been. And that's what the Sages say: that we had been here all along.

The other crews called us the Book Boys because we wrote on the walls of the tunnels. We wrote what happened. We always wrote the Truth. After a while, nobody really paid any attention to the InfoBoards anymore.

Lots of crews write on the walls in the tunnels. They do it to mark their territory, or to send messages, or just to scream. But we're the only ones who write in blue.

"If it's written in blue, it must be true," that's the word in the whisper-stream.

It's a special shade of blue. They only make it in the temple. The Rulers know this, but they can't change it. First they tried to imitate it, but they could never get the color exactly right. The whisper-stream says there's a secret ingredient in the blue that comes from the temple. Nobody knows what the secret ingredient is, but everybody agrees . . . it must come from Outside.

The temple has a link to Outside, that's what everyone believes. So, when the Book Boys write, it's not only true, it's a link to Outside, too.

The Rulers did what the Rulers always do. They made a Rule. If you break a Rule, you go to the HydroFarm. If you break a Major Rule, you go for a year.

And for a Violation, you get put Outside.

The whisper-stream says that the first Book Boys who got put Outside . . . after a long time, they found a way to come back. And that's when the temple started. So there were Book Boys before there was a temple, if that legend is true.

It doesn't matter.

It is a Violation to be a Book Boy. Even if you're a girl. There are girls in the Book Boys too, but they still call all of us Book Boys. I don't know why. In the temple, they said that, at first, we always called ourselves Book Boys so the Rulers would think that there were only boys in the crew. That way, the girls would be safe. But the Rulers know now, and I guess they could change our name if they wanted.

It doesn't matter what the Rulers call something. In the whisper-stream, we would always be the Book Boys. In the temple, they talk about tradition. How truth always lives.

"Whatever the name, the truth is the same."

That was one of the first lessons in the temple. One of the things we had to practice writing. All the Book Boys have the same handwriting. The exact same. We never sign our writings, the way other crews do. The Rulers can't tell which of us wrote any particular thing.

There's another crew. The Guardians. They don't come from the temple, but they protect us. They're a war crew, mixed skin/shades and everything. If anyone tries to sign what we write, the Guardians hurt them. And if anyone tries to erase what we write, the Guardians kill them.

Just being a Guardian is enough to get you sent Outside. That's a Violation all by itself, same as being a Book Boy.

We never meet them, but we know them. We are all One, that's another thing they taught us in the temple.

But lessons aren't important—*learning* the lessons, that's what's important. Once you learn a lesson, it's in you.

Then you go and do your work.

I have my work now.

If I get too close to her, the curtain will come down. A Jexan curtain, floor to ceiling. Come down right between us—like the laser-proof barriers they have in the Sex Tunnels.

I don't know which tunnel I'm in now, but I know I'm still Underground. Outside, there are no Rulers.

They want me to tell them things. A lot of things. But, mostly, they want to know where the temple is. Nobody can tell them that. The temple moves. All the time. When you need to go back, you just step into the Uncharted Zone and start your walk. You move until one of us finds you. If anyone follows you, all you have to do is wait—the trackers stop, sooner or later. The Uncharted Zone is full of things that can stop them.

So there's really nothing for me to tell the Rulers. Except the truth.

But they don't know that. They think Book Boys can't lie. But we can. We're not allowed to *write* a lie, but we can *speak* one. If we have to do it to survive.

The Rulers have serum. They have electrodes. They have girls who offer you sex. Or boys, if that's what you want. They have promises. They have threats. They have everything, and it's all to make you tell the truth.

But when you tell them the truth, they think you're lying.

That's what they taught us in the temple. That's what they said would happen if we were caught. The best way to lie to the Rulers is to tell them the truth.

They were right.

The Rulers have a lot of information, but they have no knowledge. They teach other things in the temple besides Journalism. That's how come we can go into the Uncharted Zone and stay there for as long as it takes. The Rulers never ask about anything else that we're taught . . . just where the temple is. That's all they care about.

I have to get close to the Questioner. When I do, I'll show her some of those other things I learned. I have to go back to the temple. I have to go back to my work.

That's the truth.

for Kamau

THE WRITING ON THE WALL

The first time I saw her, I was with my horde, so I couldn't do anything but watch. That's because everybody watches *you* when you're in a horde, and you have to be careful.

A horde's not like a crew. Not like the Game Boys or the Dancing Girls. Crews get formed by people who are . . . like each other, I guess. Or maybe people who like each other even if they're different. I don't know. I do know they're hard to get into. Everybody has to be in a crew, or you get swept up. Then you're in a horde.

My horde works the outside of the Sex Tunnels. We have to keep them clean and quiet. Especially clean. The Rulers don't allow any bad things near the entrance to the Sex Tunnels, because they want to be sure everyone who wants to can come.

I knew she wasn't one of the Sex Workers the second time I saw her. Not because she's a little fat. I know better than that. In the Sex Tunnels, there's places to buy all kinds. Whatever people like. And for every kind of person Underground, there's another per-

88

son who wants to be with them for sex. That's the way it was Outside too, before the Terror. At least that's what people say.

The reason I knew she wasn't is that she didn't live in the Sex Tunnels. It doesn't matter what the work is, the workers always live in the tunnels. They always need workers, because the tunnels never close.

When you live out your contract, you can leave the tunnel you were assigned to. But most people don't leave, they just sign up again.

There's a lot of jobs in the Sex Tunnels that don't have anything to do with sex. Just like the job my horde has—cleaning up. I mean, we don't have anything to do with sex either, but we help them run.

Our hardest job is the tunnel walls. We have to keep them *very* clean. The Rulers don't want *anything* on them, ever. The walls are pure, glistening white—so bright it hurts your eyes to look at it.

Most of the stuff people write on the walls is just silly. Sex stuff. Drawings of people doing . . . whatever. That always comes off easy. One shot of Chloroscope from a hydropistol usually takes care of it. When it doesn't, we have to use AC7. That eats the cover off the wall, but it removes anything on it too. Then we have to cover the wall again with the plastic spray-sheets. In a few hours, it always looks like new.

The real problem is the damn Book Boys. They're a crew too, like the others. But nobody knows who they are. They don't walk around in fans, and they don't wear crew clothes. You only know them by what they do. And what they do is write on the walls. In a special blue. The Book Boys are the only ones that can use it.

There's a one-hundred-thousand-credit bounty on any Book Boy. If you capture one, you collect. But you have to catch one actually doing the writing, and you have to get the special blue paint too—that's the only proof there can be.

When my horde arrived for its cycle, there it was, right on the wall near the entrance. Written in blue:

THE TERROR WAS NO ERROR
SEX WITH BABIES MAKES PEOPLE CRAZY

We all knew what it was right away, but there wasn't anyone in sight who could be a Book Boy. I did see a couple of the Guardians, but I wasn't dumb enough to ask them. That crew guards the Book Boys. Guards their work, I mean. If anyone tries to write in the same blue, and they're not a Book Boy, the Guardians take them away. Or kill them right there.

The Guardians are a warrior crew. Nobody bothers them. Sometimes the Rulers capture one of them. But never one of the Book Boys. Either the Guardians are too strong for the torture to make them tell, or they don't know where the Book Boys hide.

Every time the Book Boys write something on the wall of the Sex Tunnels, traffic slows down. That's why the Rulers make more Rules.

That's why the bounty is so high.

THEY DON'T WANT TO DO IT
AND IT'S TIME YOU KNEW IT

That was another message. It takes a long time to remove a Book Boy's message. Even when we take the whole section off and replace it, sometimes it seems like there's a little blue glow behind the new plastic. I know that can't be true, but other people have seen it, too.

PAIN'S NOT A GAME
AND WE KNOW YOUR NAME

It just got worse. The Rulers posted their own guards all around the entrance to keep away the Book Boys. But those guards, they scared some of the customers, so that wasn't any good.

I saw her again. She smiled at me. Quick. I don't think anyone noticed.

I wonder what she does in there. I know, whatever it is, she's always just finishing when my horde comes on duty.

THEY KNOW YOU RAPE
IT'S ALL ON TAPE

She was just leaving when we started to clean that one up. This time, she moved her head a little bit. Like telling me to come over to where she was.

The horde was all working. I moved toward the back. It was easy—everybody wants to be up front, so they could have a chance to capture a Book Boy.

She told me her name was Cassandra. I told her my name was Jamal. I asked her, was she with a crew, and she told me no. She didn't have a horde either, but she had to pay tolls to one to get to and from work every time.

I saw her a lot after that. Once she told me where she celled, I would go over to see her sometimes.

She's very nice. Very good to talk to. She would ask me about my work, but I never asked about hers. So, one time, she said that to me. I mean, she said, why didn't I ask her what she did. I was . . . embarrassed, I guess. She told me what she did. She was a cashier. People told her what they wanted, and she would direct them to the right arrows. They follow the arrows to what they want. After they pay her. The color of the arrow tells how many credits they have to pay.

She said most of the customers already know where to go and how much it costs, so she doesn't have to do much.

I thought that would be a good job. She said some of it was good. But some of it was evil.

I asked her what that meant, "evil." I never heard it before. She said, when people have sex with children, that is evil. I asked her why. She said because the children didn't want to do it, and the

Rulers made them. I said the Rulers make everybody do things they don't want to do. That's what the Rules are.

She said that was wrong.

How could that be wrong? I asked her. The Rulers make the Rules.

She looked real sad when I said that. She asked me, did I ever actually *read* the stuff the Book Boys write on the walls. I told her my job is to take it off, not read it.

We talked a lot. It was almost four cycles later when I asked her if she would be with me. My cell isn't even as good as hers, but if we each sold ours, we could get one big enough for the two of us.

"I love you, Jamal," she told me. "But you're not ready to be with me."

"I can get more credits," I told her. "All I have to do is—"

Cassandra slapped me. Real hard. Then she started crying. I tried to talk to her, but she wouldn't listen. I knew I did something wrong. And I knew I couldn't come back until I figured out what it was.

I thought about it every time I was at the wall. With my horde. By myself. All the time.

This morning, I got to the tunnels during the shift change, a few minutes early. Nobody was there. I saw . . . I saw a Book Boy. Writing on the wall. In that special blue. All alone.

And then I saw how I could fix what I did wrong. How I could prove to Cassandra that I was ready to be with her.

I never knew Book Boys could be girls.

for Dawn Bailey

SAFE SEX

The safest place in all Underground is the Sex Tunnels. A long time ago, the way I heard it, everything was different, and the Sex Tunnels were the most dangerous. They scared people, just being there. Nothing is forbidden in the Sex Tunnels. But that doesn't mean there are no Rules. The Book Boys wrote it on the wall. In their special blue.

IF YOU DON'T HAVE THE CREDITS
YOU DON'T GET IT

What that means is the one Rule. You have to pay. You can buy anything in the Sex Tunnels. Any skin/shade, any age, anything you want to do or have done.

The Rulers keep count. It goes on your encoder, so they always know. I mean, you don't even have to ask anyone. As soon as you go inside, the scanner tells the truth about you, and you follow the arrows to the subtunnel where they have what you want. After you see the cashier.

The only thing you need to know is that you can buy anything. That's what the Sex Tunnels are for. Nothing is for free.

Kill-sex costs the most credits, because they can only use the product once.

But nobody is afraid to go into the Sex Tunnels anymore, because the Rulers made it safe for everyone.

Only the Book Boys scare anyone. The Rulers say they are terrorists, and there is a reward for naming any of them. I heard some of them got captured once. It was on the InfoBoard. But the very next turn, the Book Boys wrote on the walls again:

> THE RULERS LIE
> THE TRUTH CAN'T DIE

So nobody ever knew what really happened. Everybody knows the Book Boys never lie. But did they mean the Rulers were lying about capturing some of them, or just . . . lying?

Nobody knows that. And there is nobody to ask.

People have sex outside the Sex Tunnels, but that has to be sanctioned—and only approved sex is sanctioned. So, if people want to have unsanctioned sex, but they don't want to pay for it, they have to go into the Uncharted Zone.

Some of those who wanted to have sex with children, that's where they went. They took the children with them. They said this was different. What they were doing was love. You shouldn't have to pay for love, just for sex. So they went where they could do what they wanted without paying.

But they never came out. They made their speeches and they went into the Uncharted Zone and nobody ever saw them again.

The Book Boys wrote:

> YOU PAY IN CREDITS
> OR YOU PAY IN DEBITS

That one was tricky to understand. A debit is a death. Everyone knows that. But . . . who died? And why?

It didn't stop anything. The people who say they love children go into the Uncharted Zone. They even sell maps of how to get to certain places where it is safe to have that kind of sex.

But nobody knows if the maps work, because none of them ever come back.

The whisper-stream says maybe they don't go to the Uncharted Zone at all. Maybe they go Outside. It's okay to do that to children Outside without paying. Here, you can only do it if you pay.

But the Book Boys say it's all a lie:

WE ARE NOT THE TERRORISTS
THE TERROR WAS OUTSIDE
THEN, NOT NOW

The whisper-stream says the Terror was just what those people do—the ones who want sex with children and don't want to pay the credits. The best way to do that is to breed your own. The whisper-stream says some do that. It is not sanctioned, and, sometimes, there are Bad Babies born that way. If the Rulers find one, it goes into the Sex Tunnels. So it isn't wasted.

I wonder if there are any Rulers at all. The whisper-stream says there aren't. It says there was a computer program. Outside, before the Terror. Because Underground had to be built *before* the Terror. It had to be ready for people a long, long time before anyone came down here. At least the life-support systems had to be in place. Some say it was prisoners who built it, the way prisoners on the HydroFarm work to make the power that drives everything here. Some say it was the children, the used children.

Nobody really cares what the truth is—people just like to talk.

Some say the Rulers don't ever put you Outside at all. That's supposed to be the ultimate punishment, but some say it never happens. They just kill you. Because some people, they *want* to go

Outside, and they can't get there. I know this one guy, Horto, he wanted to go Outside. But there is no Rule about going Outside except that's where you go if you *break* certain Rules. So Horto broke one of those, and they came and took him. The thing is, Horto said he would contact me from there. From Outside. And everybody knows there are transmissions from Outside. In the Uncharted Zone. But nobody knows if they are real, or just from some people Underground themselves. Horto never contacted me. I wish I knew what that meant.

I know secrets. Secrets even the Book Boys don't know. I was one of them. One of the children. They took me into the Uncharted Zone. They said it was love.

Here are my secrets: I grew up and I came out. There are others like me. Children, grown now. Some became just like the ones who took me into the Uncharted Zone. Now they say they love children, too.

But some are like me.

And those like me, we are the only ones who really know the ones who say they love children.

And we don't love them.

for Bror

CHARMED LIFE

I know she's in there. It was on the InfoBoard. Not her name, they never do that . . . her ID number.

I know her ID number, even though it's a secret. I know a lot about her. When she is with me, I will know everything about her. Now I have to find out. Where it is, I mean—where they are keeping her. And then I have to take her away. I know she wants me to do that. I can hear it in my head, telling me. All the time. It never stops.

The trick in here is to stay alive without doing anything to make anyone dead. Because, if you do that, you never get to leave. I know more about the HydroFarm from the whisper-stream than ever I knew from being here before. I was, once. Twelve cycles, that's what you get for what I did.

My name is Charm, and I'm Leader of the Dancing Girls. I got my name because I had none. Not name, charm. I was not charming. But

I could dance the best. Everybody knew that. Even those crazy Game Boys, the ones with the little pistols, they stepped aside for us. The pistols aren't that good. You have to be real close for them to work. And if we get close enough to dance, you're going to die. Razors never miss.

They're better for scaring people, too. A lot of people, they didn't know what the pistols were, or what they could do. But everyone knows a razor. Everyone gets afraid when they see the thin blue edge. Everyone knows how easy it goes through flesh. Everyone who knows me knows how much I like that.

A thick, heavy blanket of water comes down from above where we have to work. I don't know how they make it. One of the old men told us once that Outside, before the Terror brought everything Underground, the water came from above too, but nobody made it, it just came. Those old men are insane.

Not as mad as Radioman, though. The one who says I love him. He hears it in his head. That I love him. A boy. So crazy. I don't love anyone. I don't even know the word that they use. I know it doesn't mean sex. I mean, people who say they love, they have sex. But you never hear the word in the Sex Tunnels. Some of the Dancing Girls work there, for credits. A long time ago, the whisper-stream said, you had to live in the Sex Tunnels if you wanted to work there for credits. But it's not that way now. You just go into the main gate and tell them you want to work, and they measure you and capture your image. Then they ask you what kind of sex you will do and they put you in the right subtunnel. When you're done, you just walk out and collect the credits you earned. If you ever come back, anytime at all, they have your image and your other stuff and you can go right through the gate.

Radioman never tried to sex me. He was a Game Boy, when they still had their pistols. They were the ones who started the whole thing. With marks, I mean. You got a mark for every life you took. I had a lot of them too. I wore them on my thigh, hiding the secret. But not the secret the boys thought.

It didn't get crazy until two things happened:

The first one was the idea that if you killed someone with marks, then their marks belonged to you. So people stopped going after the easy ones and went after the ones who already had marks—you could get maybe a dozen marks for one kill that way.

But crews aren't allowed to fight each other. So a lot of people in crews got put Outside. The Rulers were confused at first, thinking everybody was breaking the Rules. But then they figured it out.

The second thing that happened, the bums made their own crew. Nobody thought this would ever happen. It wasn't such a big thing to the other crews, but it made the Rulers very upset. You could tell because they changed the Rules. The new Rules were even more tricky.

Most of the crews stopped wearing their costumes. And when they did, even then, it had to be on the fringes, near the Uncharted Zone. That wasn't much fun. People don't recognize you're moving all together in a fan if you're not dressed the same. So they don't get out of the way like they used to.

Radioman was a Game Boy. They said he heard signals in his head all the time. But he never got a signal to take a mark, so he never did. That meant he was the lowest in the crew, but he didn't care.

When he said he loved me, I just laughed at him. If he had tried to sex me, I would have sliced him. But he didn't. One of the other Game Boys did—laugh, I mean—so I ripped him. We were all going for marks back then, but the other Game Boys were scared to shoot, because the Rulers don't let crews fight and they were afraid it would look like that. We never did fight. Not as crews.

But the Rulers got it wrong. They didn't know it was about marks. And it didn't matter who you took them from.

There has to be a way to get people there. To the HydroFarm. Where they have my girl. Charm. I have to rescue her. They must have a way to get them there, and it has to be a conveyor. It's too far to walk and, anyway, the ones who come back always say it took a long time to make the trip. They couldn't see anything, but they were moving. And there's new ones back here every day. I asked a couple of them but they wouldn't tell me. After a while, I figured it out. They wouldn't tell me because they didn't know. And if a conveyor goes there, it has to be through the Charted Zone, because the Rulers couldn't have something as important as the HydroFarm out of the Zone. All the power for Underground has to come from the HydroFarm—they could never risk it.

I know who to ask. I just don't know how to ask. But the voices will tell me when they're ready.

The way they make you work here is they use what you make on you. Electricity. That works. Nobody wants it on them. And being wet all the time, it doesn't take much.

If you escape, they give you double whatever time you had left. It's easy to get away, but not many even try. Twelve cycles doesn't take long, because you can have Zoners for free on the Farm. Some of the people here, they don't feel anything, they just smile. They can still work, though, so nobody gets mad at them.

Even if you could get away, where would you go? If you have a crew, you can't go there. The Rulers will take them all for hiding you. Harboring, that's breaking a Major Rule. If you want to go back as Leader, you can't get the others in that kind of trouble. Actually, if you think about it, if you brought them that kind of trouble, there wouldn't be any of them to come back to. They wouldn't want you.

If I wait until my time is done, I can go back and be Leader again. There'll be a new girl, and we'll dance. I can't wait. That's the worst thing about being here—you can't dance.

I have a tiny little slice of nuim just under my thumbnail. It cost me a lot. Not credits, they don't have any in here. If you're caught with credits, they think you're getting ready to escape. And then you get the electricity. If you get too much, it's like you're on Zoners all the time, always smiling. But you can't even eat. They have to feed you with tubes. I paid for the nuim with sex. One of the Guards. I didn't even have to look at him while he did it.

I used the nuim and cut another straight, thin line across the front of my left thigh. The pain was wonderful. I felt something. I never usually feel anything. Except when I'm dancing. I love to cut myself, but I have to be careful, not let anyone see. And never deep. The blood dries quickly, and the moisture keeps it clean. The cuts look like painted lines now— tattoos, like some of them get. Even when the Scanners check us, they don't pay attention to the cuts. They're like marks, because I made them myself. Marks on me.

I know where it is now. I'm going there.

There's other Dancing Girls here. You're not allowed to even talk to another crew member while you're on the HydroFarm. Everything is on video. In the dark, they have infra and thermal—they can see your coding day or night. So there's no way to hook up.

But this . . . I can't believe it could be so easy. I mean, how could I even know how hard it was supposed to be unless somebody told me? A guard told me. They always want the same thing. The Rulers know the Guards are going to want sex. So they do things to them to make them not want it. But those things don't work. They don't erase things, they just bury them. You have to know how to dig down deep. The nuim helps. I do it anytime I want. The most important thing is never to let them know. I only have three cycles left now.

Charm is in my head. She will come with me. Sometimes I get a voice that says she won't. That it won't be Charm anymore. I remember once, when I was a Game Boy, she said she wasn't my girlfriend. She said it in front of some of the others too. I didn't mind, because I know Charm and me is supposed to be a secret. And that was Charm, so it didn't scare me. What scares me is the voice that says she won't be Charm anymore. The HydroFarm changes people, the voices say. I have never been there, so I don't know. But the voices know.

There's no perimeter here. You could just walk off. Back into one of the deep tunnels. I heard they don't even chase you. But you can't live out here. So I guess some people just die. If you make it back to the hub, they will video you sooner or later. That's how you get brought back.

I see Charm. I don't know if she sees me. I have to wait until she does before I take her away. I have to be quick and quiet.

Radioman has been here for three turns now. I see him, standing just outside the perimeter. He wants me to go with him. I have what he needs.

He has what I need, too. On my next turn, I'm going to go across. I can't wait anymore.

Here she comes. To be with me.

He even brought my razor.
   I'm myself now.
   Radioman was good.

for Anastasia Volkonsky

GAMBLERS

The whisper-stream says they used to have fights—sporting contests, I mean—like this all the time. A long time ago. Outside, before the Terror brought everyone down here. Way before I was born.

You can check out stuff like that—I mean, stuff that happened Before—if you really want to, but that costs credits. A lot of credits. And even then, you don't know if it's really true. The only truth in Underground is free—when the Book Boys write on the walls. Everyone knows that. If it's written in blue, it must be true. And only the Book Boys can write in that special blue everyone recognizes.

I don't care about any of that anyway. I don't need ancient Info, I need credits. Without credits—heavy credits—I can't play. And if I can't play, I can't get anything I want. That's my job, to play.

Most of the players aren't like me. They're not professionals. They don't think about the odds, they don't do the research—they just go with their blood, with their feelings. That's my edge.

You can't fix these fights. There's always rumors—about drugs and stuff—but it would be real hard to drug a Traxyl. You couldn't get a needle into them, and they only eat Zone Rats, those huge things that mostly stay out in the Uncharted Zone. I guess you could maybe drug one of the rats; then, when the Traxyl ate it . . . But I don't think it would work. It wouldn't be slick enough—everyone could tell.

That would be very bad. There's a rule against gambling on the Traxyl fights, but it's not a Major Rule, and the only thing they do is fine you when they catch you. That's part of the cost of doing business—it doesn't bother me. Anyway, one thing I learned for myself: everyone gambles, one way or the other.

And there's other rules too. Not the ones the Rulers make, but everybody knows and obeys them anyway. And if one of the Traxyl handlers tried to fix a fight, that would be the end. I saw it happen once. A handler cut his Traxyl's eye with a razor ring just before he sent him out. Traxyls can't smell or anything. And I don't know if they can hear too good either. But they need their eyes—big, huge eyes, so they can see in the dark when they go after the Zone Rats. The other Traxyl locked on to the one with the cut eye and it was over quick.

Traxyls don't eat each other. They kill for territory. Hunting space. If one comes into another's space, they fight. Everybody knows that's how they work. That's how the pit fights started, I guess. I wasn't the only one who saw what the handler had done. They just threw him into the pit and he was gone real quick.

No human would have a chance against a Traxyl. They're not that big—even the biggest ones are only about thirty kilos—but they're all armor-plated, and once they lock their jaws, there's no way to open them. Every once in a while, one gets loose, and the Police have to kill it. Shooting doesn't usually stop them. You'd have to hit them right in the eye to do that. And even then, it has to be one of the Superslugs—regular bullets won't make it all the way into their brains. So the Police have to blow them up. Anyone around gets killed when they do that. It's a Rule that no Traxyls can run loose. If people get killed to stop one, that would be sanctioned—not breaking a Rule. Besides, anything the Police do is not against the Rules.

The Rulers don't like it when a Traxyl gets loose, so the places where they hold the fights keep getting moved. Farther and farther away from the Central Tunnels. Some are so far away that you need to hire one of the Guides to take you there and bring you back. It's a funny thing about the Guides—they're all skin/shade 20+, almost a reddish color—and that doesn't make sense. I mean, if they know the Deep Tunnels—the ones far away from Central—so well, you'd think they'd be real pale from spending so much time there. But they're not.

Now almost all the fights happen near the Border, just this side of the Uncharted Zone.

Traxyls live in the Uncharted Zone. Trappers go in there to bring them back. A good fighting Traxyl is worth enough credits to live for a few years. Live *nice*, I mean, not just get by. Most of the Trappers don't succeed, which is why Traxyls are so rare. We know the Trappers don't succeed when they don't come back. So, in a way, they're just like me. I mean, people *call* them "gamblers" for going in there, but it's only the true professionals who go out and come back—the ones who make a living at it.

There's always rumors—that's what the whisper-stream is for, to carry them along—about people living in the Uncharted Zone. *Living* there, not just going in and coming out. I don't know if the rumors are true. And if they are, what would those people do about the Traxyls? I even heard the Traxyls guard the people from the rats, but that sounds so crazy—I mean, what's the odds on *that*? I check the walls every day, the same way everyone does. And, one time, the Book Boys wrote it in blue:

SURVIVE. STAY ALIVE.
BREED WHAT YOU NEED

One of the girls in the Sex Tunnels told me that meant the people who live in the Uncharted Zone bred the Traxyls to protect them from the rats. But girls in the Sex Tunnels say anything. This one said she was going to go out to the Uncharted Zone herself one day. To "join them." When I asked her what she meant, she just went back to work on me. Xyla was her name—that was about all I remembered.

But I did remember I liked her. So, next time I was in the Sex Tunnels, I asked for her. They told me she was gone. That happens all the time—I didn't pay much attention.

The only thing I really pay attention to is the Traxyl sheet. It costs fifty credits, and it comes out about a week before the fight card. It doesn't give you a won-lost record—that would be pretty stupid for Traxyls—the loser always dies, that's how they tell when it's over. The sheet tells you how many fights each one had before, weight and height, any crippling injuries—they fight Traxyls even if they're crippled, and some of them win that way for a while too—the name of the handler, stuff like that. The sheet never tells you where the fights are going to be. You have to buy that info too, but it's always hand-to-hand, and you can only get it at the last minute. The sheet gives you their records. The Traxyls, I mean. Every one has an alphanumeric burned into its side. This doesn't hurt them, just makes a mark on their armor. The hardest thing to guess is when a new one's going to be good. They don't train Traxyls or anything. Soon as they bring one back from the tunnels, they put it into the pit to fight.

You can't tell anything about how good they're going to fight by looking at them. I had to learn that for myself. At first, I would bet on the biggest one, but that wasn't . . . consistent. It wasn't a good system. In fact, *nothing* was good until I realized what the trick was: You can't tell *anything* about a Traxyl. There was one—M29X4—that won eleven in a row. That was a record. No Traxyl had ever done that. When I came to the fights that night, I saw he was matched against a Traxyl that had only fought once before. So the odds on the one-win Traxyl were about 50 to 1. And I found a Taker who was offering 75 to 1 just before the fight started, and I put up a thousand credits. And my Traxyl won. I bet I was about the only one who *did* win that night.

So that's my system. Once I realized that any Traxyl can kill another anytime, I just go with the ones at the longest odds. Now, if the odds are close, then I think about it a lot. I have to bet on every single match, otherwise the Takers would catch on to my system and I couldn't get any of them to do business with me. One of the hardest things about being a professional is to look like an amateur.

I'm not the only one with a system. When M29X4 got killed, a lot of people figured eleven wins was the maximum. So, the more a Traxyl won, the more people would bet on it—until it got close to eleven, and then they would back off. But when J44B8 won thirteen before it was killed, that theory got killed too.

I always wondered about the handlers too. It seems as if some of them even liked their Traxyls. I could never be sure, because you can't *touch* one or anything, but it looked that way. I saw one handler crying when his Traxyl died. But I figured he was probably upset because he lost so much money.

It doesn't matter now, anyway. First it was on the InfoBoard. A message from the Rulers that Traxyl-fighting had been upgraded to a Major Rule infraction. That meant a year on the HydroFarm if you were caught. But it wasn't clear about gamblers. I mean, fighting Traxyls was against a Major Rule, but was *betting* on the fights? So, in a way, I guess everyone who did it was gambling twice. You'd think that would scare people away, but it didn't.

Then the whisper-stream started flowing. It said the people in the Uncharted Zone were going to stop the Traxyl-fighting by themselves. That was crazy. I mean, it was a rumor inside of a rumor. Nobody even knows if there *were* people in the Uncharted Zone.

But no Trappers came back for eighteen cycles. And no more

would go in, even when the price for a Traxyl went up to a hundred thousand credits. It wasn't a gamble anymore; it was a sure thing—if you were a Trapper, you were going to get trapped.

There were still lots of Traxyls, though. Only one died in each fight, and there were plenty left. They just kept matching the winner from one fight against another, the way they always did.

They couldn't get more the way you'd think either. Traxyls don't mate when they're captured. I don't even know how they tell males from females, but they never have babies. Or eggs. Or whatever. I mean, you can't put two of them together to see if they would . . . have sex. Because they'd kill each other, and you wouldn't make a single credit off *that*.

I have been doing this for eighty-seven cycles. A long time. But I knew it was all going to end when the word got passed: all the Traxyls left were going in one last fight. It was going to run for as long as it took—maybe a quarter-cycle straight. Until there was only one Traxyl left.

DEATH WIND WALKING

That's what the Book Boys wrote on the walls. I figured it was proof that the last fight was coming, all right. So, when I got the last sheet, I also got the last word.

They had to hold the fight way out in the tunnels. So near the Uncharted Zone that the Police were really close. Another gamble. But that was the only way to hold a fight that size. There were over three hundred Traxyls left, and there had to be room for people to sleep, and make food, and everything—a quarter-cycle is a long time. It's hard to keep something that size quiet, and that made me nervous. But it was my last chance. I had three hundred thousand credits, and I planned to walk away with at least a couple of million. So I'd never have to gamble again.

They keep the Traxyls in little clear Jexan cages before the fights. So the gamblers can look them over if they want to. Some people think they can tell things like that. The cages have slots in the front, so all the handlers have to do is reach in and push them out into the pit once they throw the switch.

It was just before the first fight when I heard the noise. A high, humming noise I'd never heard before. Then they came in. Children. They don't let children come to these fights, but these were *all* children. Maybe a hundred or more. Holding hands, making this high noise. Everybody just . . . stared at them.

Then one of the Traxyls broke out of its cage. It went right for the first people it saw. You could hear that high noise the children made even over the screams.

More Traxyls broke out. People ran. But the children kept walking closer. Then some of them started to open the cages themselves. It was all blood and flesh and bone by then. Everyplace. If the Police heard, they never came.

The last thing I saw when I looked back was the Traxyls. They were following the children back into the tunnels. Moving toward the Uncharted Zone. But they weren't chasing the children. They were just trotting along next to them.

for Alice Darrow

JUST THE TICKET

1

It was almost two in the afternoon when the man casually strolled out of the public bathroom and into one of the long corridors of Atlanta's Hartsfield Airport. He was dressed in a conservative dark business suit and clean-shaven. Neatly combed unremarkable brown hair framed an equally unremarkable face. The most distinctive thing about him was his luggage: a beautiful alligator carry-on in one hand and a black leather computer case slung over his shoulder.

The man strolled the concourse, idly glancing into each gate's waiting area as if looking for his flight. But when he reached the midpoint, he took the escalator downstairs to the underground monorail that connects the terminals in the huge airport.

In the car, he placed the alligator bag on the floor, but he never loosened his grip on the computer case. The first stop was Concourse C. The man got off and took the escalator back upstairs.

Again he walked the corridor, checking each gate. He stopped in a bookstore, browsed the computer section for a few minutes, then went into one of the restaurants and drank a cup of coffee, slowly.

When he was finished, he returned to the monorail. He exited at Concourse D, and climbed to the Delta corridor.

Again he meandered through. Finally, he turned and sat down in the waiting area at Gate 22—a three-thirty-five flight to Chicago. The only other occupant of the area was an elderly woman reading a paperback romance novel.

The man seated himself carefully, placing the alligator bag on the floor at his feet. Then he pulled the computer case onto his lap, opened it up, and took out a gray laptop. He pressed a button and the screen gradually ripened into a complicated-looking spreadsheet, some of the numbers in red.

The man worked at his computer for about ten minutes. The elderly lady watched him covertly, eyes flicking from her book to the computer screen. She could make out colors, but that was all.

Then the man turned off the computer, closed it up, and replaced it in the case. He got to his feet, checked his wristwatch, glanced at the digital display over the ticket counter, and walked off.

In a few minutes, the gate area began to fill. The elderly woman kept her eye on the man's luggage. He hadn't asked her to, and certainly he would return in a few minutes. And this wasn't New York, after all. But still . . .

2

I was wearing an old Army jacket. I hadn't shaved in three days and I needed a haircut. Probably looked like I needed a bath, too, but that wasn't true.

It only took me a second to swoop into the gate area, pick up the alligator bag and the computer case, and start walking down the corridor like I had a plane of my own to catch.

I was almost to the very end when the cops stopped me.

"Excuse me, sir," the first one said, using "sir" like an insult the way cops do, "may I see your ticket?"

"What for?" I asked him.

"Sir, we've had a . . . That is, we've received some information. . . ."

I just stared at him. Right into his eyes. They hate that.

"Is that your luggage, sir?" the other cop asked.

"Of course it's my luggage," I told him. "Do I look like a goddamned Skycap to you?"

"May I see your ticket, sir?" the first one asked me again.

"I don't *have* my damn ticket," I said. "That's the problem. I came all the way out here, and then I find I left my ticket at home."

"And that's where you're going now?" the second cop said. "Home to get your ticket?"

"There isn't a whole lot of point in that," I said. "No way I get back here in time to make my flight."

"And which flight would that be, sir?" the first cop wanted to know.

"Why is this any of your business?" I asked him.

"Sir, do you mind if we check your luggage?"

"Check my luggage? I already told you, I'm going to miss the flight. Why in the hell would I want my luggage checked?"

"Uh, not check it on a flight, sir. Just check to see the . . . contents, all right?"

"No, it's *not* all right," I said. "I already left home without my damn ticket, now you're hassling me for no reason. This is really embarrassing," I told him, looking around at the crowd that had gathered.

"Sir, we have the right to check any luggage being carried through the airport. That's the law."

"Bullshit. There's no such law."

"Oh, you're a lawyer?" the first cop said, sarcasm dripping from his voice.

"No, I'm an ex-con, all right? You happy now? But I'm still not letting you search my luggage. You got no probable cause."

"Ah, a *jailhouse* lawyer," the second cop said. "What's your name, pal?"

"None of your business," I said. "I'm tired of this. I'm going home." And I started to walk away.

They put the handcuffs on me then. And brought the elderly lady over to where I was standing against the wall. She said she saw me take the luggage all right, but she had a plane to catch and couldn't she just . . . ?

The cops let her go, after they took her name and address and everything. Then they walked me back to the gate area and made me stand there with them while they checked the flight manifest at the desk. Then they went around the waiting area asking anyone if they lost some luggage.

Nobody said they did.

The well-dressed man never came back.

They arrested me. I spent the night in jail.

3

The next morning, the judge said bail would be ten thousand dollars. I told him I didn't have ten thousand dollars. He told me I could wait for my trial, then, unless I wanted to plead guilty. I told him I hadn't done anything. He told me I should talk to my lawyer.

He meant the public defender. It turned out to be a woman, a young black woman with a fierce, pretty face. I told her what happened. She said, did I really have a ticket back at my apartment? I told her, sure I did, but I wouldn't give the cops my address because I was afraid they'd go in there and make it disappear.

She asked me, would I give *her* the address? I looked at her for a long time. Finally, I told it to her. She said she could get the key from the Property Clerk's Office, where they vouchered all my stuff when they booked me, if I'd just sign a release. I did that.

Three days later, I was back in front of the same judge. The lady PD told him that I had a valid ticket for the same day I had been arrested. The DA told the judge they had a witness to me stealing the luggage. The PD said, where was this so-called witness? The DA said she was out of town, but they could bring her in for the trial.

The PD said I had receipts for the computer and the alligator bag too. The DA said "sure" in the same sarcastic voice the cops used.

4

I was in jail for almost three months when we came back to court. The DA told the judge that they couldn't find their witness. She wasn't at the address on her driver's license, and they wanted to drop the charges.

The PD said I had sat in jail for all that time and I was innocent. The cops had bungled, she said. And she said that if I had any sense I'd sue for false arrest.

I thanked her when they cut me loose. And I asked her, did she know the name of a good lawyer in Atlanta? Because I *did* want to sue.

The lawyer turned out to be pretty good after all. He checked out my receipts. He even got the passenger manifest from that flight to Chicago, and there was not one single person booked on it who came close to the man the elderly lady had described. Not that anyone could find that lady anyway.

5

It took almost a year and a half, but the city offered me two hundred and fifty thousand dollars to settle my lawsuit. The lawyer said he would take a third, plus expenses. So I would net about a hundred and sixty-five thousand.

I took it.

Actually, I only netted around a hundred. Twenty-five for Maggie, another twenty-five for James, plus the cost of buying that ticket I never got to use, tickets for Maggie and James to get out of town, and the computer and the alligator bag.

Still, it wasn't bad for three months' work.

for Lou Bank

SUMMER GIRL

Every summer, the rich people come out here, to the end of the island. They rent houses for the season so they can play here. Mostly on the beach or on the water. Sometimes they play inside. The real rich ones, they *own* houses, but they use them only in the summer.

The summers are perfect here, but the winters are ugly and hard. The people who live here all year wait for one thing only. Summer means money. Winter means pain.

The summer people sometimes buy little puppies for their kids, so the kids will have something to play with. But they can't take dogs back to the city, so they just leave them. The people who live here take some of them, but they can't take them all. The ones the people can't take, they live or they die. If they live through the winter, they usually make it. But you can see they will never be regular dogs again.

They call those dogs "summer puppies," because everyone knows what the rich people want them for. And what happens to them.

Lorraine was a summer girl.

It wasn't like she was the first one. Everyone said it would happen. Everyone *always* says it will happen. And every year, some girl—sometimes more than one, even—thinks it won't happen to *her.*

The summer girls are like the summer puppies. Some of them just go back home. But they're broken toys, and they're never the same. Some of them take off, and they never come back. Nobody knows what happens to them.

Lorraine probably wouldn't have even asked me if I hadn't been in prison. Everyone knew that I had been away. People out here, they don't stick together or anything, the way you'd expect if you watched a lot of movies. We get all the movies here, because the summer people want them—so there's a nice theater and all. And it's something to do in the winter, if you have the money. It doesn't matter. This isn't the movies. People look out for themselves, that's all.

So, when I killed that guy in the fight, everybody knew about it. My lawyer wasn't from out here. We don't have lawyers all the way out here. The only ones we ever see are the real-estate ones, and they have their offices closer to the city. But they sent a Legal Aid. And he was the one who told me people in these little towns always stick together. The guy I killed, he was an outsider. So probably the jury wouldn't hurt me, that's what he said.

He didn't know anything about the way things are out here but I always let him talk. It was nice to have company.

They finally offered me a deal. Manslaughter and the Minimum, they called it, like it was something you order in a diner. It means five years any way you slice it, and that's only if the parole board cuts you loose right away. So this Legal Aid, he said I shouldn't take it, because the locals—that's what he called people in the town—they wouldn't hurt me and I might get a better deal even if they didn't cut me loose. He talked about "reckless" and "negligent" and all other kinds of murder. Because that's what they charged me with—murder.

It was a hard decision. If I took the deal, I'd have to go to prison. If I didn't, I might not. But if I didn't take the deal and I went to prison, it could be for a very long time. I had to think about it. That was about all I had to think about, every day in jail.

I figured if prison was like jail I would kill someone else for sure if I had to stay there too long. And then I'd never get out.

So we had the trial. Nobody saw what happened, not really. The cops said I confessed, but that was a lie. I told them the truth. What happened. Yeah, I was on his property. But I was just looking for work. It was summer, and that's what you did—you went around asking the rich people if there was any work they wanted done. I always got work that way. So did a lot of other guys.

I knocked on the front door, but there was no answer. So I went around to the back. Lots of times, they're all out there, in the back yards.

Nobody was there either. So I turned around to go, and that's when I saw them. I didn't know him, but I knew her. Clarisse. She was a couple of years younger than me, I guess. I remembered her a little. Her red hair, mostly. They were naked. Doing it on this sofa-thing they had out back. I turned around. It wasn't none of my business. But then I heard her yell something and I ran. I knew it was nothing but trouble.

I never did see the man's face. So I didn't understand why he came up to me outside the bar that night. He told me to keep my mouth shut. I told him I didn't know what he was talking about. It was the truth when I told him that. But, like I said, I didn't know who he was then. He said he had checked, and he knew I wasn't working for his wife's lawyer, but not to get any stupid ideas. I still didn't know what he was talking about, but I figured out who he was by then. And I also figured out how he got my name. Clarisse.

I didn't say anything. He said he wasn't going to pay any lousy little blackmailer. Then he had this guy with him grab me. The guy who grabbed me, he was much bigger than the rich guy who'd been with Clarisse. He punched me in the stomach, real hard. The guy, the rich guy, he said that was nothing. If I didn't watch my mouth, I'd get a lot worse.

If that rusty old tire iron hadn't been on the ground in the parking lot, it probably would've ended just like that. But by the time it was all over, the big guy was lying there the same way I'd been. Only he was facedown and he wasn't going to get up. The rich guy ran away. The same way I had when I first met him.

The next morning, the cops came and I told them the truth. But the rich guy, he said he had been at his house the whole night before. Sure, the big guy worked for him. But it was his night off, and he'd probably gone to the bar looking for some local pussy, that's what the rich guy said to the cops. I wasn't there when they talked to him, but that's what they told me he said.

The next thing that happened, the rich guy's wife, she had a lawyer too. And he came to see me. So I told him everything, all over again. He looked real happy when I told him Clarisse's name. He said he'd be back soon and when he came I wouldn't have nothing to worry about.

When he didn't come back, I figured I knew what happened. And when I heard Clarisse's father got a new car, I knew for sure. Clarisse was a slick girl. She sold me twice, to two different people.

I had the trial. The jury found me guilty of the same manslaughter they'd offered me in the deal. And the time I spent in jail waiting for the trial, it all counted against the sentence. The public defender, he was surprised. He said he thought the town would take care of its own. I thought so too, but we thought different about how they'd do that.

The Parole Board let me go my first time up. That was the real surprise, because I'd been right—I did have to kill a man in prison. But they didn't really pay no attention. They locked me in the bing—that's solitary—for a few months, and it went on my record and all, but I never got charged by the police or nothing. When I went to the Parole Board, I told them my plan was to go home and work. I couldn't tell them what job, exactly, because I never really had an actual job. But they didn't care, even though all the guys in the block said that would blow it for me, not having a job to go to.

Lorraine knew all this. Well, not about what happened in prison, but the rest. So the reason she asked me, did I want to be partners with her, that was because of what I did. The murder, I mean. I know that was it.

What she told me was, this guy—the one who'd made her a summer girl—he had a *lot* of money. Cash money. In a safe. In his house. Not his summer house, his city house. And all we'd have to do is go there and take it.

I told her, if it was that easy, how come she hadn't done it herself?

She said she didn't have a key or anything. So we needed to get in his house when he was there, and make him tell us exactly where the money was. In a safe, *probably*. Two things: Get in the house, and make him talk. Lorraine said she could get in the house. She knew all about him. She knew when he'd be there alone. And as soon as he opened the door, I would come in too. And make him tell us.

I told her I would think about this.

Then I just listened to what other people in the town said.

Lorraine had been a summer girl a couple of times again after the first one. She hadn't been broken like the others. She knew what the deal was. She wasn't such a young girl anymore, but she looked real good.

Clarisse, she was a whore. She worked a couple of towns over, out of an apartment. She even had her number in the newspapers—one of the guys in the bar showed me. It was like they was all proud of her. A celebrity.

I saw Lorraine the next week. I told her it didn't make sense, what she wanted to do. The guy, he'd be able to identify us pretty easy. And no matter what he promised, he'd tell the cops. Or somebody.

Lorraine said she knew that. Just looked at me when she said it.

I told her I wasn't going to take the weight for a homicide. She told me she'd never talk. I laughed at her. I could see it, what she wanted. Maybe the money, sure. But she hated the guy for making her a summer girl. This wasn't really about the money, it was about making him pay. Prison was full of people like her. People who you couldn't pay with money—it always had to be blood.

But I didn't say none of that. I just told her, no way I was going to do a murder, no matter for how much money, if it meant I had to trust her.

She asked me, what would she have to do to prove I could trust her?

I told her where Clarisse lived.

for Honey & Pokey

BIG SISTER

When she didn't come on Visiting Day, I knew what it meant. There's only one thing that would make Margaret miss coming to see me.

It's always been like that, my big sister looking out for me. She's only nine years older, but it was like she was my mother. I guess she was, when I think about it. My mother died when I was born. Died giving birth to me, my father always said when he was mad. Or drunk. Which is pretty much how he was all the time.

My sister is the only one I can ever remember taking care of me. I mean, my father worked, so I guess he did part of it too—paying the rent and buying food. But it was Margaret who did everything else.

She even went to the Catholic school when they kicked me out the first time. The nuns were so impressed with her, only fifteen years old and all, they let me stay. But it didn't matter. My father said that's what he expected. He couldn't beat any sense into me, so what made Margaret think the nuns could? Margaret told him that hitting me wasn't the way to teach me anything, and my father slapped her. By the time I got the knife from the kitchen, he had stopped, but Margaret was still crying, so I tried to stab him anyway.

Everybody came to the house. The police and the social workers and people from the church and neighbors. It was like a zoo. And I was the animal.

Finally, they said it was up to my father. He went into the bedroom with Margaret and closed the door so they could talk. When they came out, my father said he wanted to keep me. So they didn't take me away.

I went to public school. It was a lot better. They didn't pay so much attention to you.

The first time I got arrested, it was Margaret who came to the station. She was all grown by then. The cops let me go back with her.

The first time I went to juvenile court, Margaret went with me too. And the judge let me go home with her.

Margaret was good at that stuff.

But when I got to be around thirteen, fourteen, I don't remember exactly, whatever Margaret did to convince people about me, it didn't work. So I didn't go home with her that time. I went away. It was only for a little while.

Then it happened again, and I went away for longer. When I came back, I was seventeen. Margaret was living with a man. He was an old man. Almost like my father. Margaret told me I could stay with them until I got a job and my own place.

What happened was, I *did* jobs. But Margaret didn't know anything about that. Everything would have been okay, maybe, if that man hadn't hit her. I don't even remember his name.

Margaret went to court with me again. She told the jury how the man had beat her all the time. She said some of the things he made her do. I started crying when I heard it. I couldn't help it.

The jury let me go home with her.

I was out for almost five years before they got me. I wasn't so surprised. I was very good at doing people, but I was never slick.

The cops knew it wasn't personal. They knew I didn't know the men I'd done. They knew I was in O'Donnell's crew too. But that was all they knew, and I didn't tell them anything. The DA said they could give me a good deal. I was a young man. I could be out in ten years at the most if I told them who ordered the hits. If I didn't talk, I was going away forever.

I didn't tell them anything. After a while, they could see I was never going to.

Margaret visited me in the jail, before the trial. I told her the truth like I always do. I told her what I did. The different jobs, all of them. I told her I wasn't going to get off. Not this time. But I promised her everything would be all right. Wherever they sent me, I could still protect her. I promised her that. She told me not to worry. She said she could take care of herself. But she didn't look at me when she said it.

O'Donnell got me a lawyer. He wasn't too bad, but I knew what his real job was. So I told the lawyer to stop worrying—just tell O'Donnell I'd never rat him out so long as he did this one thing for me. The lawyer, he said that would never be a problem, guaranteed. O'Donnell's name never came up at the trial. I never took the stand, so they couldn't even ask me.

I got twenty-five to life—that's the most they have here.

The first time Margaret visited me, when I was Upstate, she was a mess. She looked so old, I almost didn't recognize her.

She told me about it, finally.

And O'Donnell kept his word.

It didn't happen again for almost three years. Margaret tried to explain it to me. She had been in therapy to understand herself, why she kept going back to the same kind of guys. She told me that she had low self-esteem. From not being pretty and not dating when she was a girl and being too fat and . . . something she had to do with my father to keep him from sending me away.

There was nothing I could do about that. He was already dead. His liver.

I told her she was a real pretty girl, and she could get any guy she wanted. She told me her youth was gone. She wasn't a girl anymore. She was too old to do anything except work and live with guys who beat her up and took her money now.

O'Donnell got that one done too.

I didn't feel bad about it. He owed me. Anyway, they got word to me: There was a guy in here who was going to be a problem for O'Donnell, and I took care of him. Fair is fair.

After a while, Margaret must have figured out what was going on—she knew I could tell when one of those men was hurting her. Margaret never missed a visit, so, when she didn't come this time, I knew what the reason was. She was afraid I'd be able to tell.

I knew the name of the guy she was living with, and the place where they lived too. Margaret wrote me letters. She was the only one who did.

When she didn't come, I didn't need to talk to her. I knew what to do.

Margaret missed three more visits, then she came. She looked better. We didn't say anything about the guy. She told me she was still in therapy, but she was worried that she would fall back into old habits. Patterns, she called them.

Over the next few years, she fell back into that pattern four more times. Then the cops came to see me.

"We know you're the one getting these guys done," the younger one said.

I didn't say anything.

"Ah, Mickey's too smart to go for that," the older cop told his partner. "He knows another few life sentences won't matter—you can only do one of them, and Mickey's never getting out anyway."

I didn't say anything.

"You're working O'Donnell's boys pretty hard," the older one told me. "Must be averaging a hit a year, just keeping you quiet."

I didn't say anything.

"I got something to show you," he said.

I took a look at the papers he had. There were photographs of Margaret. She looked good in the pictures. Young and happy. One of them, she was getting into a new Cadillac. There was bank statements and other stuff too. And a picture of a house. Margaret was standing in front of it, smiling. Her arm was around another woman, a smaller woman, nice-looking, with short hair.

"Your sister's real smart," the older cop said. "You know she's the most reliable hitter in the city now? A contract killer. And the beauty part is, she gets O'Donnell's crew to do all the work."

I didn't say anything. I didn't look at him.

"She hasn't lived with a man in a long time, kid," the older cop said to me. Real soft and gentle. "She likes girls, your sister Margaret. Those addresses where she tells you she lives? Those aren't her addresses. They're the addresses of guys who got contracts out on them. That's some big sister you got, Mickey."

"She sure is," I told him. Proud.

for Doris

TIME SHARE

I am not an emotional man. Even the mathematical calculations to which I have devoted my life arouse no excitement in me.

Nothing does.

I live in a functioning fugue state, shielded by the implacability of numbers. Cross-trained as a mathematician and accountant, I work for an investment-banking house. I construct financial end-outcome models and convert them to macro-programs for global applicability.

Despite what is popularly believed, mathematics is not—can never be—an exact science. Viewed properly, numbers may be seen as tools to assess probability of outcome. My work is to narrow the parameters of probability.

Another man in my position would have wondered if Tessa is a whore. Another man might have tortured himself by using his skills to calculate the probabilities.

Tessa dances at a club. Dances naked, or very nearly so. She is not a showgirl in the Vegas sense of the word. Tessa does not dance at a distance. She does not remain on the stage. She . . . interacts . . . with the patrons.

Tessa says she has never had sex with a man for money. I suppose—or I would suppose, if I were a man who engaged in suppositions—it is a matter of definition. From observation, there seems little question but that the patrons are . . . gratified by Tessa's attentions. And those attentions are certainly for sale. But the equation is not so simple. And, as I possess a viable all-outcomes solution, of no consequence.

Like anyone else, I must pay to be with Tessa. As my salary-and-bonus package is quite significant, time purchase on a limited basis is not a financial strain.

I discovered Tessa is not a whore in the traditional sense. This discovery was without benefit of research. Perhaps there is a lesson in that. I proposed sex with her in exchange for money . . . whatever hourly rate she deemed appropriate. That's when she told me she does not engage in such transactions.

I might have remained in my capsule but for her refusal. Not the refusal itself. The patent disappointment she displayed—disappointment in me, I am certain—that was the catalyst.

And I am equally certain that to possess Tessa is a matter of economics. She does what she does for money. Just as I do what I do for money. A sufficient amount of money could, simply speaking, purchase her time. In total.

I think best within a structure. I see Tessa as a time-share condominium. As I wish no others to use the facility, my solution is to purchase it outright.

I pondered the possibilities. A direct purchase was out of the question. Only an income stream would guarantee the net effect I sought. My current resources, liquidated, would be sufficient to purchase Tessa's time continuously for approximately 1.44 years.

That is not a solution. The end-sum would self-determine. When my resources eventually depleted, Tessa would return to her employment. However, her employability would, necessarily, have diminished over time. Much like a conventional mortgage, where each successive payment covers more of the principal (and, obviously, less of the interest), Tessa has a limited professional life—she must either retire rather early or face a diminishing return for her services.

Therefore, an outright purchase of time is the solution, if only as a theoretical possibility. Given that my current holdings, even if they brought full-assessed value, would not amount to much in excess of a half-million dollars, and given that my calculations indicate I would need a yearly income of approximately that very same amount to maintain Tessa, a conservative estimate of the increase needed is obtained by the equation: 8% of $x =$ \$500,000/year. The answer, obviously, is \$6.25 million.

Over time, of course, I would expect to amass a relatively similar sum, assuming the tax-sheltered portion of my portfolio performs as expected throughout the next 18.6 years. However, purchasing Tessa's time *then* would be of little utility . . . albeit certainly cheaper.

Reduced to its essentials, I need the money now.

Some of our firm's clients have acquired their own fortunes by less than patrician means. From one such individual, I heard the term "bridge jumper." Apparently, this is a gambler who bets an extraordinary amount on the closest he could calculate to be a "sure thing." An example would be an overpoweringly successful racehorse—say, Secretariat—running against very inferior opposition. The bridge jumper would bet everything on Secretariat to show, the odds of such a horse's finishing within the top three being in excess of the actual price the horse would pay—the latter being governed by law. This simply takes advantage of an inherent flaw in any parimutuel system. Such a system is designed to have each bettor wager against all the others, so that the wagers placed determine the odds posted. The racetrack takes a percentage of the total amount wagered, and pays the remainder out, proportionately, to the winning bettors. However, if *all* the wagers were placed on the *same* horse, a so-called "minus pool" would result . . . and the track's own money would be at risk should that horse succeed.

This is an extremely rare occurrence, but the situation I described previously would cause an approximation of such an event. Why, therefore, do the racetracks not simply bar wagering in such situations? While that would be mathematically intelligent, the law prohibits it. The minimum payout on *any* wager is $2.10. But even if the resulting 5-percent profit appears insignificant at first blush, one must consider the implications of a 5-percent return within the less than two minutes the race itself takes. Projected out over a year's period, the percentage return would be astronomical.

Of course, nothing is certain. Even the finest racehorse may stumble. Or suffer a sudden bout of illness. Or even be subject to deliberate manipulation by its handlers. That is why, the client told me, such gamblers are called bridge jumpers. If their wager does not pay off, their choices are . . . limited.

So are mine.

I need approximately a 1,200-percent increase in my holdings . . . say 1,300 percent to be secure, given some potential liquidation difficulties. Even were I to resort to the bridge-jumping sort of wager the client described, I would need to find several *hundred* "sure-thing" candidates. And the odds of them *all* performing as expected—to say nothing of the time required—would render the wager itself ludicrous.

Arbitrage is, essentially, wagering. Should the deutsche mark, for example, be trading at $0.97 in America while simultaneously trading for $0.96 in Germany, a massive purchase of that currency (for immediate resale) could, theoretically, produce a substantial profit within seconds. Much less than the 5-percent profit the horse player would expect. But a currency race can be run much faster—mere seconds would suffice.

At roughly one cent to the dollar (slightly less than 1 percent), I would need to purchase and sell approximately point six billion dollars worth of currency to reach my goal.

My firm has access to more than twice that amount in clients' accounts.

Others have attempted what I intend to accomplish. They gambled with their companies' money, hoping a win would enable them to replace the "stake" and retain the profits. An analysis of previous attempts reveals nothing but abysmal failures, Barclay's being a sadly illustrative example. Of course, the individuals in question gambled much smaller sums, and on much riskier propositions (commodity options being a favorite).

I have targeted nineteen separate currencies. Tomorrow at approximately 3:00 a.m., I will launch the computer program in which I have invested several months of research and development. If it succeeds, the overage from the transactions will be vacuumed into my account before this office opens for business that day.

I will know the outcome before anyone else.

And once I know, I will act. Whatever the outcome, I will be purchasing Tessa's time. For the rest of my life.

for Mark

GOIN' DOWN SLOW

Saturday night, there's always a woman in a red dress. Looking over at me when my hands are down—harp in one hand, mike in the other.

I drop my hands when Big G takes a keyboard solo. Most people, their eyes go to the man with the front music. Junior does vocals, Melvin plays slide—they get most of the looks. They both play the crowd too, working them.

But when I solo, I get lost. My eyes are always closed. It's not a stage thing—that's the way it happens. So, if a woman's looking at me when I don't have my harp up and running, I know why.

But if the woman's there with a man, I know better than to look back. Woman like that, the red dress is a signal. She's a fire-starter. In the joints we play, it'd most likely be a knife, but a pistol's always a possibility.

And even if her man walks off, you can't be sure he won't be back. Slick and quiet. And maybe your next drink will be the same kind that sent Robert Johnson off to pay that debt he ran up at the Crossroads.

But if that red dress is full of juice and there's no man next to it, that's another signal. And it ain't "Stop!"

You have to play *hard* in these joints. I don't mean loud—noise won't get it. Hard *enough,* maybe that's closer to it. Sometimes we get to play big places. Even a stadium once, behind a band with a label deal and all that. In big places, you don't have to play hard. The people in the crowd make most of the sound themselves anyway. But in the clubs, you better bring it. Or they'll take you right off the stage.

That's the way I started. Tuesday nights at the Ice Pick. The house band opens up, one slot at a time, the way a flower opens, petal by petal. That's to see if anyone wants to sit in. Like, the slide man, he'll make a gesture, then take a seat off to the side. And anyone who thinks he can make steel sing, well, he can just step up and try and take the man's place for that piece of time.

It was a long time before I was ready. Longer than I thought, actually. 'Cause, the first two times, I didn't make it. It wasn't like the people booed me or nothing. They don't do that. What they do is . . . they talk. To themselves, I mean. Just go back to their conversations like they're in an elevator.

They do that, you're done.

The third time was the charm, like the people say. I just filled in behind at first. Then I put in a few figures. And when the leader stepped off and pointed at me, I made the crowd quiet right down. Most harp men, they can juke you to death, but they can't go slow. The great ones—Jimmy Cotton, Butterfield, Musselwhite—they can go either way, of course. Sonny Boy, Little Walter—they could go wherever they wanted.

I always modeled myself after Blind Owl Wilson. I must have listened to him on "Goin' Down Slow" a million times. I wanted to make people feel what I felt when I heard him. And that night, I got it right, bending the notes over slow and soft . . . *clean,* not cheating off the feedback from the mike.

After that, I sat in a lot with different bands until Junior picked me for permanent. I've been traveling with them ever since.

I can't read music, but I can hear it perfect. I told Honeyboy, and he said it was okay—he said he wouldn't trust no preacher that had to read his sermon from a script.

I'll never be the king of anything. My ambition is to be one of the thousand great harp men. Not to be in no arguments, just to *be*. Like the blues. That's one of the first things Honeyboy told me. "The blues is always going to be here. Like a convict run off from a chain gang who the Man never find. Oh, he have to lay low some-time—disco made the blues lay *real* low for a while back—but he always going be around. Always be running, though. Never be on top for long, but never be gone neither. Remember that part, son—never be on top to stay. Lotsa white boys, they made that mistake. The ones who come up in the late sixties—it was *good* then. College kids loved it. Record deals for everyone. Stadiums, TV, everything. Then the sheriff called to the hounds, and the blues had to get back in the woods. Those white boys, the ones who expected it to last forever, they stayed out in the open—and they got cut down. So what you got to remember is this one rule: They can't hang you while you running."

I never forgot that. But I don't know what to do now. It was a Saturday night. It was a woman in a red dress. It was a man I didn't know she had.

A young man. A white man. A rich man's son who crossed the tracks one too many times.

Now he's in the ground and I'm on the run.

I'll be all right if I don't go back to the clubs. I'm nobody . . . as long as I don't pick up my harp again.

I wonder how long I can go without.

I wonder how long I can go.

for Peter

WORD PLAY

1

Cigarettes killed my wife. She ran out of smokes late one night while I was out, working, so she went to the bodega to get some. A couple of guys in ski masks wanted to get some, too. It was just money until Lorna walked in, then they wanted to get some of her, too. Lorna was a fine-looking woman, but I know that wasn't it. The guns in their hands made them hard, and they wanted a place to put it. We had talked about it once. What she should do if it happened. I told her the truth. Fight. There's no way it makes them madder, like some of those idiot books say. If they didn't hate, they wouldn't do it at all.

Lorna tried. She let one get close, even took her top off, and then she went for his gun. The other guy panicked and started blasting. Shot his partner in the back. Got Lorna in the face. Then he sprayed the place and got the owner, too, and ran out the door. Without the money.

His partner talked—they have the death penalty in this state. So they found the other guy. He had all the weight that was left, so he took it. He's on the Row, over in the next building.

I'm not in here for killing the partner—the guy that lived and told about it. I mean, I *did* kill him all right. Right in here. But he came in here with a rat jacket, so it could have been anyone. That's the way the Administration looked at it.

I went in after Lorna. After Lorna, that's when they thought it all started to unravel for me. But that's really when it all began to make sense.

Words, that's what I mean. I mean, words always mean two things. At least two things. See, I wasn't going *after* Lorna, not like I was chasing her or anything. What I mean is: It was after Lorna got killed that they dropped me. When they come for you, they scream for you to get down—drop to the floor. Then you go to court and the judge drops you in here. Even in here, you can drop more. And if you drop enough, you can drop out.

That's what it really is, you know. Not suicide. Just dropping.

It was just bad luck, me being arrested—I'd planned the job for a long time and it should have worked. But coming back, that's an occupational hazard. So, here I am.

Words. Lorna went after smokes and she got smoked.

I do a lot of reading in here.

I'm in business, and you have to stay current. But you know what? Things don't change. Fads, fashions, styles . . . sure. But the real things stay the same. The principals change, the principles don't. The words sound the same, but they don't mean the same. Words are tricky. See what I mean?

One law puts you in here, but once you are locked down, another law rules. Higher law. Like Darwin's. Supply and demand, too. Some things are very hard to get in here. But not so hard that convicts can't buy them. What would be the point in that? Having a diamond worth a million bucks and no buyers with cash?

So, like with drugs. In here, it's Talwin. The best-seller. Bigger than heroin and coke together. You know why? Because they grow it here. Not "grow" like from the ground, but it grows right out of the shrink's office, on those ℞ pads they all have. The prison pharmacy is the warehouse. They order enough to get the whole joint medicated, then they dole out just enough to set the hook. Supply and demand.

So there's money. But you need partners to make it work. A network. Even when they have you in the net, you work. Words, right?

I used to see the shrink a lot. They told me I was schizoid. Not one of those paranoid loons, or a split personality, or anything. Just . . . a lot of words. That's when I found out about the ℞ pads.

I wasn't the only one. They started killing each other soon after. The blacks wanted the whole traffic for themselves, so they offed a bunch of Italians and sold to the Latins. But the Latins, they figured they could get stuff, too. For themselves. The whites use, but they don't control. The *real* whites—you know, the Aryan nuts—they don't do much dealing. They're getting ready for the big revolution. I listen to them sometimes. Always talking about forming cells when they get out. They're *in* a cell and they're talking about forming one. Words.

The real reason they say I'm crazy is because I understand. And *that's* crazy. See what I mean?

It's only other convicts talking like that anyway. The Administration doesn't think I'm crazy. They have special places for guys who are truly crazy, and I've never been in one of them, not even for an evaluation. They keep me here. They give me the meds. And they make me see the shrink. That's all.

I study words. I need to be in business, and it's very hard to be in business here.

Words are very good. Good friends. I write letters. I put a lot of work into them. I only write to women. I am very careful about that. I never ask them for money. Most women who write to men in here, they have something . . . missing. Maybe in their lives, maybe in themselves. Everybody tries to game them. That means, play a game on them. A con game. A game cons play, see? I don't do that.

I am very sincere. I am looking for a relationship. Like I had with Lorna. I tell them the truth—I am a widower. And I have no children.

It took a long time to find the right one. But time isn't a problem here. Some guys have typewriters. I could buy one, but I wouldn't. Women like the handwritten letters the best. They know it takes more work to do that. The women work—I would only want a woman who works—and they want the man to work too. I don't mean work like in the license-plate shop or in the cafeteria. Prison jobs aren't work. They don't pay you, not really. The only reason cons take those jobs is to impress the Parole Board or so they can steal stuff.

I don't have to worry about the Parole Board. I only have another two years to go. In here, they say I'm "short." It means I only have a short time to go. Some of the ones doing life sentences, they're short too. Only they don't know it. Like the guy who killed Lorna. Not the one on Death Row. I can't get to him. But it doesn't matter. If the State doesn't take him, they'll put him back here. Then he'll be short just like his partner was.

The Administration doesn't know about me and Lorna. We weren't married on paper, so our names aren't the same. I wasn't a suspect when she got killed, so the cops never even talked to me. About that, I mean. If they had known, they wouldn't have let one of the guys who killed her lock in the same wing as me. Or maybe they would—they do that on purpose sometimes. The Administration likes to game too.

I have been practicing. Not writing. I know how to do that. Practicing with words, talking them out loud. I have to get it perfect, because the woman is coming to visit. It will take a lot of vis-

its before she starts bringing in stuff for me. But I have plenty of
time for that. First I have to practice.

The one to practice on is the guard who runs the Visiting Room.
Tomorrow, I'm going to try it.

2

"I've been here a long time, right?" I asked him.

"A long time? There's guys in here got more time on the toilet
than you got locked up total," the guard said. He was a hard
one—I don't mean tough, I mean difficult—because he had no
friends.

"I never bothered you, right?" I said. "I never caused any trouble?"

"What's your point?" he asked me. He had piggy eyes.

"I never even talked to you before today," I told him, quiet and
mild and nice.

"So?"

"My girlfriend is coming on Sunday. Visiting Day. It's going to
be a wonderful visit, do you know why?"

"Why?" he asked. But he wasn't really asking, it was just a
word.

"Because you're not going to stare at her chest. You're not
going to put your hands on her. And we're going to sit at the real
nice table—you know, the one in the far corner."

"You threatening me?" That's what he said, but I knew what he
meant—what was I going to pay him?

"No, of course I am not threatening you," I told him. "I would
never do that. I have empathy. You know what that is? It just
means you can feel what other people feel. I know how I would
feel if somebody hurt someone I really liked. So I would never
threaten you. I would never threaten anyone. Especially not here.
It's not safe."

He gave me a strange look. But I didn't mind. People are always giving me strange looks. Not strange like I am a stranger, but . . . well, it's just more words.

"What makes a place safe is the neighborhood. My neighborhood, well, you know where that is. On the tier. It's not like your neighborhood. It's safe where you live, isn't it? At 325 Maple Drive. That's a beautiful house you have. And a nice car, nice kids."

He moved real close to me, dropping his voice. "You want to see what pain is really like?" he whispered. "Just even say my wife's fucking *name* and I'll—"

"Oh, I'd never say *her* name," I told him. "I'd be afraid Suzie B. would hear me. You know Suzie B., locks over on 4-Left? She probably doesn't even know you're married. She might get jealous and . . . well, who knows *what* that outrageous queen would do . . ."

Everything went fine on Visiting Day.

I'm very close now.

As soon as I learn how to play all the words, I'll be ready.

for Zak

STEPPING STONE

It's nine-forty-five. The bus is supposed to leave soon—the ten-fifteen to St. Louis—and Jasmine isn't here yet.

I wonder if maybe she had trouble getting a cab, with all the rain coming down. Or maybe it was taking her longer than she thought to get to the money. I was thinking maybe even the cops . . . But then I stopped. It always makes my head hurt, trying to figure things out.

"Leave that to me, baby," Jasmine always said. It was easier to do that. And that's what I always did.

I never could have figured it out by myself. I mean, they keep a lot of cash in those gambling joints, everybody knows that. And everybody knows they have to move it out of there sometime. But only Jasmine could have figured out how they do it.

The first floor of the joint is for the wheels and the dice games and blackjack. Where you play against the house. The second floor has poker and pool. That's where guys play against each other, and the house takes a piece.

Jasmine said it comes down to the same thing.

There's girls on the third floor. Jasmine says, even if you walk out a winner, if you walk *up*, you're going to go home with a lot less money.

That's where Jasmine works, on the third floor. She's a supervisor, she told me.

I was never there myself. Everything I know about the place is from Jasmine.

I met her by accident. I was drinking in this bar. I'm not a drunk. I was just looking for someone to talk to. A woman, that's what I really wanted. Sometimes it works out pretty easy. Sometimes it don't. I can never figure out why that is. So all I can do is go to the bar and see.

I don't go much. 'Cause I don't make much on my job. I mean, it's not bad, moving furniture. Sometimes the people give the crew boss a tip. And sometimes he splits it with us too.

The first night I met Jasmine, I told her all about my job. She was the first woman who ever wanted to know about it. She asked me, going in people's houses all the time, didn't I ever see stuff worth stealing? I told her, sure, it happens all the time. But I would never take stuff.

She asked me why. And I had to think about it. I mean, everyone knows you're not supposed to take stuff that isn't yours, right?

And Jasmine told me I *was* right. But, she said, that was only true if the people worked for it. If the people stole it, then taking it from them, well, that wouldn't be stealing—'cause the money and stuff, it was *already* stolen.

I didn't understand it the first time she said it, but she didn't get mad or make fun of me the way other people do sometimes. She was very nice, Jasmine. Very pretty too. I told her that, and she smiled.

Jasmine was my girlfriend after that. My secret girlfriend. She said it had to be that way, because she was married. Her husband was a jealous man.

I told her I could take care of her husband. I wasn't afraid. And I wanted Jasmine for myself.

She said, no, that wouldn't be smart. She said they would be getting a divorce soon, but she couldn't get caught with another man before that, or her husband would get all the money.

I knew Jasmine liked money. She was always dressed fancy. And she had a beautiful car. I felt bad I didn't have money so I could buy her things she wanted. But Jasmine said not to worry about it. We wouldn't need any money once she got her divorce.

But then things went bad. Jasmine told me her husband found out about me. He knew everything about me: where I worked, where I lived, even. He knew I had been in prison too, she said.

I was scared for Jasmine. She told me she was more scared for me. Her husband had a real bad temper, and he had a lot of connections, too.

I couldn't figure out what to do.

That's when Jasmine told me about the vacuum tube. It's this plastic tube that runs from the counting room of the club all the way up to the roof. That's how they get the money out, Jasmine told me. There's a little house on the roof. Not really a house, more like a shack. When you open the door to it, you're on the stairs. There are six floors. But when they put the money in the tube, it gets sucked right up to the top.

There's two pickups a night, Jasmine said. One at midnight, one at four in the morning. How they do it is, a guy comes from the *next* building. The roofs are all the same height. So he just jumps across—it's only about three, four feet—makes the pickup, then goes back across into the other building. That way, nobody can rob them.

Jasmine said *every* pickup is over a hundred thousand dollars. On Friday and Saturday nights, it's even more.

She said we could rob it. But they would all know it was her, and we'd have to run away together after.

We couldn't take her car either, 'cause they all knew what it looked like, and the license number and everything.

The night she told me, Jasmine put on a blond wig. She looked so different. She asked me if I liked it. I said I really did. She kept it on all that night. And she told me she'd wear it when we ran away. Nobody would recognize her.

She said the money would be a stepping stone. We could start all over with it, just her and me. In another town, nobody would ever find us.

We went over it a hundred times. Maybe more. What I had to do is start from *three* buildings away. That part was easy. Jasmine had an apartment there. She rented it a while ago, just in case I would want to move in there, so we'd be close. But she hadn't told me about it, 'cause she wanted it to be a surprise. So it was even better.

Anyway, all I had to do was step out the back window onto the fire escape and climb up to the roof. Then go across the buildings until I was on top of the right one. When the pickup man came across, I was supposed to wait. When he came out of the shack with the money, that's when I was supposed to take him.

Jasmine got a gun for me. To show the pickup man and make him hand over the money. But don't shoot, she said. No matter what. Don't shoot unless you see cops. If you see cops, honey, you have to start blasting—that's what she said.

But if I don't shoot the guy, how am I going to keep him from running downstairs and telling everyone? I asked her.

She told me all the back windows of the building were blacked out. And the whole place was soundproofed. Then she looked at me real hard. I nodded. She looked at me some more. I told her I got it.

She didn't ask me anything after that. I was proud, 'cause she knew I got it. She trusted me.

When the pickup man came across, I watched him close. He came out with the money, and I stepped out with the gun. He put his hands up. I told him to turn around. Then I took a running start and knocked him off the roof. I went back across the rooftops. It wasn't hard, even with all the rain.

I left the money in the apartment Jasmine had, just like she said. That way, if I got stopped, I wouldn't have it on me, and I would be okay.

I kept the pistol, though.

It's after ten now, but I still don't see her.

The speaker at the bus station was loud. I looked at the clock. Then I went outside to smoke a cigarette. That's when I saw the cops. All around the place, a whole bunch of them.

One of them yelled something. I took out the pistol and did what Jasmine said.

for Marty Furman, CPA

FIREMAN

When I first fell in love with Connie, I was ashamed to tell her. But I knew it, right when it happened. She was eleven then, and I was twelve, almost thirteen. We were both in the sixth grade.

The day it happened, it was after school. Raj found a butterfly on the sidewalk. I guess it was hurt or something, 'cause it couldn't fly away. Raj started to torture it, pulling off the bright-orange wings one by one, holding it up so everybody could see. Connie screamed at him to stop, but he just laughed and kept on doing it.

I said, "Only a faggot would play with bugs like that." Loud, so Raj would hear. I knew what would happen next. There's magic words you can say to make people fight you. He had to do it. And he was bigger than me, so maybe he thought he could win. I busted his face all up. He couldn't take it and he ran.

One of the other guys said, yeah, Raj *was* a faggot—that proved it. The guy who said it—he never would have tried to fight me himself, no matter what I said to him. I just looked at him until he walked away.

Then only me and Connie was left on the sidewalk. But when she thanked me, for, like, rescuing her, I was so ashamed that I hadn't done nothing until after she made her move that I just told her to get lost.

Maybe you think that's stupid. How could a twelve-year-old boy know what love was, right?

Yeah, well, love's supposed to be the other side of hate, isn't it? By the time I was twelve, I knew what hate was. For years, I knew. So I figure I should know the opposite when I felt it, too.

Connie was always sticking up for other people. When the kids made fun of Peggy because she was so fat, Connie walked home with her, just to show everyone.

She hated bullies, Connie. I figured out later, that's why she hated Raj. And that's what made me stop being one, although I never told her she was the reason.

Before Connie, I thought I got it. I mean, I thought I understood the way things worked. The guy who taught me was Sammy, my mother's boyfriend. He always beat on me, and I could never stop him—he was bigger than me, and a lot stronger. He's the one who taught me to take it. After a while, I could take a lot. But I knew that one day I'd be stronger than he was—I could feel it happening.

When it happened, then he'd stop.

I didn't know if I would, though.

In the meantime, I saw how it worked. If you were pushing people around, they weren't pushing *you* around. So I did that. Not with my mouth—I mean, I never made fun of anyone, not even William, with his twisted, gimpy leg that dragged behind him when he walked. But I'd fight over a seat in the cafeteria, or a turn on the basketball court. Or anything, I guess. Most of the time, I started it.

I liked to fight.

So I wasn't afraid of Raj that day, when he was hurting the butterfly. It wasn't that. I knew I could take him. It's just that I wasn't going to do anything about it—I was just going to let him go on doing it. But when Connie tried to stop him, I knew I should have done that myself, first.

I didn't care about the stupid butterfly. I was afraid Raj was going to hurt Connie. But I didn't know that. Or, anyway, I guess I didn't. But when I figured out that I had to keep Raj from hurting her, I knew I loved her.

Because, if my mother had loved me, she would have kept Sammy from hurting me.

A couple of weeks after the day I backed Raj down, Connie stopped me from hurting a kid. Without saying nothing, she did it. I had Bobby against the wall in the schoolyard. I wanted to fight. He didn't, but he didn't know how to get out of it—I'd said some of the magic words to him. A crowd of kids was standing around. They always like to watch. I didn't care. But then I saw Connie. And when I saw the way she was looking at me, I couldn't stand it. So I just called Bobby a punk and I walked away.

Connie's father was a very brave guy. A fireman. He went into burning buildings and he pulled people out. He even got his picture in the paper once, after he did that. Connie was so proud of him—she was always bragging about how brave he was.

I thought about how, if Connie's building was on fire, I could rescue her for real. And then she would love me, too.

It's easy to burn things. I knew a kid who did it all the time. Lawrence. But Lawrence, he—I don't know—I couldn't stand to be around him. I didn't like the way he laughed when he struck a match. Giggling like a girl. I didn't care about no building burning down, but Lawrence made me . . . all nervous-like.

So I never rescued Connie. But one day I told her I was going to be a fireman when I grew up.

Oh, man, she was *so* excited. She made me walk home with her that day. I was fifteen by then, so she couldn't really *make* me do nothing, I guess. By then, Sammy knew he couldn't make me do nothing no more.

I got arrested for that, the thing with Sammy that changed his mind about me. But the cops, I don't know, they talked to him. In another room from where they were holding me. And Sammy dropped the charges. It never went to court. I didn't have a record.

So I could still be a fireman.

I didn't know why I had to walk Connie home that day until we got to her stoop. She told me to wait there. In a few minutes, her father came out. He wasn't as big as I thought he would be, from the way Connie talked about him. He was kind of short and . . . even fat, maybe. But he was real nice. Connie said he was "on nights" that whole month. I guess that meant he was home in the daytime, that's why she made me come with her. To meet him.

He asked me, was it true that I wanted to be a fireman? I told him, yes, it was. He asked me why. I didn't know what to tell him—just I liked the idea of rescuing people and all. I never said nothing about Connie to him, and I don't think he knew.

But he listened to me, anyway. He told me about the tests and all. How you had to be in good shape. I told him I was in good shape. He said there was a bunch of tests besides the stuff you had to be in good shape for. Mental tests, like. Anyway, he said I had to wait until I graduated from high school before I could take the tests.

After you passed the tests, they put you on a list. In the same order that you scored. So, like, if you was number twenty-five, then after the first twenty-four guys got appointed you got called.

I told him that was fair, and he said, yes, it was. He had to wait to get appointed himself, he told me, but his turn came. He said my turn would come too.

It wasn't until late that night, when I couldn't sleep, that I realized what he was saying. He *knew* I was going to pass the tests. Like it was a sure thing.

But I never graduated from high school. When I was seventeen, I enlisted in the Marines. Your parents have to sign for you when you're that age. My mother did it. She said it would be best. I couldn't live in that apartment with her and Sammy anymore—and she wasn't going to make Sammy leave.

I went over to Connie's house to say goodbye. We sat at the kitchen table. I told her I was going in. But I was going to get a GED in there, and I could still be a fireman when I got out. Connie was mad. She wanted me to stay in school, so we could graduate together.

Her father came into the kitchen. He said a lot of guys got their GED in the service, and they got to be firemen just the same as if they'd stayed in school. I could still take the tests, he said. And you got extra points if you had been in, too. Veteran's points. He shook my hand.

Connie was mad at him, I could tell. I could always tell when she was mad, but that time, I wasn't sure why.

I didn't say nothing to her then, but it was like she knew. When I got out, I was going to marry her and be a fireman. She said she'd write to me, and I knew it was true when she said it.

So I went in the Marines. The basic training was nothing—I was in good shape from practicing to be a fireman all those years.

I didn't even know there was a war going on until I was in it.

It changed everything.

Connie wrote, just like she promised. At first, I wrote back. After a while, I just stopped. I didn't know how to tell her I finally got to be a fireman. In those crazy, scary tunnels. But I wasn't there to rescue nobody. That's not what we did.

She must have known I was in country, because she just kept on writing, figuring I would read everything when I got back across the line.

But as soon as I got back across that line, I went over some others.

It was almost nine months by the time I wrote to Connie. I knew it was too late. I tried to explain it to her, but I know I didn't do a good job.

I know that because she kept on writing.

So I told her what was really happening over there. What had happened to me. What people did over there. What I did.

Then she stopped.

I went back into the tunnels. Stoned most of the time, like everyone else. It was the only way to do that.

I was in a lot of stuff, but I never got hit. Never took a bullet. Never hit a tripwire. Never fell into one of those punji-stick traps Charlie had everywhere either.

Some of the guys started to call me Lucky. They always wanted to go out with me. They said I was charmed. But some of the other guys, they *never* wanted to go out with me—they said my number hadn't come up yet, and they didn't want to be around me when it did.

I just kept doing it, walking through the tunnels, carrying the fire. One day they told me I was done. I was so wrecked on H and ganja I didn't even understand them for a while. They shipped me out.

When I came home, nothing was the same.

I didn't want to be a fireman anymore. I didn't want to be anything. Every time I closed my eyes, I saw dead people. Broken, burned, torn to pieces.

I got high a lot. I stole too—the dope was expensive, not like over there.

My head hurt. I went to the VA. The shrink there said I was having flashbacks. He said they'd go away after a while.

He was a liar. But that didn't surprise me—he was just another officer, right?

I heard Connie had gone away. To college, I guess. She was already gone by the time I got back.

Her building was still there. The stoop, anyway—I never

looked inside. I walked past it a few times, but I never saw nobody sitting there. Nobody that I knew, anyway.

All I think about now is being a fireman. The kind I wanted to be, and the kind I got to be.

And the kind I know I'm going to be someday.

for Teddie Szinai Sante

DOPE FIEND

1

This all started when Charlene asked me to kill her.

You'd have to know her to understand what that means. It didn't come easy to her, to say those words. Not because she's afraid of dying—it would be a comfort for her, I know that. She just don't want to leave me alone.

It's the pain. Cancer's been eating her bones like a pack of winter-starved wolves. Gnawing right into the marrow. Charlene, she's no stranger to the pain. She was never a big woman. But she was strong. Always did her share, and more. I met her in the tobacco fields, and she was pulling a full load, even though she wasn't but sixteen, and skinny too.

When we left the fields together, we was looking for something better than seasonal. That never seemed to work out, not for a long time. I mean, I'd get work, and Charlene wouldn't be able to find none. Or she'd have to waitress or something while I got that

Unemployment. Neither of us never took the Welfare. We wasn't raised like that.

There was chances, but Charlene never would let me take them. A couple of boys where I was raised up, they wanted me to run shine into some dry counties. Real good money if you could drive, and they knowed I could.

Charlene told me I couldn't do it. I told her, I was the man in the house, if I wanted to do something I would. Being against the law don't make something wrong, and we needed the money. She didn't say nothing, just walked off and left me sitting there.

I had a beer and a couple of cigarettes, thinking about how I was going to handle this. Then Charlene came back into the room. She was all dressed up, like we was going to a dance. Except that she didn't look right. Her face was all painted, real heavy, not like she does it. And her blouse wasn't buttoned up. I asked her what she was . . . But before I could even finish, she told me she was going down to Front Street and make her some money. With men. I got so mad I . . . It was the only time I ever raised my hand to Charlene. She didn't even move, just stood there, hands on her hips. And I never did hit her. I couldn't. And she knew it.

Charlene didn't turn no tricks and I didn't haul no shine. We just kept trying.

When I got on at the plant regular, we thought that was it. I mean, it was a union job, with benefits and everything.

We wanted some babies. We'd waited long enough. Charlene said she wasn't going to put no kids of hers in the fields, and I agreed with her. Complete. So, when I got on regular, got my union card and all, then we figured it was time.

But Charlene couldn't get pregnant. One of the benefits I got was this health insurance. So we went to this place they said to go to—a clinic, like. They told Charlene her . . . insides was all rotted out. She had this cancer.

They tried to cut it out. She went into the hospital. The health insurance paid for it. And she had the operation. But the doctor told us later that it was too late. It was into her bones. Nothing they could do.

So Charlene is dying right in our trailer. She can bear that. I mean, she can bear it for herself, dying. Like I said, there ain't but one reason she don't want to go, as much pain as she's got now.

The pain is the thing. Charlene can't take it no more. But the doctors from that health-insurance thing, they said they can't give her no more of the drugs. It's against the law or something. They could lose their license.

I told the doctor plain, I didn't believe him. He showed it to me. On a piece of paper. I couldn't make no sense of it. So I told him even plainer: If it was him in all that pain, they'd give *him* all the drugs he needed. He didn't say nothing to me about that.

What they give Charlene, it comes in special little bottles. The top is rubber, like. So you can stick the needle right into it and draw out what you need.

Only Charlene don't *have* what she needs. Every time the nurses comes, Charlene asks her for more. And the nurse just says, "Doctor hasn't prescribed any."

"Doctor." Like he don't have no name. Don't need one. Might as well say "King." Or even "God."

They leave three, four of them bottles at a time. They showed me how to give the injections. It ain't even into Charlene herself. I mean, the needle's already in her, all taped down. I fill the syringe, then I push the plunger into the little spot they showed me.

What hurts her so is between the shots. When she starts to run out of strength to fight. One time, I gave her another shot before the time the nurse said had to pass. And it made her feel better. I could see it right away. She even smiled a little. But when the nurse came and she saw I only had half of one bottle left instead of the two I should have, she said she couldn't do nothing. We had to take the drug when they said so. Not more than they said. Not ever.

I asked her, nice as I could: Why? I mean, what did it matter if Charlene turned into one of them dope fiends? She was going to die. They all knew that. Why couldn't she die without so much pain?

The nurse didn't say nothing. Her lips was pressed together so tight they was the same color as her uniform.

Finally she said, if you took too much morphine it could kill you. Charlene, she started to laugh then. But the pain took that away right quick. Not as quick as that nurse left, though.

I went back to the doctor. He told me the DEA set the rules. If you prescribed too much painkillers, they would come and make trouble for you.

I asked him, was I doing it right? Could he show me? You could see he didn't want to, but he was scared, so he got one of the little bottles from this refrigerator-thing and showed me how to stick the needle in. I begged him with my eyes to give me that one extra bottle. He looked away.

2

Now Charlene has all the medicine she needs. It won't be long. If there's any left after she goes, I'm going to take it myself, so I can go along with her right away, down the same road. If there's none left, I'll let the law do it. They've been outside for a couple of days now, screaming at us through their horns. They think Charlene is a hostage.

We both liked that one. It was so funny, Charlene even smiled a little.

I guess Charlene's a drug addict now. A dope fiend. She's going to go soon. But she don't have no more pain.

Neither does Doctor.

for James Colbert

ESCORT SERVICE

1

Upscale Escorts," purred over the fiber-optic cable into the telephone receiver. "Victoria speaking. How may I help you?"

"Double D," a man's voice replied. Calm and assured, but with a tremor of excitement the woman who called herself Victoria had come to recognize over the years.

"Certainly, sir. Please hold."

"Double D. This is Tammy. Could I have your access code, please, sir?"

"Eight one eight eight one."

"One moment, please."

The only sound was the faint hum of the phone line.

"Verified. Please hold for service."

Fifteen seconds passed.

"You're calling from the Royale?" A man's voice, somewhere between oily and menacing.

"Yes, that's right. How did you—?"

"Caller ID, pal. We've got the best stuff here. Of *all* kinds, if you catch my drift. That's room 2720. A suite, if I remember correctly, right?"

"Yes. I—"

"First we ask the questions, then you talk, how's that?"

"Sure. I mean, whatever you—"

"Credit card?"

"Yes, I have a credit card. Do you—?"

"Spell it out. It's not for billing . . . You understand that all payments are in cash, right?"

"Yes. I was just—"

"The card is for verification, understand? We have to know who we're dealing with. That protects us, and it protects you too, okay?"

"Yes. I understand. The card is American Express, number 07J4 89B677R 0X91."

"Expiration date?"

"June 2001."

"Gonna put you on hold, all right?"

"Yes."

Ninety-seven seconds passed.

"Okay, Mr. Roget, we've got you."

"That's Rogét," the caller said. "It's French-Canadian."

"Sure. Okay, you're clear. What can we send you?"

"I'd like an . . . escort."

"Right. But you called Double D, so I take it you want a very deluxe escort, yes?"

"Yes."

"I don't mean to sound cold, sir, but escorts, they're kind of like cars. There's Rolls-Royces and there's Fords, you understand?"

"Yes. I—"

"And there's used cars and new ones, you understand that?"

"Yes."

"The newer it is, the more expensive. Because, once you drive it, once *anyone* drives it, well, it's not so new anymore, you still with me?"

"Yes."

"Now, we don't go below a certain . . . limit, okay? Uh, let's say we were talking about . . . oh, I don't know . . . school. High school, that's an easy way to look at it. Would you want, say sophomore, senior . . . or . . . ?"

"Freshman," the man said.

"Very expensive."

"I don't care. I just want—"

"It's five K for all night, plus whatever . . . gratuity you might wish to bestow."

"All right."

"All our escorts *are* escorted, do you know what I'm saying?"

"I think so."

"Someone will be along with the escort. That's the person you pay. In cash. The only thing you give the escort is the gratuity, got it?"

"Yes."

"Now, a little wear and tear is perfectly acceptable, okay? But damaged goods, that would be a very serious thing. Very expensive. If you—"

"I'm not going to—"

"Sure. Whatever. But, remember, we know where you live, Mr. Rogét. In fact, we know an awful lot about you now. So . . ."

"I said I'm not going to—"

"Sir, we don't care what you do. What we do care is that you understand: what*ever* you do, you have to pay for it, all right?"

"Yes."

"Would nine o'clock be satisfactory?"

"Yes. That would be—"

"They'll ring your room from the lobby," the man said, cutting the connection.

2

The man who gave his name as Roget put down the phone and got to his feet. He was medium-height, perhaps in his late forties—but close-cropped dull-gray hair, a sallow complexion, and a haggard face added another decade to his appearance. His body was not so much thin as taut. The backs of his hands were stippled with tiny dark spots. The little finger and the first segment of the one next to it on his right hand were missing.

He left the sitting room of the suite and entered the bedroom. Dropping to both knees, he opened the bottom drawer of a bureau and looked inside for a long moment. Then he shut the drawer, got to his feet, carefully removed his clothing, and entered the bathroom.

When he emerged from the bedroom a half-hour later, the man was dressed in a dark-blue suit with a white shirt and black tie. He checked his watch. Nodded to himself. Picked up the phone and ordered a chicken sandwich on rye toast, no mayo, from Room Service.

He ate the sandwich slowly, chewing each mouthful with care. When he finished, he dialed Room Service again and told the person who answered that he would leave his tray outside the door.

Then he went to the desk, took out a few sheets of hotel stationery, and began to write—tiny words so precise they might have been typed. When he was finished, he placed the sheets of paper inside a hotel envelope and sealed it. Then he put the envelope in the pocket of his suit coat.

The man sat down in an armchair and closed his eyes.

3

The phone rang at 8:58 p.m. The man picked it up.

"Yes?"

"Your escort is here." It was a man's voice. "Shall I bring her up?"

"Yes."

Less than two minutes later, there was a soft rap at the door of the suite. The man opened it. Standing before him was a tall, well-developed man with long dark hair pulled back into a ponytail. Behind him, just visible behind and below his right shoulder, was a girl with straight blond hair almost covering her face.

Roget stood aside. The tall man and the blonde girl entered the suite. Roget started to open his mouth, but the tall man motioned for silence. The blonde girl walked deeper into the suite and stood quietly, hands clasped behind her back as if terribly shy, eyes downcast. She was dressed in a school uniform: green blazer over a plain white blouse and a plaid pleated skirt with matching suspenders.

The tall man opened his palm. Roget reached into his pocket and came out with a stack of new one-hundred-dollar bills. The tall man fanned it as one might a sheaf of paper, then pocketed it without counting. He stepped so close that Roget could see the pores of his skin. "She can get back on her own," the tall man said. "And if she can't . . . you just call us, all right? But that would be extra . . ."

"All right," Roget replied.

The tall man left.

4

"How old are you?" Roget asked the blonde girl.

"Thirteen," she replied, still not looking up.

"Do you want to sit down?" he asked her.

"Whatever *you* want. That's why I'm here."

"Then let's sit down."

"Okay."

"You seem . . . afraid. Are you?"

"I'm a little . . . nervous, I guess."

"I'm not going to hurt you, child."

"Thanks. I—"

"But you're not really thirteen, are you?"

"Yes, I am. Do you want to see my birth certificate? I have it with—"

"No, thank you. How long have you been doing . . . this?"

"I never . . . I mean, this is my first—"

"What's your name?"

"Whatever you say it is, Daddy."

Roget's face tightened. He took a deep breath. Then he said: "Your name is Melody, how's that?"

The blonde girl's face twitched. "Okay," she said.

"And you live in the Heights. And go to Cables High. You're in the eleventh grade. And you were sixteen last July. Your father works at—"

"How do you *know* all that? How could you? They promised no one would ever . . ."

"No one has to," Roget said, his voice calm with assurance. "It just costs money. To find out things. To get things. You know about the 'getting things' part, don't you, Melody?"

"You don't—"

"Yes, I do. Did they show you the film about the Japanese

schoolgirls? Or start you off with a beeper in the mall? Or maybe it was—"

"What*ever*! I mean, who cares?"

"You know what 'Double D' stands for, Melody?"

"Yeah," the girl said, her voice hardening. "Daddy-Daughter."

"And how much does that pay?"

"A thousand dollars," the girl said proudly. "The most anyone gets."

"Plus the . . . gratuity, yes?"

"Sometimes. Not always."

"How would you like to start earning that money, Melody?"

"Whatever you say, Daddy."

"Don't call me that!" Roget said sharply.

"I'm sorry. I was just . . ."

"That's all right," he said, voice shifting to a soothing tone. "It's my fault. I shouldn't have barked at you like that. I shouldn't have . . . made you feel bad. That's abuse too, you know. Emotional abuse. When a parent makes a child feel bad—as though they have no worth—that hurts. Sometimes it hurts worse than anything. And sometimes the parent doesn't even know he's doing it. . . ."

"That's all right," the girl said, repeating the man's words, using his same tone, keeping the fear at bay, working hard, terrified that she had finally found that client who all the girls whispered about—the Death Trick.

Roget shook his head like a terrier with a rat. The girl didn't move.

Finally, he stopped. When he looked across at her, his eyes were clear and calm again.

"I'm sorry," he said. "The headaches . . . they get really bad sometimes."

"Are they migraines?" the girl asked, too brightly. "My mother used to—"

"No, child. It's a tumor. A brain tumor. From cancer."

"You mean you're going to, like. . . ?"

"Die? Yes. And fairly soon. I refused the chemo. It would have made it impossible to . . ."

"What?"

"Make amends."

"I don't get it."

"It doesn't matter, Melody. I've spent just about all my money. And I've done a lot of work. But your work . . . Well, you won't have to do it. Not tonight. All you have to do is talk, okay? Talk and listen."

"Sure. Do you want me to take off my—?"

"Just sit, child. If you want some soda or anything, it's right over there in the mini-bar."

"Thank you."

"You're welcome. I had—I guess I *have*—a daughter about your age. I mean, she *was* your age. When she . . . I mean, she's about nineteen now. Almost twenty. Her birthday is next month."

"Are you going to—?"

"No, I'm not going to see her. I don't know where she is."

"Did she, like, run away or something?"

"Yes, that's just what she did. She ran away. She ran away from me."

"Oh."

"Not for . . . what you think. Not for . . . the reason you're here. Or thought you were here, anyway. I never touched my daughter. Never laid a hand on her. Just words," Roget said. "Ugly, hurtful, mean words. 'You're fat. You're ugly. You're stupid. You're lazy.' I thought I was . . . motivating her. Making her work harder. The same way my . . . It doesn't matter. Do you know what I mean, Melody?"

"I . . . guess so. I mean, nobody in my family ever called me names. They just . . ."

"What?"

"I don't know . . . ignored me. Like I wasn't there. I had—I
mean, I have—nice things. And friends. And everything. That's
not why I . . ."

"Do this?"

"Yes. It's just for . . . fun. Kicks. I mean—"

"They ask you that a lot, don't they? Why you got into . . .
this?"

"Who? You mean . . . clients?"

"Yes."

"No. They never ask. I mean, you're the first one. If you're even
asking . . . I can't really tell."

"No, I'm not asking you, Melody. It doesn't much matter after a
while, does it?"

"I . . . guess not. And they . . ."

"What?"

"I don't know how to explain it. They . . . pay attention to me."

Roget nodded his head. Sadly, as though acknowledging a
great truth.

"I mean, I'm not going to be doing this much longer," the girl
continued. "When I go to college, I'll—"

"Yes, I understand, Melody. Do you have a red button?"

"A red button? On my—?"

"No. I guess the different . . . services . . . call it different things.
A beeper, a cell phone . . . some way you can call them if you get
in trouble."

"You mean, like . . . arrested? Morty said we would never get
arrested. But if something goes wrong, I have a number to call.
For a lawyer. Morty says —"

"And Morty is the man who brought you?"

"No. That's just Chester. He's—"

"So Morty is your boss?"

"Well, he's not really my *boss*. I mean, not like my *father's* boss,
like in a company and all. He's the guy who talked to me when
I . . . signed up."

"And where is Morty now?"

"Now? I don't know. I mean, he doesn't stay in one place, like. He moves around."

"Does he ever go to the Castle?"

"Oh, wow! You know about that? I was only there once. It's really—"

"Only for special guests?"

"Yeah! I wasn't supposed to even know where it is, you know what I mean? They, like, blindfold you and everything."

"But . . . ?"

"But I, like, recognized it. Not from the front. It's all dark and everything. But after. When I was . . . done. I went outside. In the back yard. Only it's not a yard. It's humongous. Like a park, even. Way out past the pool with all the lights. I just wanted to smoke a joint, be by myself. And then I realized where I was. My friend . . . well, she's not really my *friend* so much, from school, like, we went there once. Around the back, I mean. So I knew it. Where I was, I mean."

"Was your . . . friend there that night?"

"Alexia? Fat chance! I mean, it's *her* house, right? But she doesn't even know about . . . it. Only a couple of kids at school do it, and Alexia's not in our crowd, so she'd never—"

"It's pretty early yet," Roget said, getting to his feet. "We have a long time to wait. Why don't you just lie down. You can sleep if you like. Or watch TV. Just no phone calls, okay?"

"Okay."

5

It was almost one in the morning when the girl finally spoke to Roget again. She was sprawled on the couch, candy wrappers strewn in a fan around her feet.

"Look, it's, like, none of my business, okay? But you paid a lot of money. And I haven't done anything. And it's getting late and all. I mean, what did you hire me for?"

Roget got up silently and went into the back bedroom. When he emerged he was carrying a large satchel. And an ugly-looking Uzi on a strap slung over his shoulder. He put on a raincoat, sliding the submachine gun underneath.

"I hired you for just what I told them, Melody. I need an escort."

*for **Dr. Yitzhak Bakal***

STUNTMAN

"This is a matter of some delicacy, Mr. Slate," the man in the charcoal Savile Row suit said primly.

I yawned. Lux shot me one of her disapproving looks. She has dozens of them, all different.

"The studio has a situation," the Brit went on like I hadn't said a word. Lux does that too. I figured they'd get along real good.

"You see why I get paid by the hour," I told him, stifling another yawn.

"Very well," he said. "I shall be brief. Brett Kingman is being blackmailed."

"This look like a police station to you?" I asked him politely.

"*Sssst!*" Lux hissed at me. "Please sit down," she said to the Brit, flashing her cobra-killer smile. "Mr. Slate's manners are not always . . . appropriate."

"Thank you," he told her gratefully, pulling his pleated trousers toward his crotch as he sat.

"Would you like some coffee?" Lux purred. "Some tea, perhaps?"

He made another grateful sound. Lux turned around and walked off. I made a grateful sound of my own.

"All right," I asked him. "What's the deal with Kingman?"

"You are . . . aware of who he is, then?"

"Brett Kingman, the movie twit, right?"

"Sir! Brett Kingman is one of the world's highest-ranking martial artists, as well as a screen actor of the most . . . bankable magnitude."

"As a martial artist, he's mid-level on his best day. I know a half-dozen *karateka* who could kick his ass without breaking a sweat. And two of them are women."

"Mr. Kingman—"

"—is also so purely stupid he needs a stand-in for dialogue."

"I gather you're not a fan," he said dryly.

"Mr. Slate isn't a fan of anything," Lux said, coming back into the office with a small silver tray and a full tea service. It weighed about fifteen pounds. She carried it in one hand like it was a handkerchief.

"I'm a fan of money," I volunteered.

They both looked at me about how you'd expect.

"Mr. Slate, I was referred to you by the studio. I have no idea why. If you are not interested in this matter, I would be *more* than happy to seek services elsewhere."

"I don't have to be interested to do the work," I assured him. "Or to get paid, either."

"So that means—?"

"Please explain your problem," Lux told him gently, pouring the tea, doing her geisha act. The one that's about as real as Lux is Japanese.

"It started with an anonymous note. . . ."

"Damn! That's a new twist. The blackmailer didn't sign his name, huh?"

"Mr. Slate. I am *trying*—"

"—my damn patience," I told him. "Look, you've been here a half-hour and I don't know anything more than when you walked in. You're on the clock, pal. You want to keep spinning your wheels, that's up to you."

Lux gave him one of her "Forgive him—he's an idiot!" looks. He smiled. Men smile at Lux all the time.

"Very well, I shall cut to the chase, as you people say. It seems Mr. Kingman had a . . . romantic liaison some years ago."

"So?"

"So the other party was married."

"*That's* going to crimp his box office?"

"In the aforementioned marriage"—the Brit coughed delicately— "the other party was the husband."

"If this is cutting to the chase, I'd hate to see you beat around the bush. So the chump's gay—so what?"

"This isn't a matter of reality, Mr. Slate. It's one of public perception. If Mr. Kingman's fans were to see him as . . ."

"Get out of town," I said. "I've seen his movies. If this guy's a sex symbol, so am I."

Lux giggled. I wasn't offended. I'm used to it.

"That is not the point," he said stiffly. "This is not a matter of . . . sexuality. It is one of politics."

"I don't get . . . Wait a minute," I said. "Kingman. Isn't he the one who did that commercial for those loons? The one where he said gays could be 'converted' and all?"

"There were—"

"I remember now," I told him. "Sure. He went on the talk shows, too. Told everyone how being gay was a choice, and they had made the wrong one. Huh! You're right, pal. Once the public finds out that a gay-basher is a stone queen, that'll about do it."

"I hardly think—"

"That's obvious. Look, let's be real clear, okay? Paying blackmail is about as effective as putting an agoraphobic under house arrest. What you need is for it to *stop*, right?"

"Yes! That is precisely what is needed. And the studio said you were the one to—"

"Right. I remember. You told me that about ten minutes ago. How much is the payoff?"

"They want one hundred thousand dollars. In—"

"—used bills, nothing bigger than a fifty, no sequential serial numbers."

"Yes. And they—"

"—'re going to give you the *negatives*, right? Or is it video?"

"Neither. It's some letters. And an audiotape."

"Whatever. You want someone to make the exchange?"

"Yes."

"And to make *sure* your boy isn't bothered again?"

"Yes."

"You have the payoff money?"

"I do," he said, patting an oxblood leather briefcase next to his leg.

"And my fee?"

"Which is?"

"The usual. Two and a half times the bite. So, in this case, a quarter mil."

"The studio will—"

"Sure."

"It's tonight. At the bus station. How will you—?"

"Me? Hey, I don't do the drops, pal. In this outfit, I'm the brains. Lux over there, she's the muscle."

"This . . . young lady?" The Brit seemed shocked at the prospect.

"Why not?"

"She doesn't look very . . ."

I nodded at Lux. She bowed slightly and put her hands together in a prayerful gesture. When she opened her hands, she was holding a fireball. She blew gently and the fireball shot across the room, splattering against the far wall. It blazed for a second, then went out, leaving an ugly black char mark.

"Want to see what she can do with a fingernail?" I asked the Brit.

He wasn't saying anything.

"The studio knows how it works," I told him. "Leave the brief-case here. There's plenty of time for them to wire the payment into my account. The business department knows how to do it. I'm on the books as a stuntman. A special stuntman. Soon as the money lands, we'll take care of the rest. You'll have your tape and letters tomorrow. And you'll never hear from the blackmailer again."

"How can we be—?"

"Ask the studio if I've ever failed."

He pushed the briefcase toward Lux, got up, and showed him-self out.

Lux locked the door. Then she walked over and sat in my lap. "Do you think they'll ever figure it out?" she asked me.

"Nah. We solved the first one, didn't we? Eight years ago. You know Hollywood—they haven't had an original idea since they moved west. The suits never imagined we'd be at both ends of the game. Ever since, we're the studio's first choice when they get a 'situation.' And, working for them like we do, funny how much we hear, huh?"

"It's a good plan," Lux said approvingly. "And they get exactly what they deserve."

"Us too," I said. "Didn't I tell you I was the brains of this out-fit?"

Lux chuckled. It felt real fine.

for r.

PIECEWORK

"**H**ow much you go for this?"

"A yard."

"A yard? For a .357 Python? Man, this piece musta got a murder on it, be that cheap."

"Gonna have another one on it before tomorrow."

"Yeah? You really gonna do him?"

"*Got* to do him."

"He didn't actually call you out, man. It don't have to be like this."

"No? How it supposed to be?"

"It supposed to be Chill City, bro. You don't see him, he don't see you right?"

"I stay off the corner behind this, you can change my name to 'Bitch.'"

"Man, I didn't say stay off the corner. Got to corner, I'm with that. But you wasn't gonna do him *on* the corner, right?"

"I was thinking about it."

"Take him down in front of all them rats? Man, you mother-fucking big-time crazy-stupid-dumb. Half those dudes got cases on them. They trade your sorry ass in on a deal with the Man, then where you be?"

"Everybody gonna know I did it anyways."

"You mean everybody gonna *say* they know. True. And Five-Oh gonna come take you down, that true, too. So what? You ice up, don't say nothing. Without the piece, they *got* nothing, okay? But you do him on the corner, it won't go like that."

"I don't give a—"

"Man, what you come around me for, then? You know where I be. Same time, same place, every day. I be here to t.c.b. You know what I do—watch my man's back, right? So why you tell me this, show me the piece and all, you don't want my advice? I am trying to look out for you and all you do is give me attitude."

"Look, I'm . . . Truth, brother: I wasn't downing you. No way I do that. I know you been Upstate and all. I mean, you don't get to be working right under an OG without knowing things. You got my apology."

"All right! First thing is, you don't gotta do it."

"No, man. No disrespect. But he gotta die."

"Over a ho, man?"

"You calling my—?"

"Yeah, brother. That is exactly right. I *am* calling her what she is. Matter of fact, you break it down, you want to blast the one who put you in the cross, you blast *her*, way I look at it."

"She's—"

"—like all the rest of 'em, bro. You gonna let her play you into the Death House?"

"Nobody's playing me."

"You wasn't even *there*, man."

"How you know that?"

" 'Cause I *was*, bro. What she tell you? He grabbed her ass?"

"Yeah."

"Well, he did, man. 'Course, she was waving it in front of him. And everybody else, too. Got half her cheeks hanging below those shorts. The way she was staging, he *don't* grab him a little something, it's like he a fucking homo."

"He didn't have no—"

"Oh, man, you making me tired. You was gonna . . . what? Marry the ho?"

"That's my woman."

"That's *everybody's* woman, fool. You not the first, you not gonna be the last. I tell you something else too, all right? She not only won't be coming to visit you when you waiting trial, she gonna for*get* your pitiful ass soon as you get shipped Upstate. That is, if she don't testify against you yourself."

"Why you saying this, man? Why you wanna hurt me?"

"I'm trying to keep you from hurting your*self*, young brother. You gonna take a man's life over something you don't even know the truth of?"

"I don't do nothing, I got no face."

"You gonna do it, then? No matter what I say?"

"Got to do it."

"Yeah, well, listen up, then. A piece like you got there, that's a motherfucking *cannon*. You ever hear how much noise one of them makes? It's not like no nine, like I carry. This one, you can make it *quiet*. You just screw this thing in the front. See, like I'm doing here? Then you can pop someone, it ain't loud at all. That's the way a pro would do it."

"I ain't no pro."

"No. You ain't."

"Hold up! Okay. Okay, I see it. All right. I'm not gonna dust him. I let it slide, okay? Brother? Let me . . . *Please!*"

for Keith Gilyard

THE REAL WORLD

This all started over one of the silly kinds of things kids get into. The kind of things they're supposed to settle themselves. Maybe it was because we're both fathers, Hank and me.

That's his name, Hank. I don't really know much about him except that he lives a few blocks over. In a little tract house, just like we do. It's a big development, the one we live in. Built right after the war, for returning GIs. That's World War II, not the one I was in. The one I was in, they don't really have a name for it, just the place where it happened.

What I mean is, people called it different things, depending on how they looked at it. Even the guys that was in it, they called it different things. Vietnam. The Nam. Overseas. It didn't matter. All we knew, it wasn't out here. The World, that's what we used to call out here. We used to talk all the time about getting back to the World.

Nobody *in* the World ever called it that. Funny, huh? So I always thought it was a special name that only soldiers used.

Until I went to prison. In there, guys called it the World too. And they'd say it the same way—they couldn't wait to get out in the World.

The stuff they talked about doing once they got out there, it was the same thing guys used to talk about doing overseas. I don't mean the *same* same things. I mean, different guys had different . . . I don't know, goals. So some guys overseas, they talked about getting back to the World, get a job, find a girl, get married, have kids . . . like that. And some talked about dealing drugs, or hijacking armored cars. Or raping women. It just depended. But it was the same thing, the Army and prison—people talked about what they were going to do when they got out. And the guys who stayed, they got called the same thing in both places—lifers.

Another way both places were the same—people got there for different reasons. In my platoon, there were guys who enlisted. Some because they wanted to be in the war. For America, they said. They didn't keep saying that, not after a while. I mean, it got hard to tell after a while why you were there. The only thing you knew for sure is that you didn't want to be. The guys who *did* want to be there—everybody stayed away from them.

Others, they thought it was a good opportunity. Learn a trade, maybe go to college when they got out. A few even thought it would be a career, like if their fathers were in already. Then there were guys like me. Guys who had to be there—either they got drafted or it was their only choice, you know what I mean.

So, because of that last thing, I never blamed the war for me going to prison. I mean, I was going to prison before the war—or before I went into it, anyway—and I got a break from the judge. Everybody was against the war then, it seemed like, so they was looking for guys to go. When the public defender I had told the judge I wanted to go, the judge looked real serious. Then he said I was a good kid, and that fight I'd been in—the one where the other guy got hurt so bad—well, those things happened in certain neighborhoods.

That was when I lived in the city. We didn't call where we lived a neighborhood like the judge did, but we knew it had borders. The whole thing had started when those other guys crossed our border.

When I went in, I had a bad temper. A real bad temper. And I liked to drink, too. Liquor only gave me a worse temper. I knew that, but I still liked to drink. But even though there was a lot of dope in my . . . neighborhood, I never used it.

Not until I was over there.

I lost my temper in the Army. I don't mean I got mad. I mean I *lost* all my bad temper. It disappeared. I stopped drinking too, after a while. This was all after I found out stuff about myself. After I got my MOS—Military Occupation Specialty. Which was Infantry, at first. Which really isn't an MOS at all. I mean, it's not like being a helicopter mechanic or a radioman—nothing you could use in the World.

So I stopped drinking and I didn't use any more dope—which was only weed, anyway, not the other stuff.

That other stuff, it was good and bad both. Good because you stopped being afraid when you had to go out into the jungle. Which was most of the time, for us. That's what Infantry did. The bad thing was that it made you stupid. Like you didn't care if you got blown away or not. Or made you so paranoid you would just start blasting away every time a leaf moved. That could get you killed, too—we were supposed to be quiet.

One thing I learned over there, it was how to be quiet.

I got shot once. When I was still Infantry. It wasn't much of a wound. Not a "million-dollar wound," like they called it when you got shot bad enough to go back to the World, but not so bad that you was crippled or nothing. The best thing was to get shot bad enough to go back, and get Disability too. They give you that in percentages, like 10 percent disability or 30 percent or whatever.

My wound was in the leg. Not even from a bullet, from a mortar round they lobbed into where we was dug in. I didn't get to go back to the World. They gave me a medal, a Purple Heart. Some guys had a whole bunch of them. Nobody cared, except the lieutenants and the lifers—they wanted them bad.

When I got back to the World, I just drifted around for a while. A lot of guys did that. I know, because I'd meet them in the same places I hung out in.

I went to prison for stealing. Robbing, actually. There's a real difference. In the law, anyway. One is if you take something that's not yours. The other is the same, but it's when you take it from a person, not a place. Anyway, the public defender told the judge the same kind of story he did the first time. I don't mean it was the same guy, the PD, only that he told the same story. But this time, instead of saying I was going to serve my country, he said I already had, see? The judge was one of those liberals. He had long hair and everything. He was probably against the war. Or he was in law school and didn't have to go. Or something. I know he never went in, because I can tell. But now it's like . . . fashionable to give a damn about Vietnam vets. So he made a big speech and gave me five years. Instead of the twenty-five he could have given me, that's what the PD said. Like he'd done a real good job. The PD, not the judge.

I didn't care so much. I thought prison would be like the Army. And the guards would be the VC. But it wasn't like that. Mostly, the convicts fought each other. Usually over race, but it could be any stupid thing. It was like that in the Army too, but not so much. And almost never out in the field.

Except for lieutenants. Nobody liked them. You couldn't fight them—that was straight to jail, worse even—but some guys, they'd toss a grenade right into a trench where one of the lieutenants would be dug in. Everybody would see it, but nobody would say anything.

In prison, most of the guards was white. And most of the convicts was black. Kind of like the Army too, except that, like I said, nobody thought the guards was lieutenants, if you understand what I'm saying.

There was a lot of murderers in there. They never called themselves that—they always called themselves killers. If they was ever in the Army, ever in the Infantry especially, they would know the difference.

Anyway, I didn't care what they called themselves, so I never said anything.

You want to know something funny? In the Army, I never learned one useful thing for the World. In prison, I never learned one useful thing for the World either. But the stuff I learned in the Army helped me in prison. And I guess, if I'd gone to prison first, it would have helped me in the Army. Weird, huh?

Anyway, I got out of both. I came back to the World each time.

What I do now, I drive a truck. So I'm on the road a lot. I never really had a home, and that was okay. Until I met Noreen. She was working in one of the truck stops. I don't mean "working" like when they say "working girl." See, all the truck stops have hookers. "Lot lizards," they call them. You can even call ahead on the CB, make a reservation if you want. But Noreen was a waitress. She cooked too, sometimes.

I really liked her. She talked about stuff I didn't know anything about, but I always liked to hear her say it anyway. You know what I liked best about her? She wrote me letters. On the road, so they'd be waiting for me at the next stop. All the time I was in the Army, I never got a letter. All the time in prison neither.

Noreen was a single mother. That's what she said, "I'm a single mother." I wasn't even sure what she meant, until she explained. She had a son. Lewis, his name was. He was nine years old. Lewis didn't have a father. I don't mean like Noreen was divorced, she was never married. She said she knew who the father was. She said he knew it, too. But he never came around after she told him she was pregnant. She told Lewis his father died in an accident. Before he was even born. Lewis, I mean, not the father.

Noreen and I got married. She had this little apartment. Only one bedroom. Lewis slept in the bedroom, and Noreen slept on a fold-out couch in the living room. After we got married, she asked me, did I want us to sleep in the bedroom? I told her that was Lewis' room. She hugged me so tight it hurt.

I think Lewis really liked me. He never said much—but that's okay, because I never say much either. But we did some things together. Mostly watched TV and played cards. And computer games—he was real good at those. I never took him fishing or nothing like that. Lewis wasn't into sports much—he didn't even like to watch them on TV.

In the little house, Lewis still had his own bedroom. Noreen and I had one too, right across the hall. It was nice. I was always glad to come back. With Noreen and me both working, we did okay. That's how we got the down payment for the house, saving together. I bought it on the GI Bill. That was the first time I ever got anything out of being in the Army. I didn't even know you could do that, but the man at the bank told us about it.

Lewis used to ask me about the Army. I never told him much. I don't mean I told the kid to shut the hell up and not bother me or nothing—I would never do that. I just told him it was a long time ago, and it was different things to different people, depending on who you asked. He asked me something once, though. His class was going on a field trip to Washington, D.C. You know, where they have that monument to all the people who got killed over there? Anyway, Lewis asked me, did I want him to look up the names of anyone I had served with? I told him nobody I had served with ever got killed over there. I was sorry to lie to him, but the truth would have been harder. Noreen was always doing things that made it harder on herself so she could make it easier for Lewis, and that's what I wanted to do too.

I even read a book on it. Being a good parent, I mean. But it didn't make sense to me. I mean, there was nothing so great in there. It's like the person who wrote it didn't get it. Or maybe I didn't.

Lewis asked me if I got any medals once, too. I told him no. They didn't give out any medals for what I did.

I guess I'm rambling all over the place with this. Noreen says I do that when I don't like what I'm going to have to say. Say I'm going to be gone for a few weeks on the road—it takes me hours just to tell her that.

Anyway, it was just a little fight. Between two kids. This guy Hank's kid—his name is Hank, too; they called him Junior—and Lewis. I guess Lewis got beat up a little bit, but not too bad. He wasn't all that upset about it. But this guy Hank, he was mad. Even though Lewis didn't win the fight, I guess he hurt Junior.

Lewis didn't think he won, but maybe Junior didn't think he did either.

So Hank came over to our house. He pounded on the door. I wasn't home. Noreen told me about it. Hank was screaming that Lewis should come out of the house and take what was coming to him. Noreen got mad. I'm not sure what happened next, but I know Hank hit her. Slapped her, really, I guess. Then Lewis got real mad and tried to stab Hank with a kitchen knife. Hank got it away from him and he punched Lewis. Noreen really tried to get him then, but she couldn't. This was all while I was away.

I don't think Noreen would ever have told me about it. But she knew Lewis would, and she figured maybe it would be better coming from her. I told her I wouldn't lose my temper, and she believed me. That was fair—she'd never seen me lose my temper.

I went over to see Hank. He came outside. I told him what he did was wrong. He shouldn't have hurt my wife or my kid. He said Lewis wasn't my kid. That made me feel real bad. Not for me, I don't care, I guess. But I know how kids are. And if Hank was saying that then probably Junior was saying that. And maybe all the kids were saying it too. Lewis always told everyone I was his father, so it was like calling him a liar. Lewis is no liar, just like his mother.

Hank said other things too. About Noreen. I think he was trying to make me mad. He told me he was over there. In the Nam. He was a Green Beret, he said. Trained in hand-to-hand combat. He was training Junior, and Junior was going to really get Lewis one day.

I didn't get mad. I told him I'd been there too. And I learned fighting like that was stupid. I learned that over there. He said I was a punk. That was okay—I know how people talk.

He asked me, did I want to step outside? I told him we was already outside. That just made him madder.

Then he said we'd have to settle it. He asked me if I knew where this old factory was. On the edge of town. It's abandoned now, empty. Even the kids don't go there to play, because there's all kinds of busted machinery lying around and they could get hurt. Noreen would never let Lewis go there.

I told him, yes, I knew where it was.

Hank asked me, did I have a gun at home? I told him yes.

He said he had one, too. And we'd have to meet at the factory and settle this thing. I told him he was crazy. Gunfights, they don't happen in the World. He said, if I didn't do it, next time I went on the road he'd go and see Noreen. He said that was the *real* World. He said some other stuff, too.

So I'm here, at the factory. Waiting for Hank.

It won't take long. I did this before. A lot.

After I got done with Infantry, I got my real MOS. The one I could never use in the World before this.

Hank's head fills the scope. I rest the crosshairs on the bridge of his nose, tracking him as he walks forward. He has a pistol held down at his side, right against the thigh of his camo-pants.

I wait for my breathing to be perfect. Between heartbeats, I do it.

Then I go back to the real World.

for Walter Anderson

PERP WALK

1

"It's all set up, Tracy." It was the Chief's bulldog voice, thick from the pressure of all the media attention. "Bring him on down," he said.

I keyed the microphone in the cruiser. "ETA under fifteen minutes, sir," I promised.

"I'll meet you out front. And, Tracy . . ."

"Yes, Chief?"

"This case is a career-maker, son. I won't forget who cracked it."

"Thank you, sir."

I replaced the mike, glanced over my shoulder to the cage in the back of the prowl car. Wallace John Loomis sat back there, hands cuffed behind his broad back, a three-day stubble on his pockmarked face, dull eyes staring straight ahead like he was watching one of those TV cartoons he loved so much.

"You think he'll beat it? Take an NGI and go to the state hospital?" the fresh-faced young trooper behind the wheel asked me. He'd only been on the job for a year or so—he still loved the cop slang.

"Not Guilty by Reason of Insanity? Not a chance, kid. Old Wallace ain't crazy, he's just slow in the head, that's all. Real slow."

"But isn't that the same as—?"

"Nah. Remember Homer Sistrunk? He had the IQ of a potted plant. But he was smart enough to rape and kill that old woman, right? They fry retards in this state, kid. And in a case like this . . ."

2

They were all waiting for us in the parking lot. Four in the afternoon, timed just perfect for the evening news. Better to let the TV people lead off, the Chief always said. It's more dramatic. Besides, people don't read the way they used to years ago—let the newspapers hold until the morning editions.

I could see the bright-yellow Channel 29 van right in front of the steps to the station house, the blonde-woman half of the evening anchor team already set up in the floodlights, a wireless microphone in her hand. The working press was there too—I recognized the red-haired guy with the gray trench coat from the *Herald Dispatch*. A phalanx of uniformed troopers kept the crowd behind wooden sawhorse barriers.

The kid pulled the cruiser as close as he could. I got out and opened the back door, motioning for Loomis to get out, holding my hand gently over his head so he wouldn't bump it as he exited.

Then we did the Perp Walk. Loomis first, me next to him, right hand tight on his left biceps. The reporters shouted questions at him:

"Did you kill Mary Jo?"

"Do you have a statement to make?"

"Was anyone else involved?"

But Loomis didn't say anything, just stared straight ahead, putting one foot ahead of the other, moving slow like he always did.

3

Once we got him locked up in one of the isolation cells, I came back outside. The chief was talking to the press, telling them how I had found the little girl's gym shorts in a shed at the back of the falling-down dump Loomis lived in all by himself. The little girl had disappeared the night of March 31.

"Good old-fashioned police work," the chief said. "That's how these cases are solved. Not with computers, not with those FBI profiles—with classic investigative techniques. And I'm proud to say that, when it comes to investigators, we've got one of the best in the business."

He gestured with his hand and I moved in next to him on top of the steps. "I can't stop and answer any of your questions now," I told them all. "The defendant has indicated he wants to make a statement and—"

"So the Blue Moon Murderer hasn't demanded a lawyer?" one wise guy in the press corps asked me.

"No, he hasn't," I said calmly. "In fact, we've already had quite a long conversation right after I placed him under arrest. I think his conscience . . . I better not say any more at this time," I cut myself off. "Talk to the chief. He's in charge. I've still got work to do."

4

I spent the whole night with Loomis, just him and me in the interrogation cell. Loomis doesn't talk much. Hell, he *can't* talk much. Mostly just mumbles and grunts. He liked fried chicken, though—I found that out.

I got him a whole bucket of that fried chicken, all for himself. With a double order of cole slaw and mashed potatoes. A six-pack of beer, too. And a portable TV set with a VCR, so he could watch cartoons.

We smoked three packs of cigarettes between us by four in the morning. Nobody came near us, letting me do my job. When Loomis finally fell asleep, I covered him with a blanket.

Then I called the chief.

5

It was almost noon before we were ready to go. This time, the national media were there. The word had gotten out—the Blue Moon Murderer was going to walk us right to the scene of the crime.

Loomis looked pretty good. I made him take a shower and shave, and one of the guys brought him in some old clothes that were a pretty good fit.

I led the way in the Ford Explorer we used for the back country. You need four-wheel drive in some of those gullies, even in the dry season. I let Loomis ride next to me in the front bucket seat. He was handcuffed, and I controlled the lock to the passenger door, so there wasn't any risk.

We gave the media a half-hour to set up, then we started the walk. Me and Loomis, so close together I could hear his breathing.

The rest of the guys stepped back, gave us plenty of room—they didn't want to do anything that might spook him. Every once in a while, I'd lean in real close and he'd say something to me.

The ground was so hard and dry it hadn't even picked up the tracks of the Explorer—you couldn't tell the last time somebody had been in that area.

I kept talking to Loomis. The cameras watched from a distance. Even the most rabid members of the press didn't want to spoil this one chance of finding Mary Jo if she was still alive.

We walked for a long time. Finally, we came on an old shack. It was so decrepit only three walls were standing. I whispered to Loomis. He pointed toward the shack.

I bowed my head. The forensic squad moved in. Loomis just stared stupidly into space. It had taken me a long time to get him to understand he should point like I told him.

Right to where I'd buried Mary Jo's body.

for Greg Posner-Weber

GOOD FOR THE SOUL

"It ain't like I'm her father, you understand?"

"Sure. You want another smoke?"

"Thanks, man. I mean, how many guys would marry a woman with a kid, right? Her real father, it's like the guy don't exist. Never sends a dime of child support, never writes to the kid, nothing."

"She even know who he is?"

"Not a clue. You ask me, I'm not even sure the little tramp's *mother* knows, you understand what I'm saying?"

"Yeah. Happens all the time. They want to party, but they don't want to pay the freight."

"That's the truth. I mean, I work *hard*. I could be spending all my money in strip clubs, you know what I mean? But, no, I bring it home."

"The mother don't work?"

"Cheryl? You gotta be kidding, pal. I'm the breadwinner in that house. Just me. That little part-time job of hers doesn't hardly pay enough to cover her car and insurance."

"Must be rough sometimes . . ."

"Hey, I can deal with it. But . . . it just got to be too much, you know what I'm saying? I work all day, okay? Then I come home and Cheryl throws some TV-dinner crap in front of me, tells me she's gotta get to work, leaves me to watch the kid."

"She's . . . how old?"

"Nine, last birthday. Sounds like a *little* kid, right? Let me tell you something. I don't know if she gets it from her mother or what, but that is one *wise* kid, believe me when I tell you. She knows exactly how to get over."

"So when the mother . . . Cheryl?"

"Yeah, Cheryl."

"So when Cheryl would leave you alone . . ."

"No, it wasn't nothing like that. I mean, I may have . . . played with her a little before, but this . . . thing, it was only that one time."

"Why do you think—?"

"I was drunk. Simple as that. I mean, I usually have a beer or two after work. Just to unwind, okay? But that night, Cheryl said she was gonna be late, trading off with another girl on a split, and I was just watching TV and I guess the booze just got away on me. I mean, I was *drunk*. The next thing I know, it's like I just woke up. And she was . . ."

"The mother?"

"Yeah, she caught us. I mean, the kid was in bed with me. And I was still drunk. And I guess she just . . ."

"The mother?"

"No, the kid. She just—I mean, look: I was drunk. I never did nothing like that before."

"Sure, I understand. Let me ask you something: was that the first time you ever got drunk?"

"In my life? Come *on*."

"Yeah. So, when you got drunk before, you rape any little girls?"

"Huh? What're you—?"

"Me? I'm just trying to figure this out. Trying to help you help yourself. You want it to work, it's gotta *sound* right. Now, you did it because you were drunk. The booze made you do it. But you got drunk before. And you didn't do it then, right? So *something* had to be different. . . ."

"Oh, I see what you mean. Sure. I'm telling you what was different. That little slut, that's what was different. If I'd been sober, she never would've gotten over on me like that."

"Yeah. I hope you didn't say any of this to the cops?"

"Hey, man, I said I was drunk, not stupid. I ain't saying *nothing* until I see a lawyer."

"Good. No way they're gonna take that kid's word over yours, right?"

"Well, there was some . . . blood and stuff, I guess. But there's other ways it could've . . . I mean, I done some reading about it and—"

"You read about it *before* it happened?"

"Well, not about *it*. Just about—you know what I'm talking about. Hell, the guards told me you've already been in a long time—"

"Eight years, seven months, and eleven days."

"Jesus. For what?"

"Murder."

"Oh. Then what're you doing here in the County? They told me this is the pre-trial tank."

"I got another charge."

"From when you was—"

"Yeah. Downstate."

"Damn! You got nothing *but* bad luck, huh, partner? Anyway, like I was saying, you got fuck-books in prison too, right? That's what I heard. This book I was telling you about? It was called *Daddy's Doll*. I got it at the video store. And it said how these little bitches sometimes get you so—"

"Yeah. You didn't leave the book lying around, did you?"

"Oh shit! I never thought of—"

"Calm down. Just call your wife. They have to let you use the pay phone here. Tell her where the stuff is—*any* stuff, you hear what I'm saying?—and tell her to get rid of it."

"I dunno, man. She was really mad. Like I *killed* the kid or something."

"It's worth a try. What you got to lose? Look, promise her anything. Tell her about the booze. Tell her you're going to get therapy. Just make sure she gets rid of all the stuff. And if *she* won't do it, tell your lawyer to get you a power-of-attorney form. That gives *him* the right to act like he was you, understand? So *he* can get everything—go right into your house with your key. You got videos too, right?"

"Yeah. Damn, I'm sure glad I talked to you."

"No problem. Look, the important thing is, you never confess, understand? They say confession is good for the soul. That's cute. Confession, it's good for the cops, that's all. Now, your wife, she *can't* testify against you, so you're covered there. But don't say another word to anyone, all right?"

"Absolutely."

"All right. Then just chill until your lawyer shows. We got this whole place to ourselves."

"Why do you think that is? I mean, there's room enough in here for twenty guys."

"The man wants it *quiet* in here. Same as in the joint. So they keep us separated."

"I don't get—"

"They don't lock whites with niggers, man. What's so hard to understand?"

"Nothing. I mean—I just thought they didn't . . ."

"It ain't like the movies, pal."

"I . . . figured. That's what those tattoos are for, right? Like, white power?"

"Yeah. *Exactly* like that. You want another smoke?"

"Thanks. I'll pay you back as soon as Cheryl gets down here with the bail. That is, *if* she . . ."

"Don't sweat it. Like you said, you're the breadwinner, right?"

"Right. Hey, what did they bring you back down for?"

"I told you."

"No, I mean, what'd they say you did?"

"Oh. Another one."

"A . . . murder?"

"Yeah. Four, actually. They say I'm the enforcer for this prison gang. Real science fiction."

"You don't seem too worried about it."

"Me? Nah. How many life sentences can you do?"

"I guess that's right. Christ, I hope the judge cuts me a play on bail. I don't see how you did so much time already—it would drive me nuts."

"You won't be doing any time."

"You really don't think so?"

"I'd bet on it."

"Well, you've been around a lot; I guess you should know."

"Sure. The truth, it always comes out. They're going to try me for killing four men behind the walls. But they got it wrong."

"You didn't do it?"

"Sure I did it, pal. They just got the number wrong."

"Huh?"

"Those pay phones, they're really something. You can just reach out and talk to anyone. Even someone you haven't heard from in years."

"I don't—"

for Sergeant Mike McNamara

HIT MAN

"**D**on't you want to know why?" the chubby brunette asked. She was looking across at me, her elbows on the little round table in the corner of the bar, hands clasped under her chin. A damsel in distress. In case that act wouldn't fly, she moved her elbows closer to center, displaying even more creamy cleavage. Or maybe she just believed in insurance.

Her husband sure did. One point five, the finger had told me, and all hers—they had no kids.

"Anyone who'd want to know that would be a cop," I told her softly.

Her pale face went chalky.

"They don't have to prove motive in court," I said, "but they always want it when the defendant isn't the one who did it themselves, understand?"

"I . . . think so."

"Let's say, just talking hypothetically, a woman's getting beat up by her husband. She doesn't know what to do. She tells her

story to a guy she meets in a bar. That guy, he takes matters into
his own hands. And the husband, he gets killed. Maybe it wasn't
supposed to happen that way. Just a taste of his own medicine
that went wrong. Maybe the wife's a suspect. Maybe she's not.
Kind of depends on what kind of life the husband was living himself, understand?"

"He—"

"*Hypothetically*, let's say the husband had a drug habit. Or a lot
of gambling debts. Maybe he was playing around with a woman
and her boyfriend got jealous. Maybe he's got a thing for hookers.
Who knows? There's lots of reasons for a guy to get killed. Now, if
his wife has a rock-solid alibi for when it goes down, she doesn't
become a suspect automatically . . . but the cops'll still want to
talk to her. You with me so far?"

"Yes. But—"

Christ, she was a dimwit. "*Hypothetically* speaking, if there was,
say, a big life-insurance policy, then no question: The wife *is* a suspect. *Now* the cops care about a motive. I mean, the money, there's
a motive, sure. But plenty of guys carry life insurance and they
don't get whacked by their wives. Now, for the cops, greed, that's
plenty of motive all by itself. But that won't fly with a lot of juries.
They always want some more, and the DA knows it. So the cops
always ask around, see if there isn't anything else they can throw
in. You understand what I'm talking about?"

"Sure. And I—"

I held up one hand, palm out like a traffic cop. "Another thing
about cops: they're always wired. You know what that means?"

"Like on TV? With a little—?"

"Right. Doesn't take up any more space than . . . this," I said,
showing her the wireless disk I held in my cupped hand.

Her mouth made a nice round *O!* but she didn't say a word.
Finally.

"Now get up," I told her, "and go over to the pay phone. Bring
back the Yellow Pages."

She did it without another word, handing it to me. I opened it up, turned to the listing for Motels. "Trust, it's a funny thing," I told her. "People trust too easy. And there's no excuse for it. Not when they're about to go into something serious." I turned the book around so she could see the pages. "Look what's there. Motel listings. Must be a few hundred of them, just on one page alone. And there's a lot of pages, right? What I'm going to do is turn it around again, like this." I showed her what I meant, so she could read the print. "Then I'm going to turn to the next couple of pages, like this." I did that too, not looking down, my eyes right on hers. "Then what *you're* going to do is take this pen"—I handed her a red felt-tip—"close your eyes, and just make a circle, a little circle, anywhere you want on the page, okay? That's the motel we're going to go to, you and me."

"Why are—?"

"That way, neither of us could know the place in advance," I told her, ignoring the question she really wanted to ask. "Nobody makes a phone call. Nobody goes to the bathroom. We stay right in each other's sight every second, understand?"

"Yes, but—"

"Sure," I told her reasonably, like I knew what she was going to ask. "There could be a backup team in place. And we could get followed. But all they'd know is where we ended up. Not which room. And even if they could find *that* out, no way they could plant a listening device inside in advance, understand? Now: You ready to go?"

She just nodded. Then she closed her eyes and made a little circle on the page. When we looked, she had covered about three different ones. I pointed to the one in the middle. She nodded. We got up to leave.

In the parking lot, we went over to my car. I opened the trunk, took a pair of suitcases out. Hers was bigger than mine, a nice blue one. I looked at her. She hesitated. "Your car," I told her.

As soon as she got into the car and turned the key, I switched on the radio, holding my finger to my lips. She didn't say a word.

The motel was out on the highway, pretty close to the airport.

Middle-class place, mostly for business travelers, not a quick-trick joint. We registered as Mr. and Mrs. Albert Kowalski.

Once we got into the room, I put the suitcases on the bed and opened them. Then I gestured that she should look inside, satisfy herself there were no microphones. She did it, sort of.

Then I started talking off my clothes. She just stood there, not moving. When I was stripped, I stood next to her, twisted my body a bit, then turned around, holding my hands over my head the way the cops want you to do when they pat you down. "No wire," I mouthed to her, not making a sound, but letting her read my exaggerated lip movement. She didn't react. "No mi-cro-phone," I mouthed again, even slower. She nodded. Then I turned my back on her and went into the bathroom. I opened both the hot and cold jets on the shower to the max. It made a noise like a waterfall.

I motioned for her to come close. I didn't even have to tell her to take her clothes off.

I whispered in her ear, under the roar of the shower. "Nobody could pick this up," I said, putting my arms around her. "It's safe, understand?"

"Yes," she whispered.

"It has to look like a robbery," I told her. "Does he have a job, or does he work for himself?" I already knew all this from the finger who'd tipped me to this score, but I needed to see if she was going to be truthful with me.

"He owns a jewelry store," she said. "That's how I found out."

"Found out what?"

"Remember what you said before? About the kind of life he has? That's so funny. Like this—with you—was meant to be. I mean, that *is* what's going on. There's a woman. He gave her . . . gifts, I guess. Right from inventory. I know because his father complained. It's really his father's business, but he's retired. His father, I mean. Anyway, the old man comes in once in a while, just to look things over. We were having dinner at the house when he told John that there was some shrinkage. I didn't even know what that meant. His father said there were a couple of items listed on the inventory sheet but they weren't in stock. John told him he was probably wrong, and his father got *real* mad. He said John had no head for business and one of the stockboys or a clerk or something had probably just slipped it in his pocket. It happens all the time. John told him, okay, he would take care of it. And he fired Rubén. That was this Puerto Rican kid who worked there. So I figured he found out who took the stuff and that was it."

"How did you find out what he was doing with it?" I asked her. If she noticed my hand patting her hip, she didn't say anything.

"He has business dinners. A lot. He always did, so I didn't pay any attention. But one day, I was downtown shopping and I thought I'd drop in, maybe surprise him and we could have lunch. He wasn't there. Marie—she works the front counter, she's been there for years—said he had an appointment. Well, I was already there, so I went back into his office to call my girlfriend and see if *she* wanted to have lunch. That's when I saw it—his American Express bill for the month. He has a corporate card. There was maybe seven or eight or even more charges from this one restaurant. At least that's what I thought it was. But they were *huge*. I mean, the *cheapest* one was over three hundred dollars! It stuck in my mind. I looked up the restaurant in the phone book and there wasn't any! So now I was *really* curious. I asked my girl-friend had she ever heard of it. She hadn't either. I was going to just ask him, but, I mean, I *knew* something was fishy. So I . . . followed him one day. Right in the middle of the day. You know where he went? This place called the Playpen. I could see it was a strip club, even from the outside. But I didn't go in. You know what I did then?"

"No," I whispered, feeling her plump little breasts against my chest, my right hand on her thigh, just below her butt.

"I have a nephew. Michael. He's just a kid. In college. Anyway, for his birthday, I told him he could take a couple of friends to the Playpen. On me. I gave him my Visa card and told him to have a good time. Oh boy, was *he* excited! And I was too—when I got the bill. It didn't say 'Playpen' on it. You know what? It said the name of this so-called restaurant. Can you imagine? He was taking his little—whatever it was you get in there—as a business expense!"

"A lot of men do it," I told her.

"What? Pay for whores with a business account, or cheat on their wives?"

"Both," I told her, pressing against the base of her spine with my thumb. "You got dynamite proof. And a nice IRS problem for him too. Why don't you just divorce him?"

"Because his father made me sign one of those pre-nuptial things. If I divorce him, I only get a little bit. Almost nothing. We've been married nearly eight years. And we don't have kids. He'd *love* it if I'd divorce him. He told me so. I mean, I *told* him. I told him everything. If he wants that tramp so bad, he could just . . . go."

"What makes you sure it's just one woman?" I asked her, slipping my knee between her thighs. "Strip clubs, they have new girls every day."

"The jewelry," she said. "He might be giving cash to any of those sluts. But jewelry—that's what you give someone you . . . You know what I mean."

"Sure," I told her. "But if that was the case, he could just divorce *you*, right?"

"No, he can't. I mean, not without something against me. I went to a lawyer. He has to have *grounds* to divorce me. And he has nothing. So we're both stuck."

"And you want a way out, huh?"

"Will you do it?" she asked.

"I don't know. Depends on . . ."

"What?" she breathed into my ear, her hands clasped behind my back to steady herself.

"Money, for one. It's expensive to set something like this up. And it's harder when the guy's crazy."

"Crazy? John isn't crazy."

"He must be," I said softly. "Who in their right mind would be spending money on hookers when he's got all this at home?" I squeezed her bottom a little to show her what I meant.

"Oh. Stop that! I mean—John's like an . . . addict or something."

"What's he addicted to?" I asked, cupping her right breast in my hand and lifting it slightly. "Silicon?"

"What're you trying to do, raise my self-esteem?" She giggled.

"Speaking of raising something . . ." I said, guiding her hand down.

She was flushed and sweaty from the shower steam. It didn't take long.

After that, I met her a bunch of times. To set things up, make sure everything went perfect. Sometimes she picked the motel, sometimes I did. We would talk in the shower, then use the bed.

The last time we got together, she gave me the ten thousand. A down payment. I was going to get a hundred grand when I took her husband out.

That's not my idea of a hit. Yolanda had told me all about her husband. She's a stripper at the Playpen. And she fingers jobs for me once in a while. Yolanda and me are together, but I'm not the jealous type.

The husband's paying a quarter-mil for the videotape. There's no words on it, but you can see her face clear enough. And everything else. More than enough for him to get that divorce.

I'm not going to cheat the brunette, though. Old John's a dead man. And it *is* going to look like a robbery that went wrong.

Maybe a year or so from now. After he's been married to Yolanda for a while.

for Big Wayne

SEARCHER

It's hard to travel so much without a horse. But I have to keep looking. And if I stop long enough to earn money for a horse, I could be too late.

It would take me a long time to earn money, anyway. I don't know how to do nothing except lift things or pull stuff. I never learned no trade. I knowed I was bonded out when I was a little kid. The preacher told me I was going to learn a trade. But all I learned was how hard the whip cut into my back when I didn't pull the plow straight and deep enough. I learned that part good. A woman in one of the places I looked in, she saw my back. She thought I had been in prison, to get whipped like that.

But I was never in no prison. I was a farm boy. But I wasn't nobody's born boy—I was a work animal. They worked me all the time, except for Sundays, of course. I went to church then.

The people who owned me, everyone told them what good Christians they was for taking me in and treating me like I was one of their own.

I never said nothing.

I don't talk much.

But I learned.

I don't drink. I don't use tobacco. I can't read, but I can understand when people talk. And I can talk myself. All I usually have to tell folks is that I can work. I tell them how much work I can do, and they laugh at me. Then they see me do it, and they don't laugh no more.

That's the way I go from place to place. Working. Sometimes people will give me a ride. For nothing, I mean. I always offer to do some work, but some of them, they just let me ride along without doing nothing. One whole family, they was moving west to homestead. I rode with them a long way. But when they turned north, I had to get off.

Most of them, they do want me to do something. There's always something to do.

I can't fix a wagon, or shoe a horse, or shoot a gun. I never learned none of that stuff. But I can lift anything. And I never get tired.

I wouldn't let nobody whip me no more. I made them stop on the farm when I got big enough. But then I had to go. That same night. Anyway, nobody even tries anymore—you can't whip someone if you don't own them. It's better not to be a kid. Or any kind of slave.

I don't steal neither. I am trying to be a good man. I am trying to find the answer to my question. Once I find it, I know I will be a good man for certain.

But I'm not sure where to look. I mean, I know where to look, but not exactly the right place. So I keep looking.

It's hard to travel around like I do. But I met an Indian once. An old one. He had a cart he was trying to pull. His horse had died. He wanted to get home, but he had to bring his stuff with him. So I pulled the cart. It wasn't nothing. I mean, it had wheels and everything, not like plowing a field. The old Indian, he asked me how I got so strong. I told him. He didn't say nothing.

But he taught me a lot of stuff. How to get food, mostly. He didn't have no gun, but he knew how to make traps. He taught me. Some other stuff, too.

If he wouldn't have died, I would have learned more too, I bet.

When he died, it was in his sleep. I didn't know what to do. So I just kept pulling his cart. Only now he was in it, too. He didn't weigh much.

I got to where he wanted to go. There was a lot of Indians there. I told them the old Indian wanted to come there with all this stuff. They told me he wanted to come there to die. And now he could. He smelled pretty bad by then, but they didn't care. They put him in a fire. Not just him, everything he brought with him, the cart, too.

They was real friendly to me. They even told me I could stay with them. And I would have, too; but I have to keep looking. I can't stay anywhere until I find out the answer to my question. I told them that. They said that was good. They gave me a lot of food. Dried meat, mostly. They wanted to give me a horse, even. But I told them that wouldn't be right. I mean, I didn't work for it. They told me I didn't have to bring the old Indian back, so that was work. I told them I promised him I would do it, so it wasn't work, it was just keeping my word.

They said a lot of stuff I didn't understand. One of them asked me if my mother was an Indian. I told them, no, she wasn't. Then they didn't ask me nothing no more.

Yesterday, I got a ride all the way into town. It's a big town. I heared about it the last place I was. It's where the Bluebird Palace is. That's where I have to go.

I have to be careful. I learned good. I know I just can't go in there and ask my question. Not after what happened the last couple of times.

But I know my mother was there. I mean, she was there once. I even know her name. She was . . . famous, I guess. My mother. A lot of men knew her name. Before she died, anyway.

That night, I watched real careful. At the men going in and out of the Bluebird Palace. The real young ones, they were no good. I am seventeen, I think. So I got a pretty good idea of how old the man I'm searching for is. Not exact, but pretty good.

It was real late when I saw the one I wanted to ask. He was staggering around a little bit but not real drunk. So I went up to him in the alley and asked him.

But he was like all the others. He got mad. He told me I was crazy. I'm not crazy. I just wanted him to answer me. But he wouldn't. He had a gun. He reached for it. After a minute, he was dead.

I know I have to go to the next place now. I'm not stupid, like the people who worked me always said. And I'm not crazy. I know I got to go to the next place now. If I stay around, they will blame me. And then I'll never find the answer.

There's a place called Lulu's over in the next town. I heared about that one. I bet my mother worked there once too.

I hope the next man will answer my question. But if the same thing happens like it always does, I will just keep searching until I find one who will.

Only my father can answer my question.

for Jim Procter

| CROSS |

THE CONCRETE PUPPY

"**D**o you know where the Red 71 poolroom is?" the woman asked, bending forward to speak through the open window of the cab.

The cabbie took in the woman's wild mane of red hair, her heavily made-up face, and her spectacular chest. He swallowed hard, looking up.

"Lady, you don't want to go there. That's not a place for—"

"Look," she interrupted, "you're the fourth driver I asked. Two didn't speak English; the other one wanted a street address. 'Red 71,' that's all I know. And you, you *know* where it is. Come on, be a sport. I'm a big girl," she said in a husky voice, drawing in a deep breath to showcase the proof. "I can take care of myself."

The cabbie considered for a minute, then nodded toward the back seat. "Get in."

The cab left the Loop, working its way uptown. The woman sat back, crossed her long legs. "Do you mind if I smoke?" she asked politely.

"I look like one of those kinda people to you?" the driver replied. "Go ahead, make yourself happy."

The woman fired up, inhaled gratefully, watching the neighborhood change through the back window.

"Excuse me, lady," the driver said, "I don't mean to get personal or nothing, but are you . . . like an actress or something?"

"Something," the woman replied, smiling.

The cab pulled up to the curb between the rotting hulks of two abandoned cars. The driver pointed to a length of chain-link fence topped by coils of rusting concertina wire.

"There it is, miss."

"Where? All I see is the fence."

"See? Over there. That's like the gate, okay?"

The woman shot the driver a dubious look, deciding. Then she reached in her clutch bag and pulled out a pair of fifties. "Look," she told the driver, "I'll never get a cab to come to this neighborhood. Here's fifty on a twenty-dollar fare—that's pretty good, right? And here's another, for coming back to pick me up in an hour."

"Lady, you don't have to . . ."

"One hour, okay? I'll be right here. Thanks!"

The redhead stepped past the opening in the chain-link fence and carefully picked her way through a maze of debris, well balanced despite the spike heels, keeping her eyes on the "71" scrawled in fading red over a slab-faced metal door. When she neared the door, she could see that it had no handle, and was standing slightly ajar. She pushed, and the door yielded. Inside, she found herself on a stairwell, with another arrow in the same faded red paint pointing down.

She followed the arrow to the basement, where she encountered another handleless door. She pushed gently and stepped inside. The poolroom was murky, clouds of cigarette smoke mingling with darkness to create pockets of gloom. There was no overhead lighting; the only illumination was a series of shaded bulbs hanging low over each pool table. To her left was a battered wood counter. Behind it was an elderly man, watching a small black-and-white TV set from under an old-fashioned green eyeshade.

The redhead approached the counter, leaning forward, resting on her elbows, offering the same view that had so entranced the cabdriver. The elderly man didn't turn his head.

"Excuse me?" she asked in a husky voice.

The elderly man turned slightly in his chair, ran his eyes quickly over the woman, then focused on the middle distance behind her. "What?"

"I'm looking for a man named Cross."

"Nobody here by that name, lady," the old man said, pressing a panel on the floor with his toe as he spoke.

"Yes, there is. I mean, I was told . . ."

"Sorry," the old man said, turning back to his TV.

The woman whirled around, hands on hips, surveying the poolroom. She got a few looks in return, nothing else. The woman held her ground but didn't attempt to move forward. Then she felt a gentle tap on her elbow and turned to see a short, pudgy man with a vaguely Oriental face regarding her.

"Miss, the way you came through? To get here? It's pretty dangerous. Let me show you a safer way out, all right?"

"I'm looking for Cross," the redhead said.

The pudgy man moved his head in a gesture almost too slight to be a nod, but when he moved off, the redhead followed. As they passed between two tables, the pudgy man said something to one of the players. It sounded something like Chinese, but the redhead couldn't be sure.

Near the back of the poolroom, an enormous man was

patiently practicing the same shot, over and over. Given his size, his movements were surprisingly delicate. As the redhead passed his table, the huge man turned to watch over one massive shoulder.

The pudgy man moved some strands of a steel-beaded curtain to one side, held them there for the redhead to precede him. As she stepped through, she saw a man seated on an old wooden barrel, as relaxed as if it were an easy chair. When he moved to take a drag from his cigarette, the redhead noticed a bull's-eye tattoo on the back of his right hand. He was unremarkable-looking: medium height, medium build, medium face. If it weren't for the tattoo, he would be lost in any crowd.

The pudgy man held up a palm. The redhead stopped. The pudgy man rolled out another barrel from a dark corner of the room, and bowed to the redhead. She climbed onto the offered barrel, letting her skirt ride up as she did. She crossed her legs, tried a tentative smile. The man seated across from her didn't react.

"Are you . . . ?"

The man on the barrel made a *sssh*-ing gesture, finger to his lips. He took another drag on his cigarette, then stubbed it out in an inverted hubcap. The redhead noticed that most of the cigarette was still unsmoked. The man went off somewhere within himself.

The redhead understood this as some test of patience, pulled down the hem of her skirt slightly, and sat very still.

Minutes passed. Then a man with an outrageously hyper-muscled torso, barely covered by a chartreuse tank top, poked his shaven head into the room. "Okay," he said to the man on the barrel.

The man turned to the redhead. "What do you want?" he said.

"Are you Cross?" she replied.

"Sure," he said, implying that if he wasn't, he would do.

"I have a . . . problem. And I was told—"

"*Who* told you?" the man interrupted.

"Tabitha. She dances at the—"

"I know. Go ahead."

She took a deep breath, making her white silk blouse flutter. If the man noticed, he gave no sign. "I have a foster child. His name is Romeo. He's eight years old. I got him from . . . from a girl who used to work with me. She died. Of AIDS. She knew she was going, so we worked it out in front. Romeo—I've had him for years. He's my son now. But I wouldn't want the nosy social workers asking how—"

"What's the problem?" the man asked, cutting her off.

"We live in a nice place. In the suburbs. Romeo has . . . *had* a puppy. Brutus. A little rottweiler. He was run over. By a car. Romeo saw it happen. He got the license number. Brutus was just screwing around. Romeo said he ran out in the street and just laid down. Like taking a sunbath or something. It's a real quiet road, with this big hook turn, like. You can't go over maybe thirty miles an hour. Romeo said the driver had plenty of time. He *saw* Brutus. And then he speeded up! He hit the puppy on purpose."

"So . . . ?"

"So I went to the police. With his license number. They found the man. He said he never saw the puppy. And that was that."

"What would you want me to—?"

"Romeo cried for days. Nothing I could say to him convinced him—he's sure that the driver did it on purpose."

"What difference would it make? The dog's still dead."

"It makes a difference. It makes *all* the difference. If he did it on purpose, he has to pay. If it was an accident, okay, but I believe my son."

"And you want me to . . . what?"

"Not what you think. I want you to find out. If he did it on purpose. Can you do that?"

"Maybe."

"I can pay. Whatever it costs."

"Buddha will show you how to get out of here, take you back to where that cab dropped you off, all right? Give him whatever you have on the guy who hit the dog. And leave a number where I can get in touch."

The redhead climbed off the barrel and followed the pudgy man through a back door out into another piece of the yard. If she was surprised that she'd been under observation since getting out of the cab, she gave no sign.

"What you think, boss?" Buddha asked, handing over a piece of paper covered with writing. "Looks like she already has most of it."

Cross scanned the paper, checking off points to himself in a low voice. "Jon—no 'h'—Rangel. DOB 2/3/50. Drives a black 1998 Ford Crown Vic. Lives in the Heights. Two speeding tickets last three years. No DUIs." Cross scratched idly at his right cheek-bone, where only a faint unnatural whitening of the skin revealed an old scar. "Got one of those giant street maps, Buddha? Let's see if we can find his address."

The bodybuilder parted the beaded curtain and noticed Cross and Buddha studying the huge street map they had laid out on the floor. "What's going down?" he asked.

"See this?" Cross asked Buddha, ignoring the bodybuilder. "He was only maybe a mile or so from home when he hit the puppy. Look, there's a long left-hand sweeper right about here . . ." he said, pointing.

"Hey, come on, you guys," the bodybuilder pleaded.

"Cool your jets, Princess," Cross told him. "We're not done with this yet."

Princess crossed his arms, accentuating his outrageous biceps, a pouty look on his face.

Another few minutes passed. Then Cross looked up. "Princess, get Rhino back here, will you?"

The bodybuilder did an about-face and disappeared. When he came back, the huge man who had been practicing billiard shots was with him.

"We got something?" the huge man asked, his voice an improbable high-pitched squeak.

"We got something all right, Rhino," Cross told him. "We got a guy who ran over a puppy. Question is, what to do about it."

"And we're getting paid to—" Buddha said.

"He ran over a puppy on purpose?" Princess cut in, his voice gone quiet and cold.

"That's the piece we don't know," Cross said. "That's what we're getting paid for. I've got to make some phone calls first."

Two days later, the crew was gathered in a loose circle in what looked like a living room—an old living room that hadn't seen a vacuum cleaner in years. Stashed on the third floor of the Red 71 building, the windowless room was invisible from the street.

"Here's what we have so far," Cross said. "This Rangel guy is a salesman. Phone guy. Something in bonds, or penny stocks; I'm not sure. But he's got a real gift of gab, talks smooth. Two arrests as a juvenile, nothing since. Married. No kids. TRW says he's pretty much AA. House is valued around one fifty, mortgage for eighty-something. Lives within his means. Doesn't gamble. Doesn't drink either. Straight-arrow on paper."

"On those juvenile busts—he go the same route we did?" Rhino asked.

"No, he never went inside. One Intake Adjustment, one Probation," Cross replied, an edge to his voice that only his crew would recognize.

"You get what he was beefed for, boss?" Buddha asked.

"Yeah. The first one, he shot a cat with a bow and arrow. The other one, he poured gasoline on a dog. Set it on fire."

"Fucking weasel," Princess muttered. "This guy, he started it, right? And we're getting paid, too. So how about I just go over to his house tonight and snap his neck?"

"No go, brother. We're getting paid to find something out, not dust him."

"So how do we—"

"Relax, I'm coming to that. The kid said this guy actually swerved. Went out of his way to hit the puppy. Now, maybe that's what it looked like to him, but maybe the car just got pulled to the outside of the sweeper. You know, when you're driving too fast . . ."

"Centrifugal force," Buddha supplied.

"Yeah," Cross continued. "Too tough to tell. What we do first, we put a man around there. Undercover."

"Me! Me!" Princess yelped. "I never get to work undercover. Come on, Cross. You said the next time . . ."

"You got it, partner," Cross told him, looking over the body-builder's shoulder at Rhino, who shrugged elaborately. "Now, listen close. . . ."

The big pink Harley rolled through the suburbs like a pit bull at an AKC dog show. The rider looked carved out of stone, his massive arms bare under a black leather vest, his face unreadable behind a black face-shield. Princess gave the throttle an extra blip as he downshifted, then tore off down a side road onto the highway. As he approached the left-hand sweeper, he leaned the bike over until his inside boot scraped the ground.

"You were right, chief," Buddha said. He was behind the wheel of the anonymous sedan the outlaw teenagers who lived in the Badlands called the "shark car." Cross next to him on the front seat. "It's like the cops don't patrol this sector at all. That idiot Princess was making enough racket to wake the dead."

"You think that curve pulls?" Cross asked.

"Sure. See how mild it's banked . . . just that little bit? No way that's enough. Wasn't for that guardrail, you make a mistake, you could go right over the side."

"Let's take a look."

Buddha drove expertly, making the car move quickly without appearing to do so. He slid to a stop just off the road at the apex of the curve. The two men got out. The guardrail was metal, two thick bands set up parallel to the ground between posts to absorb impact. They looked past the guardrail. Looked down. It was a sheer drop, at least a couple of hundred feet. Below, the jagged rocks of a long-abandoned quarry.

"Rhino report in?" Cross asked.

"Yeah, chief. This guy drives the same route very day. Same time, same way. Clocked him for nine days now. He's never been more than a few minutes off."

"Traffic patterns?"

"Nothing, boss. Look how long we been sitting here—*you* see a car go by? Only reason to use this road is if you live in that subdivision over there, see?" Buddha pointed. "And this guy, he works seven to three, all right? Rest of the commuters, they come along much later."

"So where'd the kid come from?"

"Over there." Buddha pointed again. "See that clump of trees? On the left? Just at the bottom of the hill? The kid lives on the other side. I guess he was just going down the hill when the pup got away from him."

"You took a look? From where the kid stood?"

"Perfect cover," Buddha replied. "Sniper's roost. You thinking . . . ?"

"No. We need answers, remember? This guy can't tell us anything dead."

"What do you see?" Cross asked his crew, pointing with one finger to a white object sitting on top of one of the pool tables, maybe thirty feet away.

"It's a puppy," Princess said. "Can I . . . ?"

"Hold up a minute," Cross said. "Rhino, you see the same thing?"

The huge man nodded, waiting. Cross strolled over to the puppy, the others followed.

Princess stuck out a hand to pat the puppy, then drew it back like he'd touched a stove. "It's a fake," he snarled. "A stuffed dog."

"Try and pick it up," Cross told him.

The bodybuilder reached out one hand, grabbed the puppy by the back of its neck. "Ugh!" he said. "What the hell is this?"

"It's a concrete puppy," Cross told him. "With a lead core. Painted to look like a dalmatian. Weighs almost seventy pounds. Fong did it. Nice job, huh?"

"What's it for?" Princess asked.

"It's a lie detector," Cross said.

"You understand how this is going to work?" Cross asked the boy standing next to him. They were in the copse of trees at the base of the left-hand sweeper. The redhead stood just off to one side.

"I . . . think so."

"Okay, kid; listen good. We're gonna put the puppy—just a model, not a real puppy, okay?—we're gonna put the puppy in the road. But way off to the side, see? When this guy comes by, he'll have plenty of room to miss it. So, if he *does* miss it, you'll know it was an accident when he hit your dog."

"What if he tries to hit it?" the boy asked.

"Then we'll know that, too," Cross told him, checking his watch. He pulled a cellular phone from inside his coat. Punched in a number, waited. Then he said, "T minus three. Set it up."

The motorcycle's exhausts bubbled as the pink Harley pulled around the bend, then veered off to the side. Princess dismounted, unstrapped a white object from the back of the bike, set it in place.

"It sure looks real," the boy whispered.

"Just watch," Cross told him.

Princess positioned the puppy on the shoulder of the road, about a yard off the paved portion. It looked as though the dog was injured, one foot held slightly off the ground at an odd angle. Princess checked once more, then leaped onto the bike and vanished.

A red station wagon came around the curve, its wheels over the double yellow dividing line, giving the shoulder a wide berth. The driver didn't come near the puppy. Didn't stop, either.

The phone in Cross' jacket buzzed. Once. Twice.

"Next up," Cross said to the boy.

The black Ford came around the corner at a moderate speed, hugging the double yellow line, as the station wagon had. Suddenly, the Ford's engine roared and the big car charged forward, its outside front wheel aimed directly at the puppy. The Ford impacted as if it had gone up a ramp; the front end launched as the rear wheels lost traction. The Ford slammed sideways into the guardrail—which immediately parted as if it had been pre-cut with an acetylene torch.

Cross and the boy ran across the road, the redhead close behind. Only the Ford's tire marks were visible. The section of guardrail still standing was smeared with black paint. The concrete puppy was cracked, lying on its side, but still intact.

Cross, the boy, and the redhead all looked down. The black Ford was a dot at the bottom of the quarry. A dot in flames.

The boy was crying. The redhead knelt next to him, a comforting arm around the child's shoulders.

"What's wrong, baby?" she asked.

"He hit my Brutus on purpose," the boy said. "He killed my puppy."

The redhead caught Cross' eye over the boy's shoulder. Cross nodded. She clasped the child to her, holding him fiercely.

When she looked up again, Cross was gone. So was the concrete puppy.

The redhead and the boy walked back up the hill together.

In a few minutes, the road was deserted again.

for Shannon Jones

HARVEST TIME

The walking man was medium height, with sandy hair still lightened from a summer spent outdoors. His eyes were shielded by dark glasses; a gym bag was swinging gently in one hand. He crossed the gigantic parking lot surrounding the mall, looking straight ahead, a slight prizefighter's roll to his walk.

"I still say he don't look like much." The speaker was wearing a violet silk tank top, covering a torso so massively built, so outrageously ripped, that he looked cartoonish. His head was shaved. An emerald earring dangled from his right ear.

"Count the cars, Princess," his companion replied, pointing with the stub of his forefinger—the last digit, where a fingernail would have been, was missing.

"Huh?" Princess said. "I don't get it, Rhino."

Rhino shrugged—it looked like a boulder experiencing a ground tremor. Although he was actually much larger than the bodybuilder, there was no hint of definition to the muscles that stretched his skin to the limit. "Watch the other guy . . . See? The guy in the pretty running suit. He's jogging, right? McNamara, he's walking, okay? Count the damn *cars*, Princess. Get a fix, where they start, count to thirty, like thirty seconds, see? Then go back and count the cars."

Princess made a face, his lips moving.

Time passed.

"Damn!" Princess said. "You was right, Rhino. The jogging guy, he covered fifty-four cars. McNamara, he did sixty-eight. And he's *walking*, right? I see what you mean—it don't look like he's moving, but he is. That karate stuff, that's what does it?"

"Cross says it's kinetic control."

The man they called McNamara unlocked the door of a ten-year old Ford that had once been burgundy. He tossed his gym bag carelessly into the back seat, stuck his key into the ignition, looking straight ahead through the streaked windshield.

The rasping sound of a heavy zipper came from the back seat. "You looked real good in there, Mac," a matching voice said. "You stay at light-heavy, there's no one out there who could take you. What are you now, sixth degree?"

"Seventh," the man in the front seat said, not turning around.

Sounds of paper being shuffled. "This the whole list?"

"That's everything," McNamara said. "Every OC name in the city. Everything's there: DOB, NCJIC and FBI numbers; last known address; AKAs for each one. What the hell did you want the blood types for?"

"You don't want to know. Okay, you sure there's nothing I can do for . . . ?"

McNamara's voice dropped an octave, edged with ice. "Don't insult me, Cross."

"Sorry. No disrespect intended."

"None taken. A man like you, that's what I'd expect." He turned the key. The engine reluctantly coughed into life. "Can I drop you anywhere?"

"Don't worry about it, Mac. You just stop for the lights—I won't be here by the time you pull into your driveway."

The CTA bus rumbled to a shuddering stop at the fringe of the - Projects. The front doors hissed open and a tall black woman stepped to the sidewalk. She was dressed in a dark raincoat over a nurse's uniform, the white stockings and shoes a dead giveaway in the October night. Adjusting her shoulder bag for maximum protection against a snatch attempt, the woman turned toward a cluster of high-rises a quarter of a mile away. She walked past the bus-stop bench, carriage proud and erect despite her exhaustion. She didn't even glance at the slumped-over figure of a man, sensing rather than seeing the empty bottle of cheap wine clutched in the bum's slack hand.

"Tough working two jobs, isn't it, Clara?"

The woman whirled sharply, her eyes pinning the seated bum, one leg shifting behind the other as if to brace herself to run.

"Cross?"

"Sit down," the bum said quietly. "Have a talk with an old friend."

The woman took a tentative step forward, eyes wary. "What happened to your face?" she asked, peering into the darkness.

"Just a little help from the makeup department, Clara. It's me."

"How would I know that?"

"Come on, Clara. You recognized my voice on the phone. You knew I'd be somewhere around here tonight."

The woman's hand slid into her pocketbook. Stayed there.

"Lots of people can do voices," she said.

"Big Luke always said you were a hard woman."

The woman blinked rapidly, tears very near the surface. But her hand stayed deep in her pocketbook.

"Even when you were a little girl, he told me. One night, we were talking. Just before we went into the caves. Talking to kill the fear, you know what I mean? He told me about your pink party dress—about how you wore it to church one day and people were whispering behind their hands about it. How you just stared them down, backed them away, all their little-town gossip. He said he knew he wanted to marry you right then."

The woman took her hand from her pocketbook, walked over, and sat down next to the bum. Her nose told her the truth—whatever the man was, he was no wino.

"I still miss that fool," she whispered.

"He knows. He knows what you're doing, how good a mother you are to the girls. What sacrifices you make for them."

"You believe that? You truly do?"

"I do. He's watching."

"I feel that too, sometimes. That's why I never even thought about . . ."

"I know."

"I know things, too, Cross. I know about you. Things I hear. Who's watching *you*, then?"

"It doesn't matter."

"I have all his letters. From over there. I read them, all the time. Read some of them to the girls. He wrote to them too, you know. They were just babies. Separate letters he wrote, even though they're twins. Like he knew they would be different. I was pregnant when he went over. He never saw them."

"He sees them now, Clara. Sees you, too. Days at the Motor Vehicle Bureau, nights at the hospital. No vacations. No fancy clothes. Everything for the girls."

"I keep them safe, Cross. It's hard lines here. The gangbangers own the Projects now. I been tempted. Many, many times. Not a man for *me*—I'm waiting on Big Luke, and we'll be together again soon enough. But a man for . . . protection, you understand?"

"Yes."

"But I go it alone."

"You want to move out, yes, Clara? Out of here. To a quieter place."

"That's what I've been saving for. But the girls go to school, that comes first. That's our way. I tell them, you finish college, make something of yourselves, then you go out and earn some money, buy Momma a little house someplace."

"It's time now, Clara. You sow, and so you reap. Like the Bible says."

"The Bible? The Word of the Lord? Cross, that's blasphemy in your mouth. I told you, I know what you do. Some of it, anyway."

"Same thing I did over there. With Big Luke."

"My man died serving his country," she said, head back, eyes flashing.

"It's just another war," the man called Cross said, lighting a cigarette. "And I don't *have* a country."

The woman made a face. "I don't allow cigarettes in my house. Not liquor, either."

The man snapped the cigarette away without taking a drag. "It's time *for* that house, Clara." He reached into his voluminous coat, took out an envelope, handed it to her. "There's a piece of paper in there with the money," he said. "Names, addresses, Social Security numbers, dates of birth, copies of signatures. All you have to do is make sure each one gets registered as an organ donor when he renews his driver's license."

"Why do you . . . ?"

"You don't want to know, Clara. You worked your whole life, now harvest time is coming. The crops are ready to come in. Take the money, buy your house. There's enough there. More than enough. I'm planting my own seeds, that's all."

"One of Luke's letters, he talked about you too. He said you didn't care if you lived or you died."

"He told you the truth."

"And he cared so much. He had so much to come back to. You didn't care. But you came back and he didn't. Why is that?"

"I don't know."

She reached over, took the envelope, put it in her pocketbook.

"Goodbye, Clara."

"Goodbye, Cross."

There were five of them watching. Black teenagers with old eyes. Each already proven impervious to every "rehabilitative" service the State of Illinois had to offer, from counseling to incarceration. They were a feral crew—wolves without the loyalty of the pack.

"Bitch packs a piece, man," one said. "Heard she shot one of the Disciples last year. Shot him cold. She ain't going for no elevator jam."

"She got money," another replied. "Money in the house, too. I gotta get paid. She want to be stupid, too bad."

"You see her girls? Them twins. That's what I want. Ain't nobody had any a that stuff."

"Shut up," the shortest one said. "Everybody get what they want outa this, we do it right. A vise, that's what we need here; come at her from both sides. Her apartment's on seventeen, right? We go up there, split into two sides, wait on the stairs. Soon's we hear that elevator open, we jump her. Take her down. Her keys won't help us—the girls keep the chains on from inside. We make the bitch tell 'em to open the door. Then it's game time!"

"Bet!" one of the watchers said. "I'm gonna make them twins *dance,* man!"

"Let's move it. She making tracks now."

The pack split into two groups, cutting through the Projects to reach the building before the woman did.

The leader and two of the others waited on the stairwell, their harsh breathing loud against the concrete. The leader leaned forward, opening the door a crack.

"She be comin' soon," he said.

"Freeze!" a voice whispered. "Not a sound."

They turned slowly. The leader blinked at the source of the whisper. A white man the size of a small gorilla, his back against the far wall. A dull-black Uzi riveted their attention. In the monster's hand, it looked like a derringer.

"Hands up," the monster said. He walked over to the leader, grabbed the back of his neck with his empty hand, and lifted the terrified youth off the ground. Pain-bolts shot along the leader's spine.

"We're going upstairs," the monster said. "To the roof. We're going to walk. Slow. One man's hands come down, you all die. Understand me? *Die.* Then I just pick you up and carry you up there, see? I'm getting paid, bring you to the roof. Dead or alive, it don't matter." He released the leader, who slumped to the floor, hands still rigidly held over his head.

"Walk," the monster said.

It was only three flights, but the pack was breathless as they stepped out onto the roof. The monster herded them over to a far corner. As they approached, they saw their two partners, standing with their hands high. Next to them, a blade-thin black man in a long black leather coat and a Zorro hat.

"Oh shit!" the leader said. A visible shudder ran through his stocky frame.

The five pack members were herded into a row, their backs to the roof's edge.

The man in the Zorro hat stood before them, so finely balanced as to appear weightless in the roof's darkness. A leather thong was looped around his neck. At its end was a double-barreled shotgun, sawed off so far down that the red tips of the shells were showing.

"What they call you, man?" he asked the leader.

"Dice."

"Dice. You just rolled craps, boy. You know my name?"

"Yeah. I mean . . . yes."

"Say it," the thin man whispered.

"Ace."

"You know how I come by that name, boy? You hear about me when you was telling stories in the dorms downstate?"

"Yes, sir."

"Tell it."

"They calls you Ace 'cause you the Ace of Spades."

"Yeah, that's about right. You know what I do?"

"Yes, sir."

"The ace of spades, that's the death card, right? Me, I make people dead. That's how I make my living. I'm a contract man, understand? I take the money; I take a life, see?"

"Yes, sir."

"Now, listen. Listen real good. Listen the best you ever did in your lousy little life. That woman you was tracking, Clara? Well, somebody paid me money—*good* money, boy. They paid me this money, told me make sure nothing happens to that woman. *Nothing*. Same for her girls, the twins. Same for her apartment. Understand? Now, you boys, you got the bangers on the run 'round here, don't you? You king of this hill. That's okay. You do what you do. But now I got a job for you. You want to work for me?"

"Yes, *sir*!"

"That's good. That's real good. Now, here's the job. You watch the lady. The way you *been* watching the lady. You watch them twins too. And the crib. Anybody acts like they trouble, you *take them out*. You understand what I'm telling you?"

"Yes, sir."

"I been watching you boys. You got potential. You do this right, there's work for you. *Hard* work, understand? Hard work pays hard cash. You got the heart to do it? Not smoke some poor sucker in a drive-by—walk up to the man, put the piece in his face, and make him dead?"

"Yes, sir."

"You want to learn?"

"Yes, sir."

"Okay, then pay attention. First thing, you get the money up front, understand?" The blade-thin man's left hand went into a deep pocket. It came out with a thick wad of bills, wrapped in rubber bands. "This is four thousand dollars. One thousand apiece. For doing what I told you. A contract, understand?"

He put his left hand forward, almost in the stocky boy's face. "Take it and we got a deal. That's your word. That's your life."

The stocky boy took the money.

"Now I'm gonna give you something else. Something even more valuable than the green. Which one of you wanted to rape the girls?"

Dead silence on the roof.

"I ain't gonna ask again. Anytime you got a rat pack, you got someone in it wants to do some sex thing. Now, the thing about that, sex fiends ain't reliable. You can't trust them. Their word is no good. You get dropped, they be the first to roll. Now, which one was it?"

Nobody moved.

"I guess maybe it was all of you," the blade-thin man said in a tone of deep regret. "Too bad."

"It was Randall," the stocky boy said. "He wanted to do the twins."

"Motherfucker!" one of the boys hissed. He was a tall, well-muscled youth wearing a black-and-silver Raiders jacket.

"You Randall?" Ace asked.

"Yeah, man. But I was only playing. I ain't gonna rape nobody."

"That's right," Ace said, nodding at Rhino. The monster slid
forward so quickly Randall had no chance to move. Rhino hooked
him in the stomach with the same hand that held the Uzi. The boy
grunted as he doubled over. The monster-man snatched him by
his jacket and threw him off the roof.

One of the boys turned away, vomiting against the wall.

"You got paid," Ace said. "Anything happen to the lady or the
girls, *nobody* gonna die as easy as that punk just did."

"He's on the top of the list," the white-coated intern said into the
pay phone in the basement of the hospital.

"You're sure."

"No doubt about it. He gets the next one."

"Kiss your student loan goodbye," a voice told him.

A phone rang in the living room of a modest home in Merrillville,
Indiana. It was snatched on the first ring by a pretty woman
whose face showed hard lines of stress.

"Yes."

"It's time," a voice said. "You remember where to meet?"

"Yes."

The woman put down the phone. "Joanne, come in here," she
called.

A teenage girl walked into the living room, a paint-daubed
artist's smock covering her to her knees.

"What is it, Mom? Did they find . . . ?"

"Not yet, darling. I have to go out for a while. You watch your
brother. And say a prayer, okay?"

The girl nodded. Stood patiently for her mother's kiss.

The woman drove quickly to the parking lot of a local diner.

She pulled into an empty slot in the back, started to roll down her window; before it was all the way down, she saw a man detach himself from a motorcycle and start toward her.

He approached, leaned against the car, his face hidden from her eyes.

"He's on the top of the list," the man said.

"I know. We waited so long."

"You sure you want to go through with this? It's expensive. And they could find a donor on their own. Maybe in a real short time."

"He doesn't have much time," the woman said.

The man was so old that even his expensive cologne couldn't mask the stench of the grave. A silk suit hung limply on his wasted frame. A two-carat blue-white-perfect solitaire flickered in the neon light from the bar, the ring sliding down his bony finger toward the knuckle as his palsied hand trembled. The black Lincoln stretch limo was parked in an alley behind the bar, the old man seated in the cavernous back seat. Bodyguards flanked the limo, standing outside. The chauffeur's partition was closed.

The door opened and a man climbed inside, seated himself across from the living skeleton. One of the bodyguards closed the door behind him; it made a noise like a bank vault.

The two inhabitants of the back seat sat in silence, both waiting.

"You're good," the old man finally said, his voice a reedy imitation of a human's. "You got patience. Respect. The old ways. Too bad you were never one of us."

"There aren't enough of you left," the other man said.

"Yeah, that's true. Less of us all the time. This . . . thing you got to do, it ain't for me. Rocco, he couldn't take me down. Too many buffers. The Accountant, he calls himself. Like he knows it all. He don't know it all, see? The big thing he don't know is that *we* know. The indictment is sealed, but we know what's coming. He's going to turn. Roll over like the cowardly dog he is, take a couple a years in a Level One, play some tennis, come out and start over. You got everything you need?"

"Rocco Bernardi. That's all I need."

"Then it's done, Cross?"

"We got two things left, then it's done."

"Here's one," said the old man, handing over a thick envelope.

"Watch the news," Cross said, stepping out of the limo into the night.

A phone buzzed in the guard booth at the gates to a mini-mansion in the lush suburb of Winnetka.

"Front gate, Tony speaking," a smartly uniformed man answered.

"Have Ricardo bring the Mercedes around to the front."

"Yes, sir," Tony answered, nodding over to another uniformed man next to him in the booth. "Right away."

The other man took a holster and cartridge belt from a hook, strapped it on, walked across the manicured, floodlit lawn to a four-car garage. He pressed a transmitter on his belt and the garage door rose. The interior was as brightly lit as an operating room. The man opened the door of a black Mercedes SL 600 coupe, its flanks gleaming as if polished with oil. He started the car, sat patiently, listening to the muted purr of power. Then he slowly backed out to the circular driveway in front of a white brick two-story house. He climbed out of the driver's seat, leaving the door open.

A man came down the steps to the car, moving with an air of moderate caution. He was dressed in a conservative midnight-blue suit. His brilliant white-on-white shirt set off a red-and-blue tie in a tiny diamond pattern that rippled in the glare of the flood-lights.

"Everything okay?" the man asked.

"All quiet, Mr. Bernardi," the guard said, touching his cap with two fingers. He maintained his position even as the Mercedes shot off, firing a barrage of marble chips from the driveway at his ankles.

The Mercedes turned the corner, heading for downtown Chicago. Bernardi punched a single button on the cellular phone in the console between the bucket seats and lit a cigarette while the phone rang through the speaker system.

"Hello . . . ?"

"It's me. I'm on my way."

"Oh, *good*, honey. I was wondering when—"

"Don't wonder, bitch. That's not your job. I'll be there in an hour, tops."

"I'll be waiting, honey. I—"

He broke the connection.

As the Mercedes turned onto a winding stretch of road, a young woman in a wheelchair watched from a darkened room lit only by the sickly amber glow of a computer screen. She lifted a pair of infrared night glasses to her eyes, touched the zoom, zeroed in on the license plate: ACCT 1.

The young woman dropped the night glasses to her lap, wheeled herself over to the computer. A few keystrokes accessed a modem.

WHAT? the screen said in response.

Her fingers tapped the keys. ROLLING appeared on her screen. She hit another key and the screen went blank.

In an office on a high floor of the Sears Tower, a man turned from another computer screen and picked up a telephone.

In an after-hours joint on the South Side, Ace felt a vibration in his shirt pocket. He took out his beeper, glanced at the liquid-crystal display. The blade-thin killer walked through the club into a back room where a man was watching television. He turned from the screen at Ace's approach, waiting. When Ace nodded, he got up and walked out the back door.

A city ambulance was cruising the Dan Ryan Expressway. A round-faced Hispanic woman was driving, her hair spilling out from under her cap. A lanky white man with a prominent Adam's apple was in the passenger seat. Their radio was quiet. A *brrr*-ing sound filled the cab. The lanky man took a mobile phone from his shirt pocket, flipped it open. He didn't speak.

"Alert," the phone said into his ear.

The lanky man nodded at his partner.

"Tell Bruno that he has a deal," the man in the Mercedes was saying into his cellular phone.

The door to the truck bay of an abandoned warehouse slid up. A car slid out into the night—an anonymous smog-gray sedan, custom-assembled from several different makes, unidentifiable. It squatted on extra-wide tires, its bulletproof windows tinted dark blue. The car's license plates were made from two legitimate half-plates welded together. Its undercarriage was sheathed in a belly-pan of steel. The car weighed almost three tons.

A pudgy man was at the wheel, guiding the massive vehicle delicately with his fingertips.

"I got him on the scanner," Cross said from the passenger seat. "Probably the *federales* do too, the chump."

The pudgy man said nothing, piloting the shark car through

the warehouse district on the Near South Side, heading toward the Loop.

Cross pulled a cellular phone from a shoulder holster, hit a number.

"How close?" he asked.

"He's on the Drive," a voice came back. "Maybe ten minutes. Fifteen tops."

Cross reholstered the phone.

"He's going to his girlfriend's, Buddha. He'll have a couple of boys out front. It has to be on the turn-in, okay?"

"Sure, chief," the pudgy man said.

The Mercedes stayed well within the speed limit, its driver talking on his phone, making deals. In his head, making plans. The sleek black car turned off Lake Shore Drive, heading to the Gold Coast apartment where his mistress waited.

"He's about two klicks away now, Buddha. Stay sharp."

The pudgy man made no acknowledgment.

Cross hit a number on the cellular phone. In the cab of the ambulance, the lanky man didn't speak; just listened:

"Going down," a voice said.

"Hit it!" the lanky man told the driver. As she stepped on the gas, he picked up his radio.

"We're taking a break. Out of service for a personal. Fifteen minutes; acknowledge."

"You're clear," came back the dispatcher's voice.

"Let's try the Gold Coast, partner," he said to the Hispanic woman. "There's a little Vietnamese joint over there I want to try."

"Remind you of old times?" The woman smiled.

The Mercedes turned the corner as the anonymous gray shark car moved in from a side street.

"You got him?" Cross asked.

"Locked," Buddha said, focusing.

"It's harvest time," Cross said, adjusting his shoulder belt.

As the Mercedes slowed down for the corner, the shark car took it broadside, knocking the black coupe into a line of parked vehicles at the curb. Cross slid from the car, looking dazed, his hands empty. Bernardi emerged from the Mercedes, unhurt. And angry. As Cross approached, Bernardi's fists were balled, his face a mottled pattern of red and white.

"You stupid hillbilly sonofabitch! Look at my car."

"I'm . . . sorry, man," Cross muttered. "Look, I got insurance. Really. See . . ."

Cross reached into the pocket of his coat. The sneer vanished from Bernardi's face as the silenced handgun came up. The first shot took away the bridge of his nose. Cross walked over, cranked off two more rounds into the man's head. The shark car was off the block before the doorman at the fancy building had finished dialing 911.

The city ambulance was first on the scene.

"We're coming in, got one down."

"Trauma team?"

"No way—he's gone. But his license said he's an organ donor. May not be too late—all head wounds. We've got him all iced down—maybe they can do something."

"You're clear to fly, come on."

"ETA about two minutes."

The ambulance piled into the hospital lot. The body was wheeled out on a stretcher, rushed into OR. Then the surgeons went to work.

The phone rang in the woman's home in Merrillville.

"Mrs. Layne?"

"Yes."

"Please come right away. A casualty just arrived, too late to save him. But he was an organ donor, and his heart's in perfect condition. We've done the blood-typing, and it appears to be an ideal match. We've already started surgery."

"It's a miracle!" the woman said.

for Rex Miller

PIGEON DROP

"**W**hat?" The speaker's voice was hard-cored . . . but its edges were brittle.

"Put Carlos on."

"Who wants him?"

"This whole conversation's not going past forty-five seconds, pal. You want to spend it playing games?"

A muttered curse cushioned the sound of a palm slapped over the receiver.

"Where, when, and how much?" Carlos didn't bother with the preliminaries—he knew his voice would be recognized instantly. And he knew the man he was speaking to would do as he promised—hang up when the trace-time had run.

"Tonight, oh two hundred hours. The Paradise Motel on Twenty-fifth," the man answered. "Go around to the service entrance in the back—where the supply trucks pull in. Two fifty. Small bills, no sequence, no chemicals, and no bang in the suitcase."

"Be reasonable, *hombre*. It is almost two p.m. now. Twelve

hours, it is not very much. And that is a bad neighborhood you picked. I need more time."

"Come alone, Carlos."

A sad-sounding sigh . . . of reluctant acquiescence. "Ah, you too, Cross."

Cross hit the off switch on the cellular phone, thinking it was typical of an amateur to make sure he got the other guy's name on the tape. In case the *federales* were listening.

If he'd had a sense of humor, Cross would have chuckled at that. Amateurs never got it. And the easiest kind of amateurs were those who thought being a pro at one thing gave them the same status at another—like a dentist doing his own taxes. Carlos was near the top of a dope-smuggling pyramid, but he didn't know how to play *this* game.

Otherwise, he would have known: when you're in a war zone, it's never the name that matters—it's the address.

And Cross was already at the address. From his vantage point in the ground-floor room, he had a clear view of the service entrance in the back.

"You are really so sure he will do it?" A woman's voice, coming from the darkness in the back of the small, narrow room.

"Which? Bring the baby or bring the money?"

"The *baby*. What do I care about your money? You already *got* plenty of money. My husband's money, yes? Why did you not just make the trade, like you told us you would?"

"Carlos knows me," Cross patiently told the woman. "*Thinks* he knows me, anyway. He took your baby to make you pay, right? What your husband owed him?"

"I do not know my husband's business," the woman's voice said.

"Sure," Cross replied, nothing in his voice. "Anyway, Carlos knows the risk I took to hijack his shipment. He knows I have to get paid. I'm charging him maybe a tenth of what it's worth. Plus the baby. That would make sense to him. If I traded a couple of million dollars' worth of pure for the baby, he wouldn't like the math. You can't be paying me *that* much—that's the way he'd figure it."

"How could he know how much we would pay for our own baby? I would pay anything to—"

"Yeah, you might. But your husband, he must have drawn the line somewhere short of that."

"I do not know what you mean."

"Yeah, you do. This was always about money. You don't know your husband's business—sure, whatever you say. You think maybe he's selling used cars, that's what pays for that mansion you live in? All those servants? Fancy cars? Jewelry? Your husband, he's not so slick, figuring Carlos for just another smuggler. Telling him the powder was no good—that he wouldn't pay."

"I don't know any——"

"I guess your husband figured he had enough horsepower in case Carlos squawked. That joint you live in, it's pretty well protected. Your husband had it all covered—except for the nanny you hired a few months ago."

"Ah, Carmelita. *Puta!* I thought he hired her for his . . . pleasure. Bringing her into my own home, right in front of my eyes. But I could do nothing. You don't understand how—"

"It makes no difference to me," Cross said. "It wasn't about sex anyway. You found that out, didn't you?"

"You weren't there. You don't know what she—"

"I know what she did. She took your baby. Right under your nose. You were so busy watching to make sure she didn't get it on with your husband that you let down your guard as soon as he was out of the house. Pretty smooth, wasn't it? FedEx guy comes to the front door with a package. Carmelita goes to answer it, has the baby in her arms. You're not paying any attention—"

"I wasn't even downstairs. I was in the—"

"Whatever," Cross cut her off. "She hands the baby to the phony FedEx guy and he walks right off with him, right past the guards, the baby in his pouch. By the time you wake up . . ."

"From that poison she put in my coffee!"

"Yeah. I guess it would have been harder for her to knock you out if you hadn't used her as your personal maid as well as the baby's nurse."

"I was—"

"—trying to humiliate her. You couldn't get her fired, but you sure could break her chops. Just like Carlos figured you would. He's been ahead of you all since the beginning."

"You know everything, don't you?" the woman said, venom-laced bitterness in her voice.

"I know the same as you do," the man called Cross said to her. "Only difference is, I don't close my eyes to it."

The black Corvette pulled into the drive-up area behind the motel at 1:58 a.m. It sat idling, no sign of life visible inside.

Less than a minute later, a smog-colored four-door sedan of no particular make entered the same area, aimed windshield-to-windshield at the black coupe.

The cars watched each other like pit dogs preparing to fight. The Corvette's headlights were shrouded; the sedan's amber running lights were on.

A man exited the anonymous car and walked toward the Corvette. He was carrying a scuffed brown leather suitcase.

The door to the Corvette opened. Another man stepped out, a bundle wrapped in a pale-blue blanket held in one arm.

"Cross," the man with the blanket said.

"Time to test," Cross replied.

"You think this ain't a real baby?" Carlos asked. "Look." He gently pulled the blanket away from where it was tucked. "See for yourself."

"That's not the test," Cross said. "All I see is a baby. Could be *any* baby, right? All you see is a suitcase. You open it, it looks like your powder—but how are you going to know for sure?"

"I got—"

"Yeah, you got the stuff to test it with, I know. But it could take you a few minutes, do all that. And you have to go into your car to do it too, right?"

"Of course. Do you think I can—?"

"Don't get excited," Cross said softly. "We're both worried the other's pulling a switch, right? The old pigeon drop. An envelope stuffed full of money right there on the sidewalk. The mark spots it same time as the hustlers. They open it together, check it out. It's stuffed with cash. Big bills. No ID. Finders keepers, right? Only thing is, you gotta wait thirty days, see if anyone claims it, that's the law. And maybe there's a reward, who knows? Now, the mark don't trust the hustlers—and the hustlers act like they don't trust the mark. So they finally decide to let the mark hold the envelope, but he first has to go to his bank, take out a couple of thousand, and give it to the hustlers for 'security.' The mark figures, what can he lose? Or maybe he's planning to just vanish with the cash. Doesn't matter. When he gets to a safe place and opens the envelope, he finds it's full of blank paper."

"I know how it works," Carlos said impatiently. "So how do we do this without one of us leaving?"

"We exchange packages," Cross told him. "I take the kid. A short ride. Make sure I got the real thing. You take the powder, sit in your car, make sure you got the real thing too. Fair enough?"

"How do I know you won't just disappear? Leave me with a whole suitcase full of cut?"

"I'll stay right here. I'll put the baby in the car, turn around, and wait right here. You still got my money, right? I haven't asked you for it. Make sure your powder's good, *then* pay me, how's that?"

"The baby is my trump card, *hombre.* Not the money. How about I give you the money and I keep the baby while I check the powder?"

"No good. You can check the powder yourself. See if the test tube turns blue. I can't check the baby with no chemicals. And I got paid for the *baby.*"

"Right, I give up the baby, go back to my car. Let's say the powder's good. Probably *is* good—I know your crew doesn't deal—what else *could* you do with it but sell it back to me? So I check it out, come back to give you your money, get out of the car—and you smoke me right here. You called this spot—you probably got people all around."

"Sure," Cross told him softly. "But if that's all I wanted, your cash and the powder, I could've done it already." He put the suitcase on the ground. Instantly, a red dot bloomed on Carlos' white leather jacket, right over his heart. "Laser sight," Cross said. "Anytime I wanted, see? That's not what this is about. Lorgano didn't hire me to hit you—he just wants the baby back."

"The baby? He don't care nothing about the baby. He is no kind of man. That is his own child, his own son. And all I wanted was what he owes us. What does he do? He hires you. What could you be paid for a job like this? Not the money he owes us. Much less. He is a clever man, I give him that. This way, he cannot lose. You get the baby back, he's a little lighter in the pocket, but he still has my product and he has not paid for it. If you fail, what has he lost?"

"The baby—"

"Don't insult me," Carlos said. "You know I never return the baby without *all* the money. And you know Lorgano will not *pay* all the money—that's why he hires you. So you hijack another of my shipments, go for the discount."

"Nobody got hurt," Cross said.

"Sure. Everyone knows your crew. I don't have no rookies working for me. They seen your people—you didn't make no secret of it. Like you could disguise Rhino and Princess anyway—Christ! They got the drop on my people. What was they gonna do then, shoot it out? And now I not only don't get my money for the first shipment, I have to pay you for the second one."

"That happens sometimes." Cross shrugged.

"You know what this cost me, *hombre*? You think putting a woman inside his house to steal the baby was cheap? I had to go through Victor himself to set it up. A hundred grand just for that, for the plan and the woman. Another two and a half for you, tonight. This is a business. Business is supposed to make a profit. I never should have dealt with that slime Lorgano—he has no honor."

"Here's the way we'll do it," Cross said, unperturbed. "Give me the kid. Take the suitcase. Get in your car. Drive off, anywhere you want. Look through it, check it out, do whatever you need to do. When you know it's pure, come back here with my money."

"This is the real baby," Carlos said. "And, you know what, I believe you got the real powder there too. So why should I come back with your cash?"

"You shouldn't have snatched the baby," Cross said quietly. "You're right—he don't give a damn about the kid. Only his wife does, and she don't count. He *was* trying for a discount, just like you said. He didn't set specs on how I should get the kid back, probably thought he was buying a hit for what he paid me. What you should have done, you should have snatched *him*. Then you'd find out where your product is—and his money too."

"*Bueno!* You tell me all this *now*. Besides, there's no way we get close enough to snatch him. It would be a suicide run. And my crew, it is all *familia*, you understand? Not soldiers I can just throw into the jungle, don't give a rat's ass if they come back. You remember how that was, Cross?"

"I remember," Cross said. "We don't work for that country anymore, you and me. Go look at your powder. Come back with my money. And then I'll solve your problem for you."

"How you do that, *hombre*?"

"While you're checking out that powder, make a call. Call Victor. And ask him where he found the woman to put inside Lorgano's house."

Carlos nodded, as if thinking it through for himself. "Okay, I get it—this was you from the beginning, right? So what? No way you get another girl next to him—he'll never go for that twice."

"In a couple of minutes," Cross said, soft-voiced, "you'll have the powder. Me, I'll have the baby. I'm not going into his compound. He could decide the best way to clean the slate is to whack me soon as he has the kid. I'm going to show the baby to his wife, not to him. And then *I'm* going to hold the baby. So Lorgano, he'll have to meet me somewhere. Someplace open—like right here, understand?"

"*Sí*. How much?"

"He's got, what, three million of your money? Plus whatever this all cost you. What's it worth to get your hands on him?"

"You tell me, *hombre*."

"You already owe me a quarter-mil, right? Double it, and he's yours. COD."

"It sounds good, Cross. Too good. In fact, it does not sound like you at all. Lorgano, he will know who set him up. And they still have plenty of firepower."

"Yeah, I know. His crew, it's not like yours. They're all mercs. They work for the money. They wouldn't do anything just for revenge. It would just be Lorgano."

"So? As soon as we let him go, he could just hire some new . . ."

"You remember a kid named Juan? He was with your crew, wasn't he? Until he got smoked doing a delivery. You lost that shipment too, right?"

"Yes, Juanito was my sister's oldest son. But that was—"

"That was Lorgano," Cross said. "He had the kid hit. Another shipment he didn't pay for."

Carlos' face shifted imperceptibly, then went stony. He handed the baby to Cross. "It's a contract," he said. "COD."

for Ralph Compton Pino

TWO-WAY RADIO

The florid-faced man stared intently at the small aluminum cube. It sat pure and pristine on the mottled green surface of a crude desk fashioned from an old wood door laid carelessly across a pair of sawhorses. "You're sure it'll work?" he asked, eyeing it warily. He made no move to reach out and touch it.

"It's a half-pound of pure C4," the shadowy man on the other side of the desk assured him. "There'll be nothing left of the car. Guaranteed."

"I got to be sure," the florid-faced man said. "Myra's a vicious damn bitch. I won't get more than one chance."

"You won't need more than one."

"I'm not worried about it being traced back to me. Running a porno business, it isn't like it used to be. The Mob wants to control everything now, even little operators like me and Myra. The cops, they'll figure we didn't pay off and . . ."

"Sure," the shadowy man said, not interested.

"Cross. I been hearing about you for years. I didn't even know you was real until I reached out. They say you never miss."

The shadowy man lit a cigarette, not responding.

"Is that right?" the florid-faced man asked, a slightly more insistent tone in his reedy voice. "That you never miss?"

"You know anybody saying different?"

"No. I didn't mean . . . ah, never mind. How does it work?"

"Right now, it's as harmless as a paperweight," the shadowy man said, reaching out for the aluminum cube. A bull's-eye tattoo on the back of his hand gleamed faintly in the dim light. The man called Cross tossed the aluminum cube into the air, caught it on the way down. "The receiver's inside. All you need is the transmitter," he said, taking a black plastic box about the size of a pack of cigarettes from inside his coat. He held the transmitter up so the florid-faced man could see it.

"Yeah," the man said, wiping his brow with a white handkerchief. "It doesn't matter where I put it?"

"No. Trunk of the car's fine. Or under the dash. In the back seat. Inside a package. The whole car's going anyway. Just be sure you're at least a block or so away—there's going to be shrapnel."

"That's no problem. We got our . . . studio out on a farm. Almost a hundred acres. It'll go off when she's still on the property. But . . ."

"What?"

"This is like a radio thing, right? How do I know some idiot with a cordless phone won't set it off while I'm driving out to the place?"

"That's the beauty of it," Cross said. "This is a *two-way* radio. See these buttons? The green one arms it, the red one sets it off. Unless you press the green button, it can't be activated."

"I guess that's it, then," the florid-faced man said, pocketing the aluminum cube and the transmitter and getting to his feet.

"Give me the money," Cross said quietly.

It was almost forty-five minutes before the cellular phone rang. Cross picked it up without speaking.

"He just turned onto the dirt road," a woman's voice said. "I can see his car from the attic."

From his pocket, Cross took the twin to the transmitter he had given the florid-faced man. He pushed the green button. "Bring the money tomorrow," he said. And pushed the red button.

for Molly and Brenna

EVERYBODY PAYS

A CROSS NOVELLA

"**F**ong swears he's a snakehead, boss," the pudgy man said. The small back room was filled to capacity, but his voice was aimed only at the man seated behind a makeshift desk—a wooden door placed over a pair of sawhorses.

The man behind the desk took the third drag of his cigarette and snubbed it out in an inverted hubcap already filled to the brim with butts, exposing the bull's-eye tattoo on the back of his right hand. He was so still within himself that the movement seemed ghostlike.

"What's a snakehead?" one of the other men asked. He was so grotesquely overmuscled that he looked like a comic-book figure. His shaved head and the miniature wrecking ball dangling on a chain from one ear didn't detract from the image. His voice was that of a fascinated child.

"A smuggler, Princess," a man in the farthest corner of the room answered. That man was so enormous he appeared to be part of the wall itself, dwarfing even the massive bodybuilder by several inches and a hundred pounds. His voice was a high-pitched squeak, the result of drain cleaner forced down his throat when he was a teenager. "Only they smuggle people, not stuff, understand?"

"You mean like Mexicans across the border?"

"Yes," the huge man said, approvingly.

"I did good, right, Rhino?" the bodybuilder asked.

"It was very smart of you to figure that out," the huge man said, his tone indicating he'd doled out enough praise for one conversation.

"That ain't no cargo worth hijacking," a razor-thin black man in an ankle-length leather coat spoke up. "What's all this bullshit about, Cross?"

The man behind the desk closed his eyes. "I don't know what it's about," he said softly. "Buddha brought it in—it's on him to say where the money is."

The slim black man turned to the pudgy man. "Well?"

"Look, Ace, it's just a job, all right? I don't know anything more about it. This guy, he says he's bringing in some people; he wants cover, in case someone tipped the INS. That's what he told So Long. I asked Fong, and Fong said, yeah, the guy's a snakehead all right. Does it all the time. But he always worked the coast before. This time he told So Long he's bringing them over from Canada on one of those ore barges."

"Across Lake Michigan?" Ace sneered.

"That's what he said," Buddha replied, shrugging his shoulders.

"And he's offering . . . what?" Rhino asked.

"A hundred. Half up front, half when the cargo's gone."

"You speak any Chinese?" Cross asked Buddha.

"Boss, there ain't no such thing as 'Chinese.' Jesus. They got about a million different dialects, depending on where they're from. I mean, I can get by a little, maybe, but . . ."

"It stinks," Cross said. "How much could each of the people he brings over be worth?"

"Thirty, even forty," Buddha told him. "So Long says they'd have to work it off here, but their people'd still have to front a nice piece of it before they took off, too. All their relatives chip in. If the snakehead's got a full boat, it could be a few dozen head, that'd be huge, chief. A big score."

"I'm sure So Long knows what's she's talking about," Cross said mildly. "Your wife—"

"So Long knows money," Buddha said defensively. "You gotta give her that much."

"Fuck, even *I* give her that much," Ace acknowledged.

Rhino grunted assent.

"I'm not saying she's not right about what the cargo's worth," Cross said, voice still soft and mild. "But it's not worth that to *us*, right?"

"No, chief. Just the—"

"Yeah," Cross interrupted. "Just the thing to make us believe that it would be *worth* a hundred large for cover fire."

"You don't think—?"

"One," Cross said, holding up a finger, "a hundred grand isn't enough to get us in a firefight with the feds. Two, if we go for it, somebody's going to know where *all* of us are at the same time."

"Why would this snakehead want to ambush us?" Buddha asked.

"Who knows? Who even knows if it's him that wants to do it? Plenty do, right? Maybe he's worried some other tiger crew is looking to hijack his cargo. Or maybe some of the people he brought across didn't make it one time, and somebody wants payback. Maybe, maybe, maybe . . . Too many 'maybe's for us."

"So we pass?" Buddha asked, an undercurrent of disappointment in his tone. The shrewish So Long, his wife of many carping years, wouldn't be happy at a missed opportunity for cash.

"Buddha, ask him for the drop-off point. Tell him we need at least seventy-two hours to get dug in. See if he'll go for that."

"But boss, he probably don't even know. I mean, they'll be in radio contact with the barge, right? They'll have to send a smaller boat out, offload the cargo. No way they're gonna bring an ore barge right up to Lake Shore Drive, come on!"

"So how would he get this cover fire he says he wants to buy?"

"Oh. Yeah, well, he explained that to So Long. See, all he needs is a phone number. Cell phone. When he knows exactly where they're coming in, he calls and we can come to the drop point."

"It's an ambush," Cross said flatly. "Now we need to find out who's setting it up. Tell So Long to tell this snakehead he's got himself a deal."

"Are you sure?" the immaculately dressed man demanded imperiously from the back of the discreetly dark, long-wheelbase Rolls-Royce.

"These are the precise directions I was given, sir," the chauffeur replied.

"I pay good money for . . . Oh, never mind. Just . . . go ahead."

"Yes, sir."

A few more turns and the limo was facing a prairie. A prairie populated with junk beneath even the lowest scavenger's contempt: skeletons of abandoned cars, rotted furniture beyond salvage, broken chunks of concrete, rusting razor wire, pieces of discarded appliances. The sweep of the car's headlights reflected tiny dots of light at various points in the rubble. *Pairs* of dots, the chauffeur noted.

A six-story building stood alone some distance back from the street, the sole survivor of what had been a connected string of flats. The other buildings had long since fallen to a builder's wrecking ball. Bankruptcy had canceled the plans for "developing" an area even the most optimistic yuppie pioneer would refuse to visit in broad daylight, much less inhabit.

"*That's* it?" the man in the back seat asked incredulously.

"These are the coordinates, sir. There are no street numbers around here. I assume that is the building. We won't know until we're closer. And there appears to be no way to *drive* any closer, so . . ."

"You expect me to—?"

"Pal, you want to know the truth?" the driver asked, his formerly subservient tone replaced by something just this side of a sneer. "I don't give a rat's ass about your little expectations. You know who I work for. My orders were, bring you to this joint, play chauffeur, keep anybody from hurting you. I did that. I can do that. The rest of this stuff—mister, you're on your own. You want to stroll through that minefield over there, I'll walk point. You want to bag the whole thing and go home, I'm just as okay with that. Don't matter to me, you understand?"

"Couldn't we call—?"

"This is what I was told, all right? Only place to find this guy is right here. Or at that Double X joint he owns, but word is he won't do business there. So it's got to be here. And it's got to be now, the way it was set up."

"Do you know this man?"

"Only by rep. Never met him."

"Do you believe he could actually—?"

"Don't know, don't care."

"Your superiors—"

"Sure. Whatever. I'm not in this. You want to walk or you want to ride?"

The immaculately dressed man let himself out of the back seat for an answer, tapping one toe impatiently as the chauffeur also got out and joined him.

"Did you set the alarm?"

"What the silly fuck for? You think anyone around here's gonna call the cops? Look, the way I was told, you park in this spot—see, right across from that fire hydrant with the top knocked off it—you're covered, long as you're inside. And they're expecting you. I figure they got us scoped already. These guys, they're not car thieves, okay? Now come on. . . ."

The chauffeur walked ahead carefully, lips twisting in something close to a smile at the brief flashes of ankle-level light that exploded coldly every few steps—lighting the path and announcing a warning at the same time. The immaculately dressed man came behind him, finally silent.

The outside of the building had the number "71" scrawled in dried-blood red as its only identification. *Good enough,* the chauffeur thought to himself. A rusty metal door was standing slightly ajar. He pulled it toward himself and stepped inside. A long streamer of the same-color paint greeted him. A crudely drawn arrow at its end pointed the way. Down.

He descended the steps, chuckling at the dozen different ways he'd already spotted for an intruder who pulled the wrong move to die. The door at the bottom had the same "71" scrawled in the same-color paint. Past the door was a poolroom. At least, it looked like a poolroom—it was so murky that only the click of the ivory balls and an occasional muted movement gave any hint. The size of the room was impossible to determine.

An elderly man wearing a green eyeshade as old as he was swiveled in his wooden chair, pulling his eyes away from a small black-and-white TV set with rabbit-ear antennas wrapped in silver foil. He looked at the chauffeur, saying nothing.

"We're here for Cross," the chauffeur said.

"I ain't the boss," the old man said, cupping a hand around one ear.

"Sure, Pop." The chauffeur snickered. "I get the joke. How long do I have to—?"

He stopped speaking because he felt a hand on his forearm. A gentle hand, but the chauffeur sensed it would be impossible to dislodge. He didn't turn around.

"Count to five. Then turn around. Follow the biggest thing you see," a high-pitched squeaky voice said quietly.

When the chauffeur turned around, he saw the shapeless bulk of the largest human he'd ever seen in his life moving off between the tables. "Let's go," he told the immaculately dressed man.

The huge man cleared a path with his presence, as though he were displacing the very air. When he came to a curtain composed of thousands of ball bearings strung like beads, he stepped to one side. "In there," is all he said.

The chauffeur parted the curtain for his passenger, noting the weight—any one strand would snap bones as if they were dry twigs. As the chauffeur passed through, he felt the presence of the behemoth behind him, but there was no physical contact.

Inside, he saw a man behind a desk fashioned out of a door laid across a pair of sawhorses. The man was as unremarkable as a grain of rice. A human generic, a member of any crowd, invisible even in person. A pair of institutional-gray metal folding chairs was arranged on the other side of the desk.

"You're Cross?" the immaculately dressed man asked the man behind the desk.

"Just sit down," the chauffeur told him, embarrassed, taking a seat himself. "I'm carrying," he told the man behind the desk.

"We know."

The chauffeur nodded in acknowledgment. They knew he was armed. He knew he was surrounded. He'd disclosed his weapon only to keep things honest, that's what he told himself. But he knew the truth—he wanted to distance himself from the immaculately dressed man. He was a professional, same as the man sitting across from them. And, somehow, it was important to him that the other man recognize it.

"My friends in the State Department . . ." the immaculately dressed man began.

"Told you I could get something done. Just tell me what it is," the man behind the desk said softly.

"My daughter is a political prisoner," the man said.

Cross regarded him in total stillness, waiting. It was almost fifteen seconds before the immaculately dressed man understood that this was not going to be a conversation—if he didn't speak again, the meeting was over.

"She's being held in Quitasol," he said. "Maybe you read about it. The government claims she was working with the rebel faction, with some guerrilla outfit. But she was only there for some ecology thing. She never had a trial. Like that girl in Peru. Only these people are even worse. There's no appellate process at all. The prison they have her in, she . . . won't survive much longer. It's high in the mountains. The food is foul. There's no medical care. She . . ."

"What do you want?" the man behind the desk asked.

"Want? I want her out of there. I want her home. Where she belongs."

"Uh, maybe you didn't understand me. You came *here*. I'm not a therapist. Tell me what you want to *buy*."

"He wants an extraction," the chauffeur said, motioning the immaculately dressed man into silence before the arrogant fool said something that would end it all before they even got the offer out.

"From La Casa de Dolor?" Cross asked.

"Yes," the chauffeur replied, unsurprised that Cross knew not only where the girl was being kept, but what the locals called it.

"Not a chance. Can't be done."

"You did it before," the chauffeur said, wasting no time in playing the card his bosses had told him to hold back unless he really needed it. "Same country. A chopper made up to look like the Red Cross on one side and La Policía on the other. Dropped into the biggest drug-dealer gathering the DEA ever heard of. And took your man out."

"That was on the ground, just the other side of the border," Cross said, not bothering to deny anything he'd done in another country . . . one with no extradition treaty. "The prison is in the mountains. No way to get a chopper there without being spotted halfway up. And the camp we hit was right out in the open. This one's behind high walls. You could blast it, maybe, but there's no guarantee you wouldn't take out the client at the same time."

"We're willing to take that chance," the chauffeur said. "She's not going to last much longer anyway."

"*You're* willing to take the chance? The last thing you talked about—it cost me two men."

"High risk, high return," the chauffeur said.

"Your . . . friend here, he's way-up connected, right?"

"Sure. But this can't be a government thing. Hell, even the President called for her release; and our UN ambassador did, too. But Quitasol isn't going for it. They saw what happened with the girl in Peru when the government wouldn't release her. Nothing. Hell, Uncle's not even willing to demand Pinochet's extradition from England, for Christ's sake. We got no muscle anymore," he said, a deep trace of sadness in his voice.

"And even if the government was willing," he continued, "we couldn't do it the usual way—you know, foreign trade tariffs, Most Favored Nation status, rebuilding aid—with these guys. The only industry they got there is coke and gold. The coke market is drying up. Smack is back. So the Triangle's back in business. That's why Pol Pot had to go. And the gold they have, it's not concentrated in one spot. On top of that, the government is *highly* unstable. The rebels hold big pieces of the country, and they could make their move anytime."

"So why not throw *them* a little support? The government did that for the Kurds, they would have shredded Saddam a long time ago."

"The old guard at the . . . agency isn't real fond of the rebels. They're *way* too leftist, if you get my drift. And they got no real leadership. Not pyramid-style, anyway. There's nobody to talk to. Until the agency figures out who's going to come out on top, they have to hedge. We need a presence there, in Central America. We're going to lose our hold in the Canal Zone soon enough.

Remember, this whole shaky mess is just the other side of Mexico. And Mexico, it's got its *own* problems, especially in Chiapas."

"But you tried anyway?" Cross asked mildly.

"Yeah, we did. And you know what's funny? This guy," the chauffeur said, jerking a thumb toward the immaculately dressed man, "he's right. His daughter didn't have jack to do with the rebels. She went down there with some other rich kids. You know, spend-a-semester-in-the-rain-forest thing? So the rebels, they don't care what happens to her either. Fact is, near as I can tell, they'd kind of *like* it if she died there. Amnesty International already has her as a prisoner of conscience. It'd make it harder for us to associate ourselves with the guys in power."

"So you want her out because . . . ?"

"Because I have friends in right places," the immaculately dressed man interjected sharply. "*Grateful* friends. And all they've done is provide some . . . intelligence. I am expected to finance any rescue operation out of my own resources. And I am fully prepared to do so."

"That's nice," Cross told him. "Good luck."

"I am told," the man said, his voice doing an isometric exercise against his impatience, "that you had the only private . . . force capable of handling such an operation."

"We're not a merc outfit," Cross told him. "But there's plenty of those out of work since Rhodesia disappeared and the Congo changed hands and the French pulled out of Algeria and the Portuguese out of Angola. . . . Well, you understand. Hell, for all I know, the Count still has his little air force you can rent."

"I have spoken to . . . several such groups as you describe. It is clear to me, after consultation with my advisers, that I could spend money but would have no guarantee that the operation would ever be undertaken, much less successfully so."

"And the difference between me and them is . . . what?"

"You live here," the chauffeur said flatly. "Sorry, pal, but that's the way it is. Uncle can't reach out and touch the way it could years ago. The only outfits operating on U.S. soil are full of it. Bull-shit idiots in camouflage suits. No way they could do anything like what we're talking about. The ones that used to . . . work, they're living elsewhere. Our orders are . . . Uh, look at it like this: We got to make you do it, okay? I don't mean as a freebie or any-thing like that. This guy here"—indicating the immaculately dressed man with a curt nod—"he's got the coin; that's legit. But if you don't take the deal, we have to take you down."

"You mean . . . what?" Cross asked. "Those words, they're like from a movie. They could mean anything. You saying you're going to *kill* us, is that right? Murder us? All of us?"

The chauffeur threw up his hands, as if to defend himself against a blow. "Don't be ridiculous. I gave you respect, why not give me some? I don't know what I'm being recorded on now, but I'm not stupid enough to think I'm not. This place doesn't *look* high-tech but . . . listen, I know what I'm dealing with, okay? You don't want me to say in front of this guy"—another nod in the direction of the immaculately dressed man—"but I can show you whatever you want. You got something going here in Chicago, that's all I'm saying. We *know* you don't work out of the country anymore. All I'm saying is, we could make it kind of hard for you to work *here*, see what I'm saying?"

"Sure. And if I was running some kind of criminal enterprise, maybe that would be scary or something. But I think you got me confused with someone else."

"No. No, we don't. Look, don't you have some place this guy"—another nod of the head—"can go while I talk to you alone for a minute?"

Cross nodded. A huge hand clamped down on the immacu-lately dressed man's right shoulder. The tip of the hand's forefin-ger was missing. Not a word was exchanged, but the man got up and left the room. The chauffeur didn't take his eyes from Cross.

"You don't want Uncle to owe you one?" he asked softly.

"He's not *my* uncle," Cross said.

"You must have thought so once. Your service record—"

"I went out on a Dishonorable."

"That could be fixed. Easy enough. After all—"

"I don't give a fuck. Gonna give me my medals back too, ass-hole? I went in because I thought it would be better than prison. It wasn't."

"Ah. All right, look: that guy, you think he's got so much juice because of his cash? Fuck, the Chinese got more than him, and they *pay*. Got more politicians on their payroll than the whole tobacco industry. Reason he can call something like this in, he *knows* something. I don't know what it is. And I know if he disap-peared that wouldn't be a tragedy, if you get what I'm saying. But the . . . agency doesn't have what it takes to handle that stuff on the domestic side anymore."

"Then you don't have enough to hit us, either."

"Nobody's threatening to . . ." The chauffeur drew a deep breath. "Listen for a minute. This business with his daughter . . . I don't understand these things. You got any kids?"

Cross stared through him.

"Yeah, sorry. Okay, look, here's how it is. You got to do it. At least *try* to do it. And if it doesn't work out, if the daughter doesn't make it, *that's A-fucking-okay with us*, you understand me now?"

"I don't have the crew," Cross replied.

"You got Ace, Rhino, Princess, Buddha, and Falcon for sure. And probably Tiger too."

"You know so much, you know *this* much," Cross said gently. "Ace never worked jungle in his life—he's a city guy. Buddha, me, and Falcon are the only ones with the experience. And Falcon's not with us."

"He was with you on—"

"On some job, maybe," Cross cut him off. "In another country. Once. But he's not *with* us, understand? He's not with the crew. He's free-lance."

"Uh, first of all, Rhino was on the ground when you made the last extraction from that same country. And Princess, you took him out of there ... for whatever fucking reason we'll never know, 'cause we *do* know he wasn't part of the plan going in. And Falcon *was* there, on that job."

"Princess wouldn't know a rifle from a rock," Cross said. "He's useless. Tiger, I don't even know where she is. She decides job by job, just like Fal, anyway. And I don't have Luis or Maddox anymore. It's too small a crew."

"Money's no—"

"We never take strangers," Cross said, his voice dry ice. "Don't even go there. And don't waste my time telling me you know just the right boys."

"She doesn't have to come out, Cross. All we need is a big bang, something that'll show on the radar, got me? Then you keep the money and Uncle owes you one, too."

"I already told you—"

"Yeah. I believe you don't know where Tiger is. Because we do. And I bet she'd be glad to go along on this one. She doesn't get out much anymore."

"That right?"

"Yeah. She killed a U.S. marshal while he was in performance of his duties. Only reason she didn't get the death penalty was ... it was a little murky, all right? Anyway, she's got about another, oh, fifteen years inside. You take this deal, she goes with you."

"What, on work release?"

"You *do* have a good sense of humor, huh? No, pal. She 'escapes,' all right? And nobody looks for her either."

"Better she dies in prison," Cross said.

"Damn, you're a cold motherfucker. I thought—"

"Better she dies there," Cross said, as if the other man had not spoken. "On paper. Then it's off the books forever. Like the Witness Protection Program. Only one that *works.*"

"So you *will* do it?"

"I didn't say that. I'm only saying, if I was to do it, that'd have to be her end."

"Huh?"

"She wouldn't get any of the money. Just the walkaway. That should be enough."

"Yeah. Sure. Whatever you say. Who cares? Are you going to—?"

"Twenty-five thousand."

"Huh?"

"Twenty-five thousand ounces of gold. That's two hundred and eight bullion bars, ten pounds troy each. Half in hand, minimum of one month before we move."

"That's . . . how much?"

"At today's quote, plus or minus a few bucks, seven and a half million."

"He's not even gonna blink," the chauffeur said.

"Right. So you can tell your little asset that we're not going for his snakehead scam either."

"Ah. Look, nobody was going to get—"

"Right. Not killed, captured. In the act. Looking at forever Inside. So you could make the same deal with us you're offering to make with Tiger."

"Just business."

"Right."

"And you'll . . . ?"

"Let you know."

"It has to be something she already did . . . or something she knows," Cross said four hours later. "He has to be worried what she's going to spill when she gets out."

"Spill what, boss?"

"How would I know, Buddha? And what difference does it make?"

"I don't get it," Ace spoke up. "This rich guy, even *his* money ain't big enough, right? I mean, that's what the spook told you. So he has to *know* something; all it could be, the feds humoring him like they are."

"Humoring him?"

"The spook said, don't matter if the girl gets out alive. In fact, way you told it, they'd just as soon have it *not*. And those guys that have her, *they're* damn sure gonna kill her if they see someone trying to bust her out. So what they're really doing, they're buying a long-distance hit."

"Sure," Cross agreed. "But the agency doesn't care about that. And neither does Uncle. It's that man, he's the one that wants it. The government, they're just delivering."

"What's this got to do with the snakehead?" Buddha asked.

"The spook admitted it was a box. They were going to nab us red-handed, make us some walkaway deal. That way they'd have it all. But I suspect, the way it was supposed to happen—because our pal from Uncle snapped that we caught wise—he was going to make contact before we went in, tell us it's a trap, do us a favor, okay? And what he'd be telling us is that, we don't do them *this* favor, they won't be doing us any more in the future."

"So just another way to threaten us?" Rhino asked.

"More threats." Cross nodded agreement, his voice weary. "I already told him it was a flop. But we need to tell them stronger. Fan out. Stir things up. Make some money. We had a couple of moves waiting. Small stuff, in case we needed a stake. Let's do those. Let them know we're still here, still doing business. See if that doesn't make Uncle up the offer."

"Because . . . ?" Ace leaned forward.

"Because it's on the line now," Cross told his crew. "This deal the fed told us about? We either take it . . . or we take off."

"You're kidding me, right?" the tall, slender man with pianist's hands said over his left shoulder. He was looking down through the plate-glass window of the second floor at two men who had just exited a large anonymous sedan parked across the street. The car was a mottled gray-and-black color. It seemed to disappear into . . . no, the tall man thought to himself, to *become* a shadow. Two men were crossing the street. Slightly in front was a short, pudgy individual wearing an Army jacket over a baggy pair of cargo pants, a long, narrow black case in one hand. Just behind his right shoulder was a man so huge that his bulk riveted the eye. At least six seven, the slender man mused to himself. And he had to weigh three seventy-five, minimum. Hard to tell for sure—the monster was wearing a shapeless rust-colored jumpsuit. His hands were empty.

"No, Billy Ray, I kid you not," a man dressed in a conventional business suit answered. He was maybe ten, fifteen years older and definitely several inches shorter than Billy Ray. "That's Rhino, in the flesh."

"Kee-rist. How's he even gonna *hold* a cue? I mean, I heard he was big, but that guy's just . . . humongous."

"That's not your problem," the man in the suit said. "You're problem is beating him, remember?"

"I beat everyone," the slender man said, a hurt tone buried somewhere beneath the coldness of his voice.

"You're the best," the other man agreed. "Best I've ever seen, and I've been backing games since before you were born. There's no way he can beat you. No way anyone can beat you. Just stay cool."

"I'm always—"

"Thing is," the man in the suit said, as if the other hadn't spoken, "you don't want to trash-talk those guys. In fact, you don't want to fuck with them at all. You just want to put the balls in the holes, you understand what I'm saying?"

"I know—"

"—because you're not going to rattle those guys. You're not going to make them nervous. They're not going to talk to you.

And if you beat Rhino, there won't be any beef. But if one of those *boys* of yours gets silly," he warned, eye-sweeping the poolroom, "it would be a mistake."

"You think I'm a fucking idiot? That guy, he looks like he could tear down a house with his hands."

"Rhino? Sure. It's not him you have to worry about."

"Huh?"

"See the little fat one? Buddha, that's his name. He's the money man."

"So?"

"So, number one: No way Rhino plays pool for money. Buddha, he'll do *anything* for money, but not Rhino. Number two: They're both part of the Cross crew."

"What's that?"

"You don't want to know," the businessman said emphatically. "Just hope that . . . *Fuck!*"

"What's the problem, Manny?" the slender man, asked, looking down. "That's only one of those bikers. They come by all the time. There's a strip joint right down the block. It doesn't—"

"When's the last time you saw a biker wearing makeup and perfume?" the businessman asked.

"What? What's wrong with—?"

"Me? Nothing. Just wait, you'll see soon enough."

As the two men crossing the street disappeared into the building below them, the two men watching saw a shocking-pink Harley dock next to the shadow the big sedan had become. The rider was not only without a helmet, he was without hair entirely, his shaven skull gleaming in the neon wash from the strip joint. Even at that distance, the slender man could see the hypermuscled torso of the biker, who was wearing only a leather vest despite Chicago's September-night chill.

"That's the—?"

"That's fucking Princess," the businessman said, his voice that of a man resigned to his own doom.

The door to the second-story poolroom opened. Buddha entered first, Rhino holding the same position he had crossing the street, just off the pudgy man's right shoulder. While Buddha stepped forward toward the businessman, Rhino remained in place, his massive bulk merging with the faded nicotine-colored wall.

"Ready to do business, Manny?" Buddha asked.

"Me, I'm always ready," the businessman replied. "But you didn't tell me the maniac was coming along."

"Princess? He's not gonna bother anybody."

As Buddha spoke, the biker strolled into the poolroom. And conversation stopped. The biker's face was outrageously made up: Lipstick, rouge, eyeshadow. He reeked of perfume. And dangling from one ear was a miniature wrecking ball on a heavy chain. The biker's face was open and friendly, split by a child's wide smile. "*Awwwrrright!*" he yelled, spotting Rhino and throwing a high-five that made the watchers wince at the vicious crack when their palms met.

"When are you gonna—?" Princess asked. But Rhino held one finger to his lips, gesturing for silence. The finger's missing tip was burnished as smoothly as if it had been designed that way.

"Well, I brought my guy," Buddha said briskly. "This one yours?"

"My name's Billy Ray," the slender man said, stepping forward but not offering his hand.

"Sure," Buddha replied, indifferent. "Whatever you want." He turned to the businessman: "You know how it works, right? Nobody starts nothing with Princess. He's just a big dumb kid, wants to have fun. Anyone don't understand that should . . ."

"Give me a minute," the businessman said. He walked over to where the poolroom watchers had gathered in a silent clot, spoke urgently in a low voice for a couple of minutes, then returned. "Okay," he said to Buddha. "They get the joke."

"Good for them. You got the money?"

"Over there," the businessman said, gesturing toward a man leaning against one of the tables, an attaché case at his elbow.

"For Chrissakes." Buddha laughed. "You got a fucking *body-guard* now, Manny?"

"It's a lot of money," the businessman said, defensively.

"And you think I came here to hijack it?" Buddha sneered.

The businessman spread his hands wide in a placating gesture. "Of course not, Buddha. I know you guys wouldn't ever pull a—"

"You're a real smart guy, Manny," Buddha said, cutting him off. "Real funny, too." The pudgy man pulled a thick brown envelope from his jacket pocket and tossed it on the green felt. It didn't bounce. "Want to count it?"

"Yeah. I fucking *do* want to count it. And you want to count mine, right?"

"Nah, Manny. I trust you. You got a stupid mouth, but your mind ain't broke. No way you gonna die for twenty large."

The slender man watched his backer's face blanch. Billy Ray prided himself on the steadiness of his hands and the calmness of his face. He was there to do a job. A pro. All this bluff-and-bullshit stuff didn't interest him. He knew he was being watched, but never as closely as he watched himself.

From the first time he'd held a cue in his hands, he'd known. It was part of him, even then. And it hadn't taken so long after that. Obsession doesn't wait to rule. He played every night and slept every day. He didn't ramble the way some of the players did. Never left his home base. Where he started. Sure, in the beginning, he'd had to travel a bit. Being the best in Uptown wasn't *that* much . . . not after a while. He had to try the West Side. And the South. After that, almost three years on the circuit: St. Louis to Cincinnati to Atlanta to Miami to New Orleans to . . . *Ah, what difference?* the slender man thought to himself. Now he never moved. This was his place. People wanted to try him, they came here. That's the way it worked.

Sure, it gave him an edge, some said. He knew the tables.

They'd be strange surfaces to anyone else. There was a story about a black kid years and years ago. A legend, maybe. The kid's name was Cowboy and he played at some joint in the worst part of Cleveland. Hough, it was called. Anyway, the place had these old wood-base tables—not slate, like they used in *real* tables. And the kid was unbeatable on them. Knew every groove, every slant, every drop. But get him off those tables, he was nothing special. Good, not great. The slender man didn't know if the story was true, but he could see how it could be. And how they could say sort of the same thing about him.

But not really. Not since the all-in tournament at Huron's five years ago. Eleven straight days and nights. All comers. The slender man didn't go near the one-pocket guys or any of the other trick-game specialists. And he stayed on the standard tables, too. No three-cushion, no snooker. He played nine-ball and straight pool only. Won both categories. And the best part of a quarter-million. He didn't have to travel anymore. Every so often, some wise kid would think he had what it took, and they'd tell him, go to Chicago, find Billy Ray's place, and try your luck.

No problem.

There was something else about home-court advantage, too. Not one of those cow-pie "intangibles" sportswriters were always jabbering about. The real thing. And if these crazy guys really wanted to go through with what Manny told him, they'd see it, soon enough.

"One game of nine-ball, right?" Buddha asked, getting the terms clear.

"One game, twenty grand," Manny replied. "That's the deal. You lose—and you *will* lose, Buddha—you come back when you got another twenty. But one game at a time, understand? I don't care you walk in here with a hundred, that don't get you five games. One game, one time, period. And you agreed."

"I did," Buddha said placidly.

The slender man didn't like this, couldn't figure out why

Manny had wanted to do it this way. The longer the match, the better his chances, that's the way Billy Ray figured it. Always had been that way. This was too much like flipping a damn coin. Nine-ball, it could be over on the break. Dumb luck, and twenty grand flies. Ah, what the hell. Wasn't *his* twenty. Manny puts it up, fifty-fifty on the win. Couldn't get a better deal than that anywhere.

"Let's do it," Buddha said, opening the black leather case.

As Rhino and Princess approached the table, Buddha assembled the two-piece cue he took from its case. Billy Ray watched closely, but he didn't see anything exotic. No graphite, no fancy inlays along the thicker butt portion, which was wrapped in black electrician's tape. Just a professional's working tool—one that looked as if it had seen plenty of work. But it *was* the thickest cue Billy Ray had ever seen. *Looks like the damn thing weighs sixty ounces,* he thought. A lot of guys used heavier cues on the break playing nine-ball, putting power over accuracy, then switched to lighter ones for the rest of the game. But he'd never seen one this size . . . and it seemed to be the only one the monster had brought with him.

Billy Ray worked the odds in his head. He knew them as well as any poker player. *Only difference is,* Billy Ray thought, *me, I make my own odds. And they only work for me. Cards, they work for anyone.* So Billy Ray knew it down to a mathematical certainty: He was going to win about 85 percent of all games played if he got to break the balls. If the other guy broke, the percentage dropped to around 70. And, over time, that combination would guarantee a victory. But if Billy Ray *pocketed* a ball on the break—and *that* he did a little better than 90 percent of the time—the odds on him winning *that* particular game went up to the *high* nineties. All that kept it from being a sure thing after he pocketed a ball on the break was when a bad bounce gave him no look at the next ball up. That didn't happen often enough to worry about.

Besides, it was the element of luck that kept the suckers coming.

Billy Ray knew that the odds he'd painstakingly computed over the years were only valid for the long haul—you couldn't count on them for any one game. Still, he was better than even money against anyone who ever played the game, no matter who broke. The home tables didn't matter much once the cue ball cracked into the rack. But getting to go first, getting the break, that was the big edge in nine-ball. And on his home court, he had more than one way to do that.

A little Asian guy in a Cubs baseball hat worn backward stepped to the head of the table. It would be his job to rack the balls into the nine-ball diamond, the yellow-and-white-striped money ball in its precise center. But he didn't move, awaiting the order.

"He racks them now," Buddha said. "*Before* we see who breaks."

All right, that one was shot to hell, Billy Ray thought. But he was neither surprised nor unnerved. Any fool would know that a loose rack would inhibit the movement of the balls, making a successful break highly unlikely. If Rhino had won the coin toss for who breaks first, a loose rack would have been his reward. Now, without knowing who was going to win first shot, the little man had to rack them right. Right and tight.

Manny took a silver dollar out of his pocket. Held it on top of his fist, supported by his thumb. "Call it in the air," he said to Buddha.

"Nah," the pudgy man said. "Let's lag for the break."

Billy Ray's face stayed flat, but his mind smiled. He hadn't expected even the dumbest Hoosier to go for a coin toss anyway. So far, everything was going exactly as planned. The table they were using had a dead spot against the short rail farthest from the rack, the very rail they'd have to come to for the lag. But the dead spot was only on the right side—the side Billy Ray stepped to immediately. Rhino took his place on the left side of the same rail. They each stroked one of the colored balls toward the opposite short rail at the far end of the table; each stepped back to watch the balls hit the rail and return. Closest ball to the near short rail got the break. Billy Ray's ball had more pace on it than Rhino's, but he knew what would happen as soon as it hit that dead spot. In fact, you *had* to stroke it pretty good unless you wanted it to just plain *stop* like a magnet stuck to metal . . . and that would make anyone suspicious.

Nobody spoke as the two balls approached the short rail. Billy Ray always used the six ball. It was solid green, visually closing the gap between it and the rail by maybe a hundredth of an inch over the bright-red three ball Rhino had selected. Another edge.

Billy Ray's ball hit the dead spot on the short rail perfectly, like it always did . . . and bounced off *hard*, a good four inches away. Rhino's settled gently against the cushion, maybe an inch and a half off. Not even close.

"Our break," Buddha said.

Billy Ray sat down. Not out of courtesy to the other shooter, but from shock. How could that have . . . ?

Rhino stepped to the table. He placed the cue ball six inches from the right-hand long rail, stroked a few times, the cue's tip poking in and out from between his fingers—a gentle, steady movement, as methodically probing as a snake's tongue. Then his right arm came forward and the cue ball rocketed into the pack, sending the balls scattering as if fleeing in fear. Four balls dropped into various pockets. One of them was the nine ball in the left corner.

"*Yes!*" Princess shouted.

Rhino didn't say a word.

"Nice doing business with you," Buddha said, walking toward the man standing next to the attaché case. The man looked to Manny. The businessman shook his head. The bodyguard stood aside. Buddha picked up the attaché case in one hand and started for the door, Rhino just off his right shoulder. Princess was the last one to leave, turning to the crowd, waving. "That was *fun*, huh?" he yelled.

Then he too disappeared.

When Billy Ray heard the Harley's engine growl into life, he got to his feet and went over to the table. Unlike a few minutes before, when any close scrutiny would have been a mistake, he now pressed his thumbs against the right-hand side of the near short rail. It was alive. The dead spot had vanished. "Give me a light," he called to one of the watchers against the corner.

"Since when'd you start—?"

"Not a match, goddamn it. A . . . flashlight or something. I want to look close."

When he did, Billy Ray saw it for himself. He pulled out a penknife and went to work.

"This is a new rail," he told Manny, gesturing at a piece of what looked like black rubber. "A new rail under the old cloth. Whoever did it, he's got the best hands I ever saw. This is fucking perfect. Even if I was looking for it, I don't think I would've seen it."

"So you mean . . . ?"

"Yeah. Somebody got in here. This place don't close until two in the morning, officially. And it stays open way past that sometimes, especially when I got a game. When did you set this up?"

"About three weeks ago. I was in the Double X and Buddha—"

"Three weeks. Plenty of time. Whoever did this, they knew exactly what they were doing. And they knew me, too. Knew my game. Knew what table we'd be using. Knew it all."

"All that for twenty grand?" Manny wondered. "That don't seem like Cross at all."

"They didn't even cheat me," Billy Ray said, mostly to himself. "I mean, I was gonna do them that same way. And the monster . . . he *did* make the shot. It's even a bigger risk than you say. What if he'd missed? I *still* would've won the money. You know I would. So why would they . . . ?"

"Fuck if I know," Manny snapped at him. "All I know is I'm out twenty grand. And Buddha, he'd kill his mother for twenty large."

"Kill his mother-in-*law* for nothing, way I understand it," a Latin guy lounging against the wall said, laughing.

"You know him?" Manny asked.

"I served with him. Same outfit. He was an evil little mother-fucker even then."

"Why didn't you say something?"

"What you want me to say, *patrón*? You the big man, you running the show, putting up the money. You need *me* to tell you what Buddha is?"

"You promised!" Princess sulked in the front seat of the car. They had followed him to a spot where he'd ditched the Harley. Rhino's bulk loomed in the back.

"Look, Princess," Buddha said, "what I told you was—"

"You said if I was good, if I didn't cause no problems, we could race. You said it! Didn't he, Rhino?"

"You did say it," the monster-man spoke to Buddha, his voice an incongruous high-pitched squeak.

"I'm not saying I fucking *didn't* say it, okay? I just didn't say it would be tonight, all right?"

"I *wanna* do it now," Princess demanded.

"Fuck me," Buddha said softly, his eyes toward the heavens.

Forty minutes later, Buddha was working the shark car through a maze of twisted streets near the Badlands. The road surface was cobbled from neglect. When citizens don't vote, road repair is very slow. And when a neighborhood *has* no citizens . . .

Buddha's touch on the small-diameter, thick-rimmed wheel was as delicate as a surgeon's. "I'm not promising anything," he said to no one in particular. "Maybe we'll get some action, maybe we won't."

"You said—"

"Princess, gimme a break, okay? This is street racing, not the fucking Indy 500. Sometimes the players are around, sometimes they're not."

"Try the back of the diner," Rhino advised.

Buddha turned and shot him a look. Rhino stared back impassively. Buddha sighed. "I just put a whole new suspension underneath. Full-time four. Gotta have it, you want the beast to handle on slick roads. But I don't know if she'll tolerate a nitrous shock like a solid rear axle would, and . . ."

"Might as well find out now," Rhino said implacably. "When there's no risk."

"No risk? Fuck you talking about? The Man is down on street racing now, big-time. Too much stuff about it on the wire. They even got that damn newsletter making the rounds, giving the rankings and the handicaps and all. You let people bet money in this town on anything, you open up the action, and you don't let the cops dip their beaks; you know what's gonna happen next."

"So it's a ticket. Big deal."

"A ticket? Listen, Rhino. They'd pop me for Driving to Endanger. And I'm carrying. You too. And probably this maniac," he continued, nodding his head in Princess' direction, "for all I know. You're talking felony beefs for all of us."

"No. If that happens, Princess and I will get gone. It'll just be you."

"Isn't *that* special? They'd hold me for—"

"—a few days, max," Rhino assured him. "And nothing's going to happen to you at the County. Just make sure they know you're with Cross. You're the only one with papers, Buddha. A fall comes, you got to take it. This isn't news to you. You make bail, we juice the cops, their memory isn't so good; our shyster pleads you to some nonsense, we pay a fine, and that's all. Don't get excited."

"You think I'm worried about a few days in jail?" the pudgy man snapped. "Fuck that. What's gonna happen to my car? And who's gonna tell So Long why I didn't come home?"

"The car's no problem," Rhino assured him. "It's registered, it'll go to the Impound Lot. Cost us some money, that's all."

"And So Long . . ."

"Uh . . . you could call her from the County. They got pay phones there. Somebody'll know Cross, get you right to the front of the line."

"Thanks a fucking lot, pal."

Rhino shrugged. He wasn't going to visit So Long no matter what the inducement. And sending Princess would be . . . too gruesome to contemplate.

The shark car rolled into the dimly lit parking lot behind an aluminum-sided diner with no name that had been perched on the edge of the Badlands for as long as anyone could remember. Nobody ever ate there—it was a trading post on the outskirts of a hostile nation.

About two dozen cars were arrayed in no particular pattern around the back lot. They ranged from flamboyant to drab, but they all had one thing in common—the hardcore stance of the street racer: monstrous rear tires and skinny fronts. Superchargers poked conspicuously from some hoods. Others had painted flames pouring out of louvers. A few actually looked near-stock.

"I don't like this," Buddha said to Rhino. "Most of those ponies are back-halved. Blowers right out in the open. Look like a bunch of trailer queens too, even with the plates. Probably some running alky, too. This thing ain't no drag racer. And none of those quarter horses are going for the twisties. They'll only take on straight-line stuff, maybe even want to do eighths. If I could get them to go from a standing start, we might be able to pull a little, get off first. But they all want to run thirty-tromp now, 'cause they can't get all that torque to hook up."

"Rhino, what does he mean?" Princess asked.

"That the other cars are faster than this one."

"Hey, *fuck* that, all right? I never said that. I was just . . . There's horses for courses, you understand what I'm saying? Like, come on, Princess . . . look at it like this: What if I was gonna race a helicopter against a jet, how fair would that be?"

"But these are all *cars*!"

"Fine," Buddha mumbled darkly. "Let me see if any of these clowns want to dance." He got out of the shark car and leaned against the driver's door, lighting a cigarette.

Within five minutes, a small crowd approached.

"What you running?" one asked.

"A 698 Elephant."

"Heinous! You on the bottle?"

"Sure."

"Fuel?"

"Right outa the pump. 76 straight, not even av-gas. This is a *street* car, sonny. No tubs, no tubes, got real seats, all that. And it's all-steel, too—no fiberglass, no carbon, no titanium."

"Damn! This thing must weigh two and a half."

"Three and a piece," Buddha replied. "There's a four-wheel drive underneath, viscous coupling, full-time torque-splitter, air bags instead of springs. . . ."

"You still working on it," one young man asked, looking over the shark car's gray-black-primer flanks, "or are you going suede?"

Buddha ignored him, his eyes only on the target.

"You see the Nova over there? The blue one with the red flames?" the target asked.

"Yeah, I see it."

"Wanna go?"

"Against that?" Buddha laughed. "What'd you do, have it trailered over, waiting for a sucker? You running a Rat, right?"

"Nah. Small-block, 406 huffed."

"I'm a Mopar man myself."

"Yeah, well, want to show me something?"

"For how much?"

"You say."

"Got five?"

"Hundred?"

"Thousand."

"Oh." The young man looked around, caught a few nods. "Yeah, I got it covered."

"Okay. How many lengths I get?"

"Lengths? Nobody said nothing about lengths. We run to thirty, get in sync, go past the white post—we'll show you—then get on it to the next white post. First over takes it."

"Right," Buddha said, his voice heavy with sarcasm. "You got—you *say* you got—a bored-out small-block, a blower, and that's all, right? And I got maybe a few liters' displacement on you. *No* blower, and—"

"You got the nitrous."

"And you don't?"

"Uh . . ."

"Right. Bottom line, you got a—what?—nine-second car there? Weighs—what?—twenty-two hundred, tops? I got same-size rubber all around. I don't even have a solid rear axle, like I told you."

"Bullshit," the young man said flatly.

"See for yourself," Buddha told him, handing over a large black flashlight.

Several players crouched down as the young man played the light under the shark car's bumper. Another man grabbed the flashlight from him, lay down on his back, and pushed himself underneath with the soles of his feet. "He ain't lying," he told the others when he emerged. "I never seen nothing like it. I mean, it's supertrick under there all right, but that's an independent rear suspension, period."

"Now what you gonna do?" Buddha asked the young man. "You know there ain't no way I can even stomp it down without blowing that rear out, right? I got a throttle stop behind the pedal, just to be sure."

"So what'd you set it up like that for?"

"It's for the curves, not the straights. For *hauling* stuff, get it? I never raced against no quarter-mile pro, like you. I gotta get lengths . . . *and* the bust."

Princess suddenly emerged from the passenger seat. "Hey, Buddha, we gonna race or what?"

"Jesus, Mary, and Joseph!" one of them exclaimed. "What is *that*?"

Princess approached the crowd, grinning broadly. "Oh, man, this is gonna be great!"

"This ain't no game for—" one of them started to say, stopping when his friend elbowed him sharply in the ribs. "Shut the fuck *up*," his friend hissed. "I know who that is. Hell, I even know what this *all* is now. That's the shark car."

"The what?"

"Come on over here," he said, pulling his friend into the darkness.

When the haggling finished, they agreed to a standing start with Buddha getting a two-length lead on a quarter-mile distance. The guy and his friend got some bets down too. On Buddha.

"Oh, man! We're gonna race!" Princess yelled, pounding the dash in excitement.

"Will you fucking calm down?" Buddha snapped at him. "You're gonna smash her all up. And you're gonna *watch*, not race."

"Huh?"

"Well, you heard Rhino. If anything happens, if the car breaks or something, then you guys gotta fade. Besides, the less weight I gotta carry the better."

"But I won't be able to *see* nothing!"

"Hey, look, this was your fucking idea. At least give me a chance to—"

"We'll all stay," Rhino squeaked.

"All right!" from Princess.

From Buddha, silence.

It was a good ten minutes before both drivers were satisfied with their starting positions. They were over the Border now, deep enough into the Badlands that some of the teenage vulture packs were watching from the shadows cast by burnouts and abandoned buildings. Money changed hands there, too.

The unmuffled roar of the Nova pawed at the night. The shark car was almost silent in response, Buddha disdaining throttle-blipping games, uninterested in impressing the crowd.

"Want bleach?" the starter asked, a kid in a Day-Glo–orange jacket.

"No burnouts," Buddha said flatly. "We're already staged. Tell that boy, he didn't want to give me the bust, we gotta leave the same time, I said okay. But that's fucking *it*. If he still wants to go, let's do it. He wants to fry his tires for the fans, I got business elsewhere."

The guy in the Nova listened. The starter waved his arms, as if holding off a threat. Finally, the starter took his position between the two cars. He took off his jacket and waved it at the Nova. The driver held up a thumb out the window. The starter pointed at Buddha, who did the same.

"How come we don't rev it—?"

"Shut up, Princess," Buddha said quietly. "We launch at nineteen hundred. I'm line-locked right now. Any more, we just sit here and spin. So we don't *need* no fucking big noise, okay? Just watch that flag. . . ."

The flag dropped. The Nova lunged forward so violently that only its wheelie bars kept it from standing on end. But the shark car had already disappeared into the night. As the digital readout for the tachometer hit 6600, Buddha slapped home the plunger on the silver-nitrous bottle sitting on the transmission tunnel and the shark car shot forward like a staged rocket. The race wasn't close.

Buddha wheeled his mount back to the staging area. He and Princess got out together. "Pay up," he told the man holding the stake.

"That ain't no car," one of the watching teenagers told the others.

As in the poolroom, Buddha didn't count the money.

"Told ya, James," the skinny black kid whispered to his friend. They were both lying on their stomachs, hands gripping the edge of the building ledge, looking down.

"Man!" is all his friend contributed to the conversation, his eyes wide with fascination at the scene below. Which was . . .

A bodybuilder with a grotesquely overdeveloped physique bounced a basketball with his left hand several times, as if getting the feel of a foreign object. Then he reached across his body and gently tossed the ball to a point several feet above his head. As the ball descended, the bodybuilder stepped forward on his left foot and launched into a spinning back-fist—his clenched hand caught the ball as it bounced up from the concrete floor of the deserted basketball court and sent it flying in the general direction of the chain-netted hoop.

From somewhere in the darkness, a massive lump of . . . something . . . tossed another basketball toward the bodybuilder, who deftly caught it on the first bounce and repeated the same maneuver. Again, the ball soared toward the hoop, this time missing the entire backboard by a dozen feet.

"Aahhh!" the bodybuilder said. "Come on, Rhino, send me another."

"We've used them all up," a high-pitched squeaky voice responded. "Fifty balls. Now we have to grab them all and get back, remember?"

"Can't we do it just one more—?" the bodybuilder pleaded.

"Princess, we had a deal," the massive lump spoke. As the lump moved forward, the watching boys could see it was a man. A huge, shapeless man in a rust-colored jumpsuit that blended perfectly into the mottled light. This camouflage was meaningless in view of his partner's appearance. Not only was the hyperdeveloped man wearing a neon-orange tank top over bright-yellow parachute pants and electric-blue sneakers, he was wearing enough makeup to cover a girls' boarding school.

"Rhino, I'm telling you, I can do this," the bodybuilder said.

"I know you can," the massive boulder of a man replied. "And I'm helping you, just like I promised, right? But you don't want to go to the gym because people might see you, remember?"

"Yeah! This has gotta be a secret. I hit this shot, we're rich, right? A trick, just like Buddha's always pulling."

"Princess," the massive man said, his patience matching his size, "if you hit it on a bet, sure, we could make a lot of money. But you have to hit it that *exact* time, understand?"

"Sure, I understand. Why else you think I'm gonna practice till I can do it maybe ten times in a row first?"

"You haven't even—"

"And I been getting closer too, right?"

"Yes," the massive man sighed. "Now let's gather up these balls, okay?"

"They does this every night?" the boy called James asked his pal.

"Every night, bro. They comes about two, three in the morning, when it's all empty-like. They does this for about an hour, maybe. Then they just go away."

"White guys . . ."

"Oh, man, did you *see* them? Who's gonna bother 'em? Besides, I was here once when the Rajaz came down."

"How many of them?"

"Maybe a dozen, man. It was nasty. The one with the bald head . . . with all the girl's makeup . . . he kept asking them if they wanted to play a little two-on-everybody. No lie! Anyway, one of the Rajaz, he shows them a piece, asks them if they know they in somebody's turf. The monster-guy, he shows *them* a piece too. I seen one before, man. An Uzi. The monster, he got it on a chain around his neck, like it's a little charm or something. The guy with the muscles, he just keep picking up the basketballs. Nobody say nothing. Nobody do nothing. Then the Rajaz booked, just like that."

"That's a pair of crazy monster motherfuckers."

"You right, bro. But here they is again. And I don't see nobody running them off the court, neither."

"One thousand yards."

"One klick," the man in camouflage gear and matching cap said.

"Either you trying to play soldier boy or you trying to cheat. Either way, forget it."

"Look, Buddha, I was just saying—"

"What you was just *doing* was adding two, three hundred yards to the bet. Next thing, you'll want it right through the spade in the center too. Look, *Colonel*," Buddha said, sarcasm dripping from his voice, "you want to call it off, then just say so, all right? What we *said*, what we *agreed* to, it was real simple. I said my man could hit a playing card at a thousand yards. That's all. You said, if I recall exactly, 'Bullshit!' Then you started going on about putting my money where my mouth is . . . or were you too pitiful-drunk to remember *that*?"

"Watch your mouth, mister, You're on—"

"What? Sacred Aryan ground? Private property? Thin ice? Look, clown, it was a *long* drive up here to this fuckforsaken little 'compound' of yours. And we didn't make the trip to pick up a few spare Nazi flags, you understand what I'm saying? My man is a pro. You probably wouldn't understand that, you being a 'patriot' and all. So let me explain the way it works: you pay twenty-five grand, he'll pop somebody. Reach out and touch 'em.

Long-range. It's called being a sniper. And maybe if you'd served anyplace but fucking Stateside you'd have heard of it. Now, what *you* said, *you* said you had twenty-five grand. And what we were gonna do, we were gonna set up this target. One thousand yards. One playing card. Got one right here," Buddha said, patting his breast pocket. "I call my man out of the car. He gets one shot. He drills it, we take your money. He don't, you take ours."

The Colonel looked over his shoulder at the half-dozen assembled men. Then back at Buddha. "Maybe we could just take your money without any of this other stuff. How would that be?"

"Uh, I don't know," Buddha said, stifling a yawn. "Tell you what . . . why don't you use that GI Joe radio of yours on your belt, get in contact with your sentries, see how things are going on your fucking 'perimeter' first."

The Colonel looked at Buddha carefully. Said "Watch him!" to his man, and thumbed the radio into life. "Alpha to Red Dog. Read me? Over."

"They're all sleeping," a strange voice squeaked back through the radio. The Colonel's mouth dropped.

"You better have the money," Buddha said, stepping back a few feet. "Check your chest, chump."

The Colonel's prior military experience had been limited, but he understood the meaning of the red dot now cold-burning just over his heart.

"See, my man's a lot *less* than a thousand yards off," Buddha said. "So we got ourselves a new bet. Me, I bet you don't have no twenty-five grand here. I bet you're a fucking liar. I bet you figured it wouldn't be much trouble to sucker some Fourteenth Amendment citizen like me out here, take my money, and . . . who knows what? You don't know who *Cross* is, and you're gonna overthrow the government? I don't think you pitiful pieces of shit even know the difference between killers and murderers. You may have murdered a few people; that don't make you killers. But, see, one of the people you murdered—you remember,

that big-mouthed Jew you made an example of—he got some
family. Now, that don't mean nothing to us. But this family, they
got money. And, like I told you, we're professionals. So," he said,
pulling a .40-caliber Glock semi-auto from his jacket in a motion
so casual as to seem magical to the watchers, "here's your problem. You got me 'covered.' Only my man's got your heart in his
hands. And I got a few other men, already took out your dumb-
fuck guards. And I got this here piece on you, too. So what you
gonna do, boys?" Buddha finished, addressing the assembled
men. "Your 'Colonel' here, it's his head we came for. He's a dead
man, no matter what. He stands there, his heart's gonna go *poof*!
soon as I give the word. He runs, I'm gonna put a few rounds in
him, right up his spine. And the guys we got on the perimeter,
they got this nice stuff. You don't shoot it, you *launch* it, if you get
what I'm saying. We got *paid*, understand? So what I want you to
do, and I know this is fucking hard for you all, is just *think* for a
minute. You *really* want to die? Because . . ."

The Colonel dropped, crumpling lifeless even before the
ccccrack!! was audible. The men stood frozen.

"Well, damn. It's *already* too late, huh? Now, let's all play Army,
okay? Every motherfucker wants to live, put his hand up."

Each man raised his hand like a kid in a classroom. Buddha
sighed: "*Both* hands, you fucking morons."

Weapons hit the ground as hands went into the air.

"Good. Now . . . you have that twenty-five around here or
not?"

"No," one of the men said. "It was . . . like you said. We
thought *you* . . ."

"Sure. You were gonna see my money, then kill me and the
shooter I brought along, right? If you lames are the master race,
my money's on the mud people. All right, we got two problems
here. One for you, one for us. My problem is, you guys are like . . .
witnesses, you know. And witnesses are bad for business. Your
problem is to convince me why we shouldn't just My Lai all you
motherfuckers right now."

"Nobody'll know," the biggest one said. "We can bury him right here. Just say he went underground. Nobody's going to ask any questions."

"Well, you see, they *might*. So I got this idea. You got any shovels?"

"Yes."

"Good. Start digging."

Three hours later, a man emerged from the woods. Princess. In full makeup, his perfume overcoming even the stench of fear that hung like a murky cloud around the assembled clot of men. "Take it," Buddha told him. Princess unslung a Japanese katana from behind his shoulder, picked up the dead body by the belt with one hand, and draped it across a tree stump, poking it with his foot until the angle was satisfactory, then brought the sword down in a two-handed strike that severed the head cleanly. One of the watching men retched. Buddha pulled a heavy dark-green plastic bag from his jacket and unsnapped it so it was full-size. Princess unceremoniously dumped the head inside. Buddha pulled the yellow drawstrings tight. "Okay, there's our proof. Now throw the body in there."

The men did it, none of them looking down. Buddha watched patiently as they poured quicklime over the headless corpse and shoveled the dirt back.

"You can dig him up. Be a lot of work, but you could do it. But the forensics, they'd be *real* bad, you did something that stupid. So I figure your best bet is, leave him there. 'Course, you *could* go to the cops, tell them what happened here. Probably not a good idea, but you all use your best judgment. Revenge is for amateurs. And amateurs don't go up against pros. So, I was you, I'd go back to preparing for the Fourth Reich and forget this ever happened. Appoint yourselves a new Führer or whatever. But I see any one of you again, anywhere at all, you're dead. And don't think we couldn't find you in jail, either. Nice doing business with you."

It was hours after the intruders vanished before the first of the broken men moved.

"Look at that faggot. Christ! First time I ever seen one of them cruising on fucking *skates*," the young man dressed in a black alpaca suit over a white silk turtleneck said to another dressed in the same exact outfit. Both were powerfully built, with razor-cut short black hair. At twenty yards, they could be mistaken for twins. They lounged against the side of a glistening black Cadillac limo parked just off the grass at the lakefront.

"Got some damn body on him," the other said. "You gotta give him that. Motherfucker's ripped to pieces."

"Yeah, well, I don't go for that." The speaker caught a look from his opposite number. "Hey! I mean I don't go for that *look*, understand what I'm saying. You can lift for strength or you can lift for looks. Me, I lift for strength. But you see them at the gym all the time."

"See who?"

"Homos. Let me tell you, I think *most* of those bodybuilders are like that. I wish they wouldn't let them in there at all—who knows what they look at in the shower. They give me the creeps."

"You got a problem, Monty?"

"Problem? I don't got no fucking 'problem.' What I got is same as you got—a job. And that's what we're doing, right?"

"Sure. At least I am."

"What's *that* mean?"

"Means that freakish-looking guy with all the muscles, he's gone by us three times already."

"So? Like I said, he's cruising. Showing off."

"Maybe. This job of ours—what you think it is?"

"We're bodyguards," Monty said proudly. "We protect the man."

"What we are is bullet-catchers," the other man said flatly. "That's why they always want 'em big. We ain't bar bouncers, okay? It's not about flexing muscle. Our job, we get *between* trouble and the man."

"Yeah? The way I figure it, we get paid to *stop* trouble. That's what this is for," he said, touching his suit just over the heart.

"You talking about your balls or your piece, pal? Because, you know what, neither of them is any good without the brains."

"Which is what you got, right?"

"What I *got* is that I'm in charge here," the other man said. "And if that faggot skates by here again, we're gonna have a talk with him."

A dusty blue Chicago Department of Public Works pickup truck pulled up about fifty yards away. The driver was wearing a green baseball cap. Two men took their time climbing out of the truck's bed. They took even longer to pull on harness apparatus that carried small gasoline engines to power leaf-blowers.

"Your tax dollars at work." The other man laughed. "Look at that: You got your basic nigger and your basic Uptown Indian, which is a nigger with red skin. But they get these soft jobs, taking their time, making good money. All that civil-service crap, *we* pay for it."

"Maybe they're on work release from the County."

"No way. Then there'd be a guard with them. And there'd be more than two."

"Man, you don't miss much."

"That's what I'm trying to tell you, Monty. In our business, you *can't* miss much, okay?"

The two men with the leaf-blowers pulled the cords on the gasoline engines strapped to their backs. The machines roared into life. They then began to amble slowly in a vague pincer movement, blowing fallen leaves into a pile. One of them had a stiff leg, forcing him to limp.

"Here they come," the other man said to Monty, nodding his head toward two elderly men walking together as if on an outing from an old-age home.

"Should we—?"

"No. We stay right here. Whatever Don Moranelli is saying, it's not for us to hear. Just get the engine started so it's nice and—"

One of the leaf-blowing men shrugged out of the harness and dropped to the ground, ripping a rifle loose from its Velcro mount against his thigh. He wrapped the rifle's sling around his forearm, propped himself on one elbow, and spread his legs so that his body formed a Y. The other leaf-blower turned toward the two approaching old men and aimed the tube of his machine at them—a gush of fire erupted, engulfing both men instantly. One of the bodyguards was already running toward them when it happened; the other pulled his pistol and dropped to one knee. The prone rifleman fired twice. One each.

The shark car slid to a stop, its rear doors popping open. The workers and the truck driver all ran for it. The loudest sound was the roar of the abandoned leaf-blowers. Until the truck exploded with such force that it left a crater as a monument to its destruction. The two old men were microscopic particles. The two bodyguards were perfectly preserved. For the autopsy.

Nobody saw anything.

"I almost didn't recognize you," Cross told the woman seated across from him. They were separated by wire mesh.

"You think my hair grew in stripes *naturally*?" the woman chuckled. "They're not big on beauty aids in here."

"No. You're a lot . . . thinner."

"Why don't I take that as a compliment?"

"Cut it out, Tiger. You doing the time hard?"

"No. But it's like my hair. I can't get the vitamin supplements I need. Or access to the workout machines. The feds seem to think it's only the male prisoners who deserve that kind of stuff. So I have to make do, that's all."

"Anybody—?"

"Bothering me? You've been Inside. You get tested. It wasn't much. *Nothing* in here is much. My biggest problem is staying out of the middle, you know? I'm not going to get in anyone's car. They know that now. If I want a girlfriend, I can have my choice. But nobody's going to choose *me*."

"Okay. You got money on the books?"

"No. Going to leave me some?"

"Yes."

"You're wondering why I never told you, right?"

"Yes."

"But that isn't why you're here, right?"

"Right."

"Same old motormouth Cross." She smiled. "I know what it says on my papers, but that's a load of crap. It was out west. Some working girls got together, decided they didn't need pimps to be working them like mules and keeping all their cash. Sure, some of them, they're in the life because they got all kinds of . . . whatever, it doesn't matter. But the prostie pro, she just wants the coin. And what they were paying the pimps for, supposedly, was protection. Except that they weren't *getting* protection. So they opened up a little joint. On their own. I came on to cover it. Percentage deal. There were a few rough spots, but we finally got it running nice. Then this creep comes in, wants to turn a *hard* one, understand? Nobody wanted to play. I told him, move it on out—there's plenty of dungeons in town, they'll give you anything you want to buy. He goes into the usual 'fucking cunt' rap and I figure he's all done. But then he pulls a piece and tells everyone to face the wall. I heard the handcuffs and I thought I knew what was coming next. I spun off the wall and dropped him before he could crank one off. And *then* we find out he's a federal marshal. A kinky, sick, pervert of a federal marshal, but . . . Anyway, the lawyer I got, he made a deal. I keep quiet about what really happened, his widow gets a line-of-duty pension. And he's got three kids. That's nice, I tell him. But I'm not sitting for a murder beef when it was self-defense. My lawyer, he points out that the whores I was body-guarding, they weren't exactly my sisters, and their stories were already pretty much what the government wanted. They could take a hooker's walkaway on the pross stuff . . . or accessory to murder, if they didn't play nice. Rolling over—now, *that* was something they were already used to. I didn't have a chance.

"And if I let it ride without a squawk, I'd get manslaughter—sixty to one eighty. That's months, honey. Even on a max-out, I'm gone in seven, eight years. Or I could take my chances with a jury. With my priors, and all those girls playing parrot for the feds . . . ah, it was no contest." She leaned forward, using her elbows to create the deep cleavage inmate wardrobe didn't otherwise permit. "Now tell me . . . why are you here?"

"We got an offer," Cross said quietly. "A job. Down south. Understand?"

"Sure."

"It's a bad job. We passed. But Uncle said we had to take it or take off. I'm . . . deciding. Anyway, they said, if we took the job, they'd spring you. Provided you went in on it."

"What's that mean, spring—?"

"Means you die in here, Tiger. On paper. You don't go over the wall, you walk out the gate. And disappear."

"Sounds too good to be—"

"Sure. That 'on paper' thing would probably turn out to be true enough, this job they're talking about."

"So why would you—?"

"We're going to do it or we're not. If we do it, you want in? Yes or no?"

"Yes."

"If we don't do it, we're leaving."

"America?"

"Whatever you want to call it. Doesn't matter. It's not *our* country. Never was. Not for any of us. Except for Fal. And they *took* it from him, from his people. If we go, we're going to close everything down. Buddha'll stay. He's got the papers on everything, all legit. And nobody'd want his baggage anyway."

"You mean So Long?"

"Yeah. And his kids. Fal, he'll stay too. He's not with us anyway. Ace won't leave either. He mostly works alone. And he's got a woman too—she's not a pro. It'd just be me, Rhino, and Princess. And you, if you want."

"Spell it out."

"If we go, we're not leaving them a lot to look at. We'll all be wanted anyway. This place doesn't look like much," Cross said, glancing around. "You could finish out your time here, walk out clean. Or you could throw in with us. . . ."

"And maybe die anyway."

"Sure."

"You still don't care, do you, Cross?"

"About what?"

"Whether you live or you die."

"No."

Tiger looked over each shoulder, slowly and deliberately. Breathed deeply. She took Cross's right hand, turned it over in hers, smiling when she saw the bull's-eye tattoo was gone. Then she leaned close and whispered: "I think I'd like to leave. No matter which way it has to be."

"I'll let you know," Cross replied, getting to his feet.

"I'm listening," Cross said to the short, stocky man seated across from him. The man's face was a Central American mixture. Indian of some kind? Mayan? Impossible to tell. Impossible to read, too. Cross decided on Mayan in his mind, matching a face he could see with a name he knew was meaningless, filing it for the future.

"What is it my people receive for what you want?" the man asked, his English clear and unaccented, only the phrasing revealing it was not his native language.

"We're . . . deciding," Cross replied. "Maybe—and I'm not promising this—maybe they get some help with what they're doing."

"What help could you—?"

"La Casa de Dolor. How many of your people are there now?"

"Ah. It is *la americana* you want."

Cross said nothing.

"Your reputation is known to us," the Mayan said. "You are mercenaries. Without politics. If you were paid to rescue this woman, you believe it would benefit our cause? And that we should assist you in some way because of this?"

"No?"

"No. *La americana* has focused national attention on our struggle. She is a symbol of all that is hated in the regime. Her 'trial' . . . a collection of military swine wearing black hoods to hide their cowardly faces. She did nothing for us while she was free in our country. Just another rich *gringa*. A tourist. But the regime made an error. They assumed she was part of an international movement. A scout for what was to come. So they used what they always use: pain and fear. And *we* are called the terrorists," he said softly.

"The guards," Cross probed gently, "they can't all be so loyal? Or so well paid that . . . ?"

"None is truly loyal to the regime," the Mayan said. "You should understand this. Our country, it is not like most others. Our people, they can be blond or black; we are all the children of our former conquerors, in some way. Except, perhaps, for my tribe . . . what remains of it. But we are not like those lunatics in Rwanda or Yugoslavia, killing for such reasons. Tribe means nothing to us. And we are not like your country either—we have no class structure based on race. On our streets, you might see an Indian, an African, and a European. And we are all one. All *quitasolanos*. The regime has no tribal loyalties to keep it in power—it rules by fear."

"That just makes it—"

"Of course," the Indian continued, as if Cross has not spoken, "there are bribes possible for . . . privileges. Some decent food, a smuggled-in letter from a loved one. But escape? No. The penalty would be death. Anyone who assisted us in such a fashion would be forced to join us. Forever. There could be no return. And the sheep never believe the wolf can be defeated."

"And . . . ?"

"And we would never trust a *puta*. A man who sells himself for money is no man."

"Sure," Cross said, neutral-voiced, ignoring the clear insult, "but there are real men inside that joint, right? *Your* men. And you want them out, yes?"

"Of course we would want them out. But that place is a fortress, in a remote area. We would have to commit too many of our forces."

"And . . . ?"

"Why do you say it like that?"

"Because there has to be more. You are . . . united, right? All as one. For honor, as you say. So, if it took a hundred men to rescue one, you would do it except for something else. I just want to know what that is."

"Ah. Very well, *hombre*, I will tell you. As you said, the guards, they are for sale . . . in little pieces. And one thing we have learned from them is this: Should there be any attempt to storm the prison, their orders are to execute every single inmate. Each guard has a sector. Before he is even to return fire, he must kill all the inmates assigned to him."

"All right. Then the woman would not survive the escape attempt either. But what would it be worth if the entire place disappeared?"

"Your meaning is not clear to me."

"La Casa de Dolor is a symbol, not just a prison."

"*Sí.*"

"And the death of a symbol is a powerful thing."

"That is true. But how would the people know of this . . . death? Most have never seen the prison. For them, it exists only in rumor, the frightened words of terrified children, passed along in whispers. Occasionally, someone is released. And we know the purpose of that. It is not mercy. It is to spread the word of fear among us."

"So what you might trade for is . . . that, right?"

"I do not follow—"

"The word. Fear is a weapon, just like a gun. It can be pointed, just like a gun. It can be fired, just like a gun. What would the radio transmitter be worth to you?"

"You mean the—?"

"Yes. Not for long . . . maybe fifteen minutes or so. But . . . enough, if you have a message for the whole country, yes?"

The Mayan hesitated, but even his impassive face could not disguise the possibilities that raged behind his eyes. "Yes," he finally said. "But how could you guarantee—?"

"Guarantee? We can't do that. But we can make it COD."

"I do not understand."

"I think you do. Your English is too perfect to have been learned from books. But never mind. You get your fifteen minutes in the broadcaster's booth and *then*, when your troops hear it on their own radios, *then* you join the assault."

"You are paid for such things?"

"Sure."

"What I do, I do for love of my country. You . . ."

"I don't have a country."

"Yes. That is what I have been told. I will return here and give you the answer."

"I heard about it," the sandy-haired man wearing kick-boxing gear said to Cross. He had a towel around his neck, watching various fighters work out. The sparring ring was empty except for those attending a man lying flat on his back.

"Meaning . . . ?"

"That the *federales* are thinking about pulling your license."

"We don't—"

"You don't . . . what? Pay off the cops? I wouldn't know about that. I know you never paid me. But I also remember you offered to, so, the way I see it, you must have done it before. Or even been *used* to it. That crew of yours, it's no secret you're not good citizens. And if anyone on the job here could have dropped you, they would, I guess."

"You and me—"

"—aren't friends," McNamara cut Cross off. "There's some things you've done, I'm glad you did them. And, depending on how some people looked at it, I guess it could be said that I've been of some . . . I don't know . . . help to you over the years. I like Princess. Hell, everyone he hasn't hospitalized likes Princess. He's just a big, friendly kid. I respect Rhino. Wasn't for you, I don't think he'd be anywhere *near* crime, not with his brains. Or he could hire out as a bouncer, cover a whole arena all by himself. I know Ace is a contract hitter. That's no secret. And it's not my problem, unless one of the hits happens in my sector, especially since he only seems to whack guys that don't belong on the street anyway. Buddha, he's a miserable little bastard, but even he could earn a good living with what he knows how to do. You're the only one, Cross. Only you. You're a criminal in your heart. I don't know what glue holds you guys together; but, whatever it is, the feds can break it, if that's what they want. That Red 71 joint of yours, the Double X bar, other stuff you got, they could find a way to close it up, make you go to ground. And they could find you wherever you reassemble. Except for you, it's easy enough to pick any one of the others out at a hundred yards."

"You know this guy?"

"The spook? Never met him. Probably doesn't even know his own name. But our department made it clear. *Real* clear. We fuck with this guy, the Senate fucks with our appropriations; it's *that* big. So, if they go after you, don't be coming around here with some lawyer whining about your civil rights. In Chicago, you don't have any."

"Nice."

"Ah, gee. Next thing, you'll be telling me you're a taxpayer."

"I didn't come here for sympathy," Cross said.

"What *did* you come for, then?"

"Threat assessment."

"You tell me," Cross said to the assembled crew. "This isn't a tactical decision, so it's up to everyone."

"We're still a . . ." Rhino couldn't finish the sentence, letting his words drift off into the gloom.

"Here's the way I see it, okay?" Cross said. "We have to do this job or we have to split up. Whoever this spook is, he's got enough horsepower to make it impossible for us to operate in Chicago."

"You sure, bro?" Ace asked.

"Got it right from Mac's mouth," Cross confirmed. "Looks like they could stop us from operating, period."

"You mean—?" Buddha spoke up.

"Nah. Why kill us? We wouldn't go easy, and it wouldn't be quiet. They'd just bust our operation wherever we set up. We couldn't work together."

"Maybe it's time," Rhino said quietly.

"I ain't going nowhere. Sweet home Chicago," Ace said.

"You wouldn't have to," Cross said. "It's the crew that has to go. Understand?"

"Look, boss. You saying, if everyone left, they'd *still* shut down the Double X? Because, you know, I mean, I'm on the papers and—"

"Buddha, I don't know. I can't swear to it. My best guess is, you run it like a strip joint, the way we did, you're going to have to bring in muscle to keep the wolves away. But if you want to try, go for it. If that's the way it happens, we'll all still get our cut, wherever we are, right?"

Silence from Buddha.

"Right?" Ace asked.

"How fair is that?" Buddha wanted to know. "I mean, without the rest of us here, I'll be doing the work. I mean, all the work, isn't that true?"

"Sure," Cross said. "What we can do instead, we can just sell it, split the cash, and you use your piece to go into whatever you want to go into."

"Hey, I wasn't saying *that*. I was just—"

"—angling for a bigger slice, like always," Ace said sourly.

"I thought we were about money," Buddha replied. "What else you want to talk about?"

"I'm not doing it!" Princess shouted suddenly.

Every eye swiveled in his direction. For varying reasons, instability made every man nervous, and Princess was its volcanic personification.

"We're all together, right? I mean, we do stuff and everything. It's like Cross is always saying: It ain't *our* country, we just live here. So, if we live somewheres else, it don't make no difference. But we don't have to split up, do we? I mean, how *come?*"

"Cross just *said* why," Rhino spoke gently. "We . . . stick out too much if we're together."

"They started it," Princess hissed through grated teeth. Every man's spine went a bit colder, hearing the maniac child's muttered war cry.

"Princess . . ." Rhino reached out and put his hand on the cable-muscled forearm of his friend.

"No!" Princess jerked his arm away. "They *did* start it, right, Cross? We wasn't doing nothing to them!"

"You're right, Princess," Cross said, flat-voiced. "We didn't do anything to them. And we *can't* do anything to them. It's like punching a pillow—no matter how hard we hit them, there'd always be more of them. If we want to stay here, stay together, we have to play like Uncle wants."

"And *then* we get them, right?" Princess asked, his face as eager as a child's at Christmas. A child with a family.

"I don't know," Cross said. "I don't even know if we can. . . ."

"But you got a plan, right?" the huge child implored.

"I . . . might have. Just give me a few days to make some calls, think some things through. All right?

"Yes!" Princess high-fived Rhino.

"If we have to split up, and it looks like we do," Cross said to Rhino later, "you know we got to tranq him out. No way he's going to go quiet."

"He doesn't want to go," Rhino agreed.

"I know. But nobody else really gives a damn and—"

"I don't want to go either," Rhino said. "And neither does Ace."

"Ace would stay away. He—"

"I mean . . . go away from . . . us. I don't want to break up. Except for Buddha . . ."

"Sure."

"He probably can't wait for it to go down like that. Him and that So Long, they could take over the bar, make some money."

"I came up with Ace," Cross said. "And then you. I didn't meet Buddha or Fal until the fucking war. But there's more to Buddha than you think."

"Or less."

"Maybe they're the same," Cross said. "But I don't think he wants to split up either."

"We'll never know."

Cross took the last of his ritual three drags from his cigarette, said, "I think we might, brother. I think I know a way to do it. And without Buddha, it won't fly."

The alley behind the bar was a tiny pocket of silence in an uproar. The Friday-night combination—men with paychecks eager to drink them up and those without jobs drinking to dull that pain— was always a guarantee of a diversion if one was needed. Cross spoke softly to a man of about his own height and weight. But, unlike Cross's, this man's face was marked with more than the roadmap of his life. He was a Chickasaw Indian, his long black hair pulled straight back from his scalp and gathered tightly behind him.

"It's a real long shot."

"The full thermal will give us a chance at getting her—"

"I don't mean that. I mean getting out at all."

"I told you how that would work."

"Even if we could get to the area, clear the ground, and hold it, it's still shaky."

"Why? You know the score. Long as there's plenty of bang, it won't matter whether she comes out with us or not. A nice try is all they're looking for."

"We don't have any recon. For all we know, we could encounter hostiles before we ever got across the border."

"Sure. But it's not likely. You're going along the prospector's route. Bandits . . . sure. But not troops."

"The language—"

"I got it covered. At your end, anyway."

"A million in gold?"

"Post-assay, twenty-four K guaranteed. Half in hand before we leave."

"Sure. For everyone, right?"

"Right."

"There's no tontine in this, is there?"

"Who's Tontine?"

"Tontine is a kind of trust. A legal thing. Only you don't have to be legal to set one up. Just means the survivors get the share of anyone who doesn't make it back."

"What do you care? Even if *we* had one, it wouldn't cover you."

"I'll tell you why," Falcon said, his voice as unmenacing as a hovering butterfly. "I'm not going into anything with Buddha if he gets one dime extra for coming out alone."

"You think *any* of us would?" Cross laughed. "Truth is, me, Rhino, and Ace, we got one of those—what did you call it, 'tontine'?—things set up between us. Buddha's not in it. Never has been. The property's in his name, that's enough."

"Not Princess either?"

"What's the point? If Rhino's alive, he'll take care of him. If Princess is the only one left, what difference would it make if he had money? He'd only last a few hours before—"

"I have a family," Falcon interrupted.

"I didn't know."

"Not a wife. Not children. A family. A tribe. My brothers and sisters. Same as you all—"

"We're a crew," Cross said sharply. "Forget that 'family' stuff. This is about getting paid. We're professionals. This kind of job, we get paid up front. You in or out?"

"I'm always out," Falcon said. "My whole family is always out. So, on this one, count me in."

Cross nodded.

"As soon as the money's paid," Falcon said, disappearing into the alley's shadows.

"You said you could get some things into there," Cross reminded the Mayan.

"I did not say it was a certainty. It is . . . possible. It has happened. But it would be *carefully* inspected even if we could get it in. The punishment for smuggling food to a prisoner, or a letter—anything at all—it would be severe. Still, some of the guards take the risk. Who would inform on them, anyway? Another of their same"—the Mayan made a face of pure disgust—"kind. But to smuggle in a weapon, to assist in an escape, ah, then death would be guaranteed. And a long time coming. So they would test it unless it was impossible to be a weapon or a communication device."

"A pill. A lousy pill. A big fat vitamin pill. And they could make her swallow it right in front of them."

"If it was a *solid* pill, not a capsule. Yes. I think that could be done. But she might refuse the pill. Even if they told her it was from her father, she might not trust them."

"So they force it down her throat," Cross said evenly. "Odds are it wouldn't be the first time they did that."

"That is true," the Mayan said. "Even among vermin, they would be despised. I will make inquiries. And I will have your answer soon."

"Fal says he's in, if we decide to go that way," Cross told the crew.

"For how much?" Buddha asked instantly.

"One mil. Same as everyone."

"That leaves one-point-five," Buddha pointed out, his voice cold.

"With the plan I got in mind, that might not even be enough for expenses," Cross told him. "It's a million apiece. And we go in splits."

"Splits?" Ace said, raising an eyebrow.

"Yeah. You, Fal, and Princess go over the border. Me, Rhino, and Tiger go into the airport."

"What about me, boss?" Buddha asked.

"On this one, you start on your own," Cross said. "But you don't come back alone, Buddha. Understand?"

"No."

"You will."

"Tiger's gonna be in on this, don't she get a share?"

"Her share is getting *out*."

"How come I don't get to go with Rhino?" Princess demanded, a petulant tone in his voice.

"Because you're working . . . *undercover*," Cross told him.

"Oh, man! For real? Cool!" Princess exclaimed, beside himself with excitement.

Cross caught a hard look from Rhino.

"Princess, I mean *real* undercover, understand? No makeup, no earrings, no costumes, no . . . nothing, okay? You got to look like a *campesino*."

"Sure. I can—"

"And you have to speak only Spanish," Cross said, his tone final.

"I don't know any—"

"Yes, you do," Rhino said. Softly and sadly. "I know it's not something you want to think about, but you heard it enough when they had you . . ."

Princess sat down against the wall of the back room and started to cry like a newly orphaned child.

"I don't know the whole story," Rhino told Cross later. "They captured him when he was real young . . . but he never talks about it. He knew English when they took him. Then they trained him for cage-fighting. That's where he was when we found him, remember?"

"I remember when *you* found him. I still don't know why we—"

"Yeah, you do. He's one of us. He hates them. He hates them *all*."

"Princess doesn't—"

"He does, Cross. And you know it. I figure, they had to kill his people when they took him. He never mentions it. Never heard him say any word that sounds like . . . 'parent.' So it probably happened right in front of him. Maybe he wouldn't speak Spanish because it would be like admitting he was one of those . . . who took him. But you're right. He heard it. For years and years."

"He's been around plenty of Latinos. He never copped an attitude, never showed any—"

"He's a kid, Cross. A giant kid. But he's not a moron. He knows the people who snatched him, they're not the same as anyone who speaks Spanish, all right? Remember how he was in that cage? Always trying to get his opponent to join forces with him, make a break for it? How he'd never hit first, the other one always had to start it? He was famous for it. That's why he dresses like that. Other people have to start it. And he *wants* them to."

"Fal and Ace are real steady hands," Cross said. "But if Princess decides to . . ."

Rhino shrugged his huge shoulders. "What do you want me to tell you? He . . . might. I'll talk to him, do the best I can. But with Princess, there's a lot of little tripwires in his head. And if someone stumbles over one of them . . ."

"Sure I can fly one, Boss," Buddha said, confidently. "Planes are like cars. You can drive one, you can drive another."

"You won't get much practice time in," Cross warned him. "And we're not buying it either—just renting it."

"What kinda crazy . . . ?"

"Think about it for a damn minute. It would cost us more than our whole budget just to buy it. They take the chance you won't come back, but you sure as hell can't just run away with it . . . They're all flyboys—they'd spot it if it showed up anywhere in the world. Remember who we'd be renting it from. Besides, they have to make all those mods I told you about."

"Sure. But if I'm gonna take out *both* targets I need the cannons *and* the bombs."

"You can keep them. And the full rocket pod—that's the part we got to modify, remember? But we have to lose the Sidewinders."

"Chief, if I encounter any hostiles up there, I don't have no air-to-air, I'm just a sitting duck."

"The entire attack radius of that thing is less than a hundred miles, Buddha. That's the way they're made. You pop up, take out target one, spin around, target two, eject the pod and drop, scoop the others, and scream back across the border. They'll never even know you were there. And the Quitasol Air Force, they don't know anything about combat. Hell, way I got it, they don't have one single pilot. All they do is send up one of those foreign 'instructors' to strafe civilians every once in a while."

"But . . ."

"There is no fucking room for the air-to-airs, Buddha. Not if we're gonna evac four people. We have to lose weight up front to pick up behind. No choice. No chance. In or out?"

"Boss . . ."

Cross was silent, his eyes focused somewhere past Buddha. *Through* me, Buddha thought. And finally said: "I'm in."

"Why?" Cross asked Ace, the two of them sitting alone in the back room of Red 71.

"The money."

"You make money here."

"I do that. I earned my name. Ace. But you know what, brother? I'm the original Ghetto Blaster. You understand what I'm saying? Sure, I get paid. But I work local. Close to home. Ten large, that would be a nice price for one job. And now . . . you got plenty of those little baby gangsta wannabe motherfucking punks take someone out for nothing, just to 'blood in,' see? I ain't no long-distance man like Fal. I got to be close. I'm good, no question. But you know what *that* means, where we come from. Good as my last one. That's all. Here's what I got for all these years: I got a little crib, don't have to live in no Project again, ever. Got a nice ride. Case money, a few K deep, that's all. A piece of"—the handsome black man waved his hand as if to encompass his surroundings—"this. I *also* got kids I got to feed. I don't mean just food either. I got plans for my kids. College, the whole thing. They don't know what I do, and they ain't *gonna* know. I don't even let them go to school in they neighborhoods. So, bottom line, I got a big nut to cover. And I do cover it, but I got to hustle. You know my business. You can't be jumping at any job they throw your way, can't be too eager. One slip and I'm in Stateville for fucking ever. Death Row or on the yard, don't make no difference. I wouldn't be coming out."

"We'd—"

"That's it, right there," Ace said gently. "You'd come for me, that happened. Don't say you wouldn't, brother. Save that trick for someone who wasn't there with you from jump. Yeah. We've been back-to-back since we first locked together. You'd *try*, right? Juice it or blast it, you'd try and spring me. Everyone would, except that little bastard Buddha. You think I don't know that, you must think I'm stupid. Or maybe you think I'm stupid 'cause I *do*. I don't care. So you know what? If you all do this, I got to do it too. 'Cause if you have to leave Chicago, the whole crew, then you're taking my back away from me."

"You can't count on—"

"—what? I know what I can count on. And if I'm wrong, I pay what it costs. That's the way the world works, right, brother? Besides, my share, we make this work, I'm done. I can walk away. No more of this life. I'll have enough, I play it right, to last me until my kids are old enough to visit me in some nursing home."

"You don't have any training for this kind of thing, Ace. No experience."

"You think a jungle's different 'cause it be green instead of concrete? I may not know what kind of motherfucking snakes and all they got down there. But I know this. Know it for sure. Anyone can die. And I can make them dead. What else I need to know?"

"You'd be with Princess and Fal. If Princess loses it, you know what that means. Fal could fade into the brush. He'd have a chance. You can't carjack a ride out, brother. If the wheels come off, you're done."

"Been that way since we first locked together. Nothing changes. We ain't about change. We about not *being* changed. I'm down."

"It's not enough," Cross told the chauffeur.

"Seven and a half million? In fucking *gold*? And *that's* not enough, that's what you're telling me?"

Cross regarded the agent with a calmness the other man had only seen once before. In Tibet. Radiating from a man so ancient as to have defied the laws of nature with the mere fact of his continued life. But that man, he was a mystic. A man of such pure peace that he changed the warlike spirits of the conquerors. Or so it was said.

"What I'm telling you," Cross said, "is that we're not the fucking A-Team, okay? We have a deal. We do this job. We get paid. And part of that pay is, you go away. And you stay away. You don't come back playing the same tune. We do this, and you leave us be. In Chicago. Together. Like we are now."

"You expect the federal government to issue a license to—"

"I expect the federal government to do what it always does— look out for itself."

"Which means . . . what?"

Cross wiped his forehead, the bull's-eye tattoo clear in the dim light. "You ever wonder how come we—our crew, I mean—how come we never hooked up with any of those psycho groups? You know, the Nazis or the skinheads or the militia or the Klan or whatever else you got. There's plenty of money there, if you know where to look."

"Uh, for one thing, seems like you might have a few . . . ineligibles, right? Ace, Falcon, even Buddha—they wouldn't pass the DNA test."

"So you're saying they wouldn't want us, right?"

"Right."

"But if I walked in there alone. Or even with Princess and Rhino—Princess without his costumes—what then?"

"Well . . . sure. Hell, thank God they *don't* have anyone like—"

"That's what I'm telling you," Cross said softly. "*Trying* to tell you, anyway, if you'll just listen a little bit. If we do this, we're going to try and do it right. Which means, come back alive and get the other half of our money. And spend it too. So, I was trying to think to myself, how can we be sure you won't come back again someday? Maybe another little job Uncle wants done. And the same thing: We don't do it, you bust us up, just like you're gonna do this time. What could we do to keep you from doing that?"

"You have my—"

Cross laughed. It sounded like a heavy foot stepping on dry twigs. "I don't want your 'word,' pal. It isn't worth anything. See, I know you. You don't know me, but I know you. I seen your kind before. You're a patriot. You don't give a good goddamn who's in the White House, it's America you serve, huh?"

"That's right."

Good. So here's what I want you to tell your . . . people, or whatever you call them. We take this job, and we get back . . . or some of us get back, whatever . . . and you come to us again with this same squeeze, you know what happens?"

"What?" the agent asked, his tone just this side of a challenge.

"We're gonna kick it off," Cross said, his voice bloodless. "Race war. We've got stuff stashed all over the country. And we know how to do it. And you *know* we know. We're not a bunch of hand-job geeks reading little red books. We're professionals. And we got black covered as well as white. We start it off, it's gonna make Oklahoma City look like a cherry bomb in a mailbox. And we know the right notes to leave; the right calls to make to the media; the right idiots to step up and make noise. They always had the scenario, but they never had the skills. They don't have the tech-nology, and they don't have the brains to use it if they could get it. They give interviews. You fuck with us again, we're all going to be little play-Nazis for a couple of weeks. And when we're done, it's gonna take Uncle years to put out the flames."

"You're . . . insane."

"Sure. A stone psychopath. Check my records."

"You'd burn down a whole country just to—?"

"Survive? Be left the fuck alone? Oh yes. I fucking *promise* you. It's not *our* country. Never was. We're better off in wartime any-way, you don't let us live in peace. So go tell your pals that. Tell them the truth. Get your shrinks to do one of their little 'profiles,' ask *them* if they may think we'll do it.

"*That's* what I want. Besides the money. Never to see you or anyone like you ever again in life. Fair enough?"

"We were never going to . . ."

"Yes or no?"

"Yes."

The black van was unremarkable except for the heavy grates of steel mesh covering every window. A closer look might have revealed other indications that the van was meant to hold cap-tives, but the deserted two-lane blacktop wasn't likely to draw observers. The van proceeded at just over the speed limit, negotiating the gently curving road with grace, yielding whenever a vehicle behind it indicated a desire to pass.

The van rolled along, covering ground. Inside, two beefy men in gray prison-guard uniforms sat in the front seat. They spoke little.

After another hour had passed, the passenger said to the driver, "Seems like a waste of all that meat."

"We got our orders."

"Sure. But it ain't what the orders said, it's what they *didn't* say; you with me on that?"

"No, Homer. I'm not with you on that. In fact, I don't understand a word that comes out of your mouth."

Yeah? Okay, maybe you can follow this, all right? That bitch we got in back—when's the last time you saw a piece of ass that fine?"

"What difference does that make?"

"To me? Don't make any, I guess. I was just thinking. You know, about this job. I mean, we got nothing but little lines on a map. We drive until we find where they connect up, then we walk her over there and just drive away. And we're supposed to leave her cuffed too. Right where we drop her."

"So?"

"So that's supposed to mean she's still locked up, get it? So it's legal and all. She was never out of federal custody, understand what I'm saying?"

"So?"

"Fuck, is that the only word you know? Do the math, stupid. Whatever this is, it ain't kosher."

"No shit?"

"Yeah, you're a wise motherfucker, aren't you? I'm trying to draw you a picture here, but you ain't looking. This broad, whatever's gonna happen once we drop her off, she *sure* ain't gonna say anything about us, you follow what I'm saying?"

"No."

"All right, you stupid bastard. I'm done playing around with you. The way I figured it, we could have some fun once we drop her off. You been driving like a robot, got our ETA programmed right in," he said, nodding his head at the dash-mounted GSP system, which displayed a grid with a blinking green cursor showing their actual whereabouts and a red star showing their destination. "You speed it up a little bit, we get there *sooner*, see what I mean? That gives us a little extra time. With that hunk of stuff back there. Handcuffed. You think we'd ever have a better chance?"

"You're a sick bastard," the driver said quietly.

"A disgrace to the uniform?" The passenger laughed. "Man, you think the *real* cops look at us as anything but dog shit? Prison guard . . . that's lower than convict in their eyes. This ain't no military operation, *Sarge*," he sneered, hitting the last word with heavy sarcasm.

"Maybe not to you, punk," the driver said. "We've got orders. We follow orders. That's the way it's done."

"Yeah? Well, *you* do what *you* want. Me, I'm gonna go back there and see if that bitch wants to use that big mouth of hers for anything but complaining."

The driver kept staring straight ahead through the windshield; his hands gripped the steering wheel a bit tighter perhaps, but otherwise unchanged.

The passenger detached his shoulder belt, slipped out of his bucket seat, and walked down the aisle to the back of the van, where a woman sat in the last seat, anchored by ankle chains, hands cuffed to a belt around her waist.

"It's a long ride we got to go yet," the guard said.

The woman did not respond.

"You, uh, want a cigarette or something?"

The woman stared out the window.

"I'm *talking* to you, bitch!" the guard snarled, grabbing a fistful of the woman's thick hair and yanking it hard in his direction.

Her eyes were a strange shade, he thought, a kind of yellow-gray. He didn't like looking at them anyway, he thought, dropping his gaze to her breasts as they strained against the once-white sweatshirt she wore.

"No reason why you and me can't be . . . friends," he said softly. "You know the deal—I figure they must have told you. We drop you off, leave you chained to a tree. Now, maybe somebody's coming. Maybe not. But I guess you figure they are, or you wouldn't be so relaxed." He reached out with one hand and cupped her breast, bouncing it gently. "You grow these yourself, or did you buy them?" he asked.

The woman looked somewhere else, her mouth flat and grim.

"We got *plenty* of time," the guard said. "All I want is a few minutes. You give me that, I give you a real nice ride, you understand?"

The woman didn't reply.

The guard slapped her viciously. A dot of blood bubbled in the corner of her mouth. The guard leaned close to her ear. "I can do that. Or a lot more. Anytime I want. Nobody's gonna hear you scream. Or maybe I could . . . give you that cigarette you turned down before. Lit. Right on top of one of those big boobs of yours. You like *that* idea, cunt?"

"Did Riselle like it?" the woman asked, her voice as calm as a person asking directions.

The guard punched her just under one breast. Smiled when her face instantly lost color. "The next one, maybe you're gonna puke all over yourself. You fucking bitches think you can tease a man all day long, flash some tit, get my nose open, and nothing happens? Let me tell you something, cunt. *All* of those sluts, they wanted it. Or they traded for it. Women are all whores anyway. It's just a question of the price. You want a lot of pain, just keep it up. I got all the time in the world. Now, what's it's gonna be, whore?" he asked, his tongue touching the woman's ear. She whipped her face around so quickly into a head butt that the guard was aware of nothing but a sickening crunch against his temple. He staggered backward, dazed. Held his feet for a second or two, then collapsed in the aisle.

The guard got to one knee, shook his head to clear it. "This is gonna be fun," he said, reaching for his canister of mace.

The van pulled off the two-lane blacktop onto a gravel road. Followed it for 2.87 miles and turned left into a dirt path. The driver watched the digital odometer and the satellite tracking system carefully, nodding to himself as he spotted a clearing just ahead as the cursor and destination icons merged. He brought the van to a stop. "I'll take her out," he said to the passenger, who lay half slumped in his seat, face bloody, uniform pants stained.

The driver went to the back. The woman's face was battered, one eye fully closed. The once-white sweatshirt had been cut off her body with a knife. It lay in shreds around her waist. "Jesus Christ!" the driver said, kneeling to unlock the ankle chains. "I got a medical kit in front. Just wait till I—"

"Going *now*," Tiger mumbled to him.

"Sure, okay. Can you walk?"

"Yes," the woman grunted.

"Lean on me," the driver said, slowly moving toward the rear of the van. He threw a series of switches. The doors hissed open and a set of steps automatically descended. "You want me to lift—?"

"I said I can walk," the woman snarled. She took a step and then toppled forward. If the driver had not caught her, she would have hit the ground face-first. The driver half-dragged, half-carried her to a sitting position at the base of a tree stump. "Lady, I'm sorry," he said. "I got my orders. Just drive until we got here. I didn't know that freak Homer was gonna—"

The driver stopped talking when he saw the two men bracketing him. Both wearing ski masks, one pointing a double-barreled sawed-off shotgun, the other a heavy blue steel semi-automatic pistol. "Turn around," the man with the pistol said. The driver never considered reaching for his holstered weapon.

"Where's the other one?"

"In the van," the driver said. "Front seat. I didn't—"

"Shut up," the man with the pistol said softly. Then the driver heard him speak to the woman. "One or both?" is all he said.

"Not him. Just the other one," the woman answered, her voice thick with clotted blood.

"So the one in the van, he *started* it, huh?" the man with the pistol said, much louder than necessary for the woman to hear.

"Yes!" she answered, a moan with steel still in its core.

The driver heard noises behind him. He couldn't understand them—knew they were human, but not like any human sounds he'd heard—even with a decade behind bars for reference. He heard something crash through the brush toward the van. Heard the door torn open. Heard a body being dragged out. Heard "You started it!" screamed by the voice of a deranged maniac. Heard the unmistakable sound of something unyielding being rammed into human flesh. Over and over and over. His knees buckled but he held himself firm. Just like the Army, he told himself. I got my orders.

The driver heard the snap of bone . . . bone too large to be snapped by human hands. A thin scream escaped the lips of the other guard. Then he was silent. But the flesh-pounding assault continued—a wall of dull-red noise.

"Get back in the van," the man with the pistol said. "Don't turn around. You were transporting her to Carver. There was a huge tree limb across the road. You stopped. The other guy got out. That was the last time you saw him. Somebody slipped little plugs into your nose. When you woke up, the woman was gone too. Call HQ. Report in."

"I don't—" the guard started to say, but a giant hand closed around his carotid artery. He felt something inserted into his nostrils just before he lost consciousness.

When he awoke, he was alone in the van, parked alongside the two-lane blacktop, a mile or so before where he had originally turned off. A tree limb across the road blocked his path.

He called HQ.

Rhino was crouched over Tiger, who lay in the back seat of the shark car. "She'll be all right," he said. "Maybe a slight concussion. The cheekbone's probably fractured. And she lost a couple of teeth. No internals, no wounds."

"He started it," Princess mumbled, looking down.

"He did, brother," Cross said soothingly. "You did right. Easy now, okay?"

Ace sat between Cross and Princess, shaking his head. "We was gonna do the fucking guard anyway, right? I mean, that's what the feds paid us for."

"Yeah," Cross said quietly. "The weasel had about a hundred sexual-abuse complaints against him. About two dozen of the women were going to testify. This way, he gets himself killed, line-of-duty, all that. Must have been an escape attempt gone wrong . . . 'cause Tiger got killed too. Everybody's happy."

"Except he—"

"I know. It's on me. I fucked it up. Never thought he'd try anything in a moving vehicle, with a live witness and all. Tiger, I'm . . ."

The woman waved Cross's words away, her eyes starting to focus.

"How the girls gonna be happy, man?" Ace asked. "Their lawsuit just got killed too."

"They're amateurs," Cross said. "For them, revenge would be better than money."

"*I'm* a pro," Tiger said softly. "And you couldn't pay me enough money to let that . . . thing live another day."

"Quitasol means 'parasol' in Spanish," Cross told the assembled crew. "It's a tiny little place. Sits in a triangle, at the bottom, like it was covered by the others. Guatemala to the north, Honduras below, El Salvador to the west. Nearest jump-away is Belize. It's right on the water. And they have commercial flights to Miami and Jamaica too, gives us a lot of options."

"How much room will you need?" Falcon asked Buddha.

"I can get down pretty much on a dime. But getting *off*, at least a hundred meters . . . and that's only if there's a pretty low tree line direct ahead."

"There is no way to ensure enough time," Falcon responded. "We have to reach the zone, set up camp, and then start to work. It may take us . . . I don't know, perhaps weeks. We can't use power tools, and . . ."

"It's mostly flatland," Cross said. "Solid rock."

"And you know this from . . . ?"

"A native. One that wants this to work. One that knows if you can't clear the area Buddha never gets the signal to come in."

"Ah."

"And one who knows there isn't that much time."

"That leaves you, me, and Tiger to exit once we—"

"I know," Cross told Rhino. "And we're going to have to drive out. The place should be in turmoil. You know what it's like where nobody knows where they stand. Like a goddamn prison riot. People use the chance to settle old scores, maybe. And there'll be looting and burning and whatever. But the military, it's not gonna try and stop people from *leaving*. More people, that's the last thing they need. And we won't be the only ones heading for the border."

"Jamaica or Miami, it won't make any difference," Rhino said softly. "If I get on a plane, everyone'll remember."

"You're not going to Jamaica unless things go wrong," Cross told him. "That's just a backup. All you have to do in Miami is get *off* a plane. Then you disappear. Only you never leave the airport. I got a Lear standing by."

"I'll have to wait to RDV with Buddha, then?"

"You want Princess to make it back to Chicago from Miami on his own?" Cross asked.

"All right," the monster-man agreed, knowing the logic of the crew chief to be coldly correct, as always.

"Falcon's going straight across to Oklahoma. He's got his own people there. Ace is going to drive right up the highway. He's already got relatives in Belle Glade who'll cover for him, say he was there all the time."

"Is Tiger gonna be okay?" Princess asked. "She didn't look so good before."

"Better not let *her* hear you say that," Cross warned him. "Besides, that was almost three weeks ago, and she's been rehabbing perfectly. She even has her stripes back."

"I don't like the idea of moving around unstrapped," Ace said. "It's not natural."

"You won't be in enemy territory and—" Rhino started to say.

"And you ain't never been a nigger in the South," Ace finished his sentence.

"Or an Indian, anywhere," Falcon added.

"None of us can carry," Cross said. "We have to play it meek and mild until we get back home—I mean, to this place. Sure, you're more likely to get pulled over by some Klansman with a badge; but, without a weapon in the car, no drugs, no nothing, there won't be a lot they can do. Why bother with a flake job if they don't know you? And if they *do* try that, it just means a little time Inside until the rest of us can do what we need to do. We'll have enough money to grease anything that happens . . . except icing a cop. All right?"

A full minute of silence was followed by Ace's "All right" in response. Falcon said nothing. But he had not protested in the first place, merely supported the truth of Ace's comments.

"Okay. Everybody has their route in. Everybody has their route out. Everybody has their money. We all have the plan. Buddha gets his go from Fal, we get ours when Buddha makes his first pass."

"You sure I'm gonna be able to make this . . . rental, boss?"

"Already set," Cross assured him. "And don't be bargaining with them either. I told you the price—hand it over. You act like a decent guy, they might even give you some practice time, get familiar with it."

"This time, everybody's going," Buddha said. "If we don't come . . ."

"Then we'll be in the same place we'd be if we didn't agree to this deal."

"Huh?"

"Not here," Cross said.

"Man, I thought Chi-Town summers got ugly," Ace groused, mopping his forehead with a camouflage handkerchief. "This place *stays* humid."

"It's a rain forest," Falcon told him. "We're actually under a canopy. It's just about always raining overhead, because the moisture gets trapped in the overgrowth."

"Whatever. It sucks."

"Hey, come on, guys. This is fun, right?" Princess smiled. "We're on a mission and everything."

Falcon and Ace exchanged looks but kept their silence. As they approached yet another narrow trail, they fell into the positions Falcon had mapped out for them before they started their march—Falcon walking point, a modified M-16 carried in his right hand; Princess next, hauling a rucksack that weighed over two hundred pounds without apparent effort, constantly running up on Falcon in his eagerness to get to their destination. Ace brought up the rear, walking drag, his scattergun on a rawhide sling around his neck and his senses on full alert. They were on the fourth day of their march. As they entered a clearing, Falcon held up his hand, signaling for silence. His eyes swept the area. The only sounds were those of insects and birds. Falcon's innate sensors probed even as his eyes did, but there was no sign of humans. He was about to signal the others to move on when he finally spotted confirmation of what his internals had been screaming—a filter-tipped cigarette butt almost completely ground into the soil. Almost. Falcon walked silently over to it and unearthed it with his knife as carefully as if it were a prized artifact from an ancient civilization. Then he motioned the others to remain where they were and disappeared. In another half-hour, he was ready to report.

"At least four men, carrying light, maybe three, four hours ahead of us."

"Are they the bad guys?" Princess asked.

"In the brush, everyone's the bad guys," Fal told him. "But these . . . I don't think they got anything to do with us. According to the map, we're on course to cross a traders' road in about four klicks. What I think we've got here is a bunch of bandits."

"They gonna do a Jesse James on a stagecoach or what?" Ace asked.

"Something like that. Best guess is they're going to deploy along the sides of the traders' route and just take tolls."

"Or lives," Ace replied.

"Maybe. Doesn't really matter. I can already see where they left a clear trail. It'll be easy enough to follow at a distance, make sure we cross at a different spot."

"So we—?"

"Wait," Falcon said.

The ancient truck labored to climb the slight grade in the one-lane dirt road, hauling its precariously tied down flatbed cargo of green bananas. Falcon watched impassively, invisible. He hand-signaled to Princess and Ace to keep their distance. It was a good quarter-mile ahead of where Falcon had calculated the bandit crew would set up its roadblock, but his sensors picked up human activity on the other side of the road. Had he been alone, Falcon would have vanished. Encumbered as he was, he decided to remain still and see what developed.

It wasn't long in coming. A chubby man stepped into the road, holding what looked like an old British Enfield. He leveled the rifle at the truck's cab as another man, younger and leaner, hopped on the running board brandishing a machete. The truck stopped. Three other men emerged from the brush, surrounding the driver, who looked as weatherbeaten as his truck. And older.

Falcon didn't need to understand Spanish to decode the situation. The bandits didn't want bananas, they wanted money. And the old man either had none, or wasn't handing it over. Falcon watched dispassionately as the chubby one chopped at the old man's face with the butt of his rifle, drawing blood. Then he felt breath against the side of the face and shuddered even before he heard Princess whisper:

"Why are they hurting the old man?"

"They want his money. Ssssh."

"They can't—"

"Yes, they fucking *can*," Falcon hissed. "They're thieves. Just like us. We have to be *quiet*, understand? Our mission is on the other side, not here."

Princess lapsed into silence. The ugly tableau continued to play out, with one after another of the bandits kicking or slapping the old man. But then the game changed as the young man with the machete emerged from the far side of the truck, his hand twisted deep into the long black hair of a young girl. He threw the girl to the ground. She looked about twelve years old. The chubby man laughed and reached for the girl. She clawed at his face. He punched her sharply in the mouth and she collapsed in the road. The old man rushed to her side, hovering protectively over her body.

The chubby man handed his rifle to another of the bandits and stepped toward the girl, unbuttoning his pants. Princess screamed something incoherent and burst from cover, charging straight at the bandits. Falcon said "Fuck!" under his breath and put a bullet into the head of the man holding the rifle. The chubby man barked an order. One of the bandits leveled a pistol at the onrushing Princess even as Falcon's bullet took out his left eye. The chubby man was scrambling to reach the rifle lying on the road when a shotgun blast took him from behind, shredding his shirt and his lungs. The two remaining bandits dashed for the safety of the trees, but Falcon's next shot dropped one of them. And by then, Princess had the lone survivor in his hands. He didn't remain a survivor for long.

Years later, the little girl named her first child Espectro. And when he was old enough to understand, his mother explained that he was named for the ghost who had saved her from horror.

"They started it," Princess sulked as Falcon prodded him from behind, urging more speed.

"Gunfire brings questions," Falcon told him. "You fucked up, plain and simple. You pull a stunt like that while we're in place and—"

"My man ain't gonna do any such thing," Ace said soothingly, patting Princess on his massive shoulder. "This time we was just laying up, okay? But once we get across the border, we gonna be *undercover*, remember? You wouldn't blow our cover, right, brother?"

"No way!" Princess promised, his voice restored to its usual childish tone. Falcon wondered if his eyes were still purple—the unhuman color they turned every time the child lost control.

Seventeen hours later, they crossed the border.

The stream was a bare trickle as it meandered through a massive rock formation. Yet it was there that those *locos* from Dios-knows-where had set up their gold-panning operation. El Monstruo, the one with the impossible muscles, he was always working: chopping at the rock with a pickax, hammering heavy steel wedges deep into crevices so that the streambed could be widened . . . foolishness that would never repay him for all his effort. El Indio, ah, that one would come and go, vanishing as a spirit into and out of the surrounding trees. Occasionally, he would be seen with some sort of strange-looking telescope device in his hands. El Negrito, he worked with a machete like a machine. So skinny, yet so strong, working as if he were going to clear the jungle away all by himself.

So said the watchers. And there were many, for this remote part of Quitasol attracted those who preferred the risk and hardship of the brush to the certain poverty of working in one of the open-pit mines. The mines had the gold, it was said, but none for the people. In the mountains, the people could have the gold . . . if it could be found. Not gold ore, for digging was impossible. It was not a job for the hands—only high explosives and heavy machinery could accomplish such a task. But there was gold in the riverbeds, this was known. And it could be panned, strained, sifted . . . and, perhaps, revealed. So they were all there for the same reason.

The three men working that narrow stream were not talkative.

Only the huge one spoke at all, and that was to menace anyone who came close—drawing a line in the dirt with his digging
tool and daring others to cross it, telling them they had better
not "start it" as if he were a child instead of a grown man. Surely
it was not that the fools had discovered something so valuable.
Still, one of the watchers said, perhaps they had things of
value *with* them. Tools. Even machinery, maybe. Or a radio. It
could not hurt to look, yes? And even crazy men had to sleep
sometime.

The men discussed it among themselves. Quietly, for it was a matter of great seriousness. None of them would even consider
approaching the huge one without a weapon. His body appeared
to have been carved from stone, and even a blade might prove
useless against such a creature. Between the watchers, who were
all from the same village, they had a single rifle, and four car-
tridges. And there were three men in the camp by the rocks. Even
if they could kill them all, would the trade be worth it? What if the
locos had no firearms? With only one bullet left, the villagers
would be helpless. And, remember, El Indio, he was no stranger
to the darkness. Had he not simply *appeared* in the distance one
evening, as if out of the night itself? No, this was a bad plan. Best
to leave them in peace.

"Could it hurt to talk to them?" one of the youngest said. "Perhaps we could learn more about them. Perhaps they could be
frightened off?"

The oldest among them laughed aloud. "*You* go, Carlito. I will
tell your widow all about it when we return."

The young man said the old man had lost his *cojones*. The old
man laughed more. "El Diablo himself would not frighten such
men. If you live long enough, this is something you too will
understand."

Eventually, they all went to sleep, the matter unresolved.

In the morning, they found Carlito's body, already stiffening, the piano wire pulled so deeply into his neck that they could not determine the cause of death until they examined him closely.

The men broke camp within an hour. The spirits were wild in that area, they told themselves. But nobody challenged the old man when he laughed at that too.

"Check it again," Cross told Tiger, pointing to a computer printout in her lap. She had gained weight in the past weeks. And her hair was lustrous again, its stripes restored.

"These are square names," she said. "I can make two—no, three—from the pictures, but that's about all I could swear to."

"I can enhance the images," Rhino squeaked from the converted park bench he used as a chair, sitting before a screen nearly as large as a home-entertainment center.

Tiger got to her feet with a grace that justified her name and stood behind Rhino, one hand on his shoulder. "I can't believe you already got mug shots to look so good," she said.

"They use better cameras now," Cross told her. "And these aren't copies—you're looking at exactly what the feds have."

"But if they're not copies—?"

"We're on-line," Rhino said. "Inside their house."

"Oh."

"They don't have very good security," Cross said dryly. "But they sure keep great records."

"I know. I couldn't believe I was . . . dead. I mean, to see it, right there, it was . . . weird."

"Beats the crap out of your picture on the wall in the post office."

"It does, for a fact. Oh . . . look!"

The face on the screen sharpened right before her eyes, digitizing into an image as clear as a live TV camera could produce.

"That's her," Tiger said. "Martha Farmington, huh? Guess that's a bit short of the exotic image she needed."

"You knew her as—?"

"Tanya," Tiger yawned. "What else? It was either Tanya or Tammy or Candy or Crystal or something like that for all of them. You know how it works."

"Work. That's the key word. We need to get them across the border, and not kidnap them. They have to be greedy enough to risk it."

"Those ho's *love* scratch, baby. That's what they played for. Wouldn't have hired me to bodyguard them if they weren't looking to up the take."

"They rolled quick enough."

"In a second," Tiger agreed. "But we weren't sisters. I wasn't surprised."

"Four is all you can be sure of? Out of that whole batch?"

"Yep. *Sure* sure, I mean. Even looking at all the files from the ones who got busted with me, I can't swear to any more than that. It isn't like we spent a lot of time doing girly stuff together. I was muscle, they were pussy. Some of them, I hardly laid eyes on."

"All right. We're in luck, anyway. One's in St. Louis, one's in Tucson, the other two in L.A. We can scoop them up as we move."

"We're going to drive across?" Rhino wanted to know.

"Yeah. In a limo. That way, we can keep watch on them, no risk. And it'll make the splash we need once we touch down."

"Uh, Cross . . ." Tiger began

"What?"

"No offense, honey. But you and Rhino aren't exactly Central Casting for 'pimp.' I should—"

"You're dead, remember, Tiger? And if one of the girls you worked with sees you alive, that'd kind of blow the game, right? We can make this work. I know what it takes."

"Two weeks, fifty grand?" the woman who called herself Tanya said to Cross, her voice skeptical-hopeful.

"Guaranteed. With ten up front."

"And no lump tricks?"

"No whips and chains. I can't promise some of them won't get rough, you understand what I'm saying. But anyone gets *too* rough, you make a little noise, my man here quiets it right down."

The woman looked over at Rhino, agreeing within herself that he could quiet down a whole roomful of whorehouse customers just by shrugging his shoulders.

"Sounds too good to be true," she said, letting a vein of suspicion into her voice.

"Yeah? Well, it gets even better," Cross told her. "Whatever you work them for—tips, whatever you want to call it—you keep that too. It'll be in local currency, so you may get jobbed a little on the exchange, but you should clear another few thousand easy. These are *very* rich men. And they've never seen girls from Sweden before."

"Sweden? I'm from—"

"You're from fucking Stockholm, anybody asks," Cross cut her off. "You're a natural blonde, right? Blue eyes? That's enough for those chumps. Besides, none of them speak that much English."

"How do I know I won't end up there forever? I heard stories of girls going for a week and—"

"To where? Some Arab country, right? Or fucking Japan, if they were that stupid. This is right below Mexico. And you can tell anyone you want where you'll be. This isn't some 'white-slave ring,' girl," Cross said casually. "Truth is, if that was what we wanted, you'd already be in the trunk of the car outside, and nobody'd ever know what happened to you."

The woman's pale face went so bloodless it showed even through the heavy layer of makeup. "I got protec—"

"Who? That punk Maurice? Why don't you give him a call?" Cross sneered, tossing her a cellular phone.

The woman sat there, not moving.

"Think it over," Cross told her. "We promised them a minimum of three girls to work the house for two weeks. There's a *lot* of money in this. For everyone. You don't want to go, nobody'll make you. We wanted to do that, we'd do it. You couldn't stop us. We're businessmen, not kidnappers. This is all about money. I gave you my name. You must know people in Chicago. Ask around."

"How much time do I have?"

"Three, four days."

"Okay. And Maurice . . . ?"

"He'll be all right in a few hours," Cross told her.

"Wow! First-class!" Tanya looked at the pair of tickets in her hand.

"Yeah, so what? One of them's to L.A., right? This sounds like some kinda scam to me."

"Maurice, it's exactly like that man said. We're going to drive down from L.A. So I only need a ticket there, and a ticket home. That's what *this* one is."

"Let me see that . . . Damn, bitch, you see this? You got to fly to Mexico City, then to Chicago, then switch again and come back home to St. Lou."

"So?"

"So look at the bottom of the ticket. See, right here," he said, pointing with a manicured fingernail. "This sucker cost over seven thousand dollars! Throw in the one to L.A., we cash them in, and we just blow this place, you understand what I'm saying?"

"No."

"You one stupid fucking bitch sometimes, Tanya. Listen: These tickets, they in your square name, right? And you got a passport to prove it, the one that guy Cross told you to get. So these tickets, they're as good as cash. We just drive over to the airport, go up to the counter, and get a refund. What part don't you understand?"

"I want to go."

"Yeah! Like I said—"

"I want to go to this Quitasol place," the woman said. "It's *big* money. Much bigger than this."

The man reached over lazily and slapped her face. Hard. "You forgetting who's running this show, bitch? Are you?" he demanded, slapping her again. "Remember what that coat hanger felt like?" he asked, his soft voice throbbing with threat.

"No, Maurice. Don't do that! Okay. Whatever you say. I'll go right over and . . ."

"You *are* a stupid fucking bitch," the man said disgustedly. "You think they just gonna hand over that much cash? Now, we get some kinda 'credit' thing. So first we need a new address. For them to mail it to, see? Now go take a shower. Your fat ass is going back out on the stroll tonight. Man said you not leaving for another ten days or so, plenty of time to build up an even bigger stake. I'm doing you a favor, bitch. They could put whatever they slipped in my drink that first time they come here in yours too. And then you *never* come back."

The woman turned and meekly walked away, in the direction of the bathroom.

A little past ten that evening, the woman, now dressed in a tiny red spandex skirt and a halter top, stepped into a phone booth and dialed a number in area code 312.

"He's not gonna—"

"It'll be okay," the voice interrupted her. "Just finish your shift and come back whenever you usually do."

"He always picks me up at—"

"Not tonight, he won't be."

The man Tanya was speaking to folded the cellular phone closed. He turned to the huge man seated next to him. "This call-forwarding is a great invention," he said. "Looks like her pimp doesn't want her to travel."

"He's still in there," the huge man squeaked, looking across at an apartment building, "unless he went out the back way."

"Walking? I don't think so. His ride's parked right over there. See it, on the far corner? The white Caddy with the—"

"Got it."

"Be better if he doesn't get found," Cross said. "We don't want the cops pulling her in for questioning."

"None of the girls can even *see* you," Cross told Tiger. "That's all we need, have one of them start screaming."

"Then how are you gonna explain me . . . ? Oh no, you're not, pal! If you think—"

"Will you relax? Nobody expects you to turn tricks. And it's legit, anyway. I mean, we deliver the girls to the house, we provide the security, just like Jorge set up. And we *stay* open. Twenty-four/seven, like we promised. So we gotta live on the premises. And have someone at the door. All the time. You just stay upstairs, nobody has to see you at all. Not until it won't matter. Fair enough?"

"I . . . guess."

"You fly in direct. We got nobody on the ground. The *independistas*, they don't exactly trust us, okay? Only reason I think they'll do what they said is because it'd look better for them if they pulled it off all by themselves, see? So you just take a cab to the hotel, like you're a tourist on vacation. It's only about a half-mile to where we'll be, and you already have pictures of it *and* the address. These communicators will work as long as the batteries hold out. Just buzz when you're coming in and we'll have the front cleared."

"I should get there . . . when?"

"We'll already be set up for two, three days by the time you touch down. Then it all comes down to timing. Buddha can't move until they got the pad ready for him. And as soon as they do, everything jumps. No margins."

"You really think it'll work?" she asked.

"Which part?"

"Getting her out?"

"I make it eighty-twenty against," Cross said. "But you can flip those odds when it comes to us."

Fal walked the long, narrow strip end to end, his beloved Bedeaux-built Winchester .300 Magnum on a sling over his shoulder, heavy barrel down, eyes sweeping the ground. Ace and Princess followed behind—Ace with his machete, Princess with a thickly packed duffel bag. Every few yards, Falcon would point at a crevice in the rock, nod approval. Princess would beam like a child being praised for a perfect report card. Ace would pull a packet of putty-colored material wrapped in clear plastic from Princess' duffel bag and tamp it carefully into each approved spot. It took them the better part of the day to finish.

Near midnight, at La Casa de Dolor, about three-quarters of a mile away from where the three men were laboring, a muffled *whoomp!* was heard. The ground shook briefly. Some of the guards joked about earthquakes, but the more knowledgeable ones surmised it was an aftershock from blasting at the huge mine about a dozen miles to the west. Everyone was aware that the regime was speeding the deeper excavations with dynamite.

The next morning, Falcon walked the course again. When he was finished, Princess began to remove the largest boulders. Some he carried; some he rolled. Ace blocked off sections of encroaching trees and dead limbs. After dark, Falcon carefully rationed out the gasoline. A long fuse was trailed into the pool of flammable liquid before the sun could reduce its effectiveness. The men stood back as Falcon struck a wooden match. The flame crackled all around the perimeter, but stopped at the firebreak Ace had cut behind it. Smoke rose into the night, almost undetectable. If anyone nearby caught a whiff, there were too many ways to explain such things.

"I can make that much in two weeks right here," the bottle-blonde said, leaning back in her chair to take some of the pressure off her back. Every since the 48DD implants, her back hurt most of the time. But it was just like Reggie said—her prices got blown way up too.

"Lap-dancing? I don't think so."

"What are you, the IRS? Look, here's the way it works, okay? I average two, three grand a night, cash money. Do the math."

"I'm talking fifty grand *net*," Cross said. "You pay for the space in that joint, right? And Reggie, he takes a piece . . . maybe a big piece."

"Reggie's my—"

"Whoever he is, he don't know about your little gambling jones, right? He know you're into Skillman for twenty large?"

"I can handle my own—"

"No, no, you can't. See, I bought up your markers," Cross said quietly. "And I want the money. Right now. Or I want you to take this deal."

"*And* cancel the marker?"

"I *look* like a mark to you?"

"So what're you telling me?"

"That you owe me twenty. That you do this two-week thing with us, you come back clean, thirty grand ahead. No way you're gonna gamble down there. It's all work, like I told you. Who knows? Maybe you'll kick the habit."

"Reggie . . ."

"You can have that part any way you want," Cross said softly. "A little bonus. My man over there"—nodding in Rhino's direction—"he can fix it so Reggie's fine with anything. Or he can just fix Reggie. What's it gonna—?"

"Just fix Reggie," the woman said, reaching her hands up over her head and stretching backward to take off more of the pressure.

"Where did this come from?" the young woman asked the guard in formal, college-taught Spanish. She was thin to the point of emaciation, dull-brown hair hanging lifeless in limp strands.

"From a friend," the guard said. "It is something like a giant vitamin, they said. It will give you strength."

"And if I don't take it?"

The guard shrugged.

The young woman dry-swallowed the pill. The guard watched her throat carefully. Then he approached, ordered her to open her mouth. He probed with a filthy finger, running his other hand up and down her throat. Then he sat down on the only bunk in the bare cell.

The young woman did not speak. But she looked a question at him.

"I am to stay here," the guard told her. "With you. Until my shift is done. Then there will be another man. And another. That pill, it stays inside you, understand?"

"Yes. I won't—"

"Don't even talk. It does not matter."

"I have to sleep sometime. Or sit down. I have to use the—"

"Use the floor, *puta*. For anything you want to do. We have to make sure it stays inside you."

"Wow! I bet that's the first superstretch they've ever seen this far south of the border," Tanya said, watching through the heavily tinted back window as they passed the masqued faces of the pre-paid Mexican police.

"How long a drive is it, anyway?" Candy asked Cross, who sat on one of the rear-facing seats.

"About another eighteen hundred miles," he replied. "Two days, driving straight through, me and Rhino switching off."

"Yeah? Well, *I'm* not sitting in this seat for two days without . . . you know. Why can't we stop off and get a room?"

"We need to be there in *six* days," Cross said quietly. "Two days is about the best we could do, hugging the coast like we are. But we're not going for the max. The plan *is* to stop over. At least one, maybe two nights. Just relax."

"All right," Crystal interjected. "But remember, you promised I could call—"

"Call anybody you want," Cross told her. "You're wasting everyone's time with all this crap. Once we crossed that border—hell, once you got into this car—we could do whatever we wanted, and you know it. This isn't a van with a couple of guys in the back seat with a roll of duct tape and a broomstick handle, get it? We're professionals. You're supposed to be too. How about acting like one for a change?"

"There she is, mate," the middle-aged man with a regulation RAF mustache said to Buddha, gesturing with his finger. "One Harrier GR7, all spec'd as agreed. Take a look for yourself."

Buddha strolled over, saying nothing, taking several tours around the plane as the man next to him kept up a running patter:

"Runs about nine tons, ready to roll, and she can carry another four-plus external. Good for maybe six fifty at sea level, around six at thirty-six thousand. I wouldn't want to go beyond that much myself, although you can climb up to fifty if you need to. You don't want any extra fuel, so you're looking at a tactical radius of around one hundred and eighty kilometers, not much more. Now, you see that FLIR on the front? That's how you can tell it's a seven, not a five. This one's really brand-new, built in '94. But they've been flying these jump-jets for almost forty years—you couldn't find a more reliable design anywhere."

"Sure. What's FLIR?"

"Forward-looking infrared seeker. You attach it to your night-vision goggles, you can work at night if you need to."

"I won't."

"Fine. All right, see the pods? That's where the rockets are. You've got nineteen in each one, configured in rows. When you're done, you hit the big fat white button—I'll show you where it is inside—and the guts will pop out too. Then you close them down with the same button, only you hit it twice."

"Okay."

"Be a trifle cold on the return, but it shouldn't be a real problem. Mind, with the extra pod, we had to lose the Sidewinders. That's the way Cross said to do it."

"Yeah, I know."

"So what you want to do is—"

"Get in and get the fuck out, right? Sure."

"And the money?"

"A million bucks for a rental, that's what you're asking?"

"Oh, I'm not *asking* for anything, son. Cross made a deal. A million for the rental, the loads, any shakedown runs you want to make to test her out, fuel, and a ride to this little airport I know about when you come back. He said you had a good sense of humor . . . and I can see he was right, you acting as if you want to bargain."

"The money will be here in twenty-four hours," Buddha said, turning away. "I have to—"

"Ah, we have telephones here, my friend. Very civilized. At your pleasure . . ."

"It is as I promised, *sí?*" the Mayan asked Cross, a sweep of his arm indicating the plush foyer of the four-story house located on the fringe of the capital city's most upscale neighborhood.

"It looks fine," Cross assured him. The women were upstairs, arguing over which bedroom each would occupy as work space. Rhino was prowling somewhere within the house.

Tiger sat next to Cross, watching the Mayan, but not speaking or moving.

"Your . . . customers, they will start to arrive at the end of the week. Once word has been spread discreetly in certain circles."

"We're almost there," Cross told him.

"Almost . . . ?"

"One problem you got: You don't trust us. That's okay, I understand. But you're not taking any risk until we deliver, that was the deal."

"You believe there was no risk in—?"

"*Real* risk. You're not putting any troops into the field until that radio tower goes down."

"I tell you . . . my *compadres,* they think I am insane to even go this far. Especially with a man like you. That tower, it is guarded like it is the life of Torrando himself."

"Torrando is—?"

"He is El Presidente today. Tomorrow, he may be *muerto* if God wills it. But if he goes, those with him go as well. And so the guards are *good* ones. Not the fat, lazy swine who worked in the dungeons. They are soldiers. The elite. The best he has. It will be impossible to reach the tower with the kind of explosives you would need."

"Sure. Whatever you say."

"In any event, you did not bring explosives with you. You could not bring even a pistol across our borders on the main roads."

"That's one of the two things we need from you," Cross told him. "We need weapons. That's our problem. And you need to watch us. That's your problem. So here's how we're going to do it. You give us enough men to watch the door, all right? They do all the talking. What's the most anyone charges for whores around here?"

"I would not know this."

"Sure. Anyway, you can find out. Whatever that price is, ours is double, understand? So the guys at the door, they don't have to *be* hard, but they got to *look* hard, understand? Like they was hired to protect the place, watch the money, check on the girls. We want no phone in the place. No appointments. All word-of-mouth. Everytime someone shows up, your guys, they pat him down—no weapons allowed in here—tell him the price, ask him which girl he wants. We got photos, and if they're not with a customer, they'll be lounging around in that room you got in the back. We need someone on the front door around the clock. There's a door in the back. You got two choices with it—seal it up or put a man on it. Your own man—we're not dealing with it."

"What else do you require?"

"Weapons. We need an Uzi, a pair of MAC-10s, three shotguns, twelve-gauge, and"—looking across at Tiger, catching her nod—"a Sig Sauer nine. With plenty of ammo for each one. And we need a suppressor for the Sig. A real one."

"Those are expensive weapons. Especially with a silencer. And very dangerous to possess here. I do not know if—"

Cross handed the Mayan a plain envelope. "What you got in there is twenty thousand, American. That's enough to buy everything we want a few times over. We came over the border in a limo. Your guys go back and forth whenever they want. Buying pieces like we need in Guatemala is about an hour's work."

"Very well."

"Good. While you're there, I got a couple of other things I want picked up."

The Mayan looked a question, but did not speak.

"One's a present. For you all. It's a bit too bulky to carry in a suitcase, so make sure you've got a truck."

"What is this . . . present?"

"Your broadcasting booth," Cross told him.

"There's three of us," Cross said, looking at Tiger and Rhino. "Everybody works overlap until this is done. Five hours straight sleep every twenty-four, so there's always two of us awake. I'm not worried about the girls making a break for it, but we have to watch none of the customers gets stupid. And if they do," he said, looking meaningfully at Tiger, "we have to handle them *sweet*. We don't know who's coming, but Jorge said they'd all be big players. We total the wrong one, we might get visitors. And, remember, none of the girls can see you, either."

"I don't know how to count this damn money," Tanya whined, looking at a stack of bills on the coffee table in the beautifully appointed waiting room.

"You don't need to count it," Cross told her. "We'll exchange it once we get back to the States."

"You said—"

"—that you could keep all your tips, right? And you can. Nobody's taking a penny from you. They pay us at the door. Whatever they give you, it's yours to keep. What's your beef?"

"Well, I just like to know what I'm getting. I mean, I don't know if these guys are tipping me a C-note or a fiver, do I?"

"Fine, all right, give it to me," Cross said, leaning forward. Tanya handed it over, reluctantly, as if worried it would not be returned. Cross riffled through it, spinning the stack against his thumb. "You got about six grand here."

"Really?"

"Really."

"You said this place would be paradise; I guess you weren't wrong. That's only for two days. I only turned—"

"Nobody cares," Cross told her.

"You *have* to come to the house," Cross said reasonably. "Rhino has to show your guys how to work the thing, right? And there's no way he can leave—we won't have enough manpower to cover the place if something happens."

"If something happens . . . ?"

"Look, pal. This is cover. Deep cover. We spent a long, long time setting it up. Our base is there. If this *regime* of yours decides they want to close the place down, the game's up, understand?"

"*Sí.* But could we not . . . ?"

"Your guys, they're radiomen, right? I mean, not amateurs? Rhino wouldn't have to start from scratch?"

"No. Of course not. It is just that we have never seen such a—"

"Get the rig inside another truck. Not a pickup, something with a covered back, okay? Bring it behind the house. Tonight. Right after midnight. Don't *move* after that. Make sure there's a piece of red cloth tied onto the antenna. And when you hear three raps, open the door. No smoking, no talking, no piss breaks. You *stay* in there until you hear the raps. You let Rhino in. He's gonna have maybe a hour to show you *everything*. In the dark, with a flashlight."

"We can do this."

"You got the weapons, I'll give you that. All right, tonight. And give us an extra man on the door, just to be sure."

"You sure this'll hold?" Cross asked Rhino, indicating a four-bolt configuration screwed deeply into the wooden floor, with a thick black Perlon climbing line looped around it in a boxed-X pattern.

"My weight times ten," Rhino assured him. "And it's only dropping one floor. Too short to even call it rappelling—I can get down in one hop."

"All right. You know they're not going to speak English, unless Jorge is there too."

"Doesn't matter," Rhino squeaked. "None of the switches are marked with words anyway. I can hand-sign it all, no worries."

"Tiger will have you covered on the way down. With a silenced piece. If there's any trouble, the one thing we *don't* want is noise. . . ."

Rhino nodded, realizing that Cross was on full-auto now, reciting mechanically, not telling anyone anything they hadn't heard a thousand times. The pre-battle ritual. Meaningless now.

"This two-at-a-time thing doesn't really work with only three for coverage." Tiger smiled at Cross.

"Huh?"

"Well, let's say two of the three want to . . . get together privately . . . No way to do that, is there?"

"I guess not. When we get back . . ."

"Maybe women are different from men," Tiger said.

"Maybe?"

"All right." She chuckled. "We're about to . . . do something. I don't know how men get ready. Me, I'd kind of like to . . . let some of this energy go someplace, if you get my drift."

"Tiger . . ."

"Cross, stop playing. There's nobody watching. But you've been watching *me*. And don't even pretend it's because you're afraid I'm going to go off. I'm just as much a pro as you."

"I know."

"So?"

"So . . . what?"

"Can't we . . . be together and watch the pressure point at the same time?"

"One of us at least has to—"

"And you want that to be you, right?" Tiger whispered huskily, grinning.

"Actually, I want it to be you," Cross said, flat-faced. "But I don't know if you can keep your concentration."

"Me? I can do it better than you could."

Tiger leaned over the railing at the top of the stairs, bent slightly forward at the waist. She was nude. Cross stood behind her, already inside her. Tiger's silenced pistol swept the area below. "Looks good to me," she whispered.

"Looks better from here," Cross replied.

Tiger giggled. "I hope *so*."

"And you can stay like this until . . . ?"

"Question is, how long can *you* stay like this?" Tiger chuckled, wiggling her hips back against Cross.

It was no contest.

"They can use it," Rhino said.

"No question?"

"None. They already knew ninety percent of it. Probably could have worked it out by themselves, but it's not the kind of thing you want to test. A signal that strong, you could triangulate on it in minutes."

"Then all we're waiting on is word from the field."

"I know."

"Look, Rhino, if Princess had lost it, we probably would've heard an alarm—we're hooked up, and Fal has the transmitter."

"All we can do is wait it out," Tiger said gently, putting one hand on Rhino's gigantic forearm. "You've got your five hours coming. Two of the girls aren't working now... You want to ... ?"

"No offense," Rhino told her.

"None taken," she said.

"There's a pattern," Rhino said to Cross. It was three days later, and both men were sitting in the kitchen on the first floor, a vantage point that gave them full sound coverage without sight. Good enough for their purposes. The girls were above them, Tiger on the floor above that, asleep.

"To what?"

"We get *heavy* traffic some times; almost none at others."

"Not so surprising. This is a whorehouse, not a bus station."

"I know. And this 'siesta' thing takes its toll, too. But Buddha has to make his move in daylight, right?"

"I don't know. That's the smart way. But it's got the highest risk . . ."

"He won't want to fly at night without air-to-air," Rhino said, certainty in his voice. "Not Buddha. And he won't want to miss the pickup, either."

"He's not coming back alone," Cross told Rhino, finally picking up on the source of the huge man's anxiety.

"If he does, he'll never spend the money," Rhino said, his voice so low it sounded almost normal.

"I think it's finished," Princess told Ace, looking out across a clear-swept area of rock and dirt.

"One more day," Ace said sourly. "I don't want to give that fat little motherfucker no excuse not to land."

"Oh, Buddha wouldn't do that," Princess assured him. "We'd all be stuck here if he did that."

"Sure," Ace said. And went back to work with his machete.

"Do you believe these men can do as they promised?" a slim woman with a scar that bisected the empty socket of her right eye asked Jorge.

"They are not our people," he said. "They are not men of honor. They have no cause except money."

"And what does that mean?" an older man asked from the far corner of the darkened basement. "We have risked much for this."

"We have risked *nothing*," the woman hissed at him. "Some . . . money, what is that? A run across the border? Some of our soldiers in their little house of whores? This is nothing. And what we fight for, it is everything."

"*Sí*, Rosita. I do not mean to—"

"They only took one of my eyes," the woman said, her voice harsh in the quiet air. "And even if they took both, I could still see. I ask Jorge because, unless these men do as they promise, there will be no risk at all. And no change for our people."

"I believe they will do it," Jorge said finally.

Greeted with silence, he continued: "This man Cross, his name is known to the drug lords. And you know, they have armies greater than those of El Puerco. They know his name. And they fear it. Not because he is a man of honor. But because he always delivers. Not merchandise. He and his ... comrades ... are not mules. They are soldiers. All of them, like some army. He has his own reasons for doing this. And it is true that we do not know them. But what does it matter? La Casa de Dolor alone—if *that* should fall ..."

"Only if the people know," the woman with the scar reminded him.

"*Sí.* But Roberto says the radio they gave us, it will work. Even on the generator, for at least ten minutes. And it will reach every corner. Far beyond Quitasol."

"But how will they take the tower?"

"This I do not know. I know this man Cross cannot be a traitor, for he has no loyalty. He is a businessman. I assume he is a liar, then. All businessmen are liars. But I believe he can do it ... Do not ask why, I just do. And as Rosita said, we have risked nothing of value. Not so far. Only if the tower stops transmitting do we go into the streets, agreed?"

The nods were no less emphatic for being silent.

"You ready to take your medicine without any trouble this time, bitch?" the guard asked the woman in the shapeless bleached gray shift.

She nodded weakly, opening her mouth like a trained dog following a command.

"Too bad," the guard sneered at her. "It was more fun the last time."

"It's ready," said Fal, inspecting the runway. Dusk was falling. "I'm transmitting ... now." He flicked a toggle switch on a black box he had taken from the pocket of his jacket. A green light glowed. "Buddha knows now. He should be in after first light tomorrow. We've got a good ten hours to cover less than three klicks and find shelter. I've been there four times already. The path is marked. That part's easy. Getting back, there's where we have to work."

This was a long speech for Falcon. Ace and Princess squatted next to him by the fire, waiting.

Falcon flicked another switch, watched another light glow green. "Cross knows now, too. We wait for the acknowledge. That comes, we're gone."

"They just alerted Buddha," Cross told Tiger. "If he signals back, that means tomorrow, sometime after sunup."

"I'm ready," she said. "And I'll tell Rhino when I wake him up for his shift."

A red light glowed on the black box Falcon held in his hand. "Buddha's got it," he told the others. "Let's move out."

"I swear I'm gonna miss this place," Crystal told Candy the next morning, both of them lounging in customer-magnet negligees. "I never worked a place so nice in my life."

"Yeah. I don't know about you, but only two guys even *tried* to get rough. And one look at that monster we got, and that was the end of it."

"He *is* a big one." Crystal chuckled. "I wonder if he's *got* a big one."

"Whether he does or not, *you're* not gonna see it."

"How could you know?"

"'Cause I don't think he swings that way."

"Which means *you* offered him a little on the side."

"What if I did? I mean . . . what else is there to do here? Watch more *Baywatch* reruns? That is one lame show."

"You think they all bought theirs?" Crystal asked, flicking her hands across her pneumatic breasts.

"Sure, girl. Who doesn't? You believe even the marks think we came stock from the factory like this?"

"I guess not. Although nothing these idiots do would be that much of a surprise."

"It doesn't matter much. We only have three more days here."

"Yeah. Well, you can stay if you want. Me, I miss the States. And I don't like being locked up."

"I guess you don't," Tiger said, walking into the room, the semi-auto leveled. "That's why you were so quick to sell me to the feds, huh?"

The Harrier popped straight up out of the dense green Honduran jungle, hovered momentarily, then shot forward like a malevolent wasp. It headed toward the capital of Quitasol, less than twenty miles away, the roar of its vector-thrust turbofan engine blanketing the ground below into stunned silence. The radar found the little plane immediately, but even as the Quitasolan Air Force—four surplus Russian MiGs—was scrambling to alert, the Harrier let loose a single air-to-ground Maverick missile, the electric-optic system guiding the warhead right to its target. The top half of the radio tower disappeared—fire engulfed what was left. The Harrier banked sharply and darted back across the border before any of the MiGs could get into the air.

Throughout Quitasol, all radios went dead.

They didn't stay dead for long. As the Comandante screamed orders from the palace, electronics experts worked with triangulators trying to locate the new source. A source that was broadcasting over the single station available, and broadcasting so powerfully that it reached the remote mountain settlements, as well as the dense streets of the capital.

The streets quickly filled with people as radios were turned to maximum volume. Soldiers responded. The crowds moved back, but the radios continued to blare the news. . . .

The Harrier came shrieking across the border again, this time aimed in another direction entirely, flying over ground unprotected by radar systems.

La Casa de Dolor loomed in Buddha's vision. He fired both his 25mm Aden cannons at the walls, muttering, "Just like a fucking video game," as the walls started to tumble. The Harrier twisted back, hovered just above the prison, and released its cluster bombs right onto the tops of the exposed buildings.

Several of the guards fired their rifles futilely at the buzzing jet. The rest of them ran for cover. Buddha emptied his rocket pods, not bothering to aim, knowing he couldn't miss at that range, but being careful to hit only the south side of the prison.

Some of the guards were stalking through the prison, systematically slaughtering the inhabitants of the cells even as their comrades urged them to run for it.

Fal let loose with his shoulder-mounted LAAW at the north wall. Four more shells, and the wall itself was only rubble. Ace and Princess stood and watched: Ace with his scattergun ready in case any of the fleeing guards came their way, Princess adjusting a complex shoulder harness made of nylon, his face frozen.

Falcon dropped the antitank weapon, pulled a small scanner from his pocket, hit a switch. "Got her. Full thermal. Let's move out."

The men walked rapidly but purposefully, Princess in front, sweeping the area with his heavy machine gun, a creature from nightmares, moving robotically in response to pushes from Falcon on either shoulder.

The prison was in ruins. Humans who could still move were trying to run. To run anywhere.

The three men made their way through the carnage, Ace occasionally blowing away anyone in uniform and mechanically reloading.

The woman was in the last cell at the end of the corridor. A lone guard walked that corridor, aiming his pistol into each cell, pulling the trigger several times. He seemed to have an endless supply of fresh clips. His back was to the approaching men. Ace and Princess fired simultaneously. Pieces of the guard flew off. Falcon never looked up, his eyes only on the transmitter. He came to the end of the corridor.

"Marlene?" he asked.

"Oh, God. What's happening? Are you—?"

Falcon nodded. Pulled a pistol and, aiming parallel to the cell door, blew off the lock. Princess stepped inside. The woman fainted. Ace and Falcon strapped her into the harness on Princess' back. Falcon took the machine gun and the point. Princess followed, carrying the woman on his back, his treasured Lone Eagle Magnum in one fist. Ace brought up the rear, shotgun barrels seeking new prey.

The prison yard was no more. Everyone was dead, dying, or running. No one challenged the strange group.

"Double-time now," Falcon called back as they came upon the trail he had marked.

They reached their camping area just as the Harrier made a helicopter's vertical landing at the far end of the strip. The rocket pods popped free. Princess gently loaded the girl into one of the empty tubes, then climbed in there with her, cradling her frail body in his enormous arms. Falcon and Ace scrambled into the other. Buddha hit the switch and the pod faces closed. He looked grimly down the makeshift runway, nodded to himself, and gave it maximum thrust.

The Harrier cleared the edge of the jungle by three feet, climbed vertically, straightened out, and rocketed back to its nest.

The radio continued its denunciation of the regime. Telling the people that La Casa de Dolor was no more. That the rebels had freed their comrades and executed the traitors who had imprisoned them. Soldiers swarming through the streets were met with sporadic gunfire from rooftops—gunfire that increased as they moved farther away from the presidential palace.

"Everyone goes down," Cross said to Rhino and Tiger. "A bush moves, you blast it. Turns out it was just a pig, we have barbecue. Don't even think about telling the rebels from the government. Everyone's a hostile until we get over the border. Got it?"

Tiger and Rhino nodded, not looking at each other.

Cross looked out the back window and saw two soldiers facing away from the building. Their posture was nervous, alert. He made a hand signal. Tiger stepped out of the whorehouse and shot the two soldiers in the back with the silenced Sig. As Cross covered the area from the shadows, a MAC-10 in each hand, Rhino slipped behind Tiger and yanked the tarp off the package the rebels had brought across the border, revealing a stabilized mortar, pre-aimed. He reached down and delicately touched off a series of timed launches.

Seconds later, chunks of the presidential palace flew into the air. Tiger took the wheel of the armored Chevy Blazer waiting in the back alley. Rhino sat in back, his Uzi steady in his lap. Cross was in the passenger seat, tossing white phosphorus grenades at random as the Blazer fought its way through the clogged streets.

One of the whores trapped in the house screamed. Fire raged throughout the capital. More of the soldiers ran than fought. The Blazer rolled on through, indifferently lethal.

The Harrier touched down. Buddha hit the switches and the pods opened. Princess jumped out first, the woman still in his arms. Falcon and Ace got out more slowly. Of the four, only Ace showed any signs of recent exposure to cold, hugging himself, shivering. Princess was pumped with excitement, exchanging high-fives with everyone in the open-mouthed ground crew. Fal stood by, indifferent. The woman appeared to be in shock. Buddha climbed down from the cockpit.

"Let's go get our money," he said.

"You handled the truck beautifully," Rhino complimented Tiger as they waited for the flight leaving Belize.

"Anytime I can't out-drive that little slug, I'll start taking estrogen supplements." She laughed.

"You can't," Cross said.

"Can't what?"

"Out-drive Buddha. He's the best there is."

"Is that why you keep him on? Because, if it is, now that I'm—"

"It's not the only reason," Cross said, looking across at Rhino.

The huge man moved his head a fraction, but enough to indicate agreement.

"What, then?"

"He's one of us," Cross told her. "He hates them. He hates them *all*."

"And I don't?"

"I can't speak for anyone else."

"Yeah? Well, you do a pretty good job when you want something."

"Sure."

"What's your problem?"

"You're my problem. We had a deal. You're out of the joint, get to start over."

"And you got paid."

"And I got paid."

"So we're—what?—done?"

"I don't know what *we* are. But the crew, that's us, not you."

"Oh."

Cross said nothing, dragging on his cigarette, eyes alert. They had decided to go weaponless into the airport, but the local cops weren't as handicapped. Belize had no treaty with Quitasol, and, according to the CNN feed they could see in the terminal, the capital was still in flames. But a lifetime of watchfulness always called the shots in Cross's world.

"Because I'm a woman?" Tiger finally asked.

"Because you're a woman . . . What? Just say what you want to say, all right?"

"I thought . . . you and me . . . we've been . . . together before. And this time, I guess I . . . I don't know . . . I got no place to go. If I go back to what I was doing . . . I may be off their records, but they've got my prints and—"

"They've got all our prints," Cross interrupted. "They've had mine since I was a kid. Ace and Rhino's too. Fal and Buddha from the service, at least. Only Princess is off their screen. And he couldn't hide in a circus."

"I know. I just meant, look, Cross, you wanted me to be straight, here it is: I don't want to play house with you. I mean, I don't want to play house*wife* with you, okay? I want to . . . be with you. But I don't want to stay home. I want to work."

"You mean you want in, right?"

"Yes."

"No."

"Just like that?"

"Yeah. Just like that. You and me, we get along now. What happens if we stop—getting along, I mean?"

"You think I'd rat you out?" Tiger snarled low at him.

"No. Not for a minute. I think the reason the others go along with me is because they know I don't have my emotions in it. It would make a mess. Fucking Buddha, you know how he is. First thing, he'd say you and me, we should split one share. Okay, that wouldn't fly. But he'd put it in people's *minds*, understand? So, when we hand out assignments, the first time it looked like you got the softer piece, there wouldn't be the same . . ."

"Trust?"

"Yeah."

"But I worked with you before. With the crew, I mean."

"Sure. But that was free-lance. Same as Fal."

"I held up my end?"

"No question."

"But this is different because . . . ?"

"Fal isn't in on every job. He gets to pick and choose. He passes on most of what we have anyway. He's connected to us, but he's not. He has his own . . . None of us do, see?"

"I don't have my own," Tiger said, eyes welling.

"You had your own fucking *cell* a few weeks ago," Cross said, staring straight ahead.

"It's too big a risk," Buddha told Falcon. "Nothing was said about me *driving* back. Fuck a whole bunch of that. I want to see Chicago soon, not in a couple of weeks."

"Flying, that's what's too big a risk," the Indian said. "You can't take her on a commercial flight. Look at her, she needs a hospital, not a plane trip."

"I'm . . . okay," the woman said.

"Yes. And you may be recognizable as well," Falcon told her politely.

"But what *difference* does it make? I mean, you men are heroes. You *rescued* me. Why should you care if—?"

Falcon turned to face the woman, who was lying on a motel bed, propped up by several pillows. "Ma'am, what we did or didn't do isn't important. What *is* important is that we disappear. We agreed to do . . . certain things. In exchange for payment. We are . . . unauthorized to act by any government, despite what you may believe. Quitasol has no extradition treaty with America, but that is only because it operates as a safe harbor for drug dealers. We agreed to return you to Chicago. I don't believe you are in any condition to travel unassisted. Do you understand?"

"Yes."

"Then *you* take her," Buddha said. "*You* drive through the fucking South with Princess, see how far you get before he hammers a few people and you all end up on some chain gang."

"Buddha—"

"Man, don't even think about threatening me. I did my piece. Came back for you and all. Got you across the border. I earned my money, and I want it. What I *don't* want is to wait for it."

"Come on, Buddha," Princess exhorted him. "It'll be fun!"

"No way."

"All right," Ace said. "It ain't no big thing. I just hope none of us mess up the shark car."

"What the fuck you talking about?" Buddha demanded. "Nobody drives that car but me. And it's not exactly parked in the lot outside."

"No," Ace said, swinging a single key on a ring he had pulled from his pocket. "But I know where it is. Real close. Right over in Liberty City. Cross had it brought down here so we could have cover, in case it got bad going back."

"That miserable lowlife sonofabitch!" Buddha said. "He said a Lear. I fucking *knew* he'd—"

"Have a nice flight, Buddha," Falcon told him.

"Princess has to stay in the back seat," Buddha replied, defeated.

"She's a mess, Cross." The speaker was a white male, somewhere in his forties, with a husky chest and a wrestler's build. His eyes were a whirling miasma of compassion and cynicism.

"That's why we brought her to you, Doc."

"I don't think so. And *you* must think I'm pretty stupid. That's not like you, Cross."

"All of that means . . . what?"

First," Doc said, ticking off the points on his fingers, "this is . . . the girl the Quitasol government was holding in that prison in the mountains. You know . . . Quitasol? That place that's apparently burning to the ground."

"I heard there was some kind of revolution going on, yeah."

"Second," Doc continued, as if Cross had not spoken, "that job has your fingerprints all over it. Somebody paid you to pull that girl out. And, as usual, you got it done."

"People say things."

"Third, no way you did *anything* without being paid. At least a substantial portion in front. So, the way I figure it, you have to turn the girl over to get the rest of the money. How am I doing so far?"

Cross gave Doc a thousand-yard stare. Said nothing.

"So you leave her with me, figuring she needs medical rehab anyway, and, besides, you want her stashed where her father can't find her . . . and maybe take her back without you getting paid in full."

"You got paid," Cross said flatly.

"I did. And she's taking nourishment well, gaining weight, all that. She appears to have been subjected to . . . various forms of ugliness, but, given our knowledge of the Quitasol regime, not extensively so."

"Funny," Cross replied. "Seems like all the reports say she died in the attack on that . . . prison or whatever they call it."

"Yeah. Funny. So the deal wasn't that you bring her back at all, that's what you're saying? This wasn't about her?"

Cross just watched Doc's hands, silent and still within himself.

"But *that* doesn't work either. No way you bring someone back without there being something in it for you. You figure it out by yourself before you even brought her here?

"Guessed."

"Good guess. He didn't want her rescued, he wanted her silenced. Anyone who's done prison work would recognize the game. George Jackson tries to 'escape' with a 'smuggled' gun. And he gets smoked before he ever reaches the wall. Big surprise. But he sure stopped writing those books after that."

Cross shrugged.

"So now you're going to blackmail the same guy who paid you to kill her?"

"Doc, let's just say, hypothetically, I knew what the fuck you were talking about, okay? And let's just say the people with me, they saw it as a straight rescue. Maybe I thought they'd never pull off their end. But they did. And we got her now. I didn't get paid for a homicide. I got paid for an extraction attempt. But when we found she didn't want to go home to Daddy, we brought her here."

"And if you think I'm going to turn her—"

"She's not a girl, Doc. She's a grown woman. Pretty tough too, for someone who never had to work. But if you turn her loose, he's going to have her taken out, no question. And she doesn't have what it takes to go underground."

"I believe that's her choice."

"I believe we need to talk to her. Together."

"Do we have it *confirmed*?" the immaculately dressed man asked the chauffeur.

"No. And we probably never will. The destruction of the prison was near-total. And we have no—repeat, *no*—assets on the ground there. The press statements are conflicting, depending on which side breaks through. They're still fighting for control, but the President has made a run for it. He's in Paraguay, about what you'd expect. Anyway, the rebels say they destroyed the prison and liberated their comrades and the American woman was executed by the guards during the assault. The government says the rebels bombed the prison and killed a bunch of people, *including* your daughter, but *they* claim the prison is still standing."

"And this Cross, he says—?"

"Nothing. He says he wasn't there. It was a job. He says he got it done. Sent an extraction team in, they did their best. No question *something* big happened down there."

"I need to know."

"Yes, sir. I understand. We will do everything in our power to . . ."

The immaculately dressed man got to his feet, turned his back on the speaker, and walked from the room.

"I could never talk about it before," the woman said.

"You didn't remember . . . ?" Cross asked gently.

"I never had a day I didn't remember," the woman said, voice sharp and focused. "This isn't about 'recovered memory' or 'flashbacks' or anything else. Except him. And what he did. I couldn't talk about it because I just . . . couldn't, that's all. It all seemed so . . . useless. My mother knew . . ."

"You told her?"

"No. I didn't have to. She turned me over to him. Like a gift. She saw us. More than once. She always knew. But it wasn't until I was . . . locked away. Until I knew I was going to die. Those pigs . . . they thought they were torturing me. Rape. I'd been raped since I was a little girl. I know what hurts. They couldn't hurt me. But I knew enough to let them think they did."

"And now . . . ?"

"It doesn't matter. I didn't go to Quitasol to help the revolutionary movement. I didn't even know there *was* a revolutionary movement. All my friends go to Costa Rica for vacation. I wanted to go someplace different. Like discovering a new restaurant, I don't know."

"You say it doesn't matter, but . . . ?"

"But I need to say it now. Let everyone know what kind of a 'man' he is. I can't hurt him the way he hurt me, but I can hurt him. And I will."

"Is your mother alive?" Cross asked.

"No. She died when I was seventeen."

"Your father, he hasn't remarried?"

"No. He has . . . girls still. Our housekeeper's daughter, for one. But he would never get married again. He told me so himself. Why should he?"

"Yeah. Okay. I may have a way to fix this for you."

"Nobody can fix—"

"You stay here. Get better. Talk to Doc."

"I can't find out something like that, man. It would be in the safe. Or in one of the files. I wouldn't even know where to look."

"You don't have to look, bro," Ace assured the young black man in the pin-striped suit. "All we need to do is get inside. And you, you work late all the time, right?"

"It's expected of new associates. But I wouldn't be the only—"

"All you got to do is tap this here cell phone when the coast is clear, babe. We got a couple of boys, come in there like ghosts. Man never know we touched his stuff, you got my word."

"I don't like it."

"You like your mother living like she do? Your baby sister?"

"They're not going to be there much longer. I'm saving every dime and—"

"And you owe about a million bucks on your student loan. But that ain't what I'm saying, man. And you know it. You from where I from. And you know what it mean, a Rajaz honcho say he gonna brand your sister."

"I—"

"And you know who I am too. You know I make that stop if I want, right? You a lawyer. That's nice. When I was a kid, I stabbed a man beating on my momma. He died. So they put me in prison. I figured out how things work. You, you ain't figured it out. You know the law. I know what's true."

"I'm not promising . . ."

"Just tap the green button," Ace told him, handing over a mini–cell phone. "It's all you need to do."

"Why must *I* do this?" the Asian woman demanded of Buddha, her otherwise pretty face marred by an expression of intense hostility that had, after years of steady visitation, been granted permanent residence. She stalked in small, horseshoe-shaped movements in front of the hapless Buddha, who was half sprawled, half sitting on the plastic-covered sofa in the living room of a small house in a modest Chicago suburb.

"You're the one that talked to Fong. About the job, right, So Long?"

"Yes," she hissed at him. "So my 'reward' for trying to help you all earn some money is to risk my life?"

"Your life? Come on! Fong isn't gonna—"

"Not Fong, you fool. Fong is an intermediary. Perhaps you understand the term. The one who tried to set that trap for all of you—*that* is the one I would have to fear. And not just me, Buddha. We have children here, in case you have forgotten."

"So Long, give me a break. I didn't forget nothing. But Cross says—"

"Ah, *Cross*. Of *course*. How could I fail to heed the voice of the oracle? Let me see if I understand this. Cross, he is your business partner. I am your wife, and the mother of your children. And yet it is Cross who determines my safety?"

"We get a cut," Buddha said hopefully.

"A cut? You mean your usual 'equal share'?"

"Sure."

"Yes, and you believe *that* to be fair as well? I am not a member of your . . . organization, am I?"

You spend the fucking money like you are, Buddha thought to him self, wisely not letting such thoughts past his lips. "No, honey. But, remember, this whole job, it started out as your idea, right?"

"My idea? Don't be ridiculous. I merely passed along an opportunity that Fong—"

"Fong knows if he comes to you he's coming to us."

"How is that so?"

"So Long, that's enough, all right? You telling me this snake-head thought *you* were going to bodyguard his cargo?"

"You say that because I am a woman?"

This riposte was wasted on Buddha. Too many years of seeing Tiger in action had disabused him of the notion that there was a gender difference in combat. But he recognized the *non sequitur* for what it was: So Long was getting winded—now was the time to pounce. "Cross says, we don't do this, we can't run the Double X out in the open like we do. Cut the profits *way* down, people think they can move on us like that."

"But it didn't—"

"That ain't the point," Buddha told her, emphatic now. "He *tried*. You know what the vulture packs say about Cross's crew: 'Many tried, many died.' It cost us a hundred grand a *week* just to keep a presence at all the operations while we were gone," he said, stroking So Long's only known G-spot. "We can't pay

protection. We'd have to be pulling jobs all the time just to
break even. That ain't the way it works. We got enough money
now. From what we just . . . did. But it's only enough if we plow
it over, scrape some of it off, turn it legit. Not just the Double X, we
got to buy a couple of parking lots, some vacant land, maybe
some rental units, stuff like that. This guy—what's his name, anyway?"

"Liu-yang."

"Yeah. We know two things: One, he *is* a smuggler, and two,
the feds must have agreed to give him a pass in exchange for setting us up. So what we need to do, we need to show him that it's
all flipped now. See, when the feds came to him, they was telling
him, 'Cross' crew, they ain't got no license to drive no more,'
understand?"

"Yes," she snapped, impatient now.

"So that's why we can't dust him. He's gotta be alive. *Stay*
alive. So he can spread the word."

"But . . ."

"But fucking *what*? You're the one who met him, you're the one
who's gotta—"

"But if I do this, we are entitled to an extra share, no?"

A young black man in his twenties stepped from the back door of
the abandoned building. He was about six feet tall, with a motley
splattering of white on his hands and face, wearing a Rajaz jacket.
Another man stood about thirty yards away, hands open at his
sides. Looked almost like an Indian, but hard to tell at this distance. What the fuck, dope was dope, business was business.

The Rajaz gave the other man a hard look, then waved
him closer. The top of the Rajaz's head disappeared. He never
heard the blast of the double-barreled shotgun, the triggers wired
together to release both barrels at once. But men inside the build-

ing did. Two charged out the door, both going down immediately from rifle fire by the Indian, who was now on one knee in a rifleman's stance. The shark car pulled into the mouth of the alley. Ace jumped lightly from his second-story perch on the fire escape. Rhino heaved a firebomb into the door opening. The shark car vanished.

The cops and newspapers agreed: gang-related.

"He didn't worry about anything after he would be gone," Rhino said, softly. "There was no estate planning, nothing. All to her, in trust until she becomes thirty-five, then she takes it. She doesn't survive him, various charities and stuff. Some endowments. A chair in his name at the university. A few other—"

"Bottom line?" Cross interrupted.

"She takes eight figures. Maybe high eights."

"It was all done with sincerity," the snakehead assured So Long. "I *did* have a shipment coming. And I *did* require the services of—"

"Liar," So Long hissed at him. "I am not here to listen, I am here to speak. *You* listen," she said, and then spoke as if reading a cue card: "You will pay me one hundred thousand dollars in cash. In small bills, no larger than fifties. *Used* bills, without sequential serial numbers. You will pay this in three days. If you do not pay, you will die. This is a specific threat of death, designed to extort money. I am speaking to you on federal property"—indicating with a wave of one heavily ringed hand that they were standing at the back of the main post office in downtown Chicago. "This is a federal crime. You should report it to the FBI. Please do so. You will notice that they will do nothing. Cross will not be stopped by the federal government. Once you understand this, payment will be easy. For you. Or your death will be easy. For Cross. The exchange of money will take place here. On federal property. I trust you understand this. You made a mistake. In business, there are no free mistakes."

"I did not—"

But So Long was already on her way out the door.

"We bring him. You do it," Cross told her.

"Why are you saying this in front of me?" Doc asked.

"Had to persuade the others you'd never talk, Doc. You know how they can be . . ."

"You bastard."

"Sure," Cross said. He turned to the girl: "This isn't about anything you think it is. You think I don't know anything about you, what you went through, all that. You're right. I don't. But I know this much, and I know it good. It's you or him. I could probably get a million for your head."

"If I disclose first . . . on TV or something . . . it would be too late for—"

"—him to have you declared insane as a result of the torture you suffered in prison in Quitasol? Buy some doctors who'll say you've got things all scrambled in your brain? Get you civilly committed? Get them to do a fucking lobotomy? Think so? Ask Doc."

She turned to the husky man, eyes pleading. He nodded, sadly.

"Tell him we got her."

"You got her out? I don't fucking believe—"

"Watch the tape," Cross said, hitting the remote button.

"Who is this . . . mercenary to dictate to me?"

"Nobody, I guess, sir. Want me to tell him that?"

"No, you fucking idiot. I understand, he wants the rest of his money. Fair enough. Why can't you just make the exchange?"

"He says—"

"I *know* what he says. And even *you* can't come with me? I have to go alone?"

"I can drive you to the drop point, sir. And wait for you there. That's all."

"I . . ."

"He said you had—"

"Let's go."

"You are completely insane," the immaculately dressed man told his daughter. "I spent a fortune to rescue you, and I find out you're a raving lunatic."

"Relax, 'Father,'" she sneered at him. "I know I can't prove anything."

"Of course you can't. It never happened."

The girl started to cry.

The man looked at Cross and Doc, his face indicating helplessness at the young woman's obvious insanity.

She looked up. "I thought you would—I don't know—apologize. Say you were sorry. Say you were . . . drunk. Anything. I don't know what. Something. You hired these people to kill me, I know that now. I even thought that was what the pills they made me swallow were. And I didn't care. I . . . *loved* you. Even when you were doing that to me, I loved you. You're my father."

"You're not my daughter," the man said, fully in control. "You're too crazy to be—"

The woman brought the pistol from her lap. "I'm not crazy," she said. "And you're right. I'm not your daughter. I never was. But the law said I was. And you, you said it too. In your will."

"Don't! I can—"

The woman fired until the pistol was empty.

"We have it all on tape," Cross told her three days later.

"Why are you telling me such a thing?"

"I thought you might want it."

"Want it? A tape of me killing my own—"

"Sure. In fact, I thought it would be worth a lot of money to you. Part of a package. A nice package. We take you down south. You stagger across the border a few days later. You say the heroic Quitasolan rebels hid you out and rehabbed you. You read a statement they'll give you. Fair trade. While you were gone, your father was assassinated. Probably in retaliation, because the head of the Quitasol government—you know, the one that's fled the country—knew your father had financed the extraction. His body will have been riddled with bullets from a single pistol. Take a few years, but you'll get all his money. It's your money, anyway. Then you pay us."

The woman's voice was soft. "Yes. Everybody pays, don't they?"

"That's the way it is," Cross said.

for David and Jill

"Vachss is in the first rank of American crime writers."
The Cleveland Plain Dealer

BLOSSOM

Two things bring Burke from New York to Indiana: a frantic call from an old cell mate named Virgil and a serial sniper whose twisted passion is to pick off couples on a local lovers' lane.
Crime Fiction/0-679-77261-8

BLUE BELLE

With a purseful of dirty money and the help of a hard-bitten stripper named Belle, Burke sets out to find the infamous Ghost Van that is cutting a lethal swath among the teenage prostitutes in the 'hood.
Crime Fiction/0-679-76168-3

BORN BAD

Born Bad is a wickedly fine collection of forty-five stories that distill dread down to its essence, plunging readers into the hell that lurks just outside their bedroom windows.
Crime Fiction/0-679-75336-2

DOWN IN THE ZERO

The haunted and hell-ridden private eye Burke, a man inured to every evil except the kind that preys on children, is investigating suicides among the teenagers of a wealthy Connecticut suburb and, along the way, discovers a sinister connection.
Crime Fiction/0-679-76066-0

FALSE ALLEGATIONS

A professional debunker specializing in "false" allegations of child sexual abuse has stumbled across the case of his career—the real thing. What he needs now is a man who knows how to find out the truth, a man like Burke.
Crime Fiction/0-679-77293-6

FLOOD

Burke's newest client is a woman named Flood, who has the face of an angel, the body of a high-priced stripper, and the skills of a professional executioner. She enlists Burke to follow a child's murderer through the catacombs of New York so she can kill him with her bare hands.
Crime Fiction/0-679-78129-3

FOOTSTEPS OF THE HAWK

As Burke tries to unravel a string of sex crimes, he is caught in the cross-fire of two rogue cops who are setting him up to be the next victim.

Crime Fiction/0-679-76663-4

HARD CANDY

In *Hard Candy*, Burke is up against a soft-spoken messiah, who may be rescuing runaways or recruiting them for his own hideous purposes.

Crime Fiction/0-679-76169-1

SACRIFICE

What—or who—could turn a gifted little boy into a murderous thing that calls itself "Satan's Child?" In search of an answer, Burke uncovers mechanisms of evil even he had not imagined.

Crime Fiction/0-679-76410-0

SAFE HOUSE

In this blistering thriller, Burke is drawn into his ugliest case yet, one that involves an underground network of abused women and the sleekly ingenious stalkers who've marked them as their personal victims.

Crime Fiction/0-375-70074-9

SHELLA

At the heart of this story is a natural predator, Ghost, searching for a topless dancer named Shella, who has vanished somewhere in a wilderness of strip clubs, peep shows, and back alleys.

Crime Fiction/0-679-75681-7

STREGA

The implacable Burke has a new client, a woman who calls herself "Strega" (Italian for an erotic witch)—and a new assignment that leads him into the deepest oceans of the twisted city.

Crime Fiction/0-679-76409-7

VINTAGE CRIME/BLACK LIZARD
Available at your local bookstore, or call toll-free to order:
1-800-793-2665 (credit cards only).